TEARS OF THE WOLF

Elisabeth Wheatley

Content Disclosure

This book contains descriptions of graphic violence, blood, gore, infant death, animal death, and sex, as well as mention of war, sexual violence, miscarriage, and other content not suitable for all audiences. Reader discretion is advised.

If you would like more specific information, please email us at support@elisabethwheatley.com with any inquiries.

Hyldish Kings

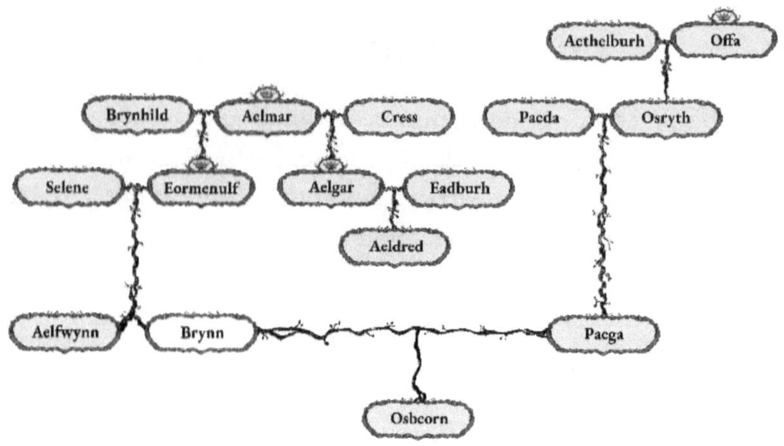

Ombra Aldermen

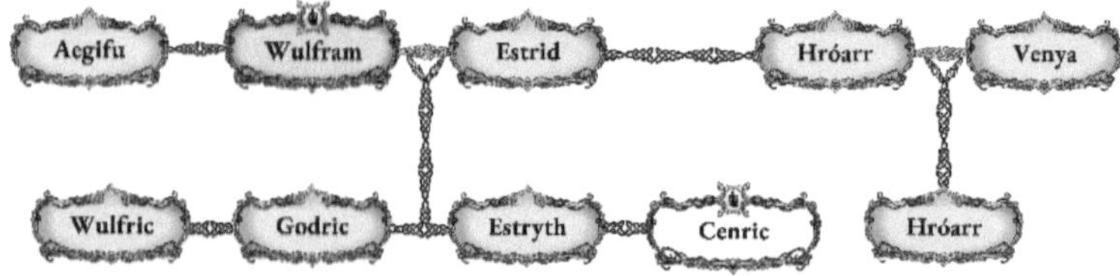

1

BRYNN

Marriage was the second fastest way to get rid of a woman, and the king was quite eager to get rid of Brynn. At least, that was the way it felt. Perhaps she should be grateful her uncle was making this simple. If he had merely wanted her gone, he could have had her murdered and been done with it.

But for King Aelgar to marry her off to the husband of his choosing, he first had to deal with Brynn's current one.

Brynn sat quietly while her maidservant braided her hair and layered strands of carnelian beads around her neck. She tried not to feel anything, her thoughts hovering above the dark chasm of grief in her chest like a seabird over the deep.

All around her, the room was alive with activity. Lady Eadburh, Brynn's aunt by marriage, oversaw the maids. She directed them this way and that, calling out commands like a shepherdess whistling to her dogs. Brynn had been invited to Eadburh's chambers to get ready. It was a kind gesture, but Brynn didn't think she would ever be ready for what she was about to do.

"Are you sure about this, Lady Brynn?" the maid asked quietly, her hands shaking as she secured Brynn's mantle with a silver brooch.

"It will be alright, Esa." Brynn's words seemed to belong to someone else. Brynn had lost nearly everything that mattered to her, but she still had Esa to consider.

Eadburh's shouting tones dropped suddenly, her voice softening.

Brynn looked up to see her aunt crouched down before a small boy, only recently learned to walk on his own. A nursemaid hovered at his back and Eadburh gestured quickly to the woman, trying to get them both out of the room, away from Brynn.

"Aeldred, Mama will come to see you later," Eadburh assured the child. "Be a good lad and go with Hilda for now." Eadburh knelt and kissed the boy's head, and he smiled up at her.

Brynn stared at them, that chasm in her chest threatening to drag her down again. The boy was herded out by his nursemaid and Brynn couldn't look away.

Aeldred was not that much older than Brynn's own son had been. Like her son, Aeldred had the bright red hair that favored the men in their family. Eadburh had kept Aeldred away from her these past months, trying to be considerate. Brynn wasn't sure if she was grateful or not. It hurt to see the child, but somehow it hurt to be hidden from him, too.

Eadburh approached Brynn, a sad smile on her face, hands held nervously before her. "Lady Brynn, how are you?"

Eadburh was a pale woman who always wore her hair covered modestly. People called her severe, overbearing, and made jokes about her behind her back. Brynn had never liked her when they were younger, but Eadburh had been kind to her these past months. At least she had tried.

Brynn's mouth moved in what she hoped resembled a smile. "Well. Thank you."

Eadburh nodded, hands clenching in front of her. "My lord husband is almost ready to see you."

"Thank you." Brynn didn't know what else to say.

Eadburh came and crouched before Brynn, taking Brynn's hands in hers. "It will be over soon."

Brynn wasn't sure what *it* Eadburh was referring to, but she answered, "Yes."

Six years of marriage. Six years of seething resentment and cold apathy.

Paega never desired to marry Brynn. He'd made it clear from the start. He had no interest in a bride less than half his age, young enough to be his child. The Istovari Mothers had chosen him for the *honor* of marrying a sorceress with royal blood and his people had needed their protection. Not to mention he'd lost all five of his sons in the war. He needed heirs. He'd had no choice.

But Brynn hadn't had a choice, either.

"Is Paega here?" Brynn asked, trying not to feel anything as she asked the question.

Eadburh's face flinched, but she looked away. "He sent his nephew as a representative."

Brynn forced back more tears at that. It wasn't as if he didn't know. She'd told him her plans explicitly when she'd left him and come here, to her uncle the king. Paega had been given three months to object, but not a word.

Brynn didn't want him to object. Not really. She just wanted him to show her something. They'd lived together for six years, had a son together. She had run his household and the even the shire of Glasney itself.

And it had meant nothing. He couldn't even go to the trouble to tell her *good riddance.*

Former husband, Brynn corrected herself. She needed to start thinking of Paega as her former husband.

At least he had sent a representative. This way, no one could claim he hadn't known.

Once again, he had done the absolute bare minimum.

Brynn sensed the handmaiden before she looked up to see the girl waiting in the doorway. Her posture and the way she held her shoulders stiff told Brynn she had a message.

Eadburh looked up, back straightening. "Has the king called for us?"

The handmaiden nodded. "King Aelgar is ready to hear Lady Brynn's petition."

Esa stepped aside, signaling that she was finished.

Brynn stood. She thought she should feel something. Something besides that churning abyss of grief and the numbness that sometimes iced over it. She didn't.

"You may go," Eadburh said to the messenger.

"Pardon me, Lady Eadburh. But the king also says to inform Lady Brynn that Alderman Cenric is here."

A jolt pierced through Brynn's numbness at that. "Alderman Cenric of Ombra?"

"Yes, lady."

Her *new* husband. The man Aelgar had found to replace Paega.

"Already?" Eadburh seemed surprised as well.

Aelgar had sent a missive to Cenric only a week ago. With sailing times from the king's seat at Ungamot to Alderman Cenric's shire of Ombra, Cenric must have set out immediately after receiving the news.

The handmaiden inclined her head. "Yes, lady."

After months of waiting, suddenly everything was happening so fast. But Brynn had set this plan in motion. Now was the time to see it through.

Brynn exhaled, letting go of any apprehension or hesitation she might have felt. This was her choice.

Eadburh came up beside Brynn. "This way, my dear." They were almost the same age, but Eadburh seemed to take the role of aunt seriously.

Brynn allowed the king's wife to lead her through the stone corridors of Ungamot, toward the king's hall. Ungamot was a collection of stone rooms chiseled from the guts of a cliffside.

No one remembered who had originally built this structure, but it had served as the seat for the kings of Hylden for generations. Brynn's father had ruled from here, as had her grandfather. Now her uncle continued the tradition.

People rushed past them, servants with messages, baskets of eggs, and buckets of water, and the well-dressed ladies of the gentry. Most recognized Eadburh and Brynn, stopping to bow to the wife of the current king and the daughter of the last king.

Esa trailed after them, the quiet girl keeping her head down as befitted a servant. She might be a sorceress, too, but she was still a servant.

Brynn caught the drone of voices as they drew nearer the king's hall. The hall served for feasts and a place for the servants to sleep at night, but during the day it was where King Aelgar settled disputes and granted petitions.

The vaulted chamber was filled with people as it always was. There was usually a festive air to the chamber. Mead flowed at most hours and a skald or two could usually be seen plucking a harp in the corner.

Today, the festive air seemed muted. Greyed. No music hummed and no strong drink poured. The laughter seemed forced and the faces solemn.

Or perhaps that was just how Brynn saw it. Perhaps that was just how the world looked through the fog of mourning.

Several aldermen—rulers of shires—gathered around the room with their sons, nephews, and retainers. Thanes—warriors who served the aldermen—stood by their sides. No weapons were permitted in the hall, and that was for the best. A few women accompanied their men, wives and daughters decked in furs and stones to flaunt the wealth of their husbands and fathers.

With so many bodies packed together, the room shimmered with *ka,* the pure energy that suffused all living things. It would be invisible to anyone who wasn't a sorceress, but to Brynn's senses, the room was aglow with power. *Ka* was not life itself, nor was *ka* magic itself, but *ka* was necessary for both.

Brynn spotted Wassa, the sorceress who attended the king. Brynn had never known her well, but she had been notably silent on this plan of Brynn's.

Near the center of the room, Brynn spotted Hrotheld, Paega's nephew. He was a young man, handsome with an easy charm. He usually laughed and joked, but today he was solemn like the rest of them.

Brynn recognized a few other faces, but she looked straight to Aelgar. Her uncle was only a few years her senior, the product of her late grandfather's appreciation for young women and aged wine. But like Eadburh, Aelgar seemed far older. His face was serious, he rarely laughed, and though she thought him a good man, he always seemed to be balanced on a knife's edge—as if he feared going too far in one direction or the other would lead to disaster.

Her uncle spotted her. He stepped away from the circle of advisors and retainers, toward his mercy seat.

It was a wooden chair set on a raised platform at the head of the room. Aelgar liked to use it for passing judgments, even when people made snide comments about him trying to imitate the great palaces of the distant southern kings.

A gradual shushing fell over the room as Aelgar took his seat.

Brynn glanced around the chamber, guessing there must be three hundred people packed into this hall. Good. That was a few hundred witnesses to the end of her marriage to Paega. More than had witnessed her wedding.

"Lady Brynn, my dearest niece." Aelgar's voice rose over the quieted chamber. He did not have an impressive voice, but it carried nonetheless.

Brynn came to stand before his mercy seat and bowed. The crowd parted, giving space to the main spectacle. She stood alone before the king.

"You have requested a petition from your king." This was all a formality for the benefit of the onlookers. Everything had already been decided.

"Yes, lord." Brynn kept her head bowed.

"You are my only niece, sole surviving child of my late

brother, King Eormenulf. Sister to Aelfwynn the Brave, as loyal a warrior as ever there was." Everyone here knew who Brynn was, but he was taking the time to remind them. Brynn wasn't sure why, but she remained silent. This was his hall. His kingdom. His decision. "Whatever I can grant you, be assured I will."

Brynn licked her lips nervously.

"You have requested a divorcement from Paega of Glasney on grounds of dereliction. Is that correct?"

Her uncle had already agreed to this, seemed eager to agree to it, even. She still felt herself tremble as she said, "Yes, lord."

"I have heard your case these past months and I am satisfied your case is valid." Aelgar gestured to the room. "Is Paega or his representative here to answer to these accusations?"

"My uncle has sent me in his stead, lord." Hrotheld stepped forward, bowing as he did. "Hrotheld, son of Hrulfan. My mother Ulstrid was Paega's sister."

Aelgar inclined his head to the young man. "How does your uncle answer Lady Brynn's accusation?"

Hrotheld looked to Brynn almost apologetically. "He offers no contest, lord."

That earned a stunned silence from the onlookers. Some of them might still remember Paega Ironarm, the young man who had been all but a legend in the warband of Brynn's father. Young Paega had, by all accounts, been a fierce and cunning warrior.

But the Paega Brynn knew was a man aged beyond his years by grief and loss. He had no interest in anything but the past.

When she'd told him she was pregnant, Paega had told her that the baby was hers and he wanted nothing to do with it. Foolishly, Brynn had hoped Paega would change his mind after the child arrived, especially when it had been a son. He hadn't.

Hrotheld nodded to Brynn again. "My uncle has sent me to return her dowry and asks that you rule in her favor for a divorcement."

Brynn closed her eyes. A heavy weight seemed to crash over her—a sense of failure. It was the confirmation that the past six years of her life had been wasted. She had poured her heart and soul into being the perfect wife, a good mother, and all for nothing.

She'd had a son and if her son had been all that had come of it, she might have had something to hold onto. Someday, she might even have thought it was worth it.

But now her son was dead and like everything else, Paega simply did not care.

Aelgar seemed to consider this situation. He asked Hrotheld several more questions. Hrotheld answered.

Brynn bowed her head, trying to keep herself together for a few more moments. This would be quick. Aelgar had already found her another husband. He'd made it clear he planned to rule in her favor. She just needed to remain composed while they observed these rituals of mediation.

A hot sensation crawled along the back of Brynn's neck. The feeling of being watched. There were hundreds of eyes on her, of course she was being watched. But something from the corner of her eye moved.

A man circled through the crowd around to her left. He studied her, head canted slightly and brows furrowed with interest.

He was around average height with chestnut hair that reached his broad shoulders and a close-cut dark beard. His red mantle was pinned over one shoulder with a wolf-head brooch and a collection of silver rings in varying sizes flashed on his forearms. He might not have stood out to her if not for the way he moved through the crowd, stalking like he was a forest predator, and the other onlookers were just trees. Brynn noticed two other men trailing after him, but the man with the wolf brooch seemed to be their leader.

The stranger studied her intently. His gaze swept over her from head to foot and their eyes met.

Brynn expected him to look away, as most men did with sorceresses, but he didn't. He held her stare, unblinking and unabashed. His boldness sent a shiver through her. She didn't know what to make of it.

Aelgar was speaking again.

Brynn tore her eyes away from the stranger and back to her uncle.

"If Alderman Paega offers no contest to Lady Brynn's accusations, then I must rule in her favor. I grant her petition for a divorcement."

Silence greeted the announcement.

Brynn made herself go numb. She could feel things in the privacy of her own rooms, not here. Not with everyone watching.

"Does anyone object to my judgment?" Aelgar searched the room.

Brynn held her breath, not sure why.

A moment later, her uncle continued. "With no objections, Lady Brynn's petition for divorcement is granted, and she is no longer the wife of Alderman Paega. Hrotheld, you are to return Lady Brynn's dowry on behalf of your uncle."

Hrotheld bowed again. "Yes, lord."

Aelgar stirred from his mercy seat, stepping down to return to his retainers. He cast Brynn a reassuring smile as he did.

Brynn forced a smile back in gratitude. Perhaps she should feel triumph, or at least relief. But this was not a victory. This was the amputation of a gangrenous limb. Just because it was necessary did not make it pleasant.

The crowd returned to their quiet conversations and Brynn felt their stares, heard her name and Paega's whispered from right and left. The name no one spoke was the name of her son. And why should they speak his name? He had barely reached his first birthday. At least half of all children died before their fifth.

Paega's first wife and their five sons had been buried in the hills outside the keep. Paega spent most his days pulling weeds from their cairns and tending the trees he had planted around them. Paega hadn't even wanted to build a cairn for Brynn's son.

"Aunt—Lady Brynn." Hrotheld bowed to her. "I…" He cleared his throat, glancing toward the king. "I hope you are well?"

"Yes. Thank you." Brynn swallowed, hands held in front of her.

Hrotheld inhaled, then exhaled. "I'm sorry to see you go. We all are."

Brynn forced a smile past the tears that threatened to come up. "Everyone except your uncle."

Hrotheld made a frustrated sound. He ran a hand through his hair, then looked back to her. "I wish things were different."

"As do I." Brynn had often wondered why her mother hadn't married her to Hrotheld instead. He hadn't been married at the time and since his uncle had no sons, he would probably end up as alderman of Glasney one day. The two of them were close in age and Hrotheld might not be a remarkable warrior or poet or craftsman, but at least he didn't spend his days pining for the dead. It didn't matter now, Brynn supposed.

Hrotheld bowed again. He stayed out of arms' reach. "You were always dear to my mother. The closest thing she had to a daughter."

Brynn nodded, looking down. Paega's elder sister Ulstrid had been kind to her. Kinder than Brynn's own mother ever had been. Brynn had called her Aunt Ulstrid, despite her technically being a sister-in-law. Even Ulstrid had put more effort into Brynn's marriage than Paega had.

Hrotheld's eyes slid past her, falling on someone at her back. "I wish you well, Lady Brynn."

Brynn turned, following Hrotheld's gaze. It was the stranger with the wolf's head brooch. He stayed a few steps back, but something about the way he stared felt like he was closing in on her.

"I don't believe we've met," Hrotheld chuckled nervously at

the other man.

The stranger's eyes snapped to Hrotheld, then back to Brynn. "Cenric, son of Wulfram, alderman of Ombra."

Brynn's heart flipped in her chest. This was the man Aelgar had found for her.

He was far younger than she expected. He couldn't be much older than her, if he was older at all. Aelgar had told her Cenric had recently become alderman of Ombra only a couple of years ago, but for some reason, she had pictured him as a grizzled veteran of the north.

Brynn opened her mouth to speak, but no sound came out.

"Cenric!" Aelgar was at Brynn's shoulder the next moment. He must have seen the other man closing in on her from across the room. "You're early."

Cenric bowed to Aelgar, but it seemed forced, like he didn't want to take his eyes off Brynn even for that single moment. "You sent for me, my king. I saw no reason to delay."

"This is Lady Brynn." Aelgar presented her as if everyone in this room didn't know who she was. "My niece and sorceress of the highest caliber."

Cenric's gaze flicked over Brynn again. His expression remained unreadable.

"Have you finished your harvests yet?"

"About halfway." Cenric glanced to Aelgar as he spoke, then his gaze returned to Brynn.

"You must be eager to return to them," Aelgar said.

"It's more raiders that concern me." Cenric looked back to Brynn. "Our shire is usually the first to be raided."

Brynn felt herself growing sick. Aelgar was sending her to the far north, where he knew raids were the most likely. Was this some kind of sick joke?

Aelgar took Brynn's hand.

Brynn started at the gesture. Her uncle was not one given to shows of affection.

Aelgar was still speaking to Cenric. "I think we can finalize your wedding tonight."

Tonight? Brynn had to fight to keep from yanking her hand out of her uncle's grip.

So fast. This was all happening too fast.

Brynn felt dazed, as if she had been spun in circles too many times.

"That seems quick, lord." Cenric, to his credit, sounded apprehensive.

"You have already agreed to accept Lady Brynn." Aelgar looked over his niece. "And she has agreed to accept you."

Brynn stared at Cenric's boots. They were worn, the sign of a man who had places to be.

Cenric shifted. "May I speak with the lady in private, my king?"

Aelgar cocked his head at that.

Cenric looked back to Brynn. "If it pleases you."

"If the lady allows it." Aelgar's tone lowered, the words clipped short, as if he was trying to remind Cenric of his place.

Interesting. Her uncle didn't seem to like this man. Why was he having Cenric marry his *dear niece* then?

"I will allow it." Brynn would rather not start her second marriage with an argument. "You may speak with me in private, lord."

Cenric inclined his head sharply. "My king." He took Brynn's free hand and tugged her after him.

Brynn was too startled to react. He was touching her? His forwardness caught her off guard as he pulled her to the side of the room. A few people stared, but the two men who had followed him formed a protective barrier, closing them off from the others.

Cenric faced her, still fixing her in that intent stare she didn't understand.

At least her second husband seemed to find her interesting.

2

CENRIC

Lady Brynn was beautiful, which was another thing that didn't make sense.

She was the daughter of the late King Eormenulf, whose praises still flowed from the lips of skalds across Hylden. Not only that, but she was a sorceress of some impressive skill, according to what he had been able to learn.

He'd waited and watched for the past few nights, but Morgi had sent no foretelling. His patron goddess usually sent warning if he was about to make any particularly bad decisions. But Morgi had seemingly failed to warn his father and brothers of their deaths, so Cenric's trust in her these days was tenuous.

Cenric inspected Brynn closer, but he couldn't see anything wrong. She had all her teeth, skin smooth and free of disease. She walked easily enough, so she was reasonably able-bodied. The king's summons mentioned that she'd lost her one-year-old, so she wasn't barren.

This all seemed too good to be true and Cenric couldn't shake the feeling it was a trap.

King Aelgar had said she was a reward for his loyalty. Cenric had pledged allegiance to Aelgar, but so did every other alderman in Hylden. Cenric had done no great service that he could think of.

Cenric held Ombra, but that had belonged to his family for

generations. And it served Aelgar—Ombra was the farthest northern holding in the kingdom. It was usually the first to be raided by Valdari ships. Aelgar's best interest was to see that Ombra remained a secure stronghold.

Who better to secure it than Cenric of Ombra? The man who was as much Valdari as Hyldish.

Cenric realized he had been staring at his intended for several moments without speaking. She looked straight ahead, not quite at him. "Lady Brynn." Cenric cleared his throat. "Are you being forced into this?"

Brynn's face remained impassive. "I am not."

Cenric looked over to where the king spoke with a man who appeared to be a thane, though his eyes remained on them. "You, a sorceress and the daughter of a king, are marrying a northern alderman?"

The same day her first marriage was ended, no less.

"If you'll have me." Brynn's tone was flat, disinterested, but her lip trembled, like she was overcome with emotion.

Cenric exhaled a long breath. He'd asked Aelgar to find him a sorceress to wed years ago when he had become alderman. Every time he had followed up, the king's servants had responded that there were no suitable sorceresses willing to marry into Ombra. Cenric had moved on with his life.

Then, last month, the king's messengers arrived with the wonderful news that yes, the king had finally found one for him. Cenric had accepted.

Now he wondered if this was somehow a mistake.

Cenric shifted. He felt as if he was missing something, as if there was some detail that had escaped him. "You left Paega on grounds of dereliction?"

"Yes." Brynn's expression closed off, reverting to that empty look she'd worn while standing before the king.

Divorcement was rare, but for it to be on grounds of dereliction was rarer. If a man failed to provide for his wife, especially if she was a sorceress, she usually had other recourse.

"If Glasney was not able to meet your standard of living, I doubt Ombra will be better." Cenric thought it best to be honest. "We are not as rich or prosperous as the shires to the south." Cenric hoped some of that would change with a sorceress in his lands, but it was fact.

Brynn shook her head, looking away from him. "It wasn't about comfort."

"No?" Cenric tried to think of what else dereliction could mean. Failure to perform his bed duties would have been grounds of deprivation or impotence.

Brynn took a deep breath. "Failure to provide defense."

A wife had the right to her husband's protection, but Cenric had never heard of a man shirking that. A man who couldn't protect his woman was bad enough, but a man who *wouldn't?*

Cenric frowned, glancing over to the king. Aelgar watched them from across the room, speaking to another man with his back to Cenric. What had Aelgar left out of that missive last week?

"Defense." Brynn stared to the floor, that vacant look intensifying.

"What does that mean?" This time of year, Cenric was disconnected from news in the south.

"Raiders attacked Glasney," Brynn said. "They came at night. Just before the spring equinox."

"Raiders attack everyone." Cenric still didn't understand. "If you have something worth stealing, men will try to steal it."

Brynn grimaced as if she was in pain. "There were no guards set. Paega and his thanes had gone hunting again." Bitterness entered her voice at that. "I managed most of the shire, but Paega's thanes were still loyal to him, and I could not manage them on top of everything else."

Cenric frowned at that. Why had she been running the shire?

Brynn's voice cracked and she blinked quickly. "I couldn't do it anymore."

"So." Cenric had the feeling she was upset and didn't like it, but he needed to know what he was getting into. "You left him because…" Cenric didn't know how to word the question. "They hurt you?"

"Not me," Brynn said quietly. "I was making rounds in the shire that night. I wasn't home." She looked down at her hands.

"Then?"

"My son." Brynn's voice was small, little more than a whisper. "They killed my son."

Silence stretched between them.

A cold feeling prickled along Cenric's spine. It was much like the sensation he felt in a fight when he knew he had made a misstep.

The king's missive hadn't specified and Cenric had assumed her son died of natural causes. Children died all the time, especially babies. But murder?

Cenric looked to Edric, one of his thanes who had been his friend longer than he'd been alderman. Edric's back was still turned, guarding them from intrusion. There would be no help there.

"If you're worried about me leaving you, don't." Brynn angled her head away.

Cenric had been worried about that, actually.

"It was hard enough for me to leave one husband. I doubt I will be allowed to leave a second." Brynn spoke her words on an exhale. She sounded exhausted.

"I am sorry about your child." Cenric cleared his throat. He wasn't sure what else to say.

Brynn's gaze finally focused on him. Her eyes glistened, but she held back her tears. "Thank you." The words were so soft, he almost didn't hear them.

Brynn of the Istovari was a grieving woman. Grief did things to people. It clouded over who they really were. For some, the fog lifted, and they returned to some semblance of who they were before. For others, the fog never lifted, at least not fully.

But Cenric had not come all this way to comfort a stranger.

He had come because his king had "offered" him the honor of becoming family. And when kings "offered" such a gift, it was as good as an order.

Even if there was some hidden caveat to this as Cenric expected, what could he do? Refuse the king? He was already tenuously in Aelgar's favor as it was. He had not been summoned to the last meeting of the Witan—the council of aldermen who served as the king's advisors. Nor had he ever been summoned to one, though it should have been his right. He was expected to pay his annual tribute to the king and host the king if ever Aelgar dared venture into the rugged north. Outside of Ombra, Cenric had very few privileges.

Cenric looked her over again. "I'm…" He cleared his throat.

Brynn smelled of some sweet perfume he didn't recognize, but it was pleasant. Her face had a pleasing shape and her lips were full, plump. Under different circumstances, he might be looking forward to tasting those lips.

Cenric wished they could wait at least one night. He only had foretellings of people he had already met and places he had already been. Perhaps now that he had met Brynn, Morgi would send him a warning if this was a bad idea. But it seemed the king was not interested in waiting on Morgi.

At the head of the hall, Aelgar now spoke with his wife, though the couple both watched him. Cenric couldn't make out their words, but if he had to guess, Eadburh was objecting.

Cenric had noticed on his past visits that the woman had a habit of arguing with her king in front of other people and Aelgar tolerated it. Cenric didn't understand why.

Cenric didn't have much time. A blunt approach might be best. "The north is not a gentle place. It's harsh. Rough." *Like me.* "You will have to endure much."

"I already have endured much." Brynn's voice had taken on that empty tone again, her eyes once again unfocused.

Yes, he supposed she had. He didn't know the details of what had happened months ago nor what kind of life she had led before then. But he did know some of what the previous king's daughters had survived in the war after his death.

"It's dangerous." Cenric pressed the issue. "It is not like the Istovari havens or the southern lands you are used to."

Brynn didn't reply.

"Lady Brynn?" Cenric grasped her chin, reminding himself not to alarm anyone watching. He pulled her face around, making her look at him. "Why me?"

From the corner of his eye, he saw movement as a male figure stepped toward them. Just as quickly, Edric blocked the figure's path. Though he might be a full head shorter than the average man, Edric could acquit himself well enough.

Cenric kept his attention on Brynn, trusting his friend to deal with the other man.

Brynn finally met his gaze. She truly was beautiful. She met his gaze without flinching, without any reaction at all.

They stared each other down. He scrutinized her closely, trying to guess what that lovely face might be hiding.

She wasn't some harmless beauty, she was an Istovari sorceress and niece to the king. She might be the most dangerous woman he had ever met.

"Marrying me will ruin your life," Cenric whispered, dropping his voice.

"Already ruined," Brynn answered, her voice barely audible.

"You will lose everything." While there was little either of them could do at this point, Cenric only thought it was fair he be honest with this woman.

"I lost everything," Brynn shot back.

Cenric tried to remember what he knew of the Istovari. What could he say to offend her? To make her see that this was a poor match? "I'm not some well-trained Istovari man. I could beat you. I could make you my whore."

Brynn was unimpressed. "Or I could make you mine."

Cenric fought to control his reaction to those words. From her dead expression, she hadn't meant them as an invitation. He released her.

Brynn's gaze dropped as soon as he let go. "I will not have another man forced to marry me." This time tears did escape her eyes. "I am not doing this under duress. But if you are, tell me, and I will release you."

Cenric considered it for a space of heartbeats. There was much about her first marriage he had yet to learn, and he doubted he could learn it all in just a few minutes.

Cenric glanced over his shoulder. Edric was still facing down the stranger, but another of his men, Ugba, nodded slowly.

They needed a sorceress in Ombra. The people made do with what the midwives and local wise women could manage, but they were not sorceresses. Sorceresses could mend broken bones in days instead of weeks, chase off fevers, and save men on the brink of death.

More than that, Brynn should be able to heal their animals, too. Healthier flocks and herds would be a boon unto themselves.

This might be a mistake. But as big a risk as this might be, there was the promise of a huge reward. It had taken Aelgar two years to offer him a sorceress as a wife. Cenric might not be offered another.

"Is everything in accord?" King Aelgar's voice interrupted Cenric's train of thought.

In his days in a warband, Cenric had once had to enter a narrow pass under dense fog. They had known an enemy warband lay in wait for them somewhere on the other side. They had known it was a trap, but they had no choice.

This felt like that. He could see nothing, hear nothing, he only knew that he didn't know everything. He also, unfortunately, knew he had no choice.

"Yes, my king," Cenric agreed. "All is in accord." He looked back to Brynn. "Can I trust you not to kill me in my sleep?"

Brynn's reply was flat, almost sounding bored. "I could kill you awake if I wanted to."

Was that a threat? Cenric frowned about to reply before a question came to mind.

Friend?

Cenric looked down as a furry body pressed against his leg. It seemed that Snapper had finished exploring the room and decided to return to him.

Snapper was a smaller, fluffier, and stockier echo of the wolves his ancestors had been. He was a dyrehund, one of the dogs gifted by Morgi to Cenric's forefathers.

Snapper studied Brynn with raised ears, tail wagging hesitantly.

"Snapper, this is Brynn," Cenric said to the dog. He looked back to Brynn. "Brynn, this is Snapper."

Brynn's face pinched in confusion. "Snapper?"

Cenric cleared his throat. Sometimes he forgot himself outside of Ombra. "He's…my dog."

Friend? Snapper asked again. He stepped toward Brynn, tail wagging.

Brynn studied the dog, not knowing what to make of him. "I…see." She had probably never been introduced to a dog before.

Sick? Snapper's question came as he wagged his tail at the stranger. He must be picking up on Brynn's body language.

Sad, Cenric sent back.

Sad? Confusion filtered through the dog's thoughts. Snapper sometimes struggled to understand human emotions.

Cenric tried to think of how to explain it in terms the dog would understand. *Her pup.*

No pups, came Snapper's challenge. The dog sent the impression of Brynn's scent that must somehow prove she had no pups.

Lost pup, Cenric replied in his mind. *She lost her pup.*

Understanding came from Snapper at that. He approached Brynn, whining as his tail wagged. *Friend?*

Brynn watched the dog as he came closer, ears pinned as he

pawed at her skirt. Instead of pushing him away, Brynn reached down and scratched behind Snapper's ears.

That was enough for the dog. *Friend!* his thoughts screamed as he leapt on his hind legs, tail lashing wildly as he tried to lick Brynn's face. *Friend!*

Brynn jumped back, startled.

"Down!" Cenric ordered, giving the command out loud.

Snapper dropped back down onto all fours, looking between them in confusion. *Friend?*

"Apologies." Cenric straightened. "He meant no offense."

Brynn seemed genuinely confused at that. Who could blame her? Most people had that reaction. "None taken," she said, more out of habit than understanding, if he had to guess.

Cenric could explain his connection to the dog later. He tried to go back to being serious, but it was difficult with Snapper standing between them, tongue happily lolling out one side.

"So we are doing this?" Cenric asked, trying not to sound too harsh, but also trying not to sound embarrassed. Even if he was a little embarrassed.

Brynn's expression had gone blank again, painfully blank. "I think so."

3

BRYNN

Brynn's first wedding had been a gaudy affair, a blend of Istovari and Hyldish traditions cobbled together like estranged relatives at an autumn feast. There had been floral garlands and the binding of the bride and groom with ivy. She and Paega had been wrapped together head to foot in the vines.

After, she had danced with her mother and the other women while Paega sulked with the men of his family. Gifts had been exchanged between relatives then toast after toast. A massive boar had made up the main course of the wedding meal, though Brynn had been too nervous to eat.

She had been wracked with anxiety for her wedding night, but she needn't have worried. Paega never turned up, leaving her to wait alone in the dark for hours.

She found out later than Paega had left their wedding to sit by the cairns of his family. Brynn had been Paega's second wife, and he never allowed her to forget it.

As far as she knew, she was Cenric's first wife. Perhaps that would count for something.

Her wedding to Cenric was an abridged affair. Everyone seemed to want it over with as fast as possible. The traditional negotiation began, led by Aelgar.

Twelve witnesses gathered for Brynn's side, including Esa, the king's wife Eadburh, his attending sorceress Wassa, and several of Aelgar's retainers.

Cenric had brought his own twelve witnesses—all thanes, as far as Brynn could tell. His men remained silent through the negotiations.

Aelgar explained Brynn would be entitled to living standards equal to Cenric's, her widow's rights in the event of his death, and Cenric's various obligations as her husband.

Brynn had made sure to require that Esa would be cared for. Cenric would be obligated to house, clothe, and feed Esa and any family she might have. He couldn't send Esa away and he couldn't punish her without Brynn's approval.

King Aelgar not only promised Cenric Brynn's original dowry, but presented a document listing gifts including grain, furs, and jars of imported spices. Cenric seemed surprised as he read the list. Hopefully, he was pleased.

Brynn would prefer it if at least one of them could benefit from this arrangement.

As the men reviewed the document, Brynn called for wine.

Was marrying a stranger really a wise decision? Then again, what other choice did she have? She was too important to be ignored, yet too insignificant to be feared. She needed the protection of a husband for political reasons if nothing else.

Brynn finished off her first cup of wine and called for another. She tried to think, tried to sort out wisdom from pain and anger from grief.

What did she want? She wanted to lie down and stay there. She wanted to curl so deep inside the past that she reached to the time when her son had been alive, a time that now existed only in her mind.

She wanted her son back. She'd thought Hylden would have peace now. She had been so wrong.

After the death of a king, aldermen and thanes arose from across the land to try claiming the title for themselves. That was the way it always happened. The death of Eormenulf had been no different.

Aldermen and thanes had splintered off into factions, each with their own claimant. After the first few months, the factions had solidified behind Brynn's uncle, Aelgar, and an alderman called Winfric.

The war between them had been bloody, lasting the better part of two years. Brynn had been barely fourteen at the start of it, but her elder sister Aelfwynn had led sorceresses and thanes into battle, wielding an axe as well as her spells.

Many people said Aelfwynn was the reason Aelgar had won. She had been charming, fierce, and unrelenting. A warrior goddess if ever there was one. Aelfwynn the Brave, they had called her.

Some had even whispered the word *queen* behind Aelgar's back. Was Aelfwynn not the daughter of the last king and a sorceress, too? Woman she might be, but Aelfwynn had won more battles than her sickly uncle.

In the end, it had not mattered. Aelfwynn had died in a muddy field, her body covered in too many wounds to know which had been fatal.

Aelfwynn's warriors had met Winfric's the way armies had met one another for as long as anyone could remember. Both armies had drawn up into formation, shields pressed together with weapons reaching over the top. Each line formed a wall of shields or a shieldwall, as it was called.

Brynn had not stood in the front, but a few rows back, able to see her sister's shining helmet among the warriors. The lines met in a great clatter and crash, the grunting of men, the clang of weapons, and the air glowing with *ka* as blood was spilled and sorceresses worked their spells.

There were only three ways to break an enemy shieldwall—smashing through it, tricking the enemy into abandoning it, or flanking and attacking from the rear.

Their flank was supposed to be guarded by a force from Alderman Ostig, but he and his thanes had not been there. Ostig's men had been positioned on the wrong hill south of the

Cerin River instead of north, miles away from the battlefield. Some people blamed a miscommunication, but some said it was spite over Aelfwynn refusing the alderman's offer of marriage. Aelfwynn had never mentioned a marriage proposal from Ostig, but Brynn's sister had received plenty, so perhaps that one had simply not been worth mentioning.

Whatever the reason, Aelfwynn's line had been flanked and it had been a bloodbath. Brynn had fled and survived by hiding in a cove created by the roots of a tree along the river. Once she was sure Winfric's men had gone, Brynn had picked her way through corpses in the aftermath. She found her sister's body naked, already stripped of the precious ringmail and armor that had belonged to their father.

Aelfwynn the Brave was buried in a shallow grave beside the Cerin River. Brynn had laid the stones herself, her shaking, bleeding hands making the work clumsy and slow.

The memory blurred with a more recent one—laying the cairn stones over her son. She had buried him in a cedar chest lined with his blankets and the wolf carved from oak that had been his favorite toy. This time she'd had the servants to help, but it had been small comfort as she watched the chest buried by rocks.

Was she cursed to see everyone she loved swallowed by the stones?

Brynn closed her eyes. She could still feel the phantoms of her son's small hands wrapping around her fingers. Sometimes at night she still woke, thinking she heard his cries, only to find it was the wind outside her window.

Her baby was gone. Rotting underground in the linen shroud she'd made from his blankets.

He wasn't supposed to die. He'd made it through his first year. Most children didn't. Even without an Istovari mother, his chances of reaching adulthood should have been good.

Brynn finished her second cup of wine before Cenric and Aelgar finished reviewing the contract.

Because she had the king's permission, Brynn didn't need the approval of her mother's family to remarry. Aelgar asked her several questions—if she agreed to this union, if she entered this arrangement of her own free will, and so on—and she spoke her consent.

Aelgar smiled at Brynn, though his expression was touched with sympathy as he did.

Wassa, the king's attending sorceress, looked on with tight lips. She'd also been opposed to this union, but seemed resigned to it just as Brynn and Cenric were. As Eadburh and Esa were.

In fact, it seemed the only person pleased with this arrangement was Aelgar. Brynn had to wonder why. As best she had determined, none of Aelgar's vassals or liegemen had spoken against it, so they must be in support as well.

The small private dining room Aelgar was using to formalize this union was barely large enough for the six large tables that now sat Cenric's men and the gathered witnesses.

"Then we are agreed," Aelgar sounded like a man who had just won at dice. "Your marriage is final. Let us feast."

Yes, this wedding was very different from Brynn's last one. She took another sip from her third cup.

Cenric took his place on her right. He had to adjust the sword at his hip as he sat down. He must have gotten it back as soon as he left the king's main hall.

Why did he think he needed a sword here?

Cenric sat with his knees spread wide, one hand resting on the table. He noticed her looking at him and met her stare. "Hello, wife." It was strange to hear another man call her that. A man who wasn't Paega. "Enjoying your wine?"

So he had noticed her sinking into her cups? Brynn held eye contact as she finished off what was left in her hand.

Cenric quirked one eyebrow at her.

Brynn raised her cup for the servants to refill.

Her mother would be furious when she learned Brynn had gotten a divorcement. Brynn needed to be remarried before then. Lady Selene was in the far southern empires, so she might not be back until next spring. She might not come back at all if she met with misfortune along the way, but Brynn doubted the gods would be so kind.

The servants carried in a rack of venison. Aelgar did his duty, stepping up to carve it as the host ought to do. The venison was so fresh, Brynn could feel the dying whisps of *ka* still in the meat. The animal would have been alive just a few hours ago.

"Having second thoughts?" Cenric asked, tone mild.

"I am prepared to do my duty," Brynn answered flatly.

"That makes two of us." Cenric jerked his head to the servants, pointing to his own cup. The young man filled it quickly, not making eye contact with either of them.

Brynn tried not to think too hard about the implications of his words. Cenric would not leave her alone on their wedding night, she was sure of that. She didn't expect him to be particularly gentle, either. But he might at least make it quick and that was something to hope for.

Hands shaking, Brynn held her cup out. Without a word, the servant filled it a fourth time.

Cenric studied her as other servants set trenchers of meat in front of them. They weren't thralls as they would be in certain parts of the kingdom, but free men and women paid to serve the king's household. Aelgar had been trying to put an end to thralldom in his lands—one of his more idealistic endeavors—with mixed results.

"Why would you go through with this?" Cenric asked.

Aelgar had finished carving the meat and had joined his wife at the head table. A skald had entered the room at some point. The lanky man with grey hair sat strumming his harp, telling the story of Eponine and Moreyne, the sister moon goddesses and their civil war.

Brynn was tired. The wine had done little to drown the knot of dread in the pit of her stomach. She wasn't in a place for intelligent conversation. "Why would you?"

Cenric inhaled a deep breath. He drew his eating knife and began slicing apart the venison in front of him.

Snapper whined from under the table and Cenric tossed down a large portion of meat for the dog. Brynn noticed that he fed Snapper the choice cuts, not scraps. The dog slurped appreciatively from the floor.

Brynn kept drinking, not touching her food. She'd rather bed him on an empty stomach. Voices chattered, though it might have just been the buzzing in her ears.

Someone toasted to her and Cenric. There were halfhearted cheers.

Wassa left the room at some point.

The "feast" lasted barely an hour or so before a young woman tapped Brynn on the shoulder. She recognized the girl as one of the handmaidens who had helped her prepare earlier.

"Your bridal chamber is prepared, lady."

Brynn glanced to Aelgar. Her uncle must have had the room prepared as soon as possible. He was quite eager to get this over with. She wanted this over with, too, but she wondered again if he wasn't eager to be rid of her.

"Show us the way." Cenric pushed back his chair, leaving a half-eaten rack of venison on his plate. He waved down his men who started to rise. He held out a hand for Brynn.

She stared at his hand—callused with dark lines around his fingernails. A scar slashed across his palm, like it had once been sliced open.

Brynn fit her hand into his—hers looking pale and dainty by comparison. All the same, Brynn was unsure which of them was more dangerous.

Cenric bowed to the king and Eadburh. He stopped just long enough to whisper a command to the red-haired man who had accompanied him. The smaller man nodded his acknowledgement.

Esa stared with wide eyes as Brynn was led away by Cenric. Brynn forced a smile for her maidservant, trying to be reassuring.

Snapper trotted happily after them. Did that dog follow Cenric everywhere? Brynn was starting to think he did.

Eadburh's handmaiden led them from the room. The fortress was dark and only the candle in the handmaiden's hand lit the way. The floor seemed to buck as they walked. Brynn's head swam and she realized she had drunk too much.

She tripped as they reached a flight of stairs. Cenric caught her without a word, and she leaned on him for support.

Brynn braced one hand on the wall and let him lead her the rest of the way down. The handmaiden took them through several more passages, barely speaking. Occasionally, she stopped to wait for them.

She took them to the same room Brynn had occupied for the past weeks. The fireplace had been lit and the bed had been made. Brynn's belongings had been neatly folded and put away in chests, but it was very much the same room.

Snapper ducked inside first. The dog circled the room, sniffing curiously.

Brynn went inside, not hesitating. She'd made up her mind to do this.

Cenric exchanged a few words with the handmaiden, though Brynn couldn't imagine what. He shut the door after her and then they were alone—except for the dog.

Snapper plopped down in front of the fire, seeming to have satisfied himself with exploring the small room.

Brynn sat on the edge of the bed, facing him. She cleared her throat and took a deep breath. It would be fine. It was just sex. People did it all the time and it meant nothing.

Cenric surveyed the room carefully, taking in the chests, the washbasin by the window. He went to the window first, checking to see what was outside—a courtyard. He drew the curtain over it. Much like his dog, he paced the entire room, checking every corner.

When Cenric turned back around, he was unbuckling his sword belt.

Brynn watched impassively as he removed his outer coat next, draping it over the chair beside the washbasin. He held onto his sword, though.

Brynn studied him. "Are you afraid of me, Cenric?"

He scoffed. "Any wise warrior would be."

"My sister was the warrior," Brynn said. "Not me."

Cenric grunted noncommittally. "Who attacked Glasney?"

Brynn's drunken mind reeled, confused. "Raiders."

"Do you think they could have been Valdari?" Cenric's question came hesitant, guarded.

Brynn shook her head. Why was he asking this? "They haven't raided this far south since the war." After the death of Brynn's father, the instability in Hylden had invited raids from all their neighbors.

Worst of all had been those from the islands of Valdar in the north. The Valdari were a savage people. They called themselves wolves of the sea and rode in ships with snarling wolf heads on their prows.

"It sounds like them. Striking at night and disappearing before dawn." Cenric studied the fire. Lights from the flames caught his arm rings. "At least that was how we did it. We didn't raid in spring, though."

Brynn hadn't thought anything could shock her at this point, but she'd been wrong. She stared at this man—her husband—speechless. "You…you've raided with them?"

Cenric shrugged as if it didn't matter. "My mother was Valdari. I fostered with them."

Brynn didn't want to process this or its implications right now. "Why are you telling me this?"

Cenric looked back to the fire.

"Ask my maid, Esa. She saw them. She was with…" Brynn's throat seemed to constrict suddenly, and she had to force the words out. "She was caring for my son. One of them ripped him out of her arms."

They'd found her baby's body at the bottom of the wall. The

servants had tried to stop her from seeing, but she'd used *ka* to force them out of the way.

Her son had looked so still and perfect, the carved wolf still held in one hand. But the moment she had reached for his *ka*, she had felt his life force was gone.

Brynn's shoulders shook. Again, she marveled that she could still weep.

Cenric was quiet. He kept his attention on the fire, not looking at her. If she hadn't known better, she'd have thought that expression was shame. "What was your son called?"

"Osbeorn." Brynn's voice broke in a sob. If she hadn't been drunk, she might have been able to pull herself together. She was supposed to be letting her new husband—who had apparently once been a Valdari raider—bed her, but instead she was melting into tears.

"I'm sorry." Cenric cleared his throat, sounding awkward.

Brynn heaved deep breaths, forcing herself to calm down. How could she have tears left after all these months?

She didn't hear Cenric move, but she sensed the shape of his *ka* rise from the trunk. She didn't look up. If he wanted to throw her onto her back and lift her skirts, she didn't care anymore.

Instead of toward her, he moved away. A screeching sound came from the door.

Brynn looked up, blinking away tears to see Cenric had dragged the trunk to block the door, one end against the wall. Fear spiked through her. Just why would he be barricading them in here?

Cenric must have seen her face. He shook his head, even as he sat back down on the trunk, across the room. "I won't hurt you."

Brynn swallowed, a little ashamed at the wash of relief she felt at that. She had told him she was ready to do her duty.

Cenric propped his sword against the trunk and settled down on top of it, his outer coat draped over him like a blanket. "Try to rest." He patted the trunk near his feet and his dog came leaping from across the room.

Snapper settled down on the trunk, draped over Cenric's legs as if they had done this a hundred times before.

Brynn frowned, confusion filtering through her drunken mind. If she didn't know better, she would think he was guarding the door. Was he really so suspicious of Aelgar? "What are you doing?" she whispered.

Cenric shook his head again, looking to the fire. "We'll talk more tomorrow. Just…try to rest for now."

Brynn wasn't sure what to make of this. Was he trying to respect her, or did he not want to touch her?

She settled down on the bed, watching Cenric from the corner of her eye. She waited a long time after that, but he never moved from his place in front of the door.

This might not be the perfect wedding night she had once fantasized about as a girl, but at least she wasn't spending this one by herself.

4

CENRIC

Having the goddess of foretelling as his patron was much like having a Valdari mercenary as a cousin—less useful than most people assumed. Just as the Valdari still raided Cenric's lands when the mood struck them, so Morgi seemed to only offer her guidance when the mood struck her.

Morgi was not a gentle goddess. She was not the motherly Eponine or the seductive Frenella. If anything, Morgi was a capricious younger sister, but she was protective in her own way.

Cenric had no dreams, only nightmares. As a child, they had frightened him. He had feared sleep, hated it. Some nights passed in peaceful oblivion, but Cenric had dreaded the nights he had visions all the same.

As he had grown older and his life had become more dangerous, Cenric had come to value his gift.

Though most of his nightmares were esoteric reflections of his own fear, dread, jealousy, and flaws, some of them were more. Foretellings were as different from simple nightmares as fire was from smoke.

Nightmares cleared away upon waking, fleeting and ephemeral. Foretellings burned themselves into his awareness, distinct and branded on his mind even in waking.

None of them were pleasant, but every foretelling was a warning. A possible future. Morgi only showed him danger, calamity, and misfortune, but it was always when it already lurked, and he could avoid it.

But either there was no calamity ahead or Morgi wasn't in the mood to warn him. Cenric woke quietly in the early dawn hours, stiff from a night on the hard chest, but with no foretellings. He'd had a nightmare of some kind, though its memory was already fading. Yet he had not seen any warnings from his goddess.

The first thing he realized was that Snapper was gone. Cenric glanced around the room, looking for his dog.

Brynn lay asleep on the bed, curled on her side. From her pinched expression, Cenric wondered if she suffered nightmares, too. At her back, was Cenric's traitor dog.

While Cenric had slept on the hard trunk with the wall against his back, Snapper had helped himself to the empty space on the bed.

Snapper lay at Brynn's back, his limbs curled under him with his chin draped over her shoulder. The dog's eyes were open, watching Cenric. The dog had absolutely no shame.

"Snapper," Cenric hissed. "Get down."

Snapper grunted in response and shifted. *Pup.*

Cenric got the image of a puppy curled against Brynn.

Lost pup, Snapper said.

Cenric closed his eyes and clamped his mouth shut, still trying not to wake Brynn. *You are **not** her puppy.*

Snapper's response was almost sarcastic. He sent back an image of himself curled against Brynn. He wasn't her puppy, but he could fill the empty space.

"She doesn't want you there," Cenric whispered. "She doesn't like you."

Friend, Snapper argued. As far as he was concerned, everyone liked him until proved otherwise.

Cenric pinched the bridge of his nose, trying to think of a way to extricate the dog without waking Brynn. He should have left Snapper with Edric last night. This marriage was off to a difficult start already, even without his dog harassing his new wife.

But Snapper went everywhere with him. He hadn't even thought about it until it was too late.

Snapper huffed, settling back down. Was he going to make Cenric drag him off the bed?

As best Cenric could tell, Snapper understood Brynn missed her son and was trying to help. But Cenric wasn't even sure if Brynn liked dogs, much less a dyrehund currently trying to be her surrogate baby.

"Snapper!" Cenric growled. "Get off her!"

Snapper woofed, hopping up on his forelegs.

"Shh, let her sleep." Cenric stood, pushing off the cloak he had used as a blanket. "Snapper, let's go."

Snapper leapt off the bed, joining Cenric across the room. *Go?*

Go, Cenric agreed, pushing aside the trunk he'd used to block the door.

Brynn still appeared asleep when Cenric led the way to look for his men. He'd rather not stay in Ungamot longer than he needed. Winter was fast approaching and there was much work to be done back home. And maybe once they were out of this place devoid of mountains and forests, he could sort things out with Brynn.

Edric, Cenric sent to the dog. *Find Edric.*

Edric! Snapper responded with an image of the small thane. He led the way, tail wagging.

Snapper led Cenric to Edric, asleep on the floor of the king's great hall. His other man lay on their blankets nearby along with other visitors to the king's keep. The roaring central fire had died down to embers overnight and several boys were shoveling away the coals.

Cenric shook his shoulder and Edric jumped, one of his many knives out in an instant. "It's me."

"You should know better than to startle me awake." Edric

waved his knife at Cenric like a chiding finger. "I could have gotten you square in the gut."

Cenric didn't bother asking how Edric had smuggled a weapon into the main hall. "Rouse the men. We're leaving as soon as I can speak with the king."

"Doesn't your pretty wife need time to get ready?" Edric rubbed his eyes, a mischievous smirk taking shape on his mouth. "How was she, by the way?"

Cenric stood and kicked Edric's shoulder this time.

"What? That bad?" His brows quirked. "Or perhaps that good?"

Cenric landed another kick to Edric's hip.

"I'm up. I'm up!" Edric clambered off the ground. "Any particular reason for your hurry?"

"We need to get home. I don't like this."

Edric yawned, stretching his back. "I take it you learned some things on your wedding night?"

"Very little. Where's Kalen?"

Edric pointed to a lump just a few bedrolls over. "I think the lad drank his weight in wine last night. First time he's had the stuff."

"Get up, boy." Cenric ripped the blankets off Kalen, his pale face gaping up at Cenric in shock.

"Lord," Kalen stammered.

"Up," Cenric ordered. "I need you to come with me to see the king." He worked a knot out of his shoulder as the boy scrambled to adjust his cloak and bundle up his belongings.

Spending the night on the trunk had been hard and uncomfortable. He'd slept on less forgiving surfaces, but he wasn't as young as he had once been.

Last night hadn't played out perfectly, but Cenric was hardly going to take a weeping woman. He wasn't yet sure he could trust his new wife, but he didn't want to hurt her.

Brynn's story played over in his mind. Something was missing.

He didn't think she was lying, necessarily, but she had described a Valdari raid. Valdari didn't usually raid in spring, and they didn't sail all the way down the coast and upriver to raid fortified inland keeps. There had been no other recent raids along the coast, which would mean that a group of Valdari would have banded together to raid a fortified keep when there were plenty of unfortified towns along the coast. Towns where they could have taken thralls, sheep, silver, and maybe even gold, but without the risk of encountering real defenses.

Most Valdari raiders wouldn't be pillaging until summer or the last few months before winter. Either when their own crops were planted or when the Hyldish villages and towns had their winter stores built up and ripe for taking.

And the raiders had happened to come on the night Brynn was gone? She seemed to accept it as just misfortune, but to Cenric it seemed quite convenient.

"I'm ready, lord." Kalen stood at attention, brushing his bowl-cut hair into place and buckling on his leather breastplate.

"Edric, make sure to find my wife's servants and ready them." Cenric might be giving Brynn time, and he might be giving her space, but he wanted everything promised to him. "Take this to the steward of the king's storehouses and get the ship loaded."

Edric took the scroll from Cenric's hand, etched on the finest lambskin vellum.

"And count everything twice. I don't want the old goat to cheat us." It wasn't uncommon for stewards to shortchange their lord's creditors and pocket the difference.

"This could take all day," Edric warned him. "We might not be ready to sail until tonight."

Cenric looked pointedly to the scroll in his friend's hand. "Just see what you can do." He marched back through the hall, stepping over sleeping forms with Kalen at his heels.

The noise of him rousing his men had disturbed several of the other sleepers. Figures rose across the hall, stirring from beneath their cloaks and blankets.

Cenric had not been to the keep of Ungamot for some time, but all Hylden spoke of the king's morning habits. Sure enough, he found the king in the garden beneath a young elm. The old tree had been cut down during the occupation of Ungamot by Winfric, during the war over kingship. The new tree was one of its saplings.

King Aelgar sat crosslegged in the shadow of the tree. A heavy fur mantle draped around his shoulders that seemed excessive in the mild autumn morning. A stack of pages sewn together on one side and pressed together by wooden boards lay in the king's lap—a codex or what were being called books. A servant waited on the king, holding a steaming cup in both hands. From the smell, Cenric guessed it was that same wretched herbal concoction the king always took for his stomach ailments.

A guard blocked Cenric at the entrance to the garden. "The king will see petitioners this afternoon."

Friend? Snapper asked, wagging his tail up at the stranger.

The guard ignored the dog.

Cenric looked the guard up and down. The man was wider than him, but not much taller. He had a crooked nose and held a spear, but no armor. If Cenric had really wanted to, he could have jabbed a knife into the man's ribs and shoved his way to the king.

"Is that my nephew?" Aelgar called, lowering his book.

It took Cenric a moment to realize Aelgar meant him. By marrying Brynn, Cenric had become Aelgar's nephew. The thought felt wrong.

"Let him pass," the king ordered.

Cenric smiled at the guard, confident he could have killed the man, and slipped past.

Snapper bounded off into the garden, loping in a large circle as he sniffed the grass.

By the time Cenric reached Aelgar, Snapper was nosing a row of shrubs and the king had gone back to reading his book.

"Have a seat, Cenric."

There was only the grass, coated by a thin layer of dew. Cenric grimaced.

"I enjoy an exercise in humility before attending to the needs of the kingdom." Aelgar kept his eyes on the book before him.

Seeing no way around it, Cenric sat, accepting that he would have a damp spot on his ass when he stood.

Kalen stood off to the side at a respectful distance with his head inclined slightly. He looked subservient, but the boy was good at watching for threats while looking harmless.

"Have you read anything by the philosopher, Jossel?" Aelgar asked it as if it was entirely possible Cenric had.

Cenric almost laughed. "Can't say I have." He glanced up at the sapling, wondering what Winfric had done with the old tree they had chopped down. A ship's mast, perhaps?

Aelgar lowered his book, studying Cenric thoughtfully. "I shall have to gift a copy to you to take home."

"You are truly too kind in your gifts, my liege." Cenric had sworn an oath to serve Aelgar in order to reclaim Ombra. It had not been an oath given gladly or lightly, but it was what it was. "I wish to return home. I came to ask your leave." Cenric held eye contact with Aelgar, keeping his face impassive.

Aelgar took just a few heartbeats too long to respond. "Is this the wish of your lady wife?"

"I have not yet spoken to her."

"Perhaps you should." Aelgar looked to his book again.

"Why me?"

"What do you mean?"

Cenric grew weary of the king's games. "You wrote me a letter mere weeks ago saying you had a wife for me. For all you knew, I'd already taken a wife."

Morgi might have seemingly sent her reassurances, but Cenric had learned by now not to make large decisions based on a single foretelling or lack of one.

"But you hadn't," Aelgar replied.

Cenric knew he had Aelgar's spies in his own home. Several of his people had confessed that Aelgar's agents had approached them for information. Cenric had told them to accept. They might as well receive a little extra coin in exchange for telling the spies what they would learn anyway. "Why me, my liege?"

"I was hesitant about you, Cenric." Aelgar must mean he was hesitant about Cenric's Valdari heritage, and that he had spent most of his youth across the sea. "But you have proven yourself so far." Aelgar took a deep breath and exhaled. "You deserve a reward for your loyalty."

"And Lady Brynn is your idea of a reward?" As soon as he said it, Cenric wondered if he had gone too far.

Aelgar blinked at Cenric long enough to make him fear the king was offended. He might think very highly of his niece, after all. "Brynn was an excellent wife to her last husband."

"Yet she left him." Cenric knew there was more to that story, and he already disliked Paega from what he had heard, but it was worth pointing out.

"Brynn and Paega were an unfortunate match," Aelgar said through a tight jaw, as if he was reluctant to say the words. "Her mother married her to him without my approval."

Cenric cocked his head at that.

"The sorceresses pressured Paega into marrying her because he is the grandson of King Offa."

Cenric frowned, trying to remember his country's history. "King Offa? The king before your father?"

"The same. Through his mother's line."

That meant Paega was king-worthy, an atheling or viable candidate for kingship if he'd ever chosen to press the matter.

From what Cenric remembered, Offa had been the first great king of Hylden. He had extended their borders into the far north, conquering Cenric's forefathers. He'd reigned long and, if the stories could be believed, he'd reigned well. But Offa had produced nine too many sons and after his death, they had been too busy slaughtering each other to stop King Aelmar and his thanes from taking the kingship.

Cenric considered that. That would mean Brynn's heirs with Paega would have had the blood of three kings in their veins, not to mention the likely support of the sorceresses. It made sense why Aelgar would be eager to end that union.

"But I objected for other reasons," Aelgar said. "Brynn is my brother's only surviving child. Her sister died fighting for me." Aelgar fell silent for a long moment. Cenric hadn't thought it was possible, but his expression grew even more solemn. "I would see her married to a man who appreciates what he has been given."

Cenric wasn't sure if that was a request to treat Brynn well, or a warning that he should be grateful.

Aelgar exhaled out his nose. "This union strengthens our northern defenses against the Valdari while ensuring my niece is wedded to a loyal man. I see this as a complete victory."

Cenric supposed, from that perspective, it was reasonable. He himself was not king-worthy, being descended of tribal chieftains and northern wild men. His sons with Brynn might still be king-worthy, but there were stronger claims in other families. Like spring water added to wine, Cenric was meant to dilute Brynn's lineage.

There was still an incomplete part of this story, though. The circumstances of Osbeorn's death were odd and Aelgar had more reason than anyone to want the boy dead. Not to mention it had given Brynn grounds to end her first marriage. But why bother with Valdari raiders?

Either way, Cenric decided it would be rude to ask if the king had murdered a baby.

"Brynn will be a good wife to you. She knows her duty." Aelgar sounded confident. "That's one way she's more Hyldish than Istovari."

Interesting. It must not be Brynn that Aelgar feared, just those who would use her.

"Even if things seem lackluster now, I have full confidence

she'll make you a fine wife in time."

Cenric grimaced before he stopped himself.

"Has your goddess told you otherwise?" Aelgar asked the question as a challenge.

"No," Cenric admitted. Morgi was oddly silent on this seemingly large decision.

"Then trust your goddess, if not your king."

The younger man cast a sideways glance to Aelgar. The response that came to mind was disrespectful, so he held his tongue.

Aelgar blinked at Cenric with a stony expression. "You could have turned her down."

Kings were tricky creatures. They didn't honor bonds and loyalties the way other men did. When a king could argue that what benefitted him benefitted the kingdom, it made for interesting justifications and claims.

"Do I have your leave to depart as soon as I can?" Cenric asked.

"You are not a captive or a hostage here," Aelgar answered.

Cenric took a deep breath. "Then I shall see that my lady wife is ready to depart." Cenric stood, dusting off his pants. Sure enough, his ass was damp.

Aelgar fixed him in a steady look.

"Yes?" Cenric had the feeling Aelgar wanted to hear something else. "Am I forgetting something, lord?"

"I hope you will grow to be fond of Brynn, Cenric." Aelgar's tone was soft, almost sad. "If not, I hope you will at least treat her fairly. Gods know the girl deserves that much."

Cenric frowned at that. "I look after what's mine."

"I would expect nothing less," Aelgar replied, his attention returning to the book in his lap.

Cenric turned to leave, calling for Snapper and gesturing for Kalen to follow. This was as close to answers as he expected to get.

5

BRYNN

When Brynn had woken to Cenric's angry voice and something heavy against her back, she'd been paralyzed with fear. When she realized it was Cenric's dog in the bed with her, the relief and confusion had rendered her speechless.

Before she had figured out what to do or say, Cenric left, taking the dog with him. She laid still for a long time after the two of them left.

When she pushed herself upright, the trunk Cenric had used as a bed was pushed back where it had been yesterday. She was still in the same dress, her hair braided up with ribbons.

A throb squeezed her skull with each heartbeat, threatening to make her head explode. She closed her eyes, rubbing her temples. She hadn't been that drunk in years.

Grey and black dog hair powdered both her dress and the side of the bed the dog had occupied. There was nothing to show Cenric had been here except his coat still lying on top of the trunk.

Brynn's chest tightened. She'd broken down crying in front of him. Last night, she had been too heartsore and intoxicated for dignity, but today some semblance of pride returned.

She was stuck with Cenric, one way or another. And he was stuck with her.

Brynn made her way to the washbasin. The water was icy

cold, but she splashed her face and neck. Her reflection in the water squinted back. Her eyes were bloodshot with dark circles beneath them, hair disheveled.

Brynn clutched her head. She channeled *ka* into her own skull and that alleviated some of the throbbing, but wine sickness wasn't like cuts or bruises. It mostly needed to heal the slow way.

A knock at the door startled her.

"Enter." Brynn didn't look up as the door opened. The outline of *ka* that stepped into the room was too small to be a man.

"Lady Brynn," Esa's voice called.

Brynn turned around. "Yes?"

"Your husband's men sent word that we are to make ready to leave."

Brynn blinked, her lashes still dripping icy water. "What?"

"Lord Cenric is having them load the ship as we speak. He's asked that you ready yourself to depart at once."

It struck Brynn as unusual. Ombra was at least two days away by ship, more than a week by land. Normally, someone who had sailed all the way down from Ombra would spend more time in Ungamot. But Cenric must have gotten what he wanted.

Brynn glanced around the small room. Besides her dowry, all she owned had been reduced to a few trunks, the rest given to her servants. She had dismissed all her retainers except Esa, sending them back to their families or finding them new positions in the wealthy households of Glasney. She hadn't known if her next husband would be able to afford their upkeep. Esa remained because she had no family and refused to leave Brynn.

Brynn cleared her throat. Her new husband wanting to leave this morning was unusual, but she had no reason to stay. Ungamot had nothing for her. "We just need to carry out the chests." She gestured to a trio of wooden chests reinforced with iron brackets.

Esa clasped her hands behind her back. "I will call some of

the boys to help."

"Good." Brynn smeared a hand over her face. She sensed the *ka* of several shapes coming down the hallway.

"One more thing, lady." Esa stepped aside as another girl came into view, carrying a wooden trencher.

She was one of the kitchen maids, her round face reddened from the heat of the ovens. A teetering trencher balanced in her hands. The kitchen maid inclined her head, setting the trencher on the bed. "Your husband said you hadn't eaten last night, lady. He told us to bring this to you."

Brynn frowned. "He…did?"

The kitchen maid nodded. "He and his men stopped by to break their fast not long ago. He put everything on this trencher and told us to take it to you."

Brynn wasn't sure how to respond. "He made me a plate…himself?"

"He did, lady," the kitchen maid confirmed. "I must get back to the kitchens now."

"Yes." Brynn rubbed the spot between her eyes, trying to soothe away the headache.

"Will you eat, lady?" Esa shut the door after the kitchen maid, keeping her attention on Brynn.

"Yes." Brynn responded with a resigned sigh. She examined the trencher her new husband had sent. It was a warrior's meal— comprised almost entirely of meat. Leftover venison, a chunk of wild boar, and several chunks of beef loin. A single cake of ryebread had been added, almost like an afterthought. Brynn wasn't going to be able to finish it, but focused on eating while Esa packed her chests and bundled up her belongings.

Cenric had sent her choice cuts, fatty and juicy portions with just a bit of charr on the outside. The bread was free of the grit that sometimes came off millstones during the grinding of flour.

Ka passed outside the door as servants and courtiers began their days. Brynn was aware of them but paid them little mind. Outside the window, *ka* flitted past as birds flew under the eaves.

45

Below her window, the constant river of *ka* that made up the streets of Ungamot flowed by.

The door opened—no knock this time—to admit Eadburh and several of her ladies. "My dear, I have just heard the news."

Brynn glanced to Esa, but the handmaiden only paused with a half-folded shift in her hands. She looked as surprised as Brynn.

"Cenric is taking you away from us." Eadburh settled down beside Brynn on the bed, on the opposite side of her plate. "Are you alright?" Eadburh pulled Brynn's face around and searched her carefully. Was she looking for bruises?

"I am well, lady," Brynn assured her.

"I can speak to the king and make Cenric stay another few days or weeks."

"I think I have intruded upon your hospitality long enough," Brynn said quietly. Was it unusual to depart so soon after a wedding? Yes. Would she be leaving behind everything she knew? Also, yes. But she'd stayed here wallowing in her loss for months. She didn't know what came next, but it was outside these four walls and outside this city.

"Aelgar should make you two spend at least your first few days here. I can't believe he's endangering your safety like this."

Brynn smiled softly. Eadburh seemed to forget Brynn had accompanied her sister in the war. "Thank you, aunt."

"You have endured the worst possible pain a woman could know." Eadburh squeezed Brynn's hands. "I can't imagine if one of my own children…"

Brynn stood, pulling her hand from Eadburh's. She didn't want to hear this again. Her child's death was like a disfiguring scar or the loss of a limb. People responded first with pity and then horror at the thought of experiencing it themselves. Sometimes, Brynn felt she had to hide her own pain so as not to upset Eadburh.

Maybe leaving Ungamot wouldn't be such a bad thing after all.

"Esa, do you know where everything goes?"

"Yes, lady."

"Good." Brynn looked to Eadburh. "Does anyone know the name of Cenric's ship and where I can find it?"

Eadburh nodded to one of her girls and the handmaiden scurried away.

"You are taking this all quite well," Eadburh said. "Last night, you seemed devastated."

Brynn shook her head. "I think…I think I can make this one work." She turned away.

Cenric seemed like a rough man. He was probably capable of terrible cruelty. By his own admission, he had been a raider. Men who raided had to be at least a little cruel. Despite that, he had treated Brynn well so far.

Her mind flashed back to this morning. He'd gotten angry with Snapper, but the dog hadn't been afraid. Hadn't even seemed to care. If Cenric was so terrible, surely his dog would have learned to fear his wrath by now.

Cenric might not be a good man, but Brynn didn't think he was as bad as Eadburh thought.

He'd asked for her son's name.

The boys Esa had called appeared, ruddy young men in their mid-teens. They tumbled into the room, awkward and fidgeting.

"Do any of you know where Alderman Cenric's ship is?" Brynn asked.

One of the boys nodded. "It's called the *Wolf Star*, lady. Docked outside the gates."

"Good. Carry these to it." Brynn waved to the trunks around her room.

She let herself focus on packing and arranging everything into the smallest bundles possible. Her cedar chest was the most valuable. It had been darkened to nearly black by years of treatments of oil and spells to keep it intact. Combs, ribbons, dresses, bracelets, and a few gold and silver torques wedged to one side. On the other side were neat stacks of parchments and diagrams she'd written over the years. Some of them were her grandmother, mother, and sister's spells, but by now most of them were her own, annotated in the margins with her own notes and reminders.

She knew her most common spells by heart, but the less common ones she needed to keep the instructions written down. *Ka* had many purposes, but its more complicated uses required weaving it into patterns and the correct designs.

Ever since the war, Brynn had made sure she practiced her use of magic daily, even if it was for minor spells. Like any ability, some people were born gifted, but innate talent could only take one so far. There came a point when honing one's craft was more important than natural talent.

"In the early days of my own marriage, I found it helpful to contemplate on the psalms of the goddess Lumë." Eadburh still sat on the bed with her hands folded before her. She stared at something across the room and Brynn realized it was Cenric's coat. She would have to make sure and bring that to him.

"I noticed you have shrines to her in a number of places around the fortress." Brynn picked up Cenric's coat, carefully draping it over her arm.

She would try. She would try to fit into this new life she'd been forced into. She didn't want to make Cenric, Esa, and Cenric's people suffer because of her pain.

They needed a sorceress in the north, and that's exactly what she'd be.

"Meditating on her faithfulness to Teshner helped me greatly."

Brynn bit her lip. Seeing as how Lumë had eventually left Teshner and sworn eternal celibacy, that might not be the best goddess to emulate.

"Eponine has watched over me my entire life." And Brynn related to the goddess now more than ever. She understood why the death of the moon goddess's firstborn had made the goddess tear the sky in two, dividing it into night and day.

Eadburh nodded as if not sure what to say to that.

They sent the girls to fetch more servants to help them carry the trunks. Eadburh seemed to be taking a good portion of time out of her morning to comfort Brynn.

The sorceress wished she wouldn't.

"I do regret I have no girl to send with you," Eadburh lamented.

Brynn canted her head in understanding. "I have Esa. And I am sure there are more girls in the north I might employ as my companions."

The trunks proved too heavy for the three young men who had answered the call, and so they had to fetch three others. While she waited, Brynn had Esa fix her hair again. Esa removed the festive ribbon, then fixed it into a simple plait down Brynn's back.

Brynn donned her traveling cloak as the last of her trunks was carried out.

Eadburh sat watching her with a narrow gaze. "This is the most activity I've seen from you since…well, since you came here."

Brynn inclined her head in the ghost of a bow. She had a mission for now. A purpose. "Please give my regards to the king." Brynn clasped Eadburh's hands. "I am sure he is too busy this morning, but please express my thanks and gratitude for all both of you have done for me."

It was the right thing to say, even if Brynn knew deep down her uncle was trying to get rid of her.

Eadburh stood, squeezing Brynn's hands. "Please send word if anything…" She took a deep breath, as if catching herself. "Go with the blessing of your gods and mine."

"Your gods and mine," Brynn echoed. She bowed over the other woman's hands before following the trail of servants with her trunks.

Brynn adjusted her cloak and covered her head the way most married women did in the open air. As a sorceress, she was beholden to her own customs and rules, but at this point, she would prefer not to offend Cenric. Best she found out what Ombra's customs were first then decided which, if any, she wished to negotiate.

The king's residence rose up overlooking the city. Homes, storehouses, and stables sprawled below the famed cliff face fortress of Ungamot.

King Aelmar, Brynn's grandfather, had constructed the wall that now guarded the city. The wall had been knocked down and burned in some places during the war and those spots were noticeable by the newer timbers in the palisade.

Occasional black splotches marked some of the buildings. Incongruous seams stood out where new wood and old had been cobbled together during similar repairs. Entirely new buildings stood in some places, erected over old foundations.

If the scars of the war hadn't remained, it would have been hard to believe. The streets were alive with activity as thousands of people bustled to and fro.

The air was alive with *ka* in the morning mist. Life teemed in all directions, people moving like thousands of lamps. Brynn breathed it in, trying to hold onto it—that feeling of life. She'd resented it when she had first come here.

Every time she'd felt another person's life force glowing like a hot coal, she remembered feeling Osbeorn's coldness. She'd even tried to shut out *ka* at one point, but she was too powerful for that. As a sorceress who had woven spells for as long as she could remember, magic knew her too well.

People stepped aside when they saw Brynn was accompanied by a gaggle of servants and porters. They led her to the docks, already abuzz with activity.

Dozens of ships lay anchored in Ungamot's harbor. A few ships appeared moored, but several ships appeared to be fishermen already returned hauling the first catches.

Cenric's ship, *Wolf Star*, wasn't hard to spot. Brynn half expected to see shields hung along the sides for all it looked like a Valdari ship.

The vessel had a single mast and oars all along the side. The sail was furled, but it appeared to be made of some blue fabric. The ship was large and might be able to fit thirty men or more, if it carried no cargo. The prow and stern both rose and arched gracefully, like twin serpents. Deer-head carvings graced the prow and the stern.

A plank had been set down and a number of men she recognized from the "feast" last night worked to load cargo from the dock. The ship's broad deck was already stacked with bundles of goods and sealed barrels.

One of Cenric's men spotted them, the short redhead who seemed to be in charge. He leapt lightly onto the docks, seeming to dance more than walk. He struck Brynn as vulpine, the way his dark eyes flickered over their small group as he sauntered toward them. "Lady Brynn! Good morning to you. I hope you're well rested."

In truth, Brynn's head still throbbed with a headache and the glare of the light off the waves threatened to make her eyes water. But she nodded and lied. "I am well, thank you."

The stranger took her hand and kissed the back of it, the proper way for a man to greet a woman of higher rank. "My name's Edric. Cenric's been stuck with me for nigh on six years now."

Six years—that would mean they had known each other long before Cenric became alderman.

"Cenric should be joining us soon," Edric said. "We can get your things loaded." He looked over the collection of trunks carried by the king's men. "Is this all of it?"

"Yes," Brynn answered. She looked past Edric, studying the ship.

Edric noticed her appraisal. "A beauty, isn't she? We took her from some Valdari who didn't need her anymore, if you know what I mean. One of the finest ships I've ever seen." He looked to the manservants. "That way. The boys will show you where to put them."

The king's porters carried the chests onto the ship, moving carefully along the narrow plank.

Edric gestured for her to follow him. "Right this way, lady. I'll show you where you can get settled."

Brynn and Esa stepped onto the boat after Edric, and he showed her to where the packs and bundles of goods had been arranged into a makeshift shelter from the sun and wind. The space was large enough for several people at once with packs of the men's belongings arranged on the decks.

Edric told her to make herself comfortable then left to oversee the loading of more barrels onto the ship. It seemed Aelgar was making good on his promises of provisions for her dowry.

"I've never been on a ship, lady." Esa's already pale face had gone yet paler as she stared at the sea apprehensively. "The water makes me nervous."

"It's fine, Esa," Brynn reassured her.

Esa's hands fiddled in her lap.

Movement near the prow of the ship caught Brynn's attention. She looked up and there was Cenric, boarding the vessel.

Regardless of how he had spent last night, he appeared well rested. He had a young boy at his back who carried a bundle of books and parchments. Odd. Brynn wouldn't have thought Cenric was the type to bring books and texts, but he was literate, she realized. He'd read through Aelgar's list of gifts himself.

Snapper trotted happily at Cenric's side, leaping ahead of him to bound onto the ship. The dog ran straight for Brynn and Esa, tail wagging.

Brynn lowered her hand, and Snapper licked her fingers. He must be able to still taste the meat juices from her earlier meal.

"Edric, how goes it?" Cenric went straight for the redhaired man. It seemed Edric was his second in command as she had suspected.

"Almost done. We're just waiting on a few casks of wine we were promised."

Wine would be harder to get in the north. Grapes didn't grow as well in the mountains.

"Good. After that, we'll go as soon as Lady Brynn arrives." Cenric took a scroll from Edric and began reviewing it, probably the list of goods that had been loaded onto the ship so far.

"Lady Brynn is already here." Edric sounded oddly smug.

Cenric glanced up and followed Edric's line of sight. Cenric looked to her, then Snapper and briefly to Esa, but quickly back to her. His expression was hard to read, but he seemed surprised.

Brynn wasn't sure how to greet him. Was she supposed to smile?

Clearing her throat, Brynn crossed the deck. She averted her eyes. "You left this in our room, lord." She held out his coat, neatly folded. It felt strange to say "our," like she was forcing something that wasn't there yet.

Cenric took it, watching her closely. He'd gone back to eyeing her the way a predator stared down a new animal, not sure if the creature in front of him was prey or another predator.

If Edric was a fox, Cenric was a wolf. It made sense that he was half Valdari. His dark eyes took her in from head to foot, devouring every inch of her without ever touching. "Welcome, Lady Brynn," he said at length. He fixed her with that same intensity for another space of heartbeats before turning to Edric. "We're just waiting on the casks, then?"

"Yes, lord." Edric bobbed his head. "And not even midday!"

Brynn and Esa settled in the small shelter Edric had indicated, waiting for the ship to finish loading. Snapper invited himself to join them, tail thumping on the deck.

In mere hours, Brynn would be out of sight of the capital and beyond the reach of her mother. Even when Selene returned, there was nothing she would be able to do. Brynn was divorced from Paega with hundreds of aldermen, thanes, and their wives to witness it. Now she was already remarried with the blessing of the king himself.

She had escaped Paega, escaped her mother, and escaped the machinations of the Istovari Mothers.

Brynn had done it.

6

CENRIC

They left Ungamot before the sun reached its zenith. It was better than Cenric had hoped, certainly.

They sailed out into the open waters, then steered toward the north, keeping two or so bowshots off the coast.

Cenric and his men took turns rowing. The wind was against them, and they kept the sails furled. Cenric took part in the first shift while Edric made sure all the goods were properly secured.

They rowed for over an hour at a steady pace until Edric and the next group of men stepped up to take their spots at the oars. "Wind's not too bad. We should make fair time."

"Don't tempt Llyr, my friend."

Edric shrugged. "What interest does Llyr have in making our lives difficult? If I was a god, I'd be too busy to meddle with the likes of me."

Cenric handed his oars over to Edric as other men did the same. Cenric accepted water from the communal barrel, ladling it out to take several gulps. In summer, the heat would have them all endlessly thirsty, but right now, the cold helped stave off thirst.

Several men brought out dice as many did during the boredom between shifts. Cenric almost went to join them, but his attention fell on Brynn.

She sat beneath the shade of the shelter. She and her maid

each held a boot in one hand, working something into the soles, but neither held a needle. Snapper sprawled a few paces from Brynn's side, napping in the sunshine.

Cenric came closer as the ship glided along. Seagulls swooped in around the vessel, probably hoping they were fishermen.

Brynn glanced up and acknowledged him with a slight incline of her head, then went back to work.

Cenric glanced over to his men at the oars. Daven, a young man just a few years Kalen's senior, was barefoot.

The space on the deck beside Brynn was unoccupied, so Cenric sat. He kept just enough distance between them so he wouldn't touch her by accident. Her maid continued working on her other side, mute and head down.

Snapper rose, ambling over to plop himself down against Cenric's side. He leaned against Cenric, tail thumping on the deck as Cenric rubbed his side. *Good pets,* Snapper sent, shifting appreciatively. *Good pets.*

As Cenric watched Brynn, she held a leather patch over the holes in the bottom of the boot. He studied the movement of her hands—deft and skilled. Her fingers moved mindlessly, easily. Whatever she was doing, she had done it many times before.

She massaged the sole of the boot and the patch. As she worked, the new leather seemed to meld with the old. The patches melted into the holes, fitting smoothly and thickening the leather before his eyes. Dark seams marked where she had worked, but otherwise the boots appeared as good as new. They should work as well as new, at least. Her maid did much the same thing, but with considerably less confidence and speed.

Cenric had heard of sorceresses healing bodies, but not shoes. "I didn't think sorceresses wasted their talents on boots."

Brynn shook her head. "Your man asked me what sorceresses could do. I mentioned mending things. He asked me to show him."

Cenric didn't know how he felt about his men treating his wife like their personal cobbler. She would be the lady of Ombra and had a pedigree that should have earned respect. At the same time, Ombra was not the sort of place where anyone was spared from work.

"Will these boots be imbued with any special properties now?" Cenric asked. "Silent movement? The ability to walk on hot coals, perhaps?"

Brynn shook her head, not responding to his humor. "The *ka* I've infused into them should make them more durable, but that's it."

"Hmm." Cenric rested an elbow on his knee, still watching her. Several golden strands of hair had worked free of her braid and lightly caressed her neck.

Brynn swallowed, probably aware of his attention. "Thank you," she said quietly. "For last night."

Cenric wasn't sure what to say to that. He didn't want anyone to know they hadn't consummated the marriage, but it was hardly something that could be proven either way.

Edric probably suspected things hadn't gone well, but he knew better than to press the issue.

"You seem close with your dog." Brynn's tone was careful, like she wasn't sure how he might take it.

"Snapper is a dyrehund," Cenric explained. "They were gifts to my family from the goddess Morgi."

Snapper's tail wagged as he recognized his own name.

"Morgi is your patron?"

"She is," Cenric confirmed. "Her other gifts run through my family. On the father's side, at least."

Morgi's gifts passed from father to child, unlike Eponine's gifts, which passed from mother to child.

"Do you know of my family's gifts?" Cenric thumped Snapper's ribs as the dog stretched out beside him.

"I've heard rumors," Brynn answered softly. "But I would rather you tell me."

"I dream of the future." Cenric quirked one brow at Brynn, studying her reaction.

Upon hearing of his gift the first time, most people asked Cenric if he could look into their futures. As a boy, he'd gotten so tired of being asked that he'd stopped telling people he had a gift at all.

Brynn, to her credit, did not ask about her own future. She blinked at him for several moments as if she wasn't sure whether she believed him.

"Parts of the future," Cenric conceded in the face of her skepticism. "Misfortunes, calamities. And only if they will happen in places I have already been, involving people I have already met."

Some gods were said to grant oracles visions of the futures of kings and nations, but dreams from Morgi always concerned the dreamer. Morgi could be unpredictable, but she looked after her own first and foremost.

"Did you foresee any misfortunes last night?" Brynn asked.

She was asking if he'd foreseen any misfortunes involving her. It was akin to the questions he usually got, but she wasn't directly asking about herself, which earned her some credit in his eyes.

Cenric shook his head. "I had no foretellings last night, no. But it's not unusual during times of peace. Sometimes I go months without them." During Ovrek's campaign to conquer Valdar, Cenric had foretellings almost nightly, but that had been wartime.

"I see." Brynn was silent for a moment. The furrow between her brows deepened as if she was thinking. "Is every dream you have a foretelling?"

"No, I have regular nightmares, too."

"Nightmares?" Brynn caught onto his wording. "You have no good dreams?"

"It's not so bad," Cenric assured her. "I don't remember most of the regular nightmares and I'm used to it by now."

Brynn was quiet for a time. "That seems a dubious gift."

"It really isn't bad," Cenric promised. "Besides, Morgi also lets me speak to my dyrehunds."

Brynn shot a glance to Snapper. "You can speak to him?"

"Images, smells, and simple sentences." Cenric looked down to his dyrehund. "About what you'd expect from a dog's mind."

"You can speak in your minds?" For some reason, Brynn seemed to accept him hearing his dog's thoughts more readily than his foretellings.

"Two or three words at a time," Cenric explained. "It's like talking to a young child."

Brynn's face fell and Cenric realized a moment later he should have chosen a different description. He felt the impulse to apologize, but that might push her to discuss her loss, and she might not be ready for that. After a moment, Brynn broke the silence herself.

"Do you have family in Ombra?" She was likely trying to change the subject.

"No," Cenric answered.

"Oh. Do they live elsewhere?"

"Dead." Cenric looked toward the sky. The gulls had mostly left them alone, but one or two of the birds still appeared to be holding out on hope. "I have an aunt who lives on a remote farm, but everyone else is gone."

"I'm sorry."

"I don't remember them," Cenric replied. "Not really. I was sent to Valdar as a child, then my father was killed fighting for Aelgar before I returned. My older brothers with him. I don't remember my mother or my sister at all."

"I see." Brynn's hands slowed as she worked.

He feared she might burst into tears again at the mention of dead relatives, but her face remained impassive. She must be doing better today.

"And you? Any family?"

"My sister is dead," Brynn replied. "Just my mother."

"The sorceress Selene."

"Yes," Brynn confirmed. "My mother never married Eormenulf, but he acknowledged my sister and I."

"That's all that matters." Cenric wondered if she noticed those tendrils of hair brushing her neck. Could she feel them? "Why didn't you go back to her, Brynn?"

This morning, he asked in the city about Brynn's mother. Selene was powerful, and revered. She was not yet the Istovari Elder Mother, but many thought she would be someday. Selene had friends and allies from Hylden to Mynadra in the far southern kingdoms. She could have arranged a much wealthier man for Brynn's next husband. One who lived in much safer lands, too.

"I don't want to go back to her." Brynn seemed to focus harder on her work, if it was possible.

On Cenric's other side, Snapper laid down, snout resting between his paws. The dyrehund sent an impression of utter contentment and happiness.

"You have a right to my protection, as my wife," Cenric said. "I will do all in my power to keep you safe, but Ombra can be dangerous. We are raided more than anyone else."

"Every decision we make is one between safety and freedom, in one way or another." Brynn blinked quickly. "I traded the latter for the former far too quickly last time. In the end, it was for nothing." A muscle in Brynn's cheek tightened as she clenched her jaw.

"Done, lady," her maid said, voice soft.

"Good." Brynn inspected the girl's handiwork. "Excellent. Return these to Daven."

The girl picked up both boots and scurried off.

Learning his men's names already? Impressive.

Cenric studied her. She was mesmerizing with the sea wind in her hair and her skin smooth as butter. Lovely.

"You think being a border lord's wife will be freedom?" Cenric wanted her to know the truth. If she had idealized life in

Ombra, he'd debase her of those notions quickly. He loved the northern land with its rugged peaks and mighty rivers, but it was harsh. Most of their farmland barely got them by and while the grazing in the hills was good for sheep and cattle, they had to constantly fend off raids from Valdari and sometimes southern Hyldish who thought they could get away with it. "It will be a hard life."

"You think I've had an easy life?" The question came softly, gently.

Cenric thought back to Aelgar's words about Brynn. About succession. He'd never thought that perhaps Brynn wanted herself out of talk of the crown as much as Aelgar did.

Aelgar was young, but he had always been sickly. He was a competent king, but his son was a toddler, and he had no other male relatives. If the Istovari wanted to make a play for the kingship…

But Cenric was a northern savage. He had no kings in his lineage, not even a far-flung legendry one. The other aldermen would never accept him as a ruler, probably not even as a consort. That Brynn seemed to have married him without her mother's consent had probably lost her the support of the Istovari.

"You've destroyed your chances of power by marrying me," Cenric said, both understanding and not.

"I don't want it." Brynn clasped her hands on her knees, pulling her legs closer. "And I knew what I was doing."

She was not as helpless as Cenric had thought. She was intentionally running away.

"What do you want, Brynn?" Cenric asked, being blunt. He could be subtle when necessary, but he would be bringing her home in a matter of days. He wanted to know. "From this arrangement?" He gestured between them.

Brynn was quiet for a long moment.

The sounds of the oars creaking, dipping, and splashing took on its steady rhythm. The heartbeat of a ship. Overhead, the gulls still circled hopefully.

Brynn watched the gulls as they fluttered and bobbed on the breeze.

Cenric found himself watching her. There was softness in the way she spoke, in the way she carried herself, even in the way her full lips parted while she looked across the water, but there was a vein of iron underneath.

"I am prepared to do my duty as your wife and as sorceress to the people of Ombra." Brynn kneaded her fingers in her skirt, head down. She had not answered his question.

Cenric kept his attention on her, though she still stared ahead. Always ahead. "Don't lie to me. And don't keep secrets from me. I will do the same with you."

Brynn took just another moment before she nodded. "Very well." She pulled her knees against her chest, hugging her legs.

Cenric could see now that many of his fears had been unfounded. Brynn came with her own wounds, some of them still bleeding. Her family might still be a problem, but they might not. She'd gotten drunk on their wedding night, but he forgave her for that, all things considered.

She was willing to work as hard as the rest of them, judging by how easily she had taken to mending a stranger's boots. She'd shown him respect in front of his men and hadn't kept them waiting at the ship for her.

She didn't expect to live in comfort. She wasn't the spoiled sorceress he'd feared. She was…

"I want a life I chose," Brynn finally confessed. "Not one that was chosen for me."

Brynn was saying she would rather be an alderman's wife on her own terms than something greater by the will of someone else. She fascinated him, this king's daughter who had chosen to marry a stranger because it was the one choice she could make for herself.

She stirred something deep in Cenric's chest. Something warm that tugged him toward her.

Loose tendrils of her hair whipped against her cheek and neck as the wind picked up. Those few strands were so at odds with the rest of her—controlled and restrained.

"Brynn."

She turned to him, her face tight, like she was bracing herself for what he had to say.

"May I touch you?" He didn't realize that was what he was going to ask until the words left his lips. Out loud, it sounded awkward as a boy wooing his first girl—but Cenric very much wanted to touch her.

Brynn searched his face for just a moment. "Yes," she whispered, her voice little more than a croak. She lowered her knees, leaning against the barrels at her back so she wasn't closed off from him. She uncrossed her arms, though her hands remained knotted in her lap. She might have given permission, but it was like she braced for a blow.

Cenric caught the loose tendrils of her hair, feeling them between his fingers. They were just as silky as he imagined. He traced his fingers along her jawline, feeling the softness of her cheek as he tucked her hair behind her ear.

Taking a breath, Cenric dropped his hand, facing the front of the ship again. He hadn't wanted to stop touching her, but didn't want to frighten her. He suspected her previous experience with men had been unpleasant. It might take time before she was ready to trust him.

Several of the men at dice shot them covert glances but left them alone.

Brynn's maidservant had returned the boots to Daven and now seemed to be intently studying the shoreline.

"You asked permission…for that?" Brynn's voice shook with quiet surprise.

Cenric quirked a smile in her direction. "Would you like me to touch you more?"

"I told you I'm prepared to do my duty" Her voice was barely more than a whisper.

That word again—duty. Cenric wasn't sure why it annoyed him.

Brynn wasn't going to stop him from touching her. He realized now that she wouldn't have stopped him if he'd wanted to bed her last night.

"Are you *sure?*" Cenric cocked his head toward her. He held eye contact until she shifted, but she didn't look away.

Brynn cleared her throat. She fluttered her hands in her lap and adjusted her skirt. "You're mocking me?"

Cenric was trying to tease her, but he supposed they were not at that point, yet. "Tell me about Selene. Will she cause problems for us?"

"She respects the wishes of her king," Brynn said.

"But will she be against this marriage?"

"My mother knows there is nothing she can do."

Cenric's eyes narrowed. "You are dancing around the question, lady."

Brynn looked up, frustrated.

"I take it she approved of Paega?"

Brynn grimaced at the name of her first husband. "She did."

"But you and the king did not?" Cenric asked.

"I was young." Brynn's voice turned sad again. "I thought my mother knew best." She glanced down to her hands. "My mother has many opinions, and she wants everyone to share them."

"I see," Cenric said, though he didn't, not fully.

"It was little things for the most part," Brynn continued. "She wanted me to always wear red in public, as is proper for a sorceress. I was to wear ermine in the winter, especially when receiving guests. No pigs at our table unless they were wild boars, and she always sent us a list of recommended visits and gifts to surrounding shires." Brynn paused, blinking several times before she went on. "They were called recommendations, but I know my mother meant them as orders."

"I see." And this time Cenric thought he did see, at least in part.

Brynn swiped a hand over her face. She might be batting away tears.

"Some people might say that you're ruining your life in order to get away from her."

Brynn didn't argue like he expected. "Some people might."

"But?"

Brynn almost whispered her response. "I need a husband."

"You need protection," Cenric corrected. That seemed to be the truth of it. Brynn needed protection from her mother, from the schemes of the Istovari Mothers, and maybe even Aelgar.

Brynn looked to their port side and the expanse of trees sliding by. Her jaw had gone hard.

"You need not worry." Cenric followed her gaze across the water, wondering what he'd gotten himself into. Marrying a sorceress would solve many of his problems, but it might create a host of new ones. That did not change that he'd committed to Brynn, and she seemed committed to him, or at least this course of action. "I protect what's mine."

Unlike Paega, he wanted to add. Cenric had only Brynn's version of events, but that so many people agreed with her did not reflect well on the man.

Brynn cleared her throat. "Even from the Valdari?"

Cenric laughed at that. Several heads turned in his direction, but he waved them back to their work.

"You are mocking me." Brynn sounded wounded.

"Not at all." He shook his head. "Yes, from the Valdari, too. Especially from them."

Brynn looked askance.

"Like I told you, my mother was Valdari," Cenric said. "I was sent to foster with her brother not long after I was weaned. His name was Hróarr. His wife was Venya." Cenric watched her reaction carefully, but she gave him none. It was impressive how well she could do that—drain her face of emotion. "They raised me like one of their sons and I loved them like my own mother and father."

Brynn remained still. "And you raided with them?"

Cenric quirked one eyebrow. "Does it make a difference that I did?"

Brynn held his stare, not blinking, still not giving anything away.

"We never raided Hylden," Cenric conceded at length. "My uncle felt it would be discourteous to his sister."

"Where did you raid, then?" Brynn's tone turned hard. Some of that steel he'd seen at their first meeting showed once again.

"Do you really want to know?" Cenric wasn't going to defend himself to her.

At the same time, he found he genuinely wanted her approval. He didn't need it. She'd gotten herself into this situation and she could make her own peace with it. But...

"Northern Kelethi. We took sheep and goats. Not much else worth taking in those parts."

Cenric's uncle had wanted to go further south, but Venya had forbidden it. *You can take those boys into real danger once they have beards to braid,* had been her demand.

"Then my uncle was murdered," Cenric said quietly. "A nearby jarl came in the night. He burned my uncle's longhouse with most of the family inside."

Cenric's uncle had sworn allegiance to Ovrek, the first king of Valdar. His jarl had not appreciated that.

"I'm sorry," Brynn whispered softly.

"It was a long time ago." Cenric felt that the time for condolences over his loss was long past. "My cousin and I survived because we were late bringing in the sheep that night. We returned home to find it aflame."

"I see." A vacant look flickered over Brynn's face and for a moment he wondered what memory had just been resurrected for her.

But he would hunt for her secrets another time. Right now, she had asked for his.

"We ran for days to find Ovrek's camp."

"Ovrek?" Brynn frowned, then seemed to recognize the name. "The king of Valdar?"

"He wasn't king then," Cenric qualified. "Just a warlord with ambition fresh back from the Kelethi Empire."

"What was he doing there?" Brynn sounded confused.

"Mercenary work. The Kelethi always have use for violent men." Cenric had once considered sailing south to seek work there himself, but the desire to reclaim Ombra had been too great. "Ovrek returned with a band of veterans and more gold than any of us had ever seen in one place."

Brynn glanced at the rings on Cenric's forearms. Ovrek had given him a pair of gold arm rings, but these were silver, sturdier and commissioned by Cenric himself after becoming alderman.

"He promised my cousin and I revenge and a place in his warband. We took it." What followed had been years of hard rations, sweat, bloody knuckles, and constant yelling as they were drilled by the veterans of Kelethi. It had been brutal and many of their friends had not survived.

Brynn shook her head. "How old were you?"

"Thirteen." Cenric had been younger than Kalen was now. Sometimes he wondered how he had ever been that young. "My cousin is also named Hróarr. He docks in Ombra from time to time. You will meet him eventually."

Brynn seemed resigned. "Unless he attacks us, I have no quarrel with him."

That was fair enough. Honestly, much fairer than he had expected.

"I tell you this to say that while I count some Valdari as my friends, my brothers, even, that does not apply to all of them." Cenric had mortal enemies among the Valdari still. Though Ovrek had ruled for years now, not everyone had accepted his yoke happily. "I have no problem killing those who cross me. Regardless of who they are."

Brynn did not seem frightened or even impressed by those

words. He was beginning to realize she wasn't easily impressed, but he enjoyed a challenge.

Cenric shrugged. "From what you have told me, your mother is still going to hate me."

Brynn's voice was hoarse, but firm when she said, "I hope so."

Cenric allowed himself a smile at that. He was already growing fond of his wife.

7

BRYNN

They anchored their ship at the mouth of a small river and camped for the night. Cenric said they were making good time, but it would probably be another day before they reached Ombra.

The men gathered wood and Brynn had Esa practice starting a fire. A sorceress's power was always welcome.

Several of the younger boys with Cenric's crew distributed smoked fish and bread that had probably been fresh that morning.

Snapper bounded in circles around the people as they worked, sometimes disappearing off into the trees.

They had no tents but roped lean-to shelters of oiled canvas between the trees. They spread cloaks and blankets on the soft soil of the riverbank.

Dinner was a quiet, if good-natured affair. Esa stayed close by Brynn's side as she had for most of the journey.

Throughout the day, the men had taken turns at the oars. Cenric had spent every one of his off shifts at her side. It had been strange, but…not unpleasant.

After that first conversation, they'd talked about nothing and everything. He asked her questions about spells and magic, what she could do. She asked him about Ombra. She didn't think she wanted to know anything more about his past just yet. And she wasn't ready to discuss more of hers.

He seemed genuinely interested in what a sorceress might be able to do. He asked specific questions—could a sorceress work with metal? What were the limits of their healing? What success had she had using the blood of animals to fuel spells?

When he spoke of Ombra, it was the way some men spoke of beloved mother or a patron goddess. He described the hills and cliffs and mountains of his lands, the way the rivers looked in spring. Even the winters he spoke of fondly, describing the beauty of snow-capped mountains as almost enough to make the cold worth it.

Cenric wasn't expecting trouble tonight, so only one man was posted as a guard.

A chill blew in off the ocean, despite them being mostly shielded by the trees. Brynn had slept in the cold on the hard ground before, but it had been some time. She'd have to get used to it again.

Brynn lingered outside the light of the campfire after relieving herself behind the trees. She drew her cloak tighter around her against the wind. *Ka* churned on the breeze, rising from the forest. Looking up, the sky was clouded, concealing the stars and the face of Eponine, goddess of the moon.

"You and your maid can share a tent," Cenric said.

Brynn jumped, startled by his voice. She'd been distracted by looking for the moon.

"Sorry." Cenric caught her elbows, steadying her. "I've had the men set your tent up over there. The ship's hull will help block the wind."

Brynn shook her head. "Will I not be sharing one with you?"

Cenric's face was mostly hidden in shadow, but she thought she saw him grin. He shifted, closing in on her. "Do you want to sleep with me?" The words were soft, yet laden with implication.

"No. Yes. I meant…" Brynn cleared her throat. "Thank you." She was making a fool of herself.

Cenric's hold on her elbows tightened just enough to feel significant before releasing her. "You can sleep beside me, if you wish, but I assumed you would prefer your maid didn't sleep next to one of my men." Cenric tilted his head. "And it is cold to be sleeping alone."

Everything he said made sense, so why did she have this odd sense of...disappointment? They had spent the day talking and Brynn found she enjoyed his company, at least so far.

Brynn didn't see him reach for her until a weight rested on her shoulder, its warmth seeping through her wool cloak.

Brynn's heart hammered, unsure what to think or how to respond. She had gotten drunk last night because she'd been so wracked with anxiety over letting him touch her.

Cenric leaned in closer. He smelled of salt air and sweat, like a man who had been working at the oars all day.

"Brynn," he whispered in the darkness.

"Cenric?"

His hands found her face. His fingertips traced the curve of her mouth, thumb sliding along her lower lip. He dipped down and she felt his breath on her skin.

Her heart thundered in her chest and fear rippled through her, but with something else this time. She shook, but she wasn't cold at all.

Cenric fingered the hair at her temples, smoothing it back. His hands were rough and callused, the hands of a warrior, but his touch was gentle.

He traced up her jawline and around the shell of her ear. Then his fingers brushed lower, down her throat.

Both she and Paega had done what they had to do. It had been all business between them, but Cenric...Brynn had never been seduced before, but she thought this might be what it felt like.

Did he want her to kiss him? She wasn't sure, but she wanted to please him. After the disappointment of last night, she felt that she owed him that much. She should at least try.

Brynn pressed her mouth to his. He didn't move.

Had she made a horrible error? Was this not what he wanted? Before she could pull away, she felt him smile against her lips. Suddenly, his hands were framing her face, and he was kissing her back.

Panic and excitement rose up, as intense as they were surprising. This was frightening, as all new things were, but Brynn didn't want it to stop.

Brynn let him lead, hoping he couldn't tell she'd never been kissed before. Cenric seemed happy to take control, his mouth and tongue stroking against hers with experienced mastery.

Cenric couldn't see it, but the *ka* in the air around them shimmered and crackled, picking up on Brynn's emotions. The golden sparks matched the bursts of heat shuddering through Brynn's body, invisible to anyone unable to sense *ka*. *Ka* was the energy that inhabited all living things, that drifted off all living things. Life itself responded as Cenric kissed her. For the first time in months, perhaps years, Brynn felt alive.

Brynn rested her hand on his side and felt the muscles ripple through his body as her other hand squeezed his bicep. A fluttering sensation worked through her chest and down to the pit of her stomach.

She knew his strength from watching him work the oars all day. But his kiss was gentle, even more so as it deepened and slowed.

Brynn had never been with a man this close to her own age. She had wondered during her first marriage but had shut those thoughts down as wrong. But now...

Cenric was young and strong and *alive* and kissing her so thoroughly it made her head spin.

His hand found her hip, seizing her in a fierce hold. He took a fistful of cloth and Brynn kissed him harder, pressing closer. She forgot the cold, she even forgot duty as he drew her in.

A howl rang out from the treetops, halting their kiss. A cold gust swept in, making the trees shudder and several of the men laugh as it passed. Down the river, Brynn heard the waves smacking against the shore harder, splashing and roaring.

Cenric held Brynn tight against his chest until the wind settled. He had a solid chest—broad and muscular. She wondered what it would be like to touch it without his tunic between them.

Cenric caressed her temple. "We should sleep," he whispered in her ear. "We have another long day of sailing."

Brynn nodded against his chest.

He nipped the top of her ear, not hard enough to be painful, but hard enough that she couldn't ignore. A jolt shot through her, a shiver that made her toes curl.

"When we get home, I am going to take you to my bed," he murmured, voice hoarse and low. "And I am going to show you how good it can be."

Brynn tried to speak, but all that came out was a soft whimpering sound.

Cenric held her, stroking her back as if he understood.

Cenric had been serious when he had said he wanted to get home as soon as possible. They broke their camp early the next morning, then sailed for at least twelve hours the next day until the men were too tired to row.

Daven was so pleased with his repaired boots that several of the other men brought items to Brynn in need of repair. She and Esa had nothing better to do, so she spent her own day mending boots and tunics between speaking with Cenric and learning to play dice. Edric insisted on teaching her and Esa, saying it was a vital skill for sailing.

"Boredom is our most common foe when we're on the water, you see," the redheaded man said with a wink at Brynn.

They camped again that night, this time in a small harbor with a village. They were able to moor the ship in a safe enough harbor that they spent the night on board, only going ashore to cook and refill the water barrels.

They slept on the deck of the ship. Esa bedded down on one side of Brynn and Cenric on the other.

Brynn woke on the third morning after their marriage to find him still asleep at her side. He didn't touch her, but it felt intimate. Maybe even vulnerable.

Cenric barely knew her, but he seemed to enjoy being close to her. His words implied he desired her.

What would that be like? To have a man who wanted her? Dare she hoped for that much?

A nagging voice at the back of her head told her she couldn't trust him. She couldn't open her heart so easily. Even if he did find her interesting now, there was nothing to ensure she would keep his interest. She couldn't let her happiness become dependent on how a man treated her.

But Brynn didn't need a husband who loved her. She would settle for one that didn't hate her.

Brynn clambered ashore to relieve herself and splash cold water on her face before climbing back aboard. Everyone was beginning to wake.

The young man called Kalen distributed their rations of bread and fish. Brynn was quite ready to be eating anything else.

They gathered on the deck of the ship as everyone roused. Cenric was now seated on one of the rowing benches and beckoned to her, handing over her portion of dried fish and bread. "Did you sleep well, wife?"

"I'm not used to sleeping on a ship's deck." Brynn didn't want to complain, but her entire body ached. All the same, she had been the one who had committed to this course. She knew freedom would come with some loss of comfort.

"We'll be home soon," Cenric promised. "Before nightfall." He rested a hand on her side. "Then you can tell me if I have done Ombra justice."

"I'm eager to see it," Brynn said. "I've never seen mountains before."

Cenric's eyes sparkled. "Yes, we have those." His gaze wandered to her lips.

Brynn cleared her throat. "Don't work yourself too hard today."

"Concerned for me, wife?"

Brynn was new at this, but she made her best effort. She rested a hand on his shoulder, though it felt bold, almost too bold. "I expect you'll be working hard tonight."

"And why's that?"

Brynn was trying to be subtle, but maybe she had been too subtle. "Didn't you promise to show me your bed?"

Cenric didn't smile, but his expression turned mischievous. He stared up at her, drawing her close enough her legs knocked into his. "Well, now I'm going to be rowing as hard as I can, lady."

Brynn's chest fluttered. She was being seduced, she knew it, and she found it rather pleasant.

"With that promise, I could row this ship home by myself," he said.

Brynn shook her head. "You'd just make it turn."

"If we start sailing in circles," Cenric winked at her, "you'll know who's to blame."

It was an absolutely ridiculous thing to say, but laughter burst out of Brynn. She covered her mouth a moment later, surprised.

Across the deck, Esa shot her a furtive glance, eyes wide then the girl's face softened and she smiled shyly at Brynn.

Brynn cleared her throat ducking her head. She didn't remember the last time she'd laughed.

Cenric grinned at her. He didn't seem to care that they were in plain sight of Esa and his men. He caught Brynn's hand, leaving a kiss on the back of her knuckles. "Tonight, wife."

His promise sent Brynn's heart racing. Briefly, she thought to warn him that she wasn't skilled or particularly good.

But Cenric's mouth took hers in a fierce kiss, his tongue sweeping greedily into her mouth.

Kissing him was like dancing in a storm—exciting and terrifying all at once. It made her knees weak and her head spin and she wasn't sure how he did it.

She realized now what he had been doing for two days. He was making her comfortable. Putting her at ease. He wasn't smashing through her walls, he was taking them down stone by stone.

They made good time, but Brynn noticed Cenric was quieter. He kept watching the horizon, peering ahead.

Brynn had the sense he was anxious but didn't press him.

The mountains came into view by midmorning. They were hazy blue outlines, ghostly and faint.

Brynn watched them grow larger and larger as the time slipped by. Strange excitement welled in her chest, almost like when she had been a girl, and her sister helped her ride a pony for the first time.

As the shapes of the mountains grew, Brynn was sure she could stare at them forever. They were beautiful. Massive. Like monuments made by the gods.

Pine forests spread in all directions, broken by open glades and farmland. The ship reached the wide mouth of a river and turned down it.

Kalen and several of the other younger men lowered the sail, marked with a dark pawprint stitched on a blue field.

Another fishing village stood along the bank, no more than a ramshackle collection of huts. Brynn stood at the prow of the ship, staring at everything as it passed. She studied the people in their woolen caps, shawls, and coats. They didn't appear impoverished, but true to what Cenric had said, Ombra was not a wealthy land.

They sailed up the river for the better part of an hour. Farmland dotted the river on either side, mostly wheat and barley as best Brynn could tell.

The leaves had begun to turn the color of flames—an inferno of yellow and red as far as the eye could see. Workers harvested the fields. Many stopped and appeared to balk in alarm at the sight of them, then cheered and waved at the sight of the sail.

The ship continued until they reached what appeared to be a village. The village had been built along the riverbank and docks had been constructed for the collection of boats and smaller ships bobbing in the water.

The homes were low, made of wattle and daub with thatched roofs and squat chimneys. Children ran barefoot along the river, shouting at the ship.

"What do you think, wife?" Cenric asked, coming up behind her. "You can see the longhouse up there."

Brynn followed his pointing finger to a large, imposing structure at the top of the hill. A palisade had been constructed around the foot of it, looking newly built. The longhouse stretched at least a hundred paces from end to end, much larger than Brynn had expected.

"My hall is inside." Pride colored his tone. "The finest in the north."

Several smaller versions of the longhouse dotted the surrounding foothills, probably belonging to his thanes and their families.

"We finished repairs over the summer and it's as fine as it was on the day it was built."

Brynn smiled at the excitement in his voice. He seemed genuinely eager for her to see. "I'm sure it's lovely."

Cenric kissed her cheek, touching her low back. "You're lovely."

Brynn looked down to her hands. "You don't have to flatter me." If he was trying to get something from her, she wasn't sure what. She had no intentions of holding back from him. He didn't have to keep trying.

"Don't call me a liar, wife. It's hardly fair." Cenric's hand on her back drifted lower, not quite to indecency, but near enough to it.

His affection wasn't unpleasant, she just didn't always know how to respond. She'd seen men be affectionate with their lovers before, but no one had ever been this way with her.

The thanes hauled the ship partially ashore with the help of the villagers on the riverbank. Cenric helped Brynn down from the ship, though it was something she could do herself now.

The rest of the men unloaded, and ropes were attached to the ship so they could haul it the rest of the way ashore.

Brynn stood to the side, waiting. Esa hovered at her side, glancing around them nervously.

A crowd of perhaps fifty people of all ages gathered around them. Brynn noticed many of them stared in her direction, low voices speaking between each other.

She wondered if any of them had ever seen a sorceress before. Few of her sistren chose to come this far north. There were better fortunes and aldermen with more silver in the south.

"They're staring at you," Esa said.

"Wouldn't you?" Brynn asked. "If a strange woman had just come to marry your alderman?"

Esa glanced furtively around her. "I've never seen so many strangers."

Brynn thought that might be an exaggeration, the girl had just spent months in Ungamot, but she didn't argue. "Hopefully, they are future friends." Brynn looked away from Esa to the people gathered nearby.

A young woman with a baby in her arms stood watching. *Ka*

flickered around the young woman's ribs, an unusual amount. It seemed to be concentrated along her ribcage. It might be a new injury or something else, but it looked painful.

Brynn steeled herself. She planned to live with these people so she must make a good first impression.

"Lady?" Esa glanced at her in question.

Brynn approached the young mother, hands clasped before her.

The young woman bowed, only a hint of fear in the way she did. "Lady."

"I'm Brynn." She looked over the stranger, lean and tanned from hard work, her hair wrapped under a kerchief. "Sorceress of the Istovari. Newly wed to Alderman Cenric."

The young woman bowed her head again. Brynn wondered if she imagined the woman's grimace of irritation.

Several other people bowed nearby. Nervous eyes watched Brynn, uncertain of what to do.

Brynn inhaled. "What is your name, if you don't mind?"

"Melain, lady." She adjusted the baby in her arms. "Forgive me."

"Melain, have you hurt your ribs recently?"

Melain shot her a sharp look that was answer enough. Suspicion edged the young woman's eyes. "Yes, lady. I slipped while milking and our cow stepped on me. It was a few days ago."

Brynn nodded. That sounded about right. "May I try to heal you?"

"Heal me?" Melain blinked up at her.

"I don't know how much you know of sorceresses, but we can heal most injuries, yes. Speed the recovery might be a better way of putting it, I think." Brynn had never had to explain to anyone what a sorceress did. The people of Paega's household and most of Hylden had no problems seeking one out. "I won't know for sure until I try, but I think I will be able to mend it."

Melain looked to someone at her side, another woman who

might have been a sister for all they looked alike. The other woman nodded, though her eyes stayed on Brynn.

They didn't trust her. Not yet.

"Thank you," Brynn said. "May I touch you?"

"Yes," Melain consented, jaw tight.

Brynn rested one hand over the other woman's ribs. As soon as she did, she could feel the truth of what Melain had said.

"Can you give your child to someone else for a moment?" Brynn asked.

Melain appeared anxious, but the woman at her side took the baby. Melain looked to Brynn, outright fear now in her eyes.

Brynn was going to make sure this risk paid off for Melain. She pulled on the *ka* already within Melain's body and gentled it into place. She could feel where bones had been cracked and the cartilage bruised. Brynn guided the pools of energy into their correct spaces.

A body *wanted* to be whole—that was what most people didn't understand. It just needed help knowing the way sometimes.

Something snapped into place and Melain gasped, grabbing Brynn's shoulder for support. There had been a broken rib. That explained it.

"Hold on," Brynn said softly. "Almost there."

"What are you doing to her?" someone demanded.

Brynn ignored the voice and kept working. This wound was already several days old, and some healing had already taken place. It wasn't hard to finish, guiding the broken pieces of Melain's body back into wholeness.

Melain gasped, leaning against Brynn. She looked up at the sorceress, eyes wide.

"How is it now?" Brynn asked. "Can you test it for me?"

Melain stood, one hand going to her side. She twisted slowly to the right, then to the left. She looked back to Brynn. "It...I can breathe."

Brynn nodded with a small smile. "It might be tender for a

few days after this, so be as gentle with it as you can."

Melain bowed to Brynn. "Thank you, lady."

The child Melain had handed off squalled and whined, reaching for his mother.

Brynn's chest wrenched at the sound. Her hands shook, fighting the impulse to search for Osbeorn.

"Oswiu." Melain took her son back and he snuggled against her as she bounced him up and down.

The name was even similar. Why did the name have to be similar?

Brynn forced herself not to look at the little boy. Not now. She didn't want to break down crying.

"Are you sure you're alright, Mel?" the woman who'd held the baby asked. She shot a glare to Brynn, outright hostile.

"I'm fine," Melain assured her. "You can check me over when we get back to your house."

For some reason, that only made the other woman glare harder at Brynn.

People were staring at them. More than a few whispered back and forth, but that was fine. Brynn wanted this story to spread. It was better for people to hear about what she could do than for her to tell them.

Melain shifted her baby in her arms. "I might need more healing for this one once he learns to walk," she said in an attempt at humor.

Brynn tried to smile politely as Melain continued.

"He's already trouble enough right now and he can only crawl."

Brynn had been fine seeing the baby in Melain's arms, but somehow those words hit her like a slap. Osbeorn had just learned to walk. His steps had been unsteady and wobbly, but he'd beamed with joy as he'd toddled toward Brynn's outstretched hands.

"Thank you for healing me, lady." Melain seemed oblivious to Brynn's distress.

The woman at Melain's side never once stopped staring at the sorceress. Brynn wondered if she had offended the other woman somehow, but she'd worry about that later.

Brynn inclined her head to the two women. "If you'll excuse me, it seems my husband has finished unloading our ship. I must go."

Brynn was exaggerating somewhat, but she needed to go before she started crying. She found several of the village men had stepped in to help.

Esa fell in behind her and followed her back to the ship. All of her trunks already lay on the grass, ready to be carried up to the longhouse.

Cenric saw her approaching. "Making friends?"

"I hope so," Brynn answered. She focused on breathing, not her empty arms or missing child.

8

CENRIC

Cenric had not been in such a good mood since the summer he and his men had sailed to Ufma for a day of trading and a night of debauching.

He had what he wanted. He had a powerful, beautiful Istovari wife who seemed genuinely interested in Ombra and was already getting along with his people as best he could tell. Thanks to the king, he had enough salt, wine, and spices to get his people through winter. Not only that, but the king would be sending the rest of Brynn's significant dowry north in wagons come spring.

Cenric looked forward to a night of eating, drinking, and then tumbling into his own bed—with Brynn. She was no longer the cold, mournful woman he had met in Aelgar's hall. Already, she had warmed to him and no longer stayed rigid as a meat skewer when he touched her. She'd even started teasing him back.

She was awkward at times, almost like she didn't know how to tease, but he didn't mind teaching her.

Yes, he had high hopes for this evening.

They climbed the hill to his longhouse. Servants carried the food to the half-underground storehouses at the bottom of the hill.

Brynn walked beside him, carrying a satchel since that was

all he had allowed her to carry. She was lady of this house, and he wanted her to meet her new servants without looking like one herself.

Word had spread through the village and the household, and the relief that he was back was almost palpable. He'd been gone for less than a week, but that could have been plenty of time for Valdari raiders.

Barking rose from up the hill. First yips, then howls.

Pack! Snapper's thoughts cried. *Pack!*

Cenric looked up to the house as the dyrehunds came bounding down to meet them. The fluffy creatures came running out of the longhouse, running in circles as they greeted him and the men with wagging tails.

Snapper's thoughts were drowned out as dozens more thoughts rose from the other dogs.

Cenric!

Cenric home!

Mostly the dogs excitedly repeated his name along with impressions of the smells they picked up on him and his companions. They were simple creatures, loyal and affectionate.

Brynn's maid yelped, shrinking back. "Lady, are those wolves?"

"I don't think so." Brynn sounded unsure. "They're too small." She glanced to Cenric, a question on her face moments before they were mobbed by the creatures.

"Dyrehunds." Cenric grinned as the animals gleefully hopped in around them, tongues lolling, tails lashing wildly.

Like Snapper, they were grey and fluffy with triangular ears, an echo of the wolves their ancestors had been, but as Brynn had noticed, they were smaller, stockier.

A large female bounded up, pawing at Cenric's legs. "Ash!" Cenric rubbed the female's sides, making her tail wag harder. "Did you guard the house for me? Did you keep everyone safe?"

Ash whined and barked in excitement. *Cenric!*

All the dogs were loyal to Cenric as they had always been

loyal to his family. Snapper was *his* dog, the one that had bonded most closely with him, but they were all Cenric's dogs.

The dyrehunds had been another gift to his family from the goddess Morgi. Legend said they had once been fierce wolves large enough to ride, but these days, they settled for being excellent companions.

Ash paused, leaning against Cenric, noticing Brynn. *Stranger?* Ash sniffed at the air in Brynn's direction even as the other dogs gathered around her. Most the dyrehunds didn't often meet new people.

A large male with a coat more grey than black stood rigid, facing down Brynn. It was Thorn, an old dyrehund with one eye who was sire or grandsire to most of the dyrehunds now living in Cenric's hall

Brynn's maid shrank back, seeming frightened. She kept her gaze up, not making eye contact with the dogs.

Brynn knelt, offering the back of her hand to Thorn. "Here, boy."

Stranger, Thorn sent to Cenric, aggression in the word.

Thorn had been his father's dog. He had followed Wulfram into the war and refused to leave his master's body even after he had been wounded. Wulfram's thanes had found Thorn with a bloodied face, standing guard over his corpse.

Cenric hadn't really known Thorn before, but these days he was the most bad-tempered and suspicious of all his dyrehunds.

Thorn sniffed Brynn's hand. *Stranger,* the dyrehund patriarch repeated. A low growl rumbled in his throat even as Brynn made a chirping sound, beckoning the old hound toward her.

"Thorn, be good." Cenric stepped forward to intervene, but Snapper bounded to Brynn, getting there first.

Friend! Snapper sent toward Thorn. *Friend!*

To prove it, Snapper flopped down on his back and wiggled around Brynn's feet like a beached fish, entire body thrashing in time with his wagging tail. Brynn crouched down to scratch his belly, and he leapt up, paws on Brynn's shoulder and slopped his tongue over her cheek.

"No!" Brynn cried out, even as she laughed.

Thorn's tail swayed begrudgingly from side to side. *Friend?*

Friend, Cenric and Snapper answered in unison.

The other dyrehunds joined in then, mobbing Brynn with kisses and thrashing tails in exchange for pats and scratches. The younger dogs came first and then the older ones. Only Thorn hung back, but he wasn't the affectionate sort.

Cenric had to pull Brynn up by the arm before the animals dragged her to the ground. "Back!" he shouted, shooing them away. "Down! That's enough attention for you greedy curs."

The dogs backed off, respecting their master. Their tails slowed, but their gazes still focused on Brynn. She'd probably have them at her beck and call within a week.

Brynn laughed, her head covering askew and muddy pawprints marked her dress, but her face was flush and bright with the most beautiful smile.

Cenric realized it was the second time he'd heard her laugh. "You like dogs, then?" He hadn't found a way to broach the topic before.

Brynn was still smiling, even if her eyes lowered a little. "I suppose so."

"Come. Let me show you to the house. Then you can play with them again."

Brynn looked to Snapper. "They're good dogs."

Good dog! Snapper agreed, hopping up and down as he recognized the words. Brynn had just paid him the highest compliment possible.

Brynn looked happy surrounded by Cenric's dogs. Far happier than she had looked surrounded by the majesty of Ungamot.

With a strange tugging in his chest, Cenric realized he wanted her to be this happy always. He wanted to be the reason she smiled and the reason her face flushed with delight. At least she would never want for friendly dyrehunds.

"This way." Cenric led her up the path to the longhouse.

The main doors at the end were open, as were most of the side entrances that let in light and air during the warmer months. Come winter, all those side doors would be sealed and packed with straw until spring came once again. Wooden beams supported the outside of the walls and fresh shingles covered the roof.

"What do you think?" Cenric asked as he pulled her through the entrance.

Brynn looked up at the ceiling as they approached.

Beams crisscrossed the roof, most of the timbers had been blackened with age, but some were new, replaced by Cenric and his men this past summer. Tables and benches took up a good portion of the hall, but there was also a massive pit at the center for cooking fires and braziers for smaller fires in the winter.

Come winter, many of Cenric's people would come here, especially on the colder nights. They'd pack in for warmth and spend the late nights around the fires, sleeping, but also singing and storytelling while the women spun wool, and the men repaired tools or sharpened weapons.

This was definitely not what Brynn was used to, but...

"What's this?" Brynn's hand brushed one of the wooden pillars that supported the roof of the great hall.

Shapes had been carved into the pillars, runes that appeared in threes, twos, and some lone symbols. Some of the runes had begun to wear away, but others were fresh. They were Valdari runes, made of straight lines, characters originally meant to be etched in stone.

"Honors from my guests, though some are from my father's guests, or even his father's."

Brynn looked to him in confusion, calling for more explanation.

"In the north, if we are received well, we leave the mark of our names on the pillars of our host's hall." It was an old Valdari custom, one of many that had crossed the sea and been adopted by the people of Ombra over the years, even before Cenric's birth.

"I see." Brynn looked toward the ceiling, where the marks had been scratched all the way to the top of the first two pillars. "You're running out of space."

"I am," Cenric chuckled. "My son's guests may have to use the next row of pillars."

Brynn smiled, though this time it was tinged with sadness.

Edric and the rest of the men came, carrying the trunks and barrels, and boxes, and various packs of belongings.

"Where do you want these, lady?" Kalen asked, carrying one of Brynn's trunks.

"In the head room," Cenric said. "Put all her things there."

Brynn looked around the longhouse. Her expression shuttered, becoming hard to read again. She was retreating, drawing back behind a barricade of neutrality.

Disappointment flickered through Cenric. He wanted her to be pleased. Had he said something wrong? Was Ombra disappointing her after all? "Come, lady. Let me show you the rest of your servants." He glanced around. Everyone would probably be outside tending the animals, but just the same…

"Lord! Welcome home." A slender woman with her hair pulled back under a kerchief bowed to Cenric.

"Gaitha," Cenric inclined his head to her. "I trust you've managed the household well."

"Right as you left it, lord," Gaitha said.

"This is Lady Brynn of the Istovari. My wife."

Gaitha bowed to Brynn. "Welcome, Lady Brynn. I have run the household for the past few weeks, but I understand you will be taking that over."

"Yes," Brynn answered, voice wavering just enough Cenric caught it. "I will be."

Gaitha bowed again. "It will be good to have a lady of Ombra. I can only civilize these savages so much on my own."

"We're plenty civilized," Edric laughed, grabbing her from

behind. "Miss me?"

Gaitha whirled on her husband. "And welcome home to you, you great fool."

The smaller man cast her a wicked grin. "And how was the past week without me?"

"Splendid. I finally got a full night's sleep without your snoring."

"Oh, I can promise that it won't be my *snoring* that keeps you up tonight."

Brynn watched their interaction, then looked to Cenric in question.

He shrugged. He had never understood Edric and Gaitha's relationship—but that was their business.

"Gaitha, show my wife to our room. Then you can continue berating your husband."

"Best jump to it, love," Edric quipped. "I know how much you love to berate me."

Gaitha swatted at Edric, and he laughed. "At once, lord, but you should know that your aunt sent word for you."

Cenric braced himself. "What now?"

"One of her girls came to the longhouse yesterday and said she had Nettles locked in her barn."

"Nettles?"

Nettles had been the dyrehund bonded to Cenric's older brother, Godric. Thorn had taken the loss of his master badly, but Nettles had taken it worse.

Death was difficult for the dyrehunds to understand, but they usually grasped when people or other animals were gone.

Nettles didn't seem to understand that Godric was dead. Thorn would often linger by the family graves, guarding the silent mounds. He must know that was where his master lay now. But years later and Nettles still often waited by the riverbank, her thoughts calling Godric's name. Sometimes she disappeared for days or weeks at a time and Cenric thought she must be looking for him. Perhaps it was that Godric had left her behind in Ombra when he had sailed south for the war. She'd been a pup, so perhaps she hadn't been able to recognize the rotting corpse as him.

Nettles had disappeared at the start of harvest and Cenric hadn't seen any signs of her for months. Cenric had feared she was gone for good.

"It didn't make much sense to me, either," Gaitha admitted. "Old Aggie said the mules were safe, but that her sheep were now trapped in the cold. She wants you to come deal with the dog."

Cenric's good mood shattered. His aunt might have Nettles trapped in her barn or it might be a badger.

Last time Aegifu had sent for him, she'd sworn a mountain lion was carrying off her geese. It had turned out to be a young lynx barely bigger than a barn cat.

"Go tomorrow," Edric said. "If Old Aegifu has survived one night with the beast, I'm sure she can survive another."

Cenric grimaced, thinking. It was at least three hours to his aunt's home in the hills, two if he took horses. That would still mean he wouldn't arrive until sunset.

If the stupid old woman would move closer to the longhouse, they wouldn't have this problem. But she had been given her farm as part of her dowry and swore she would die there. As her lands had been a gift from Cenric's grandfather, then the alderman of Ombra, it was Cenric's duty to honor their agreement. Part of that agreement was that the family would always see that her needs were met.

Her son had died in the war between Aelgar and Winfric as had her husband and Cenric's father and brothers. Her daughter's family had moved into the south long ago. Cenric was her only relative within three hundred miles.

And if he started breaking the contracts of his fathers…well, he wouldn't do that.

Brynn looked between Cenric and Edric, probably trying to guess what was happening.

"Brynn, I will be back tomorrow." He touched her shoulder. "Gaitha and Edric will see that you have anything you need."

Brynn swallowed and he could swear disappointment flickered across her face. "I understand." She angled her head down. "Never fear for me, lord. I shall be fine."

She had gone quiet again, making herself small. Keeping his family's promises to his aunt felt like he was breaking his own promise to Brynn.

Cenric wished he didn't have to leave her alone. "Kalen," Cenric called. "You're coming with me. Get my horse ready and meet me at the stables."

Kalen hastily set down a barrel he'd carried up. "Yes, lord."

"Bring whatever we need to stay the night."

Kalen was already out the door as his next "Yes, lord" carried on the breeze.

"Brynn?" Cenric turned back to her.

"Yes?" Brynn's eyes had sunk to the floor.

Cenric rested a hand on her shoulder, tugging her around to face him. "I'm sorry."

Brynn shook her head, still not quite meeting his gaze. "You don't have to apologize."

Cenric caught her chin, tilting it up to bring her gaze to meet his. "I'll make it up to you," he promised, stroking his thumb along her chin.

Brynn inhaled a deep breath. "It's alright."

It didn't *feel* alright. Cenric rested his forehead against hers. From the corner of his eye, he saw Edric open his mouth, but Gaitha elbowed her husband, cutting off the interruption.

Brynn tensed for just a moment, like she hadn't expected that. Then she seemed to relax, easing into the closeness with him.

That odd feeling in his chest twisted once again. Her trust in him was such a tentative thing, just now putting down roots. Cenric wanted to cultivate it, protect it, but just now he had to leave her, if only for a day.

Cenric almost claimed her mouth, but instead pressed a kiss to her forehead, just over the space between her eyes.

Brynn softened against him, a slow exhale escaping her lips. Her fingers found the front of his wool mantle, clenching into the thick fabric, careful to squeeze just the fabric.

It was so innocent, so sweet, and yet so timid. Brynn was always nervous when she touched him, like she feared his response every time. Just what had her first husband done to her?

Cenric cradled her cheek as he pulled away, reluctant to let her go. "I will see you tomorrow."

"I will wait for your return." It was a soft vow, patient and meaningful.

He held eye contact with her for a long set of heartbeats to make sure she meant what he thought she meant. She bit her lip, just the edge, her eyes falling to his mouth again.

Cenric silently cursed his aunt as he pulled away. What difference would it make if he took his wife to his bed for an hour or so, and then set out? But no. Some things shouldn't be rushed.

"Edric, Gaitha, look after her. See her settled in. I'll be back tomorrow." Cenric stormed out of the longhouse. If his aunt's captive dyrehund turned out to be another badger…

9

BRYNN

Brynn was surprised by the weight of disappointment that bore down on her as Cenric disappeared out the longhouse doors. Perhaps it was because he was the most familiar person here. Perhaps she really had been looking forward to tonight.

Maybe she just wanted to be the center of a man's attention for once.

Brynn had always done the right thing—and Cenric was tantalizingly *wrong*. He was her husband, true, but she'd married him against her mother's wishes. He was unsuitable, forbidden.

He had said he would show her how good it could be. Cenric had shown he wanted her body, at least, which was already an improvement.

It shouldn't matter, but Brynn caught herself hoping it was more than that. Did he *like* her? Was it just attraction or could he possibly be fond of her as a person?

In many ways, it felt that what she had been through—the war, the loss of Aelfwynn, the loss of her home, six years of a miserable marriage, and the loss of Osbeorn—had aged her far beyond her twenty-three summers, but in some ways, she was still a naïve little girl.

"This way, lady," Gaitha said. "Let the men finish bringing in the trunks. They can do something useful for once." She shot a glare to Edric. "I will show you to your room and around the longhouse.”

“My thanks.” Brynn’s gaze lingered where Cenric had gone.

“Never fear.” Gaitha caught Brynn’s arm and hooked it through hers. “Our lord might be inconvenienced at the moment, but he will be back in no time.”

“Does his aunt often have these emergencies?” Brynn asked.

“Old Aegifu? From time to time. If you ever meet her, you’ll understand.”

“I see.” Brynn let Gaitha lead her toward the back of the hall.

A large hearth took up the center. That would be where most the cooking was done. Two rows of tables and benches lined either side, though they had been stacked out of the way for now. In the back was what appeared to be Cenric’s room, a ladder leading up to the loft over it.

Brynn looked up, taking in the beams that crisscrossed the roof and the carved runes that decked the support pillars. Some of the tables and benches had symbols carved into them, but most were worn smooth with years of use.

It wasn’t a stone keep like Ungamot or Paega’s home, but she could feel the history here. The wood had been scuffed and stained by people long since dead. She could see where Cenric had recently replaced timbers, his own handwork side by side with that of his grandfather.

Brynn had to admit the longhouse was hardly what she was used to, but she felt a pluck of envy in her chest. This was Cenric’s ancestral home. His family had a legacy, a history with the land.

“How long has the family lived here?” Brynn asked, still studying the beams. “How old is this longhouse?”

“Must be over a hundred years,” Gaitha answered. “But Cenric would better be able to tell you. His grandfather expanded it into what it is now.”

The longhouse might be a hundred years old or more, but Brynn could *feel* that this place had been lived in for longer than that. *Ka* had sunk down into the earth, rooting deep into the bedrock of the soil.

It was an accumulation of debris—rushes on the floor, scraps of food, and generations of people living over the same spot. Some places in Ungamot felt this way, but not even Paega's keep was yet this old.

"This place has memory," Brynn mused. The longhouse appeared ordered and reasonably clean, if well-used. "There have been people here for a very long time."

"Is that your sorceress powers telling you that?" Gaitha smiled. At least she didn't seem afraid of Brynn being a sorceress.

"Yes," Brynn confirmed. "It's…there's power in the earth below us."

Gaitha shook her head. "You're a strange lot, you sorceresses. Never understood you."

"Have you known many sorceresses, then?" Brynn looked over her head, noticing the twisting shapes of leaping animals carved into the uppermost beams.

"I knew a sorceress who owned a brothel," Gaitha said. "Strange creature, she was. But she kept the men from hurting us too much and always patched us up if they did." Gaitha shrugged. "Treated me better than other masters I've had."

Brynn shot a surprised look at Gaitha. She managed to stop herself from blurting out the first words that came to mind, but her face must have given it away.

"Aye. I was a whore, once. It was another life." She looked to where Edric was directing several other men with barrels of salted pork. "Now I only have to worry about satisfying one man."

"But I have the lust of ten men, so be sure to pity her just a bit, aye?" Edric shouted over his shoulder.

Brynn's face burned. Was this considered normal conversation in Ombra? Would Cenric expect her to banter like this at some point?

"Edric!" Gaitha scolded. "Don't speak that way in front of the lady."

"I speak that way in front of you," Edric countered.

"And I'm not a lady," Gaitha snapped back.

"You're my wife and you're a lady if I say you are!"

Brynn watched the exchange with consternation, not sure if she should intervene or not.

Gaitha rolled her eyes. "Right this way, lady. We'll leave that animal to his business. I'll show you to your room."

Brynn followed her, stepping carefully around the cold hearth in the middle of the room.

Cenric might have recently repaired this place, and his grandfather might have built it, but the roots of the building were deeper than that. Brynn wouldn't be surprised if wattle and daub huts had once stood in this same spot, or even tents made of animal skins. Envy returned, twisting in her chest.

Istovari sorceresses had no roots this deep, no place this old to them. They kept up their network of connections, a sisterhood of women spread across Hylden and beyond. They married their daughters to aldermen and wealthy thanes and gathered to make decisions. Many served in the households of those who could afford them. A few traveled from place to place like journeymen, taking coin for work where they could get it.

But they had no homeland. Not really.

Brynn's mother had told her the goddess Eponine had given them a gift in depriving them of their own country. It meant they were free to belong anywhere, or nowhere, as they chose.

Brynn had tried to remember that as a child when they were shuffled from shire to shire after her father's death. Selene had left Brynn and her sister behind, going to seek the help of the Istovari Mothers, but Winfric's armies had been after the girls, forcing them from their home.

Aelfwynn had pragmatically decided to ally with Aelgar, recognizing him as king. Brynn's sister, for all her brashness and defiance, had known Hylden would never accept a woman as ruler.

Their mother had been furious when she'd found out. So furious that Brynn had wondered if her mother had wanted Aelfwynn to make a claim to the kingship anyway.

All through the war, the sisters had fought for their homeland, starving in forests and freezing in fields, all the while knowing their home at Ungamot would be forfeit even if they won.

Through those hard years, Brynn had ached for stability. She had wanted desperately to go home—never really knowing where that was. She'd hoped to find that in Glasney, but Paega never let her feel at home.

"Here you are." Gaitha pushed aside a wooden door at the very far end of the longhouse. It slid open on well-oiled hinges. Above it, a ladder led up to a loft overhead. "The younger boys and unmarried thanes sleep there." Gaitha pointed up. "They know to be quiet, but they sleep and guard in shifts, so you might hear them stomping around at night every so often. The girls have places around the main hearth."

Brynn stored the information away for later.

"But this is your place in here." Gaitha stepped inside, pushing the door open the rest of the way. "Cenric had me get it ready for you."

Brynn stepped after the other woman, not sure what to expect. Inside, her trunks had already been set down at the foot of the bed.

A fireplace sat at one side, one of the few stone features in the longhouse. Brynn realized the chimney went through the loft, providing a source of warmth above. The fireplace was cold for now, but a pyramid of sticks sat ready to be lit. The bed had been covered in animal skin pelts.

At first glance, Brynn thought a man stood in the corner, but it was a full suit of chainmail with greaves, bracers, and a shining helm with the design of a snarling wolf.

"That might be your husband's most prized possession."

Gaitha nodded to the armor.

Brynn could see why. Mail was rare, much less a full-length tabard of it. That alone was probably worth three good horses or more. It might be as fine as Aelfwynn's had been and hers had belonged to their father.

"This is Cenric's room, then?"

"Well, both of yours now."

Brynn hadn't shared a room with Paega. He had been wealthy enough that they had separate chambers, but she'd already known Cenric wasn't as rich.

"I've tidied it up." Gaitha smoothed a hand over the furs on the bed. "I imagine you'll be wanting to rearrange the furniture. In fact, I suggest you do. It will be a good lesson to teach that husband of yours after leaving you alone on your first night here."

Brynn frowned at Gaitha. "Isn't he your lord?"

"Aye, and I'm as loyal to him as much as anyone. But it's best a wife never let her husband get away with anything, trust me. Next thing you know, the men are walking all over us."

Brynn exhaled slowly. "I've been married before." And she'd learned from her mother that not all women could be seen as allies.

"Ah." Gaitha paused, taking in Brynn with a pensive look. "What happened to him?"

"I left him," Brynn answered. "The king gave me a divorcement."

Gaitha's brows rose in surprise. "How long ago?"

Brynn considered it. "I left my first husband three months ago. The king granted a divorcement a few days ago."

"I'm sorry," Gaitha said sincerely.

Brynn frowned. "I…why are you sorry?"

"Leaving husbands is a messy business, hardly something a woman does for amusement. I'm sorry."

Brynn looked down. She expected judgment, not acceptance, and certainly not sympathy. "Thank you. I didn't want to do it, but…after my son…" She trailed off, not sure how to explain it.

She knew that if she stayed with Paega, her mother would push her to have another baby with him. And she couldn't do it, *wouldn't* do it—to herself or to her children.

Gaitha fluffed the pillows at the head of the bed. "You have children, then?"

Brynn opened her mouth, then shut it, unable to give voice to the words.

"I see. No need to explain, lady." Her face softened in understanding before she glanced around the room. "I'll oversee the evening meal. I'll send one of the girls to show you and your maid to the bathhouse. Would you like that?"

Brynn wasn't sure what that meant, but a bath sounded pleasant. "Yes. I would."

"You must be tired from your journey, lady. We can introduce you to the servants and the rest of the household tomorrow."

Brynn inclined her head. "I am grateful, Gaitha."

The freckled woman took Brynn's hands in hers. "Please send for me if you need anything at all, lady."

Brynn waited until the door shut before sitting down on the bed. The mattress crunched as she did, probably filled with pea shells or something similar. She touched the furs on the bed, soft and clean.

She didn't need an easy life. She didn't need a safe life. Like she had told Cenric, she wanted a life of freedom. From the lack of ceremony and the comparative humility of this place, it seemed to her that it was exactly what she was looking for.

Brynn inhaled a deep breath, still hearing Edric and Gaitha banter on the other side of the door. She closed her eyes and counted backward from ten.

This was nothing like what she had expected, or what she was used to. Yet, she had been uprooted many times in her life and survived every one of them.

But she was tired. When she had married Paega, she had been sure she would spend the rest of her life in his lands, living out her days among a people to call her own.

Now here she was, starting over once again, for what felt like the hundredth time in her life.

10

CENRIC

Aunt Aegifu's plot of land was mostly untilled pastures used for grazing sheep. She had a cohort of young women—orphans and runaways, mostly—who worked for her and kept her house. But when it came to the hard labor of repairing walls or slaying monstruous beasts, she called on Cenric.

He'd never particularly liked the old woman. He liked her even less in this moment, but it was a matter of principle. He had a promise to keep.

Not to mention she had been the first person in Ombra to recognize him as alderman. He owed her, whether he liked it or not.

Cenric spurred his chestnut stallion, Bada, faster up the winding mountain road. Kalen rode close behind him on a dun colt. The horses seemed to be in a good mood, and flicked their tails, wanting to run faster. Snapper ran alongside them, projecting his usual unadulterated joy.

But it was a long journey, and they needed to pace the animals. Cenric reined in Bada a few miles from the longhouse of Ombra, on a ridge overlooking the river and the settlement.

"Did you see the fields on our way in?" Kalen asked. "It looks like much of the crops have been gathered in already."

"Yes," Cenric answered. "I did notice. Looks like Gaitha drove the ploughmen as hard as she drives Edric."

Kalen laughed at that. "I wonder how much fishing they were able to do."

"I want to finish that wall on the outer banks," Cenric said, thinking of the partial barrier that currently enclosed the village.

He'd been working the past couple summers to narrow the lines of attack, especially from the river. There was always the risk the Valdari could go down the coast, up one of the river's many tributaries, and cross the land to attack them. However, if anyone wanted to do that, they'd have to carry whatever goods they pillaged over land. It would be a time-consuming and dangerous venture. And there was always the chance a local lord—like Cenric—would hear of their coming and attack first.

Unlike Valdari raiders, Cenric would be able to muster mounted horsemen and archers. If he had the chance to attack first, both he and any potential raiders knew who would win.

That left the river and the coast as his most vulnerable points.

"Do you think Lady Brynn knows any spells that could help protect us until the walls are finished?" Kalen asked.

"I imagine if she did, she would have used them to protect her son," Cenric answered. Not that he hadn't wondered about it himself. He did want to ask her if perhaps she could make the existing walls stronger, like she'd done with the boots.

It was different, he supposed, but he wasn't especially familiar with what sorceresses could do.

They rode in silence for much of the journey. The sun sank lower, transforming the sky into streaks of yellow and gold with swaths of purple and blue. Ombra at sunset simply took his breath away.

From here in the foothills, everything as far as the eye could see belonged to him. The lands had been a part of his family for generations. Sometimes, Cenric was sure he could feel his own heartbeat when he touched the soil, it was so much a part of him. But certainly not everyone in the shire felt the same.

Many of the farms of Ombra were now empty, their

inhabitants having migrated south years ago. The southern lands had been ravaged by Aelgar's war, leaving swaths of more forgiving land uninhabited. Not only that, but Cenric's father and brothers had died, leaving the shire of Ombra without an alderman for several years before Cenric himself had returned. The uncertainty combined with the promises of land from southern aldermen had pushed hundreds of people into the south.

Cenric spotted several deer and one startled covey of pheasant—a good sign that there was still time for hunting before the winter set in.

Hunt! Snapper cried, woofing in excitement.

Not now, Cenric responded. *Later.*

Snapper made a low grumbling sound, but he stayed beside the horses as he was told.

They came upon Old Aegifu's lands as the sun was just touching the distant mountains. Her flocks of sheep were being brought in by the gaggle of shepherdesses, their sheep dogs harrying the animals to and fro. They came down off the hills in a stream of white, brown, and black.

Several of the girls called out to them. One ran toward the cottage tucked among the trees.

Cenric was usually recognizable on his large chestnut stallion. Bada stood out, even from a distance.

By the time they reached the cottage, Old Aegifu was waiting for them, leaning on her cane. She had been his father's older sister, though Cenric had never figured out just how much older.

Her hands were knotted with age and her back stooped with a lifetime of labor, but her eyes still glittered bright as a polecat's. She stood in the doorway of her cottage, shawl drawn tight around her shoulders.

Aegifu and her girls kept bees, geese, sheep, and spun some of the finest cloth in Ombra. They were far enough inland with the mountains at their backs that few people ever came this way by accident. And it was too far for raiders from the coast to venture.

"There you are!" Aegifu called. "I'm pleased to see you, Alderman Cenric."

Cenric might be alderman of Ombra, but the way the old woman spoke the title had unnecessary emphasis. Sometimes, he wondered if Aegifu was taunting him with it. She'd given her allegiance suspiciously easily when he had landed in Ombra two years ago with a band of warriors to retake the shire.

Geese scattered before Bada as he and Kalen's horse drew to a stop.

Aegifu inclined her head, bowing to Cenric. "I am most grateful, lord. Thank you for troubling yourself with the likes of me. You must doubtless be very busy."

Friend! Snapper trotted up to the old woman.

Aegifu, whatever her opinion of Cenric, did stoop to pet his dyrehund, murmuring sweet nothings as she stroked the dog's back. Her own dyrehund had died some years ago and she hadn't gotten another.

Cenric dismounted Bada, lashing the stallion's reins to the fence outside the farmyard. "Busy, lady?"

"It took you two days to respond to my request," Aegifu said. "I know you would only do such a thing if you were most busy."

Snapper spotted something in Aegifu's garden and rushed over to investigate.

Cenric decided not to tell his aunt he had been in Ungamot fetching a new bride. She'd find out eventually, but the fewer words he had to exchange with this woman, the better. "Where is Nettles?"

Aegifu's mouth snapped shut. She was probably offended by his terseness, but Cenric didn't care. "In the barn." She pointed to the low structure with her cane. "Killed two lambs before the girls were able to get the rest out. They locked the doors and we've been waiting ever since."

From the outside, all Cenric could see was the sealed doors

of the barn. "Is she responding?"

Like Cenric, Aegifu could speak to the dyrehunds. Morgi's blessings passed along the father's bloodline, so while Aegifu's children hadn't inherited it, she had.

"She isn't speaking, no."

"How do you know it's Nettles, then?"

"I know your brother's dog when I see her." Aegifu raised her chin and sniffed as if he had just paid her some great insult.

Cenric jerked his head at Kalen and the boy followed. With a little luck, they might be able to deal with whatever was in the barn and head back to the longhouse tonight. Though it would be dark, it might be worth the risk to see his wife tucked into his bed.

The barn was a low building with stone walls and a thatched roof. It housed a hundred or more sheep and Aegifu's collection of geese and goats in the winter.

Cenric marched toward the doors of the barn. They were thick and sturdy, meant to protect the animals from the cold. A bar had been placed across the front, sealing it shut.

"Snapper!" Cenric shouted.

His dog came running, leaping over the garden fence. *Cenric?*

Hunt. Cenric pointed to the sealed doors.

Snapper stepped closer, sniffing at the ground. *Sheep.* Snapper knew he wasn't supposed to hunt sheep, and his thoughts dripped with disapproval.

Nettles?

Snapper snorted. *Sheep.*

Cenric grimaced, glancing over his shoulder to Aegifu. *No Nettles?*

Meat. Snapper paused, his tail stiffening as he paced carefully back and forth. He perked up his ears. *Friend?* Snapper could smell another dog, but he just wasn't sure if it was Nettles.

"Snapper, back." Cenric made a shooing motion.

Friend? Snapper looked up in question.

Back, Cenric repeated, this time sending the thought.

Making that grumbling sound, Snapper backed up as Cenric reached for the barred door.

"Be careful!" Aegifu shouted. "Don't need her mauling you or that plump little boy you brought with you."

Kalen made an indignant sound.

Cenric ignored his aunt. "Kalen, my sword. Get your spear." Morgi forbade him harming dyrehunds, but it might not be Nettles inside the barn. It might be some other feral dog.

The younger man jogged to Bada and pulled Cenric's sword from the horse's saddle. Kalen handed over the weapon, bringing his own spear.

Cenric held his gaze. "If it charges, stab it. If you miss, I'll get it."

Kalen nodded solemnly. "Yes, lord."

Cenric stepped up to the door and lifted the bar. He pressed his ear to the door, listening. *Nettles?* He sent the thought toward the barn.

Nothing.

Cenric glanced to Kalen. "Ready?"

"Yes, lord."

Cenric ripped the door open and stepped to the left. Kalen stepped up beside him, spear at the ready.

Inside was dark, especially with the waning sun. The smell of dung, sheep, and the stench of death burst out. Aegifu must have told the truth about two dead lambs, at least.

"Get us a torch!" Cenric called to Aegifu.

The old woman swatted at one of her many charges, yelling for the girl to get them a torch. "You'd best not burn my barn down with only weeks to the first snows!" Aegifu shouted.

The girl returned carrying a lit torch, her head down. She tried to give it to Kalen, but Cenric snatched it out of her hand. With a spear, Kalen would need both hands.

Cenric and Kalen searched the dark, waiting for their eyes to adjust. There were several stalls made up from wooden slats, but they all appeared open.

"Stay back, girl," Aegifu said, probably speaking to the girl who'd brought them the torch. "Let the men handle this one."

Nettles? Cenric squinted into the darkness of the barn. He might have wanted to close the door after them, but he'd rather not be trapped inside.

Something stirred from the shadows. It fled from the torchlight, shrinking back.

Kalen glanced that way. Spear out. "Did you see it?"

"Something small," Cenric muttered, pointing to the darkness. "No bigger than a cat."

Kalen let off an awkward sigh. "Well. That's something."

They edged toward the movement. The stench of death grew stronger.

Cenric raised his arm, lifting the torch as high as he could without setting the thatch on fire. Movement scuttled back from the torchlight.

It must be another lynx.

"Come here," Cenric beckoned. "Come here and let us kill you, little thief."

He came a step closer, Kalen at his back.

A low rumble vibrated through the air. It took Cenric a moment to realize what he had heard.

Kalen grabbed Cenric's shoulder and jerked him back as a snarl ripped through the air.

"Hold!" Cenric snapped, facing squarely forward. "If we run, it will chase us."

"What is it?"

"Not sure." Cenric raised his torch, catching a glimpse of a grey, white, and black coat. It was some sort of canid, but he couldn't make out the details.

A low rumble came from the dark. The creature was trying to project strength, hiding its wounds behind aggression.

"I don't think—"

Cenric never heard what Kalen thought.

An explosion of fur and claws and teeth burst at them from

the darkness. Kalen jabbed straight for the beast's chest, but instead of spearing it through the heart from the front, the spearhead scraped along its shoulder.

The animal stumbled to the side with a yelp and snarl. Cenric spun to face it, sword ready. He blocked the animal's path to Kalen while the boy raised his spear again.

By the torchlight, Cenric finally got a good look at the animal. It was a dyrehund. An exceptionally aggressive, starving dyrehund.

"Nettles," Cenric exhaled the name.

Wherever she had been these past months, she had not fared well. She was far thinner than she should have been, making her legs look too long and displaying her ribs under her thick pelt.

She tried to circle the two men, ears flat and teeth bared. She favored her left shoulder, where Kalen's spear had sheared her pelt open.

Crouched to the ground, Cenric lowered his weapon. "Easy, girl."

Nettles? came Snapper's confused thought from beyond the open barn door as he recognized her. *Pups?*

Back, Cenric repeated to his dog. He kept his attention on the growling female. *Nettles? Friend.*

She pinned her ears, lips curled. *Go.*

Friend. Be calm. Cenric had been told his father could command dyrehunds like soldiers. Either that was an exaggeration or Cenric just lacked the skill.

Godric, Nettles demanded.

Cenric shook his head. *Godric is gone.*

Godric! The female snarled, canine teeth flashing. However Nettles had gotten here, she was frightened and in no state to be reasoned with.

Regardless, Cenric couldn't harm dyrehunds, not intentionally. As the dyrehund's teeth flashed, Cenric wondered how Morgi would feel about self-defense.

"Kalen." Cenric kept his voice level, not taking his eyes off the animal. "She's going to lunge again."

The dyrehund pinned her ears, head crouching low.

"Easy—"

The dyrehund leapt, but not for Cenric. She shot past him, barreling for Snapper.

Hurt! Snapper yelped as the female crashed into him, her teeth finding the scruff of his neck. He pinned his ears, tail going between his legs. *Nettles hurting Snapper!* Whining, he dropped down low, trying to show submission.

Nettles wasn't having it. The female latched on, yanking her head from side to side.

Snapper and Nettles had known each other for years, slept around the same hearth and run in the same pack, but none of that seemed to matter now. Nettles attacked him with a crazed fury.

Cenric rushed over and smashed the pommel of his sword down on Nettles. She let go and spun, lunging for Cenric.

Her body was thin, but she was strong and in her prime. Her teeth clamped on his left arm tearing into his sleeve.

Cenric let off a shout at the same time Kalen did.

Snapper lunged for the female even as she bit Cenric. The dog hadn't defended himself, but he leapt to protect his master. *Bad Nettles! Bad!*

Snapper nipped the female's haunches, and she let go of Cenric, spinning back to Snapper.

Kalen was on the dyrehund the next instant, stabbing at her side. Kalen was fast, efficient.

The dyrehund let off a yelp of pain. She jerked back to Kalen.

Cenric had dropped the torch—in the dirt, not the straw— but his sword arm was fine. He jabbed straight for Nettles' neck as she twisted on Kalen.

The dog's body seized, and her paws clawed at the empty air. Nettles let off a strangled snarling, gagging sound.

Kalen pulled back and speared her in the neck. He drove her

to the ground, her body flailing like a fish.

She kept fighting, even with her blood soaking the ground. She struggled, getting weaker and weaker, then went still, mouth still open in a snarl.

Nettles hurt? Snapper's ears pinned back. He stepped toward the dying female. *Hurt?* He looked plaintively up at Cenric. *Help Nettles?*

Cenric shook his head. He'd wanted to help Nettles, but the choice between Snapper and this feral dog hadn't been a choice at all. Things had escalated too quickly, too violently.

Kalen and Cenric looked at each other, both panting. The dead dyrehund lay before them, seeming much smaller now. Cenric ripped his sword out and Kalen freed his spear.

"Good fight." Cenric smoothed the dog's coat. "Rest now, girl."

"She bit you." Kalen gestured to Cenric's arm.

He grimaced, raising his arm for a better view. His sleeve had been torn open and he had several bruises in the shape of teeth, but shockingly no broken skin. Pain still throbbed through his entire arm. "Good thing my new wife is good at mending, isn't it?"

Cenric looked over to Snapper. *Hurt?*

Snapper whined, coming over to Cenric with his ears flattened.

Cenric looked his dyrehund over, not seeing any blood on him, either. It seemed that the thick fur around his neck had come in useful. Dogs usually sustained wounds on their faces and forelegs in fights, but Snapper had dropped to the ground as soon as Nettles charged.

"Forgive me, lord." Kalen cleared his throat awkwardly.

Cenric shook his head. "You did well." He wiped his sword blade on the dog's pelt. "Exactly as I taught you."

"Still, I—"

Movement rustled from the shadows of the barn.

Kalen's spear was up the next moment. He glanced to

Cenric.

Snapper's ears flicked up. *Pup?*

Realization hit Cenric. *Oh no.*

A squeaking whine came from the dark. Something stirred.

"Can you carry the torch?" Cenric knew what they were going to find already. *Stay,* he ordered Snapper.

This time, the dog dropped to his haunches, whining beside the dead female.

Kalen picked up the torch from where it burned on the ground. He led the way into the dark, spear at the ready.

The whimpering took them to a corner of the barn, in one of the stalls. The gnawed bones of a goat lay cracked and chewed across the entrance. From the look of it, the dyrehund had even cracked open the bones to lick out the marrow.

A flurry of motion, the shape no bigger than a cat, yelped and leapt into the light.

Kalen reached for it but missed. The small shape scurried toward Cenric, and he used his boot to block it.

The shape ran straight into his foot and yelped, scurrying back as the torchlight fell on a dyrehund pup. Its coat was the same shade as its mother. It flattened its ears and growled even as it balled into the tightest coil it could manage.

Kalen reached for it, and the pup dodged again. It ran straight for Cenric, and he grabbed it by the scruff of its neck.

He lifted the puppy with his bruised arm, though it was starting to ache. The puppy weighed no more than a pound or two, face still plump and limbs too short.

It wiggled in his grip, making a squeaking sound like a wounded rabbit, calling for its dead mother.

The puppy appeared well-fed despite Nettles' almost emaciated shape. That was probably why she'd been desperate enough to come this close to humans. It was a wonder that Nettles had gone into heat so late in the season. This pup should have been weaned and learning to hunt by now.

Cenric wondered if there had been more pups somewhere

in the woods. There probably had been at some point. Cenric grimaced, looking over to the corpse outside the barn. He wasn't sure what else they could have done. Maybe he should have put Snapper inside Aegifu's house, first. Regardless, he couldn't take back what had happened.

"Do you want me to take it, lord?" Kalen asked, holding out a hand.

Cenric held the pup to the light. It had drawn itself into a ball again, whimpering.

"No…" Cenric said after a long moment. "No. Find a basket for me."

"A basket, lord?"

Cenric thought about it. Foretellings were Morgi's only way of telling him what *not* to do. Her ways of telling him what he *should* do tended to be more symbolic.

It wasn't often Cenric was sure he was seeing a sign from Morgi, but this seemed too coincidental to be anything else. He had found an orphaned dyrehund puppy the same day he brought his new wife home. A dyrehund puppy that had been born months out of season.

"This is for my wife."

"Lady Brynn?"

Cenric shrugged. "She likes dogs."

"Cenric!" Aegifu's voice shouted from the entrance to the barn. She jabbed at the dyrehund's carcass with her cane. "Are you just going to leave this here?"

"Kalen, find something we can use to wrap the body. We'll take her home and bury her with my brother." He would reunite Nettles with Godric, if he could do nothing else for her. "After you fetch me a basket."

"What happened to your sleeve, boy?" Aegifu demanded. "And what's that?"

Cenric sheathed his sword and moved the pup to his right hand. "It's a gift," Cenric answered.

"Well, that does seem fair." Aegifu extended one hand.

"After you forced me to put up with that crazed dyrehund for days."

"Not for you."

Pup? Snapper came nearer, cautiously.

Pup.

Puppy? Snapper's excitement was almost palpable. *Puppy!*

Kalen returned carrying a basket that looked deep enough the pup couldn't crawl out.

Cenric shoved the pup inside. Immediately, the little animal huddled into a corner, crying. Cenric felt a bit guilty at that, but its mother had attacked Snapper, attacked him. What should he have done? "It's for my wife."

"Your wife?" Aegifu squinted at him. "Did you marry that Rowan girl? Well, it's about time, but she can't speak to the dyrehunds. She has no right."

Cenric shook his head. He and Rowan had parted ways months before. "Not Rowan. Someone else."

"Oh? And when was this?"

Cenric thought for a moment. "Three days ago."

Aegifu snorted. "Short notice, it seems. Did you get a baby in some thane's daughter?"

"She is Brynn of the Istovari sorceresses, niece to King Aelgar, and lady of Ombra." Cenric set down the basket.

Snapper leaned over the edge of the basket, seeming to have forgotten the dead dyrehund. *Puppy!*

"Ah," Aegifu nodded as if Brynn's name explained something. "I still have more right to that pup than she does."

"The puppy is for her," Cenric repeated. "If she doesn't want it, I'll bring it back."

"It's like that, is it? Fine. Come inside, alderman. It's too dark for you to travel home tonight."

Cenric glared up at the sky, but had to admit Aegifu was right about that last part. He picked up the basket with the puppy, cursed at nothing, and followed his aunt into her small, thatched house.

In the barnyard, Kalen had found a threadbare blanket and was working to wrap Nettles' body for travel.

11

BRYNN

The bathhouse was delightful, even if Brynn had to walk to the foot of the hill to use it. Built over a hot spring, the wooden structure was constructed of logs with an open roof.

Brynn had heard tales of hot springs, but never seen one herself. Her mother had theorized that the waters must be rich with *ka* and that was what made them hot. Now Brynn could see that the water held no more *ka* than usual, maybe even a little less. Perhaps she would never know what made some waters warm all year long.

Brynn washed her hair, then every inch of her skin with Esa's help. She combed her hair while seated on the steaming rocks, her feet soaking in the warm water.

It wasn't bath night, so they had the place to themselves. Gaitha told her the women bathed together at the second day of the week, the children the first and men the third. The heat from the stones seemed to melt away Brynn's tension and chase away the autumn chill.

When they were done, Esa helped Brynn into a clean dress. Brynn daubed her hair dry, and Esa helped her braid it into a neat plait. After, Brynn braided Esa's hair in turn.

The girl had soft auburn hair, almost red. It was as fine as eiderdown in Brynn's hands.

Brynn caught herself humming as she worked, an old lullaby

Aelfwynn had sung to her, and she had sung to Osbeorn. That surprised Brynn a little. She hadn't sung in months. If Esa noticed, she said nothing.

When the two of them returned to the longhouse, Gaitha greeted them. The other woman continued her tour of the inside of the longhouse with promises of showing her more tomorrow. Gaitha led the preparation of the evening meal for the residents of the longhouse.

Brynn observed for the most part, chopping onions, radishes, and carrots with the household girls. They poured them into a cauldron that was already boiling with chunks of lamb. The household girls stirred the pot while Gaitha oversaw the closing of all the longhouse doors and windows for the night.

Brynn went with a few of the girls to bring in the geese and stable the goats. Cenric's flocks and herds appeared healthy, with plenty of young animals. His home was prosperous enough.

The dyrehunds sprawled on the floor for the evening meal, snapping up scraps and gnawing at the discarded bones and organs of the slaughtered sheep. The one Cenric called Ash pawed at Brynn's leg, whining under the table.

Edric shooed the animal away. "None of that, now!"

The dog backed away, whimpering.

"Sorry, lady," Edric said. "If you give the animal any space at all, she'll be walking all over you!"

"Sounds like someone I know," Gaitha muttered. She grabbed Edric's face, pulled him around, planting a hard kiss on his mouth.

Brynn returned her attention to her cup of ale. There was no wine tonight, only ale. Brynn accepted it as she had accepted everything else so far. The stew was filling and well-salted. She picked out the chunks of vegetable and meat with her fingers, then drank the broth. Pieces that were too large, she cut into smaller pieces with her eating knife.

"I am grateful to have you here, Lady Brynn." Gaitha extracted herself from Edric's lips long enough to let him finish his meal. "I'll finally be able to get back to my own household now."

Brynn nodded. "I'm grateful for you looking after the longhouse."

Gaitha stroked Edric's shoulder, brazen and shameless. "Of course," she said. "When my lord requires the service."

"Who looked after it before you? His Aunt Aegifu?"

"Mad Aggie?" Gaitha scoffed. "No, she hasn't been here since Cenric became alderman. A girl from the village. Rowan."

Brynn's mouth went suddenly dry. "I see." A cold tightness grew in her belly. She didn't want to think what that might mean. She was afraid to ask.

"She's a fine girl. Hard worker. Left the longhouse in good order when I took it over."

So Cenric had some village girl, presumably unmarried, running his home? Brynn wasn't naïve.

Brynn forced herself to go empty, to not think. She wouldn't care. She wouldn't.

"I'll be back tomorrow to finish showing you around," Gaitha assured her. "You've run a much larger household than this, it sounds like. I'm sure you'll take to it in no time."

Brynn softened her mouth into a smile, but inside everything had gone tight and cold as if she'd been splashed with a bucket of water.

They finished the evening meal and fed the leftovers to the pigs. The dogs fought with several large sows for their fair share.

Esa was given a place in the main hall with the other girls. She had slept on a cot inside Brynn's room back in Glasney, but she didn't complain when she was shown a pallet on the floor.

"Are you going to be alright?" Brynn asked, giving the girl a significant look.

"Fine, lady."

Brynn touched the side of Esa's face. Esa was barely fourteen. Brynn had fought in a war at her age, but somehow Esa seemed like a child to her. She wanted to protect the girl, that was all she had ever wanted for her. Maybe she was trying to protect Esa the way she wished someone had protected her. "You don't have to punish yourself," Brynn said quietly. "It wasn't your fault."

Esa had been the one tasked with watching Osbeorn that terrible night, after all. But what could she have done? She was one girl, still inexperienced in her power. Brynn had been older than her when she'd hid while Aelfwynn and her thanes were slaughtered.

Esa's lower lip trembled, but she looked away. "I'll be fine. Send for me if you need anything?"

"I will."

Esa canted her head, adjusting her pallet in the midst of the other household girls.

The sun had already set by the time Gaitha saw Brynn to her room—her and Cenric's room. She kissed Brynn on either cheek in the way of sisters or good friends, then bid her good night.

Brynn stood alone, hands clutched before her.

Overhead, she could hear the household boys and men clambering up to the loft for the night. The girls were bedding down by the central hearth and would keep it tended through the night.

Brynn's own fire had been banked. In winter, a servant would stay awake to tend it and watch for stray embers, but it was not yet cold enough to need one now.

The floor was made of slats of wood, not earth like the main longhouse. That would help keep it warm, she hoped.

How long had Cenric been lord of Ombra? She didn't remember. But he had to have been lord for years.

Looking at the bed, it now seemed too large and too cold for just one person. Married or no, aldermen did not sleep alone for years at a time. Paega was the exception.

Brynn herself had not slept alone in a long time. Esa had slept in her room, as had Osbeorn.

Some nights, Brynn would lie awake watching him sleep,

listening to the soft rise and fall of his tiny chest. He had been so small, so delicate. So precious. Her entire heart. So many of her hopes and dreams were wrapped up in that little boy.

The silence of this bedchamber was deafening. The loneliness was an achingly frigid thing that latched icy claws around her heart. A lump formed in Brynn's throat, and she fought to swallow it.

Alone. She was alone.

It was just for the night, perhaps, but it felt deeper than that. Her father was gone, her sister was gone, Aunt Ulstrid was gone, and so was Osbeorn.

Children who died young went to the home of their patron gods—or so it was said. Osbeorn would grow up in the home of Eponine, the goddess who was ancestress to all Istovari. She would raise him as her son, free of pain, hardship, and fear. Osbeorn would be happy, never knowing the struggles of a mortal life and Brynn tried to take comfort in that. She tried very hard, repeating to herself with every beat of her heart.

Somehow, it was not comforting at all.

Brynn removed her overdress and the wraps around her ankles and calves. Her legs were instantly cold, but it was the only way to avoid waking up with the wraps tangled around her legs.

This might be a lonely bed in a lonely room, but it would still be warmer and more comfortable than the past two nights. Brynn adjusted her pillows and smoothed her blankets.

As she shuffled to the edge of the bed, something hit her foot. Most of the floor had been swept clean, spotless, but something poked out from under the bed. It was all but hidden, easily missed.

Brynn drew aside the blankets. A comb lay mostly wedged under the bed. She pried it free, inspecting closer.

It was carved of bone and decorated with careful etchings. It had been darkened with age, probably a family heirloom. A woman's comb.

Another woman had lived here, very recently. Maybe up until a week ago when Cenric had received the orders that he was to marry her.

Brynn had already suspected, if not known. So why did it hurt so much?

Brynn set the comb on top of one of her own trunks. She didn't want to weep again. She'd already wept so much.

What had she expected? Any lord who could afford them kept concubines as well as wives. This was a political arrangement between her and Cenric, just as it had been between her and Paega. Cenric was to provide a safe home for her, and she was to run his household and serve as his shire's sorceress. They were to help each other continue their respective bloodlines and that was it.

Cenric had fulfilled every expectation so far. There was no reason for her to be upset. None at all.

Brynn woke before the rest of the household, while it was still dark. She layered on her linen chemise, wool overdress, and belts. They were clothes for work, not for travel. She strapped a pouch onto her belt with her eating knife, thread, needle, and a few basic tools. Lastly, she bound her hair back under a large kerchief.

Brynn stepped out into the longhouse. A few of the animals stirred, but she didn't see movement yet. She went outside to relieve herself. Several dogs followed. The older male, the one Cenric had called Thorn, watched Brynn the whole time, his remaining eye trained on the sorceress.

The air was crisp, fresh. Frozen dew crackled beneath Brynn's feet and a few dyrehunds rushed around her, tails wagging.

The small pack only stopped when they saw her heading into the longhouse. It seemed they had more interesting places to be.

In the central longhouse, Brynn found Esa still asleep, but one of the girls was already awake, kneeling before the fire pit at the center of the longhouse. She was a slight thing with dark hair that hung around her face in whisps.

"What's your name?" Brynn asked.

At Brynn's words, the girl jumped. She kept her head down, almost shaking. "Seva, lady."

From what Brynn had seen, Seva appeared to be the youngest of the longhouse girls. She might be ten or eleven.

"Seva, I'm Brynn." The sorceress motioned to the fire pit. "Show me what you were doing."

Seva complied, showing Brynn how they stoked the fires and placed the dough for the morning's bread into the coals with paddles.

Brynn watched her carefully and when the other girls roused, she had them show her their tasks as well. Brynn needed to know their duties if she was to manage them.

Esa woke and hastily dressed, shadowing Brynn dutifully.

Brynn followed the girls for the morning milking and healed the chapped udders of an old nanny goat. The girls collected the extra milk and what wasn't set aside for the morning meal was poured into a pot for cheesemaking.

Gaitha came by the time the boys were stirring in the loft. Hot bread with soft cheese had already been prepared on the table.

Brynn threw herself into work, having the girls and Gaitha show her how the geese were kept, what they were fed, and who cared for them. Same for the household's dogs and sheep, though the latter seemed to be the responsibility of the household boys. The dyrehunds seemed to be treated more like children—shooed from underfoot, but indulgently tolerated for the most part.

Brynn visited the stables where most the horses were kept

along with the pigs and sheep. She had the boys tell her how the animals were cared for, who was responsible for their care, and so on.

For now, she needed to know the state of everything. There would be time to change things later, if she wanted to.

All morning and into midday, she worked, or rather watched other people work. A meal was prepared for later that afternoon and the house girls seemed to have that under control.

Brynn grabbed her cloak, Gaitha, and Esa, and headed down to the village. As they descended the hill, a few dogs followed them, then went bounding back up when they realized there wouldn't be a hunt or other sport.

"Is there anyone ill in the village?" Brynn asked Gaitha, the wind whipping up in her face. "Anyone injured or in need of mending?"

Gaitha considered it. "There might be a few," she said. "I can show you."

Brynn had Esa carry her bandages, clean scraps of cloth, and purifying herbs. It was much as they had done back in Paega's lands, Esa working the part of her assistant—except when she had been watching Osbeorn.

They entered the village to find it abuzz with activity. The fishermen were just bringing in their catches and sorting through their bounties on the beach.

Gaitha took her first to a hut beside one of the fisherman's homes. It seemed that the elderly resident had cut his hand cleaning nets a few days ago and the wound had been slow to heal.

Brynn was able to fix it with *ka* in a few minutes. The old fisherman didn't smile, but he thanked her solemnly before going back to his work.

By the time the three of them left the hut, it seemed that word had spread of Melain's healing yesterday. A young boy came to meet them, asking with downcast eyes if Lady Brynn would come see to his sister.

It turned out the girl had burned her arm cooking. Burns were more of a challenge than cuts, but Brynn was able to coax the flesh back into wholeness. It was still tender after, but the skin was no longer raw and weeping.

They tended to a spattering of minor injuries, thankfully nothing too serious. Cenric's people were generally in good health.

A few younger children had coughs, which was not unusual. Brynn was able to alleviate some of the distress, but the phlegm would need to clear on its own. She left them with herbs and tinctures, all infused with *ka*, and instructions to come see her if anything got worse.

It was late afternoon by the time they finished.

"Well, we've probably missed the midday meal." Gaitha glanced toward the longhouse. "I wonder if Cenric's back."

Brynn had a feeling Cenric would have come see her if he had returned. But maybe not. She barely knew him.

"Gaitha," Brynn's voice nearly cracked, and she had to clear her throat. "Do you know where Rowan lives?"

Gaitha shot her a quick look. "I do. Everyone knows where everyone lives here in the village."

Brynn took a deep breath. "Could you show me to her house? I think I have something that belongs to her."

Gaitha studied Brynn for a long moment, then looked to Esa.

Esa didn't know who Rowan was, so why would she care?

After a moment, Gaitha said, "This way."

Rowan appeared to live with her family in a much smaller version of the longhouse. Pigs and a few goats rooted in the fenced enclosure around the house.

A young boy greeted them, hair dark like most the people here. "Gaitha." The boy bowed, though he didn't use a title.

"Rod, this is Lady Brynn. Lord Cenric's new wife."

The boy's eyes went wide, and he bowed.

"Is Rowan here?"

The boy hesitated just long enough for Brynn to notice. He shot a look at her, the stranger behind Gaitha.

Did he know she was a sorceress just yet? Brynn wasn't sure what reputation sorceresses had here. No one had seemed too reluctant to accept her help, though they had been wary. It might just be how they were with all strangers.

"I'll fetch her," Rod said. "One moment, lady." He bowed again to Brynn.

Brynn waited. She looked toward the longhouse up on the hill. From here, she could see the longhouse staff at work with the animals and tending chores.

The household was well-ordered and hard working. It was a household to be proud of.

A vaguely familiar young woman appeared, her hair bound back, though not covered. She wiped her hands on her wool apron, face smudged. She looked as if she had been at work when they summoned her.

"Lady Brynn." Rowan's expression was guarded, closed off. She looked to Gaitha, almost as if she was seeking the other woman's help.

Gaitha smiled at her. "Hello, Rowan."

Brynn didn't want to feel anything. Rowan was a member of this village, of Ombra. She was one of the people Brynn was supposed to protect now.

"Forgive me for interrupting you." Brynn forced a smile. "It will be brief." She glanced to Gaitha and Esa. "Could you give us a moment?"

Esa withdrew. Gaitha arched one brow at Brynn, then took a few steps back to join the handmaid.

Brynn slipped inside the gate of the small farmstead. The young boy and an older woman watched them from the doorway of the small house.

Rowan stood straight, face neutral.

She was beautiful, Brynn supposed. Rowan reminded Brynn of a mink with her bright eyes and the easy, sinuous way she moved. Brynn remembered then where she had seen the girl before—yesterday on the riverbank.

"Lady." Rowan inclined her head.

"I hope Melain is well."

"My sister is much better." Rowan's words were clipped, terse. Brynn noted that Rowan did not thank her.

Brynn inhaled slowly. "I think this is yours." She reached into the pouch at her hip and offered the ivory comb, folded in a scrap of cloth to keep it safe.

Rowan took it and her eyes widened in recognition. "I thought I had lost this."

Brynn forced a smile. Rowan eyed her coldly in response. They stood there, staring at each other.

Sooner or later, Brynn would have had to face Rowan. She hadn't wanted to be surprised by meeting her husband's former lover, but Brynn had no idea how to do this. For all his faults, Paega had no other women during their marriage. To him, Brynn supposed she had been the other woman—the unworthy replacement to his beloved first wife.

"Do you feel Cenric treated you fairly?" Brynn asked at length. There it was. Now Rowan at least knew that Brynn knew.

Rowan let out a bark of laughter. "As his concubine, you mean?"

Brynn trained her face into one of composure. She had a responsibility to Rowan. Regardless of her own complicated feelings, she had a duty.

Rowan sighed, tucking the comb into her own pouch. "He never made me promises, but…"

But Rowan had hoped he would. That was clear enough from the way she avoided eye contact, her jaw tight.

Brynn didn't trust herself to speak. She didn't know what to say.

Rowan looked over Brynn's shoulder, not quite at her. "He's paying my dowry along with that of my younger sister. I'll get to choose my own husband, too."

"When did he dismiss you?" Brynn wasn't sure why she asked. It seemed relevant, but she wasn't sure if the question arose from honest concern or petty jealousy.

"Would you have rather turned me out yourself?" Rowan snapped.

Brynn remained impassive. "I don't want to be your enemy, Rowan."

"Then why did you come here?" Rowan's tone turned hard, sharp.

"I'm sorry," Brynn said softly.

"You're a southerner. You don't belong here." Rowan made a derisive sound. "You know you don't."

Brynn forced herself not to react. She was used to the sting of rejection by now. "Are there many girls like you in the village and surrounding farms? Ones he's taken to his bed?"

Rowan shrugged. "Not that I know of."

Brynn lowered her voice, trying to soften her next question. "Has he taken any of the household girls? Or any of the village girls?" Brynn told herself she was asking these things because she was worried about Esa, but she knew deep down that wasn't the only reason.

Rowan shook her head. "He keeps one woman at a time."

"Are you sure?" As lord of Ombra, Cenric had full rights to the women in his household under law. It was the Valdari way of things, after all.

"Cenric has taken concubines. Maybe a few whores here and there."

Brynn almost thought to ask Gaitha if she had ever bedded Cenric. But that question would be extremely inappropriate, even if Gaitha had been rather open about her past life.

"But not the household girls and not random village women." Rowan sounded certain. "He's a good man, Lady Brynn."

Brynn closed her eyes. She hoped Rowan was telling the truth. "Thank you, Rowan." Brynn forced a smile. "I appreciate your time."

Rowan looked over Brynn from head to foot, like she was seeing her for the first time. "Why did you come here?"

"I wanted to return your comb," Brynn answered honestly.

"No. To Ombra. I've asked about you. You're a sorceress. Niece to the king. You could have married anyone."

Brynn couldn't have married anyone, actually. Cenric had been the only unmarried man of suitable status to marry a king's daughter who wasn't an atheling. Cenric had no kings in his bloodline, which meant he couldn't use her to take the throne after Aelgar's death. Aelgar and Brynn had discussed as much, but Rowan didn't need to know that.

Brynn inclined her head in a bow. "I think I have kept you long enough, Rowan. Thank you for speaking with me."

Brynn stepped back through the garden gate before she lost her composure. Her husband had kept concubines before, but he seemed to treat them fairly and wasn't exploiting the household girls, if Rowan was to be believed.

That was far better than Brynn had feared and yet…it wasn't as much of a relief as it should have been.

12

CENRIC

Cenric spent the night on a hard floor that was definitely not his own bed. He had to listen to the whining of the pup in a basket, too. Aegifu's girls gave her a bowl of milk and she lapped up the goat's milk greedily but went right back to whining after.

Snapper tried to console the puppy, but she missed her mother. He leaned over the basket and nosed at her, licking the puppy until she finally fell asleep.

The next morning, Aegifu had several errands and chores for "big strong men."

Cenric's bruised arm ached, but he tended to the fence and chopped wood with Kalen, enough for a week. It was more than his aunt deserved. The girls chopped their own wood most of the time, after all.

They finished around midday and made to ready their horses. Kalen carried the puppy's basket on his saddle.

Aegifu came hobbling out of the garden, leaning on her cane. "Leaving so soon?"

"Yes," Cenric answered. "I have completed your errand and dealt with Nettles."

"I have holes in the thatch that need to be fixed," Aegifu said. "You might as well take care of it while you are here."

Cenric gritted his teeth. "The time to mention that was this morning. Before we spend the whole of it chopping wood."

"So, you will not do it?" Aegifu asked, a challenge in her voice.

"No."

"Morgi told me last night that if you leave now, you will meet with a rockslide on the way home."

Cenric cast the old woman a sardonic smile. "Well, she didn't tell me." Nettles' body wasn't stinking yet, thanks to the autumn chill, but it wouldn't be long. They needed to get home, and Cenric needed to get back to his people. Not to mention his wife.

Morgi did also speak to his aunt, but Cenric doubted that the goddess would share something like that with Aegifu and not him. Aegifu could lie, after all.

Cenric and Kalen had to move slowly down the mountain paths. The pup went back to whining, but after the first hour, it finally quieted.

Cenric pulled his mantle closer around his shoulders against the chill autumn breeze. It was getting cold. That was yet another reminder of the coming snows.

They came into sight of the longhouse a few hours after noon. It made Cenric's teeth grind to think of all the work he'd missed. Not to mention that his new wife had spent most her first day in Ombra without him.

He should have been there to introduce her and show her the village and surrounding farmland. He might still get to do that, but Gaitha and Edric had probably already started.

They reached the longhouse as the midday meal was being served to the household servants. They were just approaching the stables when the dogs began to bark and howl.

Ash, Thorn, and the rest came flocking around their horses, dog bodies wiggling and tails thrashing madly. Their thoughts were a chorus of excitement. Cenric and Kalen dismounted, a few of the stable boys coming to take their horses.

The older female, Ash, came close to the basket with the pup, sniffing with interest. Inside, the pup began whining again.

One of the dogs barked and then all the animals were howling and barking in a rancorous chorus.

Cenric scooped up the basket with the pup while Kalen saw to their horses with the other boys.

"Lord!" someone shouted from the longhouse. "Lord, you're back!"

Edric appeared at the doorway of the longhouse a moment later. "Cenric!" He greeted his lord and old friend with a hearty embrace, though the red-haired man was a full head shorter. "I was going to take a group of men to fetch you right after this meal."

"There was no need to worry," Cenric scoffed.

"That's what I told Brynn, but she was worried."

Cenric noticed Edric called her Brynn, with no title attached. Maybe he had grown more familiar with the new lady of Ombra. "Where is she?"

As if summoned, Brynn appeared in the doorway. Flour smeared the front of her dress, and her hair was drawn back in a kerchief, but those same stubborn strands of hair flew loose about her neck. From the look of her, she had been hard at work.

Cenric's face broke into a smile before he thought about it. "Wife!"

Brynn came outside, followed by several of the house girls and Gaitha. "Cenric." She kept her hands in front of her, neutral. Was that relief in her face? "I'm glad you're back, lord."

"Edric says you were concerned for me."

Brynn glanced to the smaller man. "I was, lord. I'm glad you're back safely." She looked at the basket. "What's in the basket?"

"Let me show you." Cenric set the basket on the ground. He had to shoo back dogs as they crowded around. He reached inside and picked up the dyrehund pup by the scruff of the neck.

He held it toward Brynn, supporting its back legs. "The pup and its mother were eating goats in my aunt's barn."

Brynn's eyes widened. "What happened to the mother?"

Cenric grimaced. "Nettles never recovered after my brother died."

Brynn looked to the puppy, sadness creasing her face. "You killed her." The words weren't an accusation, just a statement of fact.

Cenric lowered the pup. He felt it had been justified, but felt a little shame, nonetheless. "She went after Snapper."

"Is he alright?" Brynn looked over to the dyrehund in question.

"Fine, just a little shaken at the time."

Brynn's shoulders relaxed a little. "I see."

Cenric followed her gaze to Snapper, currently gazing fondly up at the puppy. "I can take her back to my aunt."

Brynn frowned, looking at the small ball of fur in his hands. "I don't understand."

"Because you like dogs and I thought…" Cenric's chest deflated. He'd hoped Brynn would be happy. "I thought having your own dyrehund, might…help."

"She's…for me?" Brynn seemed genuinely surprised.

Cenric shrugged, feeling awkward. "A gift." He wasn't sure why the word came out sounding like an apology.

Brynn hesitated, looking between him and the puppy. "You brought me a gift?" She licked her lips, almost like she didn't believe it.

"You don't have to accept it," Cenric said. "She's going to be a handful, and I don't blame you if you don't."

"No," Brynn said quickly. "No, I want her." Brynn scooped the puppy from his hands and cradled it against her ribs. Naturally and easily, like she'd missed having living things in her arms. The pup still whined, but it burrowed in the crook of Brynn's arm, small tail flicking. Brynn shushed the pup, stroking her grey fur. "She's beautiful, Cenric." Brynn's voice cracked with emotion.

Cenric watched as his wife petted and soothed the small animal. Had no one ever given this woman a gift?

Puppy, Snapper snorted with approval.

Cenric allowed himself a sliver of satisfaction. "I need to tend to the docks and check the fields. But I will return."

Brynn's mouth pressed into a stern line. "Do what you must." There was a shortness to her tone. Anger?

Cenric arched one eyebrow. His return wasn't going the way he had expected. "Has something upset you?"

Brynn broke eye contact, looking away even as she nestled the puppy into the crook of her elbow.

"I did not mean to spend last night away. Believe me, I would have preferred to be here." Yes, he would have much preferred to sleep with Brynn instead of on the hard floor of his aunt's cottage.

Brynn looked down at the pup in her arms. The small creature peered up at her, whimpering. Brynn stroked its head and cuddled it against her chest. "I believe you. I'm glad you're home."

She didn't sound glad.

Cenric would sort this out later. He looked to Edric. "Anything I should know before I head to the fields?" For now, he needed to check the progress of his fieldworkers, fishermen, and shepherds. He'd already been gone for too long.

13

BRYNN

Brynn bit the inside of her cheek as Cenric walked away, heading to the fields. Her heart felt like a tangle of brambles, knotted and slicing her every time she tried to sort it out. She hadn't realized how fond she'd grown of Cenric in such a short time.

She thought her heart had been seared away, yet despite everything, the stubborn organ had survived years of an unhappy marriage and the loss of her only child.

It would hurt to share Cenric. There was no way around that.

The puppy wiggled in Brynn's arms and she stroked her head, shushing gently.

"What did the lord give you?" asked one of the girls, a freckled young thing that was all knees and elbows.

"A puppy." Brynn turned to show them.

More of the girls crowded around, crying out with equal parts delight and sadness.

"Is that a dyrehund?"

"She can't be more than a few weeks old."

"Late in the year for a litter, wouldn't you say?"

"Look at her tiny paws!"

Brynn let them fawn over the pup as they headed back into the house. The household workers were finishing their food and heading out to chase down Cenric. They probably wanted to be hard at work in the fields by the time he reached them.

The girls set to the tasks of cleaning trenchers and clearing scraps from the table for the dogs and the pigs.

Brynn sat by the fire, the small fur bundle in her lap. She examined the puppy carefully, feeling at the small creature's *ka*. She had a few scratches. Urine stained her paws, and she was still too young to be weaned.

Brynn set to work while the girls cleared the table. She washed the pup in a basin, close to the hearth so as not to get her too cold.

Several of the dogs including Ash came and sat beside Brynn as she bathed the small creature and folded her into her apron to dry. She poured some of the morning's goat milk into a shallow dish and let the puppy lap it up.

Thorn, the one-eyed patriarch of the pack, sat back on his haunches, observing silently.

Once she was done, Brynn folded the puppy into the crook of her arm and went back to overseeing the girls. The kitchen maids were already working to ready the evening meal. A slab of cured pork roasted over the fire and the dough for the evening's bread was kneaded beside the hearth.

"It's alright, little girl." Brynn caught herself kissing the top of the fuzzy head before she quite knew what she was doing. She hadn't had a pet in a long time. In Paega's keep, dogs had their place. Here, the dogs seemed to be allowed everywhere.

Brynn headed out to the longhouse gardens to see to the harvesting of the peas and carrots, the dyrehund pup still tucked under her arm. She wiggled at first, but settled after a few moments, falling asleep, her belly plump and mouth stained with milk.

The weight of holding something living in her arms made something wrench in Brynn's chest. That hollow ache that was fast becoming familiar.

Brynn kept careful track of time as the day wore on. She headed into the village with Esa and Gaitha again that afternoon to see to injuries and ailments she hadn't gotten to the day before.

Some villages had healers or priests who saw to their sicknesses, but Brynn quickly learned that there was nothing like that here. A few of the older women were skilled in midwifery, but their old healer had died a few years ago.

Brynn had Esa hold her puppy when she needed both hands and held the puppy herself when she didn't.

Brynn learned from a fisherman's wife that Rowan's father had a cough, and so Brynn went back to their house. The man was old, perhaps in his sixties. His gnarled hands showed a lifetime of hard work, and his right leg ended just below the knee.

He eyed Brynn suspiciously as she put her hands on his chest and back. She suspected he didn't want her touching him at all, but the way his young daughter, Fern, Rowan's little sister, stared pointedly at him, she'd gotten him to agree to her ministrations.

Coughs and illnesses were always difficult. Brynn spent the better part of an hour channeling *ka* into the old man's body while working to draw out the bad *ka* causing the infection. Much damage had been done to his lungs and she could sense scarring.

Fern, Rowan's sister, sat on the floor of their home and petted the puppy with Esa. They sat quietly, waiting while Brynn worked.

Apparently, Rowan was with their mother tending the goats. For that, Brynn was grateful.

While Brynn couldn't fix the scarring without risking additional damage, Brynn was able to guide the elderly man's body through mending as much as she could. By the time she finished, he breathed easier and no longer wheezed when he spoke.

After, Brynn looked up and saw the sun was sinking toward the mountains. Cenric should have returned to the longhouse by now.

"Esa." Brynn gathered up her box of healing tools. "We need to be going."

Fern leapt to her feet. "Lady, can you heal animals, too?"

Brynn hesitated. She needed to get back to Cenric, but he had lasted a whole day already and she was already here. "I might."

"Our best milker hurt her leg a few days ago. We've been worried we'll have to make her into stew, but maybe…" The girl glanced at her father. "If it's not too much trouble?"

Brynn forced a smile. "I can't make promises, but I can take a look."

She followed the girl outside to the goat shed attached to the cottage. Inside, a white nanny goat with magnificent horns waited, refusing to put weight on one hoof.

Immediately, Brynn saw the accumulation of *ka* in the goat's fetlock. "It's broken," she muttered. "Can you tie her for me so I can get a better look?"

Fern did as she was asked. She grabbed the nanny's rope collar and hooked it to a notch in the wall.

Brynn knelt in the dirt, trying to sense as much as she could without touching. She chewed her lip, thinking.

The bones were misaligned, or at least she thought they were. So much *ka* had swelled around the injury, it was hard to be sure. She'd have to make sure the bones were properly set before she fused them back together, or else the goat would always walk with a limp. That could be life-threatening since most animals grazed on open pastures.

"Esa, hold her against the wall."

Esa handed the pup to Fern and stepped up to obey.

Motion at the entrance to the shed caught Brynn's eye. Rowan's father stood at the door, leaning on a cane. Sadly, Brynn had no way to repair a severed limb.

"Papa, you shouldn't be outside," Fern protested.

"I'm fine," he said. "Don't let me interrupt."

Brynn looked to Esa to make sure she was prepared. The girl

gave a short nod.

No point in waiting, then.

Brynn carefully reached out to touch the goat's leg.

The nanny writhed, head snapping from side to side against the rope.

"Sorry, girl," Brynn crooned. "Hold on. I'm going to fix it."

The nanny goat let off a wail, still thrashing.

Brynn grabbed the foreleg and slammed the goat's shoulder sideways with her own. She locked the animal into a steadying hold as best she could. Not waiting for the goat to stop thrashing, she grabbed the injured fetlock.

The goat screamed again.

Brynn focused. She'd worked on uncooperative subjects before, mostly animal, but a few human. Brynn guided the *ka* in the animal's body, forcing the bones back into place. She felt something snap—it was a soft sense of something sliding into place. Barely there. Bones did not align in straight lines unless helped. It took skill to recognize the correct positioning.

Brynn got the bones as close as she could and clamped her hands around the injury. She poured *ka* into the animal's limb, feeling *ka* sear the broken pieces like molten lead.

The goat wailed, kicking and flailing. The puppy whined from across the shed and Brynn had to fight not to be knocked over. The rope snapped and Brynn had one instant of seeing the nanny's horn swinging toward her before her head snapped back and she sprawled on the dirt floor.

"Lady!" Esa shouted.

"Lady Brynn!"

Brynn pushed herself onto her elbow just as the nanny wrenched free of Esa. The goat hopped awkwardly for several steps before putting weight on her injured foot. The goat flicked her tail indignantly and sniffed her fetlock, then trotted to the far side of the shed.

Esa was at Brynn's side in a moment. "Lady?"

"I'm well." Brynn felt carefully at her cheek. The goat's horn had just missed her eye, thankfully.

"I'm so sorry, lady!" Fern was at her side the next moment. "I should have tied her better. I'm so sorry!"

Brynn patted the girl's arm. "It's fine." She took her puppy back. Brynn looked to the goat, now pacing back and forth, indignant and wholly ungrateful, but using all four hooves now. "Make sure she stays inside for a few days, alright? That leg is set, but it will be tender for some time."

"Yes, lady. Thank you so much."

"I think we need to be heading back to the longhouse, but send word if you need anything else, alright?"

Rowan's sister clutched Brynn's hand. "Yes, lady. Thank you, lady."

Brynn stepped outside, inclining her head as she passed Rowan's father. "Same goes for you. Please send word if you need anything."

The old man jerked his head once. Like most of the village, he was probably still deciding what to think of her.

"Lady, your face." Esa frowned at her.

Brynn shook her head. She could feel *ka* building up beneath her skin. "I'll deal with it later."

Brynn had been working magic all day. She wanted to rest before she tried healing herself.

On the way back to the longhouse, they passed several fishermen and farmers coming in for the night. The shepherds and swineherds brought animals down from the hills into the pens. There might be an hour or so left of daylight, but it was fading fast.

"I'm not sure Rowan will appreciate you helping her family," Esa said.

Brynn looked down to the puppy in her arms. "Rowan can feel how she wants. Her family are my people and it's my duty to care for them. Not to make her like me."

Esa let off a long sigh. "You will do your duty, lady. No matter what."

Brynn wasn't sure what to say to that.

"Don't you…hate anyone?" Esa asked, almost hesitantly.

Brynn frowned at the girl, not sure where this was coming from. "Esa?"

The girl shook her head. "King Aelgar took your father's kingdom."

Brynn couldn't let the girl speak like this. "The aldermen would never follow a woman." Her sister had known this. "My uncle took nothing from me."

"Paega was horrible to you." Esa's voice came out softer. "He always found something awful to say behind your back if not to your face, but you never did anything."

Brynn swallowed. The reminder of her former husband's contempt stung like nettles in her chest.

"But you never said anything back. And then…" Esa's voice broke. "And then when I failed you…"

Brynn stopped halfway along the path to the longhouse, facing the girl. "Esa?"

Tears plucked at Esa's eyes. "I failed you, lady. You loved your son more than anything and it was me who failed to protect him."

"No, Esa." Brynn grabbed her by the shoulder. "No, it wasn't your fault."

"But it was!" Esa's voice broke into a sob. "I was supposed to look after him, but when the raiders came, I just…froze. I didn't run, I didn't fight, I didn't…"

Brynn choked down her own tears, wrapping the arm that wasn't holding the puppy around Esa. During all those months grieving in Ungamot, it hadn't occurred to her that Esa might be grieving, too.

Esa sobbed against Brynn's chest, her slight frame wracked with sorrow. "Why don't you hate me?" she wept. "Why haven't you punished me?"

Brynn closed her eyes, tears running down her cheeks to soak the top of Esa's head. She couldn't speak for several moments, dragging herself into composure. "When you told me what happened…" She stared over Esa's head to the distant mountains. "How you froze, how you couldn't think." Brynn cleared her throat, trying to rid herself of the lump catching her voice. "It reminded me of the day my sister died."

Esa drew in a shuddering breath, finally looking up to the other sorceress. "Lady?"

Brynn brushed back Esa's pale hair, soaked in tears and snot. "When my sister's shieldwall broke, I froze. Just like you did. I didn't know what to do. I was so afraid."

Esa watched Brynn with brimming eyes, pale face reddened and blotchy.

Brynn shook her head. "I ran and hid, and I don't think I've ever forgiven myself for it."

Rationally, Brynn knew she couldn't have saved her sister, the same way Esa couldn't have saved Osbeorn. She still felt the oily filth of shame whenever she remembered that day. Her sister had been Aelfwynn the Brave, but she had turned out to be Brynn the Coward.

"But lady, there was nothing you could have done," Esa protested, her voice small. "They were hundreds of armed thanes, and you weren't strong enough."

"Yes," Brynn agreed. At the time, she had been too inexperienced and lacked the power to do anything. Ever since, she had practiced using her magic daily as a kind of penance, but it still wouldn't bring her sister back. "So can you forgive me for Aelfwynn?"

"Of course," Esa said, almost whimpering.

"Then I forgive you for Osbeorn."

Esa burst into tears again, burying her face once more into Brynn's shoulder.

The puppy squirmed uncomfortably in her arms, whining, but Brynn held onto her and Esa while the girl wept.

She could only hope Esa would be able to let go of the guilt. Out of everyone Brynn had ever tried to forgive, forgiving herself had always been the most difficult.

14

CENRIC

Cenric ate with his people while Brynn bustled around the longhouse. She never stayed still for long, speaking with the house girls and Gaitha.

According to Edric, Cenric hadn't missed much in his absence. There were still fields to be harvested and the young aurochs to be rounded up for the autumn slaughter. There was a reason the eleventh month was called Blydmoth—Blood Month.

No word yet of any raiding ships. Some people thought they might not come this year. Cenric doubted it, especially if the raid that killed Brynn's son had been Valdari, as he suspected.

They were a pragmatic people—you had to be to live in the harsh wilds of Valdar. They wouldn't care that Cenric had once served Ovrek Fork-Beard, the first and current king of Valdar. All they would care about was that Cenric's land had fat sheep, silver, and good grain.

Unless the Valdari had found somewhere else to raid, they would come to Hylden. Being the farthest northern shire, Cenric was sure his people would be attacked first.

He would need to check the defenses of the other villages in his lands. All had been either repairing or building palisades, but not all were finished.

There were just a few precious weeks before the weather

turned, and the treacherous winter seas would make sailing too dangerous. Until then, they needed to be vigilant.

As Cenric sat with his people, Brynn stopped briefly to eat then went back outside, saying she needed to take care of the puppy and help the girls with the cows and goats.

The meal was finished and Cenric's people returned to their homes. It would be an early morning tomorrow and a long day's work. The barley was close to being harvested and they needed to finish soon.

Cenric walked with Edric to the cottage he shared with Gaitha, speaking of the harvest, their defenses, and the coming Blydmoth preparations. And Brynn.

"She's been here a day and already healed the whole village as far as I can tell," Edric said. "Always on the move."

Cenric nodded. "I've noticed."

"Fair warning, lord." Just like that, Edric's usual humor was gone from his tone.

"Warning?"

"Gaitha tells me your wife went to visit Rowan's house. Spent over an hour there."

Cenric had the sudden feeling of…what was this? Embarrassment? Why should he be embarrassed? He hadn't done anything wrong, had he?

"Gaitha said everything seemed civil, but…" Edric shrugged. "Thought you might want to know."

Suddenly, Brynn's apprehension at seeing him again made sense. "Thank you, Edric."

"Good luck." Edric sounded sincere. "Maybe she's not the jealous sort?"

Cenric doubted he would be so fortunate. He walked with Edric to the house the thane shared with Gaitha before returning to the longhouse to find it dark, most of the household girls and boys ensconced in their pallets. Snapper greeted him, tail wagging as he trailed beside his master.

"Good lad." Cenric petted the dog's ears, earning several

slobbery licks of appreciation.

Cenric headed to his bedchamber, unable to deny the shiver of excitement at the prospect of Brynn waiting for him. They had known each other for less than a week, but he had seen nothing to indicate she was anything other than what she appeared—the kind of woman he was lucky to have.

Perhaps it was safe to get his hopes up. Perhaps his new wife really was as remarkable as she seemed.

He opened the door to find the room dark and empty. Brynn's chests were there from where they had been placed yesterday, but his wife was missing. "It's late. She should be here."

Snapper looked up to Cenric, tail wagging slowly. *Brynn?*

Cenric glanced down to the dog. "I suppose we'll have to go find her."

Snapper's tail wagged faster, probably just happy to be included. *Find Brynn?*

Find Brynn.

Snapper scampered off, sniffing the floor, searching for her scent.

The main hall was dark and Cenric couldn't tell which pallet belonged to Brynn's handmaiden. He remembered the basket for her puppy was empty, so she must be outside with it.

Brynn!

Cenric followed Snapper back outside the longhouse. The air was crisp with the chill of late autumn, his breath creating little clouds in the moonlight. The sky was clear tonight, displaying the stars like a canopy of gems.

The household and the village were mostly quiet. A few horses whickered and geese honked softly. His home was drifting off to sleep. So where was Brynn?

As if in answer to his question, Snapper bounded ahead, tail wagging. Cenric followed, the late autumn grass rustling underfoot.

Brynn! Snapper rounded the longhouse and stopped before

a crouched shape, tail wagging. *Puppy!* He woofed happily and raced back to Cenric, bouncing and hopping the whole way.

"Brynn?" Cenric patted Snapper's head in thanks.

"Here." Brynn's voice came soft. She crouched on the stoop of one of the side doors, a grey shape sniffing in the grass at her feet. "I was just taking Guin out one last time."

"Guin?"

"It's what I named the puppy." Brynn reached down to pet the small grey shape as she said it. A strip of linen had been tied around the puppy's neck in a loose collar. Cenric noted with satisfaction that Brynn truly seemed to have claimed the puppy as hers.

The puppy growled at Snapper, and he knocked her over easily, tail wagging as he did. Guin snarled, a sound that was comical in her squeaking tones. Snapper woofed and knocked her over again.

Brynn didn't interfere, letting the older dog teach the puppy manners.

Cenric leaned against the wall, watching the dogs play. Or rather, Snapper was playing and Guin tried to fight.

"I'm sorry I had to leave yesterday," Cenric began.

"You look after your family," Brynn said quietly. "There is no need to apologize for that." She sounded sincere, but also sad. She still watched the dogs.

"I heard you've met Rowan."

Brynn flinched, looking up to him. He couldn't see her expression in the dark, but she shifted on the stoop. Maybe this wasn't a conversation she wanted to have, either. "I found her comb in your room. I returned it." She drew her mantle closer around her shoulders, like it was ringmail that could protect her. "Her father was ill, and their goat had a broken leg, so I visited them a second time."

Cenric wasn't sure what to make of that. He'd expected accusation or anger, not this unspoken…pain. "Are you upset?"

"I have no reason to be upset." Brynn inhaled a deep breath.

"You've lived your life as I have lived mine."

That was eerily like the defense he had prepared for himself. Hearing her speak it first was oddly disarming. "Are you jealous?"

Brynn shook her head. "I have no right to be."

Cenric studied her for a long time, not sure what to say.

Brynn went back to watching the dogs, now chasing each other in small circles.

"I would understand if you were jealous," Cenric said quietly. "Angry, even. I should have told you about her sooner."

Brynn ducked her head. "I'm not angry. I'm not..." She shook her head. "I know what the right thing is. I will do it."

"And what is that?"

"I will..." Brynn's voice hitched ever so slightly, but Cenric was listening close enough to catch it. "I will do my duty to you and the people of this shire. Heal them, help them, and be the sorceress you need."

Silence stretched between them again, broken only by Snapper's playful growls and Guin's less playful attempts at snarls.

"You always do the right thing, don't you?" Cenric surmised. "Even if it makes you feel like shit."

Brynn looked up to him, her shoulders stiff. "What do you want me to do, Cenric?" This time a hint of frustration or maybe even anger crept into her tone. "Should I have refused to heal that old man because you bedded his daughter? Should I have struck the whole family with boils, perhaps? Would you have been happy then?" Brynn's mouth snapped closed, and she ducked her head, cutting off her tirade. She covered her face with her hands and dragged in sharp breaths. "I'm sorry. I'm sorry. I...just...just tell me what you want, and I will do it."

"I would understand if you were jealous of Rowan." Cenric crouched down to her level, grasping her wrist to pull her hand from her face. "I'm jealous of Paega."

"Why?" Brynn sounded genuinely confused.

"Because he had you." Cenric wasn't sure what pulled that confession from him, but it was the truth. He hated that so much of Brynn's youth had been wasted on a man who hadn't appreciated what he'd been given. He hated that she'd given six years to that wretch and even borne him a son only to be neglected to the point she fled.

Brynn made a sound that might have been a laugh but was too sad to be a real one. "He never wanted me. He still pines for his first wife."

A trickle of understanding came to Cenric then. "I'm not pining for Rowan."

Brynn flinched again at mention of the other woman's name.

"Rowan is a good woman, and she will make someone a fine wife, but…we didn't work." Cenric had cared deeply for Rowan and her for him, but that hadn't been enough.

Rowan had soothed the aching loneliness of his first year back in Ombra, far from his friends and family in Valdar. But Rowan was not prepared to be an alderman's wife. It hadn't been right for either of them. Their relationship had died a slow, lingering death.

Brynn looked down to her knees. "You don't have to do this."

"Do what?"

"Try to make me feel better."

The problem was that Cenric wanted her to feel better. "No lies, Brynn. Like I told you. Only the truth."

"Yes?"

"The truth is that I've had other lovers, and Rowan was my *frilla.*"

Brynn's brow wrinkled. "A what?"

Cenric tried to remember the Hyldish word for it. "A woman who has an arrangement?"

"You mean a concubine?" Brynn's tone turned dry.

"Yes. Rowan was my concubine." For some reason, Cenric didn't like the sound of the words as they were spoken to Brynn.

"But you're the only woman I've called *wife*."

Brynn looked up to him then, her eyes shining orbs in the moonlight. She might be crying, but he couldn't tell. "Don't denigrate her to make me feel better."

"I'm not denigrating her." Cenric tried to smother the frustration in his chest. "Like I said, she's a fine woman, but…" How could he explain it? "It's over."

"I see." Brynn didn't sound convinced.

"You're the only woman I've called *wife*."

"And what does that mean to you?"

Cenric considered telling her about Morgi's feelings on polygyny but didn't think that would help right now. That wasn't what Brynn needed to hear. "I'll show you. Walk with me?"

"It's dark," Brynn protested.

"The moon is bright." Cenric glanced overhead. "Your goddess Eponine will light the way." He glanced to the dogs. "Snapper can lead us." He stood, reaching down to her.

Brynn hesitated but took his hand. "Where are we going?" she asked, scooping up the puppy in her other arm.

"I'll show you." Cenric tugged her away from the longhouse, up the path leading to the hills beyond.

Brynn walked beside him, silent with her head bent partly down.

Snapper, to the cairns.

Cairns! Snapper trotted ahead, leading the way.

A chill breeze whipped up, rippling the grass and lashing at their mantles. Brynn wore a thick wool mantle, the puppy tucked under it.

Cenric took her up the narrow curving path, under the pine trees. Brynn looked up through the pine branches, their skeletal fingers splayed overhead like spiderwebs.

"Not far," Cenric assured her, though she hadn't spoken.

Snapper bounded ahead of them, sniffing along the trail, then racing back and looping around them again. Several of the other dogs followed in a loose formation, escorting them through the shadows.

They cleared the line of trees, coming to a series of sloping mounds set atop the hill. Some were ancient, sinking down into the earth. Others rose new, their rocks not yet overtaken by moss and grass.

Cenric had once tried counting them, but it was hard to know which slopes were natural and which might be old barrows, worn down by the passage of time. Either way, there were a hundred or more of them in varying sizes curving along the hillside.

Brynn gave a little shudder as she realized what these things were. "Graves?"

"My family," Cenric confirmed. He looked around them at the expanse of barrows. "Over two hundred years of them, if the stories are true."

Brynn was rigid at his side.

"This is…" Cenric tried to explain it. "The land. It belongs to me, but I belong to it."

Brynn shook her head, just the barest motion. She didn't understand.

Cenric hadn't had to explain this to someone before. Aunt Aegifu, despite being the single most annoying person he knew, did understand, but she might be the only one. He tugged Brynn after him, past the newer cairns that rose around them like dark beasts.

Brynn looked to the right and left as if she was frightened. That was the last thing he wanted.

Cenric led her to a felled log near the center of the massive graveyard. He sat down, guiding her to sit beside him.

Brynn sat, if a little stiffly. She let go of his hand to readjust the puppy in her lap, bundling the edges of her mantle around the small dog.

Cenric exhaled sharply. "This…" He gestured around them. "It's…" He frowned at the dark shapes rising from the soil.

"The dead?" Brynn asked, her voice small.

"No. Yes, but that's not all." Cenric chewed his lip. "This place is filled with people who I never met, some whose names I don't know, but they are still a part of us." Cenric singled out a large mound not far from where they sat. "The children from the village play on that mound in the summer. The sides are covered in grass, so they like to roll down it."

Brynn still didn't speak, listening patiently.

"They climb that one over there." Cenric gestured to a newer mound, one taller with steeper sides. "When Valdari attacked the village in my grandfather's time, he and his men tricked the raiders here so the women could pelt them with stones from above." Cenric almost went into gorier detail but noticed that Brynn had gone rigid. He went back to something lighter. "Come spring equinox, we'll hide baubles amongst the cairns for the little ones to find. There is dancing, singing, and we light a bonfire up on this hill."

"That sounds lovely." Brynn sounded wistful. "But I still don't understand."

Cenric gestured to the silent watchers around them, his dozens of ancestors lying beneath the rocks. "All these men and women are gone, but they aren't. They are still a part of our lives, and they still mean something to us."

Brynn followed his gaze to the cairns.

"My mother, father, sister, and brothers are dead, but they are still here." He pointed to the large cairn that had been made for all of them. They had died close together thanks to Aelgar's war. A fresh corner of the cairn marked where Nettles had been buried only today. "They are with me." Cenric wasn't sure how else to put it. "Here and now."

Brynn still didn't speak, but she softened a little, seeming to relax.

"Legacy," Cenric said after a long moment. "This is legacy." He looked at Brynn. "I am a part of that legacy." He inhaled, feeling suddenly vulnerable. "And so is my wife."

One day, Brynn would be buried here with Cenric. They

would become a part of the landscape, a part of the spring festivals and the children's summer games.

"It's not that I look forward to dying," Cenric said. "I plan to live a good while yet, but it gives me peace to know that even after I am gone, I won't be. Not really."

Brynn inhaled a shuddering breath.

The puppy in her arms squirmed and she set the small beast down. Guin hopped over to where Ash and Snapper sniffed the edges of a cairn, probably scenting a mink or rabbit or any of the other creatures that made their homes among the stones. The older dogs greeted Guin with wagging tails as she joined them.

"Brynn?" Cenric wondered if it would be unwelcome for him to touch her. "Am I making sense?"

Brynn sniffled. Had she been crying again? "I think so. I'm part of your legacy."

"I want you to be a part of my legacy," Cenric said. "My family."

Brynn looked up at that word.

Cenric had wanted a sorceress's power. He had wanted a woman skilled enough in politics to act as peace-weaver with his neighbors. He had hoped for a wife with enough noble blood to bring prestige to his household. Brynn gave him all of those things, but somehow it wasn't enough.

For so long, a sorceress wife was a faceless goal in his mind. The idea was practical, a rational choice.

Now Brynn was in front of him, a real flesh and blood woman and very little of what she made him feel was rational. She was everything he had ever wanted, but she was here out of desperation.

Cenric couldn't shake the feeling he was exploiting her. Somehow, he had never considered how one-sided this bargain was until he was faced with the woman who had taken it.

Cenric ventured to touch the side of Brynn's face, cradling her cheek in his palm.

Brynn inhaled sharply, but didn't pull away. Her lips parted, her shadowed eyes watching him. She was lovely, even in the sunless darkness. Maybe even more so.

"I want you, Brynn," he whispered, letting the double meaning creep into his voice. "And I want you to be happy here."

"Happy?" Brynn choked, speaking the word like she had never heard it before.

"It doesn't have to be right now." Cenric remembered her son, her loss and grief. "But someday. Hopefully soon." He brought his other hand up to frame her face.

Brynn licked her lips, tension fluttering through her.

"Only you, Brynn," Cenric said. "No one else." Taking other lovers would hurt Brynn and he didn't want to hurt Brynn. Not to mention several of Cenric's relatives had learned the hard way what Morgi thought of infidelity.

From the way her brow furrowed, Brynn seemed genuinely surprised by that promise.

"Until one of us dies or until you leave me." As soon as he said it, Cenric wasn't sure why he had added the last part.

"I won't leave you." Brynn blurted the words out in a jumble. She shook her head. "Please don't send me away."

"What are you talking about?"

Brynn swallowed. "You sent Rowan away."

It was more complicated than that, but he didn't argue. He could explain the details of that relationship some other time.

"You're not Rowan." Cenric brushed his thumb over Brynn's lower lip. "And I'm not Paega."

"No," Brynn whispered. "You're not." She searched his face, watching him with a coiled intensity.

Cenric brushed a kiss on her chin, at the corner of her mouth. He gently suckled her lower lip, urging her to open for him.

Brynn leaned into him, her breath coming faster. She returned his kiss, despite the tension shuddering through her whole body.

Cenric wanted to devour her. He wanted to taste her secret places and hear his own name gasped from her sweet mouth.

He slid his arm around her waist, drawing her close against him. She let off a little yelp of surprise, but rested her hands on his shoulders, continuing to return his kiss.

Even through their woolen mantles, Cenric could feel her warmth. She was soft in his arms, melting against him as her mouth welcomed him.

He shifted, kneeling on the grass in front of her. Brynn whimpered at his withdrawal, then met his kiss again as he drew close.

Brynn kissed like a young colt learning to run—awkward, but no less eager. She let off a little moan, her fingers stroking the back of his neck.

Cenric had only ever known nightmares, but kissing Brynn must be what dreams felt like.

She framed his face in her hands, her breath coming faster. Cenric kissed her harder, drinking her in.

He found her boot and slid his hand up to her ankle. Brynn shuddered, but didn't break their kiss.

Cenric ran his fingers up the woolen wrap around her calf, past her knee. All the while, Brynn kissed him as if she couldn't get enough, as if she wanted it. As if she enjoyed it.

Shifting closer, Cenric touched her bare thigh under her skirt.

Brynn jolted, her palms slamming against his shoulders. In an instant, her whole body was rigid, eyes wide with fright.

"Brynn?" Cenric dropped his hand, head cocking as he watched her. "What's wrong?"

"I'm sorry," Brynn gasped, her breath still coming in heaves. "I'm just not used to…" She shook her head. "It's fine."

Cenric rested a hand on her knee, carefully, on top of her skirt this time. "I'm sorry."

Brynn tensed for just a moment, but relaxed when he didn't go any further.

"It's alright." Cenric was ready to take her on top of their mantles and among the graves of his ancestors. His own need pounded through him hot and greedy, wanting to know if the rest of her felt as good as her mouth did.

But Brynn's fearful tremor was all he needed to know.

"We have time," Cenric said. "We have all the time you need."

Brynn sucked her lips between her teeth. "I'm sorry. You don't have to stop."

"Don't be sorry." Cenric shook his head, rising to his feet. "It's late. We should be getting home."

Brynn let him pull her up. She collected the puppy and tucked her under her mantle.

They walked back to the longhouse in silence down the path, back through the trees, and into the soft warmth of his home. Neither of them spoke, but when they returned to their room, Brynn stopped at the threshold and kissed him one last time before retreating to her side of the bed.

15

BRYNN

Life in Ombra was…strange. In a good way.

Brynn worked from early morning until after sunset. The days were growing shorter, for which she was grateful. It meant less time to work.

Cenric found her with Guin again the next night and they walked to his family burial mounds again. He did the same the night after that and the next. It became something of a ritual as the days wore on.

Brynn had thought it morbid the first time. She didn't want to be shackled with yet another man who idolized the dead at the expense of the living.

To Paega, his family's graveyard had been a shrine to his worship of what was gone. It had been a place for him to wallow in grief until it had fermented into self-pity.

Cenric seemed to regard his family's cairns the same as he did the forest or the mountains. They were a part of his history, but they did not bind him to it. To Cenric, the monuments seemed more a way to bring his dead family into the present than a way to anchor him to the past.

Brynn and Cenric spent their evening walks talking for the most part. He told her of his days in the field, the state of various villages and farms around the shire, and his plans. The storehouses and palisades he wanted to build next summer, the land he wanted to clear to plant more barley.

Cenric asked Brynn about growing up as Eormenulf's daughter, her sister, and her lost son. Cenric listened. It occurred to Brynn that Cenric showed more interest in her dead baby than Osbeorn's father had the entire time the boy was alive.

Cenric kissed her often on those walks, making her head spin and her heart pound. But he never made advances anywhere else, not even when they were in bed.

A part of Brynn was grateful, another part of her wanted him to just take her and get it over with. A third, more confusing part of her, squalled in protest every time his kisses ended. That third part demanded to know if he would make love the way he kissed—like she was fire, and he desperately wished to burn.

But there were other things to occupy them both beyond her conflicted feelings.

Winter was fast approaching along with the festival of Blydmoth, when the young cattle and pigs would be slaughtered.

It was also the last chance for raiders to strike before winter.

Why not strike when your own fields and animals were harvested? When your neighbors had already gathered their grain into barns and their young animals into slaughter pens? When people came into the towns, easy pickings as thralls?

Brynn could do nothing about that, so she focused instead on what she could control. She tended the injured and sick. She treated agues, aches, and mended broken bones.

A week after her arrival, Cenric and his men headed to the fields for the day to cut barley. They left at first light and Brynn sent a barrel of water along with bread and cheese to the men near noon.

Now the sun drifted closer to the horizon and Brynn guessed that they should return in the next few hours. The longhouse was a flurry of activity as chickens were plucked for the evening meal, bread kneaded, and turnips, carrots, and leeks chopped and thrown into the pots.

Several of the dyrehunds waited hopefully for scraps,

watching plaintively at the girls' feet. Guin slumbered in a basket a safe distance from the fire, curled into a tiny ball of fur.

Brynn and the women of the village had spent the morning harvesting peas and collecting them into baskets. It was tiring, back-breaking work, but soon they would all be able to rest for a few months.

"Riders!" cried a youth's voice, out of breath. "Riders approaching!" The boy burst into the longhouse.

"Riders from where?" demanded Gaitha, standing with a clutch of cabbages in her arms.

"I don't know. But there must be fifty of them headed this way!"

"Gannon." Brynn stepped up to the boy. He couldn't be more than ten and had stayed behind to care for the animals kept in the stables. "How far are they?"

"Coming up the way, lady. From the direction of Olfirth's lands."

Cenric had mentioned Olfirth. He was a wealthy thane who had refused to swear allegiance to Cenric these past two years. He had not been outright hostile, but disrespectful.

"Perhaps it is a messenger." Gaitha set down the cabbages and picked up a knife to begin chopping.

"No! They're armed! Carrying spears and shields and everything!"

Brynn squeezed the boy's shoulders. "Show me."

Gannon raced back outside, only too happy to oblige. He led her straight back out the doors and across the small yard. Outside the longhouse, the shouts of alarm and surprise rippled up from the surrounding buildings.

Brynn followed Gannon around the corner of the stables.

"There, lady."

Gannon had exaggerated when he'd said fifty. Brynn estimated twenty or so riders, but he had told the truth about the rest. The men rode stout, muscular horses and carried shields and spears. They trotted along the road leading toward the longhouse. They appeared to be Hyldish, but there was no reason for so many armed men to be heading this direction unannounced.

Brynn took in the sight, thinking quickly. In all her worry of foreign raiders, she hadn't considered that perhaps she should have feared her own countrymen.

Twenty men. Armed men, but she didn't see any archers. It wasn't ideal, but it might be manageable.

"You see, lady?" the youth panted. "That's Olfirth right there!"

Grabbing Gannon's arm, she dragged him back toward the longhouse. "You're sure it's Olfirth?" she demanded.

"Absolutely," Gannon blurted. "He's a terrible, awful man. Heart as black as a cythraul demon, that one."

Brynn knew she couldn't trust Gannon entirely, but Olfirth and her husband were not friends. She dragged the boy around to face her, gripping his shoulders. "Gannon, this is very important. I need you to find out if there are any more of them, then tell Gaitha. Do you understand?"

"Someone needs to tell Lord Cenric!"

"I will see to that. I need your help dealing with those men in the meantime. Can I trust you with this?"

"How are you going to do that?" Gannon's eyes were wide, staring up at her.

There wasn't time to explain to this boy along with everything else she needed to do to prepare. "Can I trust you?"

Gannon bobbed his head hastily.

"Good lad. Stay out of sight and don't let them see you. Come back and find Gaitha and report to her. Now go." Brynn shoved the boy toward the village where he would be able to circle around unseen from the main road.

Not wasting time, Brynn headed straight back to the longhouse. Several women and girls hung around the entrance, partially dismembered vegetables, knives, and cooking implements in their hands.

"Continue as you were," Brynn ordered. She grabbed Gaitha's arm, pulling the other woman aside. "Gannon should come looking for you shortly. Find a way to relay whatever he tells you to me."

"What's happening?"

"Olfirth is going to learn a lesson."

Gaitha nodded once, though her usual humor was gone.

Brynn found her handmaiden where she worked to grind flour with a mortar and pestle. "Esa."

Esa's flushed cheeks and wide eyes made her look much younger as she looked up to Brynn. "Yes, lady?"

Brynn pulled the girl outside the door, wanting to impress urgency on her without causing panic in the others. She lowered her voice, squeezing the girl's hand in both of her own. "Run as fast as you can to the barley fields. Tell Lord Cenric there are twenty armed men here. Likely from Olfirth. Can you do that?"

"Yes." Esa's voice trembled just a little as she said it.

Brynn smiled in what she hoped was a reassuring way. "Go child. Hurry."

Esa took off across the garden. Brynn waited just long enough to see her climb the stone fence and disappear into the trees before marching back into the longhouse.

The meal preparations were still well underway, though with a new edge of anxiety. Brynn was a little surprised none of the girls had tried to run. It seemed they trusted her enough to at least let her attempt to save them.

"All of you go about your business." Brynn did her best to project confidence and control. "Follow my lead. And have another lamb prepared."

"What about the men?" one of the women demanded.

"Leave them to me." Brynn marched past their frightened stares. "If it goes wrong, get away from this place. All of you." Brynn paused for just a moment, singling out Seva, the youngest of the house girls. She scooped Guin out of her basket, stirring the small pup awake. "If you need to run, just make sure she gets out of the house."

If Olfirth decided to attack, he would likely try to burn the longhouse down. Brynn didn't want the puppy to be trapped inside if that happened.

Seva took the puppy, cradling Guin in her arms even as the pup whined. "Yes, lady."

"Brynn." Gaitha shook her head. "You're the lady of this shire. We can't let you face them alone."

"I am the *sorceress* of this shire," Brynn corrected, reaching the door facing the stable yard, where the horsemen would most likely approach. "You will all do as I have told you."

No one spoke another word in argument.

Brynn stepped out into the afternoon sunlight. The sun was making a speedy descent toward the west. Leaves had turned gold, red, and orange on most of the trees. The world was preparing to sleep through winter, but it was still very much alive.

Brynn could feel *ka* bursting through the world around her. She pulled it in strand by strand, drawing in power. Standing in the middle of the stable yard, Brynn drew strength around herself like a whirlwind. Hopefully, she would not need it, but she would have it just in case. Brynn waited, calming her breathing as she drew power around herself.

Never do with force what you can do with charm, had been one of her mother's lessons. As much as Brynn hated the woman, she had remembered that particular lesson.

The trail of men came into view with the barking and baying of dogs. The dyrehunds ran in circles around the strange horsemen, leaping and jumping, their tails wagging, oblivious to the danger.

A dark shape settled at Brynn's side. She looked down.

Thorn sat back on his haunches, his one remaining eye trained on the approaching riders. A low rumble started in his throat.

"Steady," Brynn said to him.

Thorn's ears perked and he lifted his head to her.

"Steady, boy." She wasn't sure if he understood or not, but he remained silent as the riders drew near. Brynn trained her face into a gentle, gracious smile. She counted nineteen men, all of them armed.

They rode into the stable yard as if they belonged here, as if they had a right to be here.

Brynn singled out their leader—or at least the oldest of their number. He looked to be past fifty, if she had to guess. His face was weathered a dark tan and though his hair and beard remained thick, they were snow-white. "Welcome to the house of Alderman Cenric of Ombra." Brynn smiled, though she didn't bow. "I am Brynn of the Istovari, wife of Cenric, daughter of Eormenulf."

She made sure to clearly enunciate, letting her voice carry. It took a breath before she saw realization dawn on the men—they addressed a sorceress. Some drew back in fear, some leaned forward in curiosity, others looked to their leader.

"I must have forgotten my husband telling me to expect visitors. How should I address you?"

The snowy-haired man didn't respond for a long moment. Brynn waited, hands clasped easily before her.

These men had come fully armed, close to the middle of the day when Cenric and his warriors were most likely to be in the fields.

However, they had come along the main road and there were only nineteen of them. They had allowed the rest of the village to see them coming, to inspire fear.

Fear—that was what they wanted, so she gave them the opposite.

Instead of frightened servants and panicked stable boys—they found themselves facing her. Here was a woman at ease as if their spears, shields, and glares didn't exist.

When people didn't see what they expected to see, it made them question things. If she wasn't afraid, perhaps it was because she had no reason to be afraid.

"I'm Olfirth." The snowy-haired man looked her over from head to foot. It was an appraising look, an old bear sizing up the she-wolf in his path.

"Welcome, Olfirth," Brynn smiled, keeping her expression mild, not too exuberant, but at the same time sincere. "I am afraid you are several hours early. My husband and his men are not yet home."

Olfirth glanced around the stable yard, empty save for the motley collection of barking dogs. "You mean the young wolf left his home undefended?"

Brynn smiled sweetly at that, though it was likely meant as an insult, if not a threat.

In truth, Cenric had left more than a dozen men in the village and scouts along the mouth of the river to watch for any sign of raiders. But her husband, like her, had assumed any threats would come from the water, not from the hills and not with so little warning.

"You need not worry for us, my lord." Brynn turned around his jab, pretending she had misunderstood. "The house and the village are as well-defended as they can be."

"They are?" Olfirth's white brows rose.

Brynn kept smiling. "I am here, aren't I?"

One of the men laughed and then a few others, but they fell silent when Olfirth didn't join them.

When the snowy haired man spoke again, it was deliberate, careful. "I heard the young wolf had petitioned Aelgar to find a willing sorceress. I didn't think any of you were daft enough to do it."

So perhaps they hadn't expected to find a sorceress here after all.

Brynn feigned ignorance. "Why not?"

Olfirth grunted noncommittally.

"I am fond of this place." Brynn looked to the village visible at the bottom of the hill, then back to the old thane. "And its people."

Olfirth gave no visible reaction, but she hoped he caught her meaning. She would protect the people of Ombra, standing over his corpse if need be.

"As I said, my husband and his men have not yet returned." Brynn continued, projecting that this was a mild inconvenience, but nothing too serious. "You will have to stable your own horses since the stable boys are gone, but we will do our best to make you feel welcome until the food is prepared."

"Food?" Olfirth cocked his head at her.

"You have come to eat with us, have you not?" With her soft smile held up like a shield, she forced herself to show calm, friendliness, and hospitality.

Thorn remained at her side, rigid as stone, glaring right back at the men.

From the way he blinked at her with a mild scowl, Olfirth had not expected her to say that at all. His mouth tightened as he took her in.

One of the warriors at Olfirth's side nudged his horse toward the older man. "Lord—"

Olfirth raised a fist, signaling for the young man to stay silent.

Brynn and the old thane stared each other down. She could see his mind spinning behind his dark eyes.

Ash came along Brynn's other side, whining as she too dropped down to sit. She nosed Brynn's hand, probably confused why the strangers weren't dismounting.

Brynn petted the dog's head, keeping her attention on the riders.

She might not be able to kill all nineteen men before they ran her down, but she could kill Olfirth and perhaps three or four others. If the dyrehunds attacked the horses to create a diversion, she might even be able to take down half of them before they even reached her.

It wasn't good odds, and it had been a long time since Brynn had used killing spells. But she would sell her life dearly and Olfirth would gain nothing but his own demise by attacking her.

She saw from the way he looked at her that Olfirth understood.

Brynn couldn't outright threaten Olfirth, especially in front of his men. A threat would be an insult. For warriors like him, insults had to be avenged, else he would appear weak.

By inviting him to her table, she was offering him a way out. He could accept her hospitality, or he could find out exactly what Istovari sorceresses did to mere men who encroached on their husband's lands.

Olfirth seemed to wrestle with the decision for a long moment. His warriors remained silent at his back, showing a better level of discipline than many Brynn had met.

Finally, Olfirth straightened atop his horse, nodding slowly. "We are grateful for your hospitality, Lady Brynn. Despite us arriving so early." Then he dismounted.

Thorn made a low huffing sound as if to say, *That's what I thought.*

"Lord?" It was the same younger man who had tried to speak earlier.

"Dismount, Evred. Show some respect for the lady."

Olfirth's men followed his lead, stepping down off their horses. As the last man's boots hit the ground, Brynn knew she had won.

16

CENRIC

It was Edric who spotted the small shape of the girl racing down the road as if the hounds of the Dread Marches were snapping at her heels.

"Aye, what now?" Edric grumbled, wiping his brow.

They'd been cutting barley all day, the fruits of their labors in sheaves around them. Everything would be gathered up in wagons and taken back to the longhouse for threshing.

Friend? Snapper rose from where he had been lounging in the shade of a wagon.

Cenric turned his attention back to the stalks in front of him.

"Lord Cenric! Lord!" The girl was out of breath and bright red from the effort, but she kept shrieking for him.

Friend afraid? Snapper barked, rushing over to meet the girl.

Cenric looked back up, recognizing the girl as she drew closer. That was his wife's servant. A pit of dread opened in his chest. "What's happened?"

"Lady Brynn said…" The girl's voice broke off as she gasped for breath.

At his wife's name, Cenric dropped his scythe. He heard Edric swear as he sprinted over to where the girl leaned panting with her hands on her knees. "What is it, girl?"

"Lady Brynn said to tell you…" Another gasp of air. "Twenty men."

"What?" Cenric paused, wondering if he had heard wrong. "Esa, was it? What did you say?"

Esa shook her head. "Twenty armed men on horses. From Olfirth. Lady Brynn…said to tell you."

Cenric leaned down. "Olfirth attacked?"

"I don't know," Esa whimpered. "Lady Brynn sent me as soon as she saw them."

"Cenric!" Edric came running after him, but Cenric was already sprinting back up the road.

Snapper raced after him, barking in confusion.

By the time the longhouse came into view, Cenric had already exhausted every curse and insult he knew. He would rip out Olfirth's guts and stuff them down the old man's throat. If that whoreson had laid a hand on Brynn…

Smoke rose from the longhouse, but only from the roof opening meant for that purpose. The village appeared intact, nothing unusual.

Everything was peaceful, as far as Cenric could tell. He slowed, his breath coming in sharp heaves. What was this? Had the girl lied?

No, she had seemed sincere. Had she been mistaken somehow?

Or was this some manner of trap?

Cenric slowed to a walk, trying to hear the sounds of the longhouse over the thundering of his own heart. He always carried his sword in the fields, and it thumped reassuringly against his back.

"Everything looks fine," Edric muttered, coming up behind him.

Cenric held a finger to his lips, motioning the other men to be quiet. Half of them had come with him, also carrying their scythes, swords, and spears. They'd taken their weapons into the field. It was best to be prepared.

As they came closer, several of the dogs came out to greet them, led by Ash. Their tails wagged as they met their master, licking his hands and pawing at his legs. He shushed them carefully.

Brynn? he asked the dogs.

House, answered several of them at once.

He looked around at their smiling canine faces, missing one. *Where is Thorn?*

With Brynn, Ash answered.

Thorn? Cenric tried reaching out for the old patriarch.

Strangers, came Thorn's distant reply. *Strangers in the house.* His thoughts were edged with aggression.

Cenric's heart jolted at that. *Brynn?*

Brynn, came Thorn's affirmative answer. Thorn was with Brynn. Dare Cenric hope that meant she was safe?

Cenric considered calling out for her, but that would warn any intruders who were lying in wait for them. "Edric, take the other men and circle around. I'm going to check the house."

"Alone?" Edric's scoff said just what he thought of that.

Cenric should probably send someone else. He could see the wisdom of it.

But Brynn…

"Just go. If I send Snapper to you, attack."

Edric exhaled sharply. "Sounds like a plan." The redheaded man motioned for the others to follow him, taking them through the treeline around the longhouse.

Cenric climbed the garden fence, keeping to the shadows. The sun was setting and the shadows lengthening. He could hear the usual sounds of work, women's voices, knives hitting wood, pots clattering.

A male voice drifted through the open door, words indistinct.

Cenric drew his sword. It might be nothing. It might be the old goat had taken his wife hostage. He considered sending Snapper ahead to scout, but if this went wrong, he would need to send Snapper to warn Edric. Signaling for Snapper to hang back, Cenric went first.

Drawing close to the door to the kitchens, Cenric hovered at the edge. He could see the flash of skirts bustling to and fro as the household girls worked. Surely if they were under attack, the girls would have fled?

One of the girls spotted him and yelped, then gasped. "Lord?" She was a thin creature with freckles, clutching a bowl filled with shelled peas.

"Where is Lady Brynn?" Cenric demanded.

The other girls took notice of him, glancing between themselves.

"She's in the hall." The voice that answered was Gaitha. The tall woman stood with hands on her hips, a faint look of amusement. "She's been speaking with our guests."

Cenric's eyes narrowed. "Guests?"

"Olfirth dropped by for a surprise visit."

Cenric had to fight down panic at that. "He has Brynn?"

Gaitha smirked, but only briefly. "I rather think she has him." She gestured for Cenric to follow. "I'll show you. Though you might want to put away the sword."

Cenric hesitated a moment, but he trusted Gaitha. He slipped his sword back into its sheath, but not before he adjusted it to hang at his hip for easier access.

He followed Gaitha into the longhouse. Two girls carrying a spent cask of mead passed them. Cenric bit back his questions as male voices rose from ahead.

Gaitha stepped aside to give Cenric a view of the hall.

Cenric spotted Brynn seated beside the empty space at the head of the table. She was smiling and appeared unhurt.

Brynn handed an overflowing mug of mead to the man across from her—Olfirth.

Thorn crouched by Brynn's feet, his single eye watching the strangers.

Olfirth sat on his side of the table, his shield and spear leaning against the wall at his back. Cenric counted eighteen other men seated along his side of the table, their shields and spears likewise placed.

Cenric's relief at seeing Brynn unhurt was almost instantly drowned out by rage. "What is this?" he demanded.

Brynn's eyes snapped to him along with Olfirth and the rest of his warriors.

The men tensed, ready to lash out. The ones nearest Olfirth looked for direction and those on Cenric's end of the table eyed him distrustfully.

Brynn rose, easily, airily. "Husband," she said, her voice too bright, too gentle for this situation. "We have guests."

"They look like intruders to me." Cenric glared at Olfirth.

If the old man was offended by it, he gave no sign. "Your wife's hospitality is remarkable, young wolf."

"Lord?" Brynn rose. She came toward Cenric, her face maddeningly serene.

There were nearly twenty armed men at his table who had come here uninvited and unannounced. They could not have made their intentions clearer if they had pissed in his bed.

Yet here was Brynn, acting like this was a social call.

Brynn met him at the doorway. She took his arm, carefully, but her fingers dug into his skin, a warning, if he hadn't known better. "Olfirth will be joining us for supper this evening."

"Will he?" Cenric glared past his wife to the white-haired goat.

The old man sipped his mead, watching Cenric and Brynn curiously.

"Gaitha, please stay with our guests. I will be back in a moment."

Gaitha inclined her head. "Of course, lady."

Cenric hated leaving these men in his house, but he let Brynn take him back out the small door of the garden. They were barely outside before he was pulling her around to face him. "Explain."

The serenity she had projected in the hall fractured. "Olfirth appeared over an hour ago with his men. I invited him to eat with us tonight."

"And he accepted?" Cenric demanded.

"Yes."

"What else?"

"Nothing else." Brynn looked back to the open door to the longhouse, probably checking for prying eyes. "I was able to make him see reason."

"What reason?" Cenric gestured back to the hall. "That is a threat, Brynn. He came here with armed men on a day he knew I would be gone to harry my wife and frighten my servants. He's trying to intimidate me."

"You think I don't know that?" Brynn exhaled a sharp breath. "You are his new neighbor. He knew your father and your brothers, but he never knew you."

"He is testing me," Cenric growled.

"Cenric!" Brynn grabbed his arm, stopping him from storming back into the longhouse. "What are you doing?"

"I will show this man what happens when he tries to cross me."

Brynn raised her chin. "You'll kill him?"

"He threatened you!"

Brynn shook her head. "Think, Cenric. Just *think!*"

Cenric yanked his arm free of her grip.

Hurt flashed across Brynn's face, but she stepped toward him. "So, you kill him." Her voice went cold. "He has two sons. What will you do when they come to avenge him?"

"I'll kill them too," Cenric growled.

"And their sons?" Brynn didn't back down. "Their nephews, cousins, brothers-in-law, and thanes?"

"That is the way of it." Cenric had a nagging feeling she was trying to make a point, but he was too angry to see it.

"And your other neighbors? There are four other aldermen within three days' ride of here. After you slaughter every last man in Olfirth's bloodline, and they decide you are too great a threat to be left alone?"

"Get to the point, woman." Cenric's hand ached to seize his sword. He wanted to ram the blade through Olfirth's gut.

"You cannot kill everyone," Brynn snapped, her voice low, but with an edge of desperation. "It does not matter how strong you are, it does not matter how dangerous you are. Sooner or later, you must learn to live in peace with the people around you."

"I have wanted to be left alone. That is all I have ever wanted."

"Does Olfirth know that?"

"What?"

Brynn smeared back several loose strands of hair. "According to Olfirth, he has only met you a handful of times. He doesn't know what to make of you."

Cenric flung an arm back toward the hall. "That is not my fault."

Brynn made a brief grimace, as if perhaps she thought it was his fault, but had decided against saying as much. "You wanted a sorceress to bring peace between you and your neighbors. This is me, making peace between you and your neighbors."

"He does not respect me." Cenric gripped his sword again. *Snapper?* He sent a thought toward the dyrehund, ready to signal to Edric and the others and make Olfirth pay.

"No." Brynn cut him off before he could give the mental command. "Olfirth fears you."

"That is the same thing!"

"It is *not.*" Brynn clenched her hands into her skirt and then let them go, seeming to do it with effort. Her hands shook, but she inhaled a long breath, looking up to him. "All he knows is that you were raised by Valdari. He fears your allegiance lies with them and that you will attack him. Or perhaps that you will strike bargains with Valdari raiders to use your lands as a harbor."

"The old man told you that?"

"Not in so many words." Her voice trembled along with her whole body. She appeared more upset arguing with him than when she had been facing down a host of armed men by herself.

That hardly seemed fair. Cenric was the one whose home had been violated.

"So, what am I supposed to do?" Cenric had not been this angry in years, but he managed to lower his voice. "Olfirth insults us, and we let him eat our stores and drink our mead?"

"Yes," Brynn hissed. "Then, if he wants peace, he will invite us to eat his stores and drink his mead."

"You're assuming he's like the men of Aelgar's circle. You don't know these northmen."

"Men are the same everywhere," Brynn retorted. "Always looking for a way to save your pride." She shook her head again. "Don't you understand? Olfirth is conceding. He realized he made a mistake and he's taking the risk of eating with us because it's the only way he can save his life *and* pride."

Cenric could see what she was saying, even if it was hard to see anything past his own blinding rage.

Brynn glanced back toward the hall. "Olfirth has seen sorceresses in battle, it seems."

Cenric muttered a string of curses in Valdari. They were the only ones that seemed adequate.

"Please, Cenric." Brynn's voice went soft, pleading. "I am trying to do my duty to you." She looked down. "I want to do my duty to you."

From the way she didn't make eye contact, Cenric wondered if she meant something more by that.

She looked back up, meeting his eyes again. Her lips parted slightly, and she took in a shaky breath. "Let me do my duty."

Cenric folded his arms across his chest. He took several long and slow breaths. "Did he hurt you?" Cenric glared back toward the hall. "Any of his men?"

"No." Brynn looked startled by the question. "They haven't touched me. Or any of the other women."

Cenric forced himself to inhale until he felt his lungs might burst, then exhale slowly until he thought he might suffocate. He looked back at his wife. "Fine."

Brynn's voice sounded fearful. "Cenric?"

He paused at the doorway back into the house. "We'll try it your way." He marched back into the house, past the hearth, past the wide eyes of the women. No doubt they'd been eavesdropping.

Cenric heard Brynn following but didn't look back as he marched into his hall—*his* hall—currently occupied by Gaitha and his unwelcome guests. He smiled, though it probably looked more like a baring of teeth.

Cenric was aware of every eye in that room on him as he took his place at the head of the table, right beside Olfirth. Cenric made himself comfortable as Brynn watched him with a stony expression from the door.

Several of the women paused beside her, holding another cask of mead. Cenric bit his tongue when he recognized it as one of the ones he'd been saving for Blydmoth.

"Don't just stand there, girls," Cenric said. "More mead for our guests and get me a cup while you're at it." He turned to Olfirth at his side, leaning on the armrest of his chair. "Welcome to my hall, Olfirth. I do hope our hospitality is to your measure."

Olfirth belched, setting down his half-finished mead. "I am sure it will be, Alderman."

The girls brought the mead casks to the center of the table and the feast began.

17

BRYNN

By the time the mead was drunk, and the lamb eaten, it was too late for Olfirth and his men to ride home. They bedded down in the hall with their cloaks, the household boys around them. The household girls settled into the loft, where the boys usually slept.

Brynn and Cenric went to bed without speaking, without going on their evening walk. Cenric unsheathed his sword and set it next to the bed. He looked at Brynn as he did it, but she didn't argue. If Olfirth decided to attack them in the night, the weapon would be useful, but Brynn doubted he would.

Cenric had been polite to Olfirth, even if he glared just a little bit when he thought no one was looking. When Edric and the others had arrived from the fields, Cenric had urged them to join the meal. Her husband had cooperated with her plan, at least from appearances.

Brynn feared perhaps her husband might still try to murder Olfirth in the night. She stayed awake for a long time after lying down, listening to the sound of his breathing at her back.

But the morning came without incident, even if a spike of terror shot through her when she woke to find Cenric gone. Thankfully, only the usual sounds of a rousing household were heard through the door.

Brynn dressed, scooped Guin up from her basket, and

ventured out of the bedchamber, still bracing herself for what she might find.

What she found was Cenric and several of his thanes including Edric speaking with Olfirth. Brynn overheard enough to guess they were discussing the upcoming Blydmoth and fears that it would bring raids.

Near the top of the northmost brace, Brynn noticed a fresh set of runes had been etched into the wooden pillar. It gave her fresh hope.

Brynn would have liked to stay and shepherd the men's conversation, but she couldn't do everything for them. She spared a moment to greet her husband and Olfirth, then sent one of the girls to fetch them a few loaves of yesterday's bread, cold meats, and cheese.

She went on with her duties for the morning, seeing to the milking of the goats and the tending of the geese.

Guin chased after a gander five times her size, then turned and fled back to Brynn when the large bird hissed and flapped his wings. Brynn scooped the puppy back up, shooing away the large male goose.

The geese had already stopped laying eggs, the chickens had slowed, and the goats were producing less as the days grew shorter. There was just enough milk to make butter and cheese to preserve through the cold months.

The sun had just cleared the far mountains when Brynn spotted Olfirth and his men riding back out toward their own land. They rode at an easy pace with all nineteen men in a line.

Brynn let out a sigh of relief. A part of her hadn't been sure Cenric would let them leave unharmed.

She found Cenric leaning against the doorway of the longhouse, watching Olfirth and his riders disappear down the road. She sent the girls ahead to the kitchens, carrying baskets of eggs and jars of milk for preparation. It would be another day of harvesting the gardens once they were done.

Brynn paused a few paces from her husband. Guin whined,

so she set the puppy down, letting her sniff in the grass with the other dogs. Brynn folded her hands in front of her, trying to project composure to anyone who might be watching them. "Well?"

Cenric remained with his arms crossed, not taking his eyes off the other men until they vanished around the bend. "Olfirth has invited us for a feast in three weeks' time. You probably saw he left his mark on our pillars."

A little of the tension in her shoulders eased. So Olfirth did want to be friends, after all. Whether he'd wanted it before yesterday didn't matter. Olfirth was seeking peace in a roundabout way and that was good enough for Brynn. She could only hope it was good enough for Cenric.

"How did you do it?" Cenric let off a laugh on an exhale. "What trickery was it?"

Brynn shook her head. "There's no trickery about it."

"You faced nearly twenty thanes by yourself. Convinced them to lay down their weapons and sup without a single show of force." Cenric must have heard from the household girls what had happened. "We call Olfirth the *old man* because he's nearly three times the age of any of his thanes, but he still fights. He's tough as the tusks of a boar and fierce as a bear in spring."

"Most people are reasonable." Brynn glanced at the empty road. "And old bears are the ones who have learned to choose their fights wisely."

Cenric pushed off the doorframe and stepped toward her. He exhaled a long breath, breaking eye contact. "I was wrong. You were right."

Brynn wasn't sure she had heard correctly. "What?"

"Are you going to make me say it again?" Cenric half-laughed, though he seemed genuinely pained. "You handled that well. Better than I would have."

Brynn had barely expected him to go along with her plan, much less acknowledge she was right. "Thank you." The words came out stiff, uncomfortable. "I suppose we'll see how things go at the feast in three weeks."

Cenric chuckled, but it was awkward. Forced. Like he wanted to say something else but didn't know how.

He was a proud man, this new husband of hers. It had probably cost him a great deal to admit he was wrong about his own neighbors. That she, a foreigner barely in his lands for a fortnight, had made better progress than he had in his two years as alderman.

"When your girl told us, I thought we'd been attacked." Cenric reached for her wrist. He pinched the edge of her sleeve, not quite touching her, but tugging ever so slightly, like it was as far as he dared to go.

Brynn's mouth went suddenly dry. "The house is fine," she assured him. "All the cattle and crops and—"

"I wasn't worried about the house."

Brynn's heart, the wretched thing, did a flip in her chest. It was folly to create expectations that had never been between them. It was foolishness to hope and yet...

"If anyone hurts you, I will kill them. I don't care who they are." Cenric released her sleeve, straightening.

Brynn smiled, trying not to feel disappointment at the loss of his touch. "Lucky for him, Olfirth didn't hurt me."

Cenric jerked his head in agreement. "Lucky for him."

Brynn's chest fluttered. She could have killed Olfirth herself and he'd known it, but Cenric's vow still made her feel lighter somehow. She didn't know where to go from here. "We should be done harvesting the leeks tonight." She offered him the option to change the subject.

"The barley will be done tomorrow if not today," Cenric answered.

Brynn tried to sound reassuring. "We will be secure through winter."

"Yes." Cenric scratched at his beard thoughtfully. He looked back to her. "Can I make this up to you?" He asked the question quietly, like he feared being overheard and perhaps he did.

"What?"

"Yesterday."

Brynn still didn't understand.

"How I spoke to you."

Brynn tried to remember how he had spoken to her. They'd argued, but she'd won. He'd already admitted he was wrong. "You don't need to make it up to me."

"A gift, then."

Did he think he could simply buy her forgiveness?

"If I wanted to give you one."

"I don't need anything," Brynn answered. She had brought her chest of jewels and baubles that was the more mobile portion of her dowry. The entire longhouse was at her disposal. Ombra might not be as wealthy as the south, but she wasn't lacking. "Guin was already a fine gift, thank you."

"There is nothing you miss from your old life?"

"No." She wished she could explain to him that her old life had been its own torment. Paega had treated her as an ignorant child and all those closest to him had followed his lead. In Ombra, Brynn was barely a step below a queen.

Cenric was not used to impossible tasks, it seemed. "Nothing?"

"It's not something you could give," Brynn answered softly.

Whatever else he might be, Cenric was persistent. "Tell me and we'll see."

"Osbeorn is the only thing I miss," Brynn answered, looking down. She inhaled a deep breath, determined not to cry first thing in the morning.

"I see," Cenric answered quietly.

"I'm sorry." Brynn forced down the lump in her throat.

Cenric brushed his fingers along her jawline, just the ghost of a touch. "I would bring you the head of his killer if I could."

Brynn shook her head, feeling tears well beneath her lashes. "There's no point. We don't know who it was."

Cenric frowned at that. "Have you never wanted revenge?"

Brynn drew in a shuddering breath. "I am too full of grief to have room for bloodlust." She had wanted revenge for her sister. Called for it, demanded it from her mother, Aelgar, and anyone who would listen. She hadn't just wanted the blodgild, the payment owed to the family of a murder victim. Brynn had demanded the men's heads.

But it had not mattered.

In the end, they didn't know which of Winfric's thanes had killed her. It was impossible to know and after two years of bloodshed, everyone was ready for peace.

All the same, Brynn held onto her bloodlust for years until it had wrung her out. Finally, she had lacked the strength to hold onto it.

Perhaps if she could have hunted those men down, but she had not been willing to sacrifice her obligations to Esa and the other people of Glasney to do it.

Revenge was for those with power and patience. Brynn had long ago recognized she did not have enough of either.

She was the type of person who would have to suffer the indignities and offenses of life. She was one of those who had to endure.

Cenric exhaled a long breath, looking past her. Brynn was sure her husband would have wanted revenge, would have found a way to get it. Perhaps he was stronger than she was, or maybe just more spiteful.

Cenric would be fierce as a father. She had tried to avoid thoughts of making him one, but it was oddly comforting to realize. He would protect their children and failing that he would extract bloody revenge.

"Brynn." Cenric reached for her, and she let him fold her into him.

He didn't kiss her as she expected, but he pressed her to his heart. Resting his chin on top of her head, he held onto her, sheltering her in the circle of his arms.

Brynn closed her eyes, her fingers digging into his back. She savored the now familiar smell of him and the firm solidness of his chest.

"You should be more selfish," Cenric murmured into her hair. "This wretched world owes you something for a change."

Brynn wasn't sure what to make of that.

Cenric kissed the top of her head, pulling away, though he grasped her hands. "I'll see you tonight?"

"You will," Brynn promised.

He smiled down at her with what Brynn thought must be genuine affection. "I missed our walk last night."

"Me too."

18

CENRIC

"Valdari ship! Valdari ship!" Kalen came racing along the riverbank, full speed toward Cenric and the other men.

"Where?" Edric demanded, straightening. There was a wild, almost eager light in the short man's eyes. It had been some time since they'd had a good battle.

They'd finished bringing in the barley and threshing it over the past several days. All of them were glad to be done with that.

Today they were salting fish and packing them into barrels. The past few days had been an unusually good catch and the boys responsible for the fishing boats had asked for help. Cenric and all his men were in the sheds near the docks, up to their elbows in scales and fish guts.

Kalen pointed back the way he had come. "Coming up the river! With red sails!"

"Red sails?" Cenric already had his sword in his hand—he never went anywhere without it this time of year—but that gave him pause. "How many ships?"

"Only one, lord," Kalen panted.

Cenric glanced to Edric.

"It could be him. Or not." Something in the way Edric said it suggested he was hoping for the latter.

Cenric grinned at his friend, but he didn't sheath his sword. If it was raiders, they'd chosen an unlucky time. All the village's men happened to be here along the riverbank. If they'd come hoping for easy prey, they would be disappointed.

Not to mention they had a sorceress to heal anyone who was injured. Cenric was hardly worried as he strode out from the shed with his thanes following behind.

Several voices called out, but no one seemed to be panicked just yet. At the sight of Cenric striding calmly along the beach, the people calmed, though they backed away.

Friends? Snapper appeared from wherever he had been napping, excitement shivering through his furry body.

The ship came into sight—a thing of beauty with seventeen oars, same as the number of steeds owned by the First of Fathers, Havnar, the king of the gods. The usual wolf head prow of a Valdari ship was replaced by the likeness of a deer so as not to frighten the good spirits in friendly waters.

The vessel neared slowly, its shields hanging on the sides. These were men in a friendly harbor, not raiders.

Cenric recognized the ship before he recognized the figure perched near its prow. Not sheathing his sword, he raised his voice to be heard across the water. "Who dares to sail into my lands?"

Thirty-four rowers manned the ship, crouched over the oars. Several other figures moved to and fro, at least two women.

The figure near the prow was a large man, a full head and shoulders above most. The wolf's pelt around his shoulders made him look even larger and broader than he was. Silver and gold rings banded his massive forearms. He swept a bow to Cenric with a grin. "Only us poor travelers come to exploit your hospitality and delightful company."

Edric made a disappointed sound from behind Cenric. No fights today, at least not the sort the red-haired man had been hoping for.

"Presumptuous, as always." Cenric allowed himself to grin back at the Valdari. "Kalen, show them where they can dock."

Kalen stepped a little apart, signaling to the man at the prow and led the way, jogging down the riverbank.

Snapper raced after him, barking. *Hróarr! Vana! Friends!*

One of Cenric's first constructions after becoming alderman had been a series of docks so that ships didn't need to be dragged ashore for loading and unloading. Though they still stored the ships on land over winter, it had made life much easier during the warmer months.

Cenric finally sheathed his sword. Word had begun to spread through the village, but no alarm had been raised. Hróarr tended to inspire excitement and curiosity.

The ship docked and Cenric walked to meet it. Some of the thanes he sent back to work, but Edric walked with him to meet Hróarr.

The big man was the first to leap from his ship and to the docks. He paused to help a svelte woman down after him.

"Snapper! How are you, you mighty beast?" Hróarr rubbed Snapper's sides, scooping him up like he weighed no more than a rabbit. He wrestled with the dog, Snapper's tail thrashing wildly while his thoughts squealed with delight.

Hróarr! Hróarr here!

Hróarr finally set the dog down and bounded to meet Cenric on the shore.

"Cenric!" Hróarr met Cenric in an embrace that was more a grapple than a hug. They both squeezed, each one trying to push the other off balance, laughing.

They shoved until they were out of breath and had to either let go, or wrestle on the ground. They clasped forearms, shaking in the more traditional way.

Cenric laughed, slipping into the Valdari language. "Ah, it's good to see you, brother."

They were cousins, but Cenric had known Hróarr far better than his own siblings. They'd been raised together, though Hróarr was a few years younger. In Cenric's mind, Hróarr was his little brother. The dead men who had been his father's sons were strangers.

"I couldn't miss Blydmoth, now could I?" Hróarr scoffed, like the thought had never occurred to him, also switching into Valdari.

"I'll be happy to have the extra hands for the slaughter," Cenric replied.

"You know me and my men are always good for a bit of bloodletting." Hróarr chuckled at his own joke. "Vana, my beauty."

The woman from before joined them. Her hair had been gathered and tied back with gold rings at her temples and a narrow gold torque around her neck. Hróarr must be doing well for her to be so well dressed.

Vana stepped up beside Hróarr even as she smiled at Cenric. "Cenric. So good to see you."

Cenric smiled and kissed the back of her hand. "Welcome, lady."

Vana! Snapper yipped with happiness, licking her hand furiously as she reached down to pet him.

"Good lad," Vana chuckled before turning back to Cenric. "I hear you have taken a wife." Vana glanced around the beach. "A sorceress?"

"Word travels quickly." Cenric was a little impressed Vana had already heard, but she had that particular talent. She always seemed to know things before anyone else did, at times she seemed omniscient.

Hróarr made a sympathetic sound. "A sorceress? My brother, do you hate yourself?"

Cenric shook his head once, not smiling. "She's a good woman and a fine wife thus far."

Hróarr seemed to catch Cenric's meaning—Brynn was here to stay. "I see. Well, I wish you much happiness and many sons. But not too many, lest you spend your old age breaking up their fights."

Cenric allowed his smile to return at that. "Gods have mercy."

The three of them made their way to the beach while Hróarr's men unloaded the ship. They had brought their own tents and gear, along with what appeared to be chests of gifts, though Cenric pretended not to notice.

The people of the village had mostly gone back to their work, but some stopped to stare at the newcomers. Hróarr had come several times over the past two years, but he still caused a stir whenever he docked in their river. A few of Cenric's thanes helped with unloading, the villagers letting their curiosity get the best of them and drawing closer.

They walked toward the longhouse. Hróarr and his people usually pitched their tents in the field between the longhouse and the village.

"Why do you stink of fish?" Hróarr sniffed in Cenric's direction. "Gah! I think you got it on me."

"Salting fish for winter." Cenric shook his head.

"Ah, you've become domestic. I always forget." Hróarr heaved a sigh. "Well, so long as you're—"

"Cenric!" Brynn blocked the path ahead, her hands at her sides, elbows slightly bent, and fingers flexed. She had called his name, but her eyes were on Hróarr. She held a wide stance, not unlike one he used for fighting.

"Brynn." Cenric stepped ahead of his guests. He cleared his throat, switching back to Hyldish. "This is Hróarr and his lady, Vana."

Brynn glanced to him briefly before looking back to the others. "Your friends?" Her voice was uncertain as she looked them over. She noticed Vana's jewelry and her expression changed, but Cenric couldn't interpret it.

"My cousin. I mentioned him to you."

"Yes." Brynn's arms relaxed, though a new kind of tension took her over. She no longer seemed a warrior bracing for a fight, but a beaten dog bracing for a blow. "I see." She forced a smile. "Welcome to Ombra. I take it you are here for Blydmoth?"

"What else?" Hróarr grunted, his Hyldish coming reluctantly. "I was just telling this one that you always need some Valdari steel when there's killing to be done."

Brynn visibly flinched at that before recovering herself. She cleared her throat, raising her chin. "Well, I am sure my husband will appreciate the help."

"No need to fear us, lady," Hróarr chuckled. "We Valdari are not as awful as the stories claim."

Cenric shook his head again, but it was too late.

Brynn's face turned blank, a shield slamming into a defensive formation. She spoke to Cenric. "I will have additional food prepared. Was it thirty-six?"

"Thirty-seven," Hróarr corrected.

Brynn did not look at him as she inclined her head and turned. She made her way ahead of them back to the longhouse. The girl Esa had been hiding behind one of the houses but ran after her as she did, carrying Brynn's puppy.

Cenric grimaced. Perhaps he should have warned Hróarr sooner.

"Not a very welcoming sort, is she?" Hróarr grunted, sliding back into Valdari. "You'll have to teach her manners."

Cenric loved his cousin, he truly did, but the man could be dense as a rock. "Valdari killed her son."

"Oh." Vana made a soft sound of understanding, as if that explained everything. "She knows you fraternize with us?"

"I told her, but…" Cenric watched as Brynn disappeared into the longhouse.

When his uncle had been killed, Cenric had been angry. He'd wanted to slaughter every last man who'd had anything to do with it. And he had. Beside Hróarr, they had avenged his father twofold. The lucky ones had received a quick beheading or a stab to the chest. The less lucky ones had met drawn-out, gruesome ends.

Brynn's grief looked different most of the time, but he saw the anger there. It had shown on their wedding night when they had first discussed her son.

The difference was that Brynn had no way to avenge her son. She didn't even know who had killed him. Instead of being used to fuel the fire of vengeance, her grief was drowning her. Cenric could see she kept her head above it most of the time, but all too often the waves dragged her under.

Maybe she just needed time, but Cenric wished he could do more. Things always seemed simpler on their nightly walks, but they couldn't spend their whole lives walking in darkness among the cairns.

"What?" The big man shared a look with his concubine. "I didn't know."

Vana shook her head. "You really should leave some things to me, my love."

"I didn't know. Cenric didn't bother to tell me."

"It's fine," Cenric interrupted. "I will talk to Brynn."

"You should apologize to her," Vana said.

"Me?" Hróarr blinked down at Vana. "Apologize to a Hyldish witch?"

Vana smiled sweetly up at him. "No, you should apologize to *your cousin's wife.*"

Hróarr let a long breath out his nose. He let off a string of curses, but all three of them knew he would do it. Eventually.

They continued walking toward the longhouse, much slower now. It was best to give Brynn time to prepare. They kept their conversation in Valdari. It felt good to speak the language freely again after so many months.

"Brynn helped me make peace with Olfirth, the great thane to the east."

"That one called the old man?" Hróarr scratched at his beard.

"That one. I didn't think anything could make us friends, but Brynn has made the opportunity."

"You are sure you can trust her?" Vana asked mildly. "I am surprised Aelgar gave you a sorceress. You're sure she isn't a spy?"

"Yes," Cenric answered confidently. "She asked for me."

That surprised Vana. "Oh? You two had met?"

"No," Cenric had to admit. "She wanted to get away from Ungamot."

"I see." Vana didn't sound convinced. "Forgive me, Cenric, dear, but you are not always the best judge of people, much less women."

Cenric's hand clenched before he thought about it. What Vana said was true, but he desperately wanted Brynn. Not just in his bed, but in his life, in his future. She made things easy that had once been difficult. She brought solutions where he had only seen problems. She made him feel…important.

He hadn't wanted anything this much since he had set out to reclaim Ombra as his inheritance.

"I believe her," Cenric said.

Vana dropped the matter.

"So much change these days," Hróarr sighed. "At least I haven't taken up farming yet."

Most Valdari raiders were farmers looking to make a bit of extra wealth. They might steal a few sheep, take a couple slaves, and carry off whatever silver they could find, but they weren't particularly ambitious. They would sail home at the end of the season, and many would never raid again.

The true professionals like Hróarr lived their lives the other way around. They had bases along the coast of Valdar, but their true home was the sea. These men lived their lives as warriors and mercenaries first, farmers and fishermen only when necessary. It carried with it extreme risk, but also great reward.

"Speaking of raids, do you claim that fishing town to the north of here?"

Cenric stopped, fixing his cousin in a hard look. "I do."

"Ah." Hróarr smacked his lips, still looking toward the longhouse. "Well, there's a raiding party headed that way. Only one or two ships, but you might want to do something about it."

19

BRYNN

Brynn had been hospitable to her husband's enemies. She supposed she should be the same to his friends.

Even if his cousin seemed a bit of a boor and the beautiful woman on his arm smiled at Cenric with a little too much familiarity. Even if she doubted Hróarr would be the kind of man to share, everyone had a past. What was to say that this lithe beauty had always been with Hróarr?

In her first marriage, Brynn had always failed to measure up to Paega's previous lover, even if Mildreth was dead. Whether Mildreth really had been so perfect or whether because it was easiest to idealize the dead, Paega had never gotten over her. He sulked among the cairns and went hunting with his thanes and waited for his life to be over.

Despite her resentment, Brynn had laid flower wreaths of evergreen and offerings of butter and barley meal on the graves of Paega's first wife and children every single new moon. So now, she served Hróarr and his companion with her own hands as befitted honored guests.

As always, Brynn did what was expected of her.

Cenric invited her to sit with them, but she declined, saying there was work to be done overseeing the household girls. Brynn thought Cenric looked displeased, but she doubted she would be able to keep herself together in front of Hróarr and Vana.

She was struggling as it was, though she wasn't quite sure why. Maybe it was that Hróarr was so obviously Valdari. Maybe it was how he had looked down on her with obvious disdain. He didn't like sorceresses, and it showed. Maybe it was that Vana seemed more at ease with Cenric than Brynn was.

Or maybe it was that Brynn's first reaction to hearing of a Valdari ship approaching had been fear for Cenric. She'd known he was working near the river today and she'd rushed to the riverbank to find him.

She'd been ready to use the full strength of her power to protect him from the Valdari, only to find him laughing and speaking like a native with their leader. Rationally, Brynn could acknowledge that was a good thing, but she couldn't shake the overwhelming sense of embarrassment.

Here she had raced across the entire village to rescue him, only to find he had never been in danger. The fear, the desperation, and the blind terror of those few moments had all been for nothing.

In that moment she had realized she cared for Cenric. It wasn't that she was afraid of losing her place in Ombra. It wasn't fear of losing her excuse to stay away from Ungamot and Glasney. It was fear of losing *him*.

Perhaps some of it had been the age difference, but she had always seen Paega as the final judge of her actions. If Paega was displeased with something she did, he must have his reasons. He was so much older and wiser that surely, he must have known better.

Then as the years had worn on, she had realized Paega would never be pleased with her for the simple fact that she was not his first wife. He was a man shattered by grief who had no interest in piecing himself back together. Nor did he care if his jagged edges left a thousand tiny cuts in the heart of the young sorceress who was as trapped with him as he was with her.

With Cenric, Brynn still had some of that same desire to please him, to do her duty, but it was more than that. She admired him. Cared for him. It felt too early in their relationship for her to care this much for him.

Cenric might be precious to her, but she was still a newcomer in his life. He had people close to him, people who had known him for years, who had fought alongside and loved him. He was becoming the center of her world, and she feared that she was still in the periphery of his.

Brynn refilled the mead cups for Cenric, Hróarr, and Vana, leaning over the table.

Snapper and Ash greeted the Valdari like old friends, lounging at their feet and begging for morsels. Even Guin tottered around the older dogs' legs and accepted pets from Vana. She didn't even growl. Brynn felt betrayed.

Cenric glanced up at her. "Thank you, wife."

Brynn tried to smile, but only succeeded in a grimace.

"Sit with us," Cenric urged, gesturing to a seat at his side.

"I still have much work to do," Brynn demurred, repeating her earlier excuse.

"I trust it's not poisoned?" Hróarr chuckled, lifting the overflowing cup to his lips. The ends of his thick mustache dipped into the foam as he drank.

Brynn's jaw tightened. "Do you prefer your mead *with* poison?"

Hróarr grinned up at Brynn, but it was a calculating grin, more a flashing of teeth.

Anger flared in Brynn's chest, hot and viscous. This foreigner, this sellsword, was more at home here than she was. He moved about the house with easy familiarity, like he belonged here. This was her house by rights, but this animal acted as if he was in his own territory.

In the back of her mind, she knew she wasn't being courteous, but her mouth seemed to move of its own accord.

Brynn kept her tone sickly sweet. "If it is not to your liking, I can provide you with a dose of hemlock. Or perhaps you would prefer nightshade?" She planted one hand on the table, leaning toward the Valdari. "Personally, I recommend the nightshade. It will be the most painful."

"Brynn." Cenric frowned. "What are you doing?"

Brynn quailed at that simple question. Was it not enough that she worked herself to exhaustion every day? Was it not enough that she had saved his face in front of his men several times now? Was it not enough that she served his former concubine despite her insults? He had to let his friends disrespect her like this?

Tears stung Brynn's eyes, and she marched away. There was nothing she could say that would explain what she was feeling or that could smooth over what she'd just done.

She had threatened a guest, an honored guest at that. It had been grotesquely inappropriate, and she would owe Cenric, Hróarr, and Vana an apology, as soon as her anger subsided.

The next time she noticed the three at the head of the table needed more mead, she sent Esa. It might be a snub to send her servant instead, but Brynn didn't trust herself to be near them again.

She saw to serving the next round of baked bread and even instructed the servants to open one of the wine casks gifted by her uncle. They had been saving those for Blydmoth, but hopefully Cenric would take it as a peace offering.

The Valdari crew howled their delight as the household girls began pouring the purple vintage. Grapes couldn't be grown this far north, at least not well, and wine was a luxury.

Anger and frustration mingled with self-loathing. She was furious with Hróarr for his disrespect, Cenric for allowing it, but most of all she was angry with herself for not being able to ignore it. Why couldn't she just do what she was supposed to do? She had done it for years with Paega. Why couldn't she just take it like she had before?

Because you thought this time would be different.

Brynn simmered through the rest of the night. She saw the kitchens cleared and the fires banked. The Valdari began to withdraw down to their camp near the village.

Vana managed to catch Brynn as she was helping clear away bowls and making sure no one had forgotten their eating knives on the table. "Lady Brynn."

Brynn tensed but faced the woman. She couldn't make herself smile but managed a neutral expression. "Yes?"

"I wanted to thank you for hosting us tonight. It was quite short notice."

Brynn inclined her head. "It was an honor." The words came out by rote.

Vana hesitated, as if Hyldish words came to her with difficulty. "Hróarr can be…abrasive. He means no harm."

Brynn wasn't ready to apologize. She was still too hurt, too angry. Too raw.

"But I wanted to apologize on his behalf for any offense he might have caused." Vana said it mildly, calmly.

Brynn thought she sounded sincere, but she didn't know the stranger well enough. Standing before this woman with her gold jewelry and poised demeanor, one might have thought she was the lady of this shire, not Brynn in her stained apron. "Thank you."

Vana's lips arched up in a gentle smile. "Cenric speaks highly of you."

Brynn swallowed, not sure why shame bubbled up at that.

"I look forward to getting to know you better," the Valdari woman said.

Did this imply that Vana and, more importantly, the Valdari, would be here often?

"Good night, Lady Brynn."

Brynn forgot to smile with the effort of keeping a neutral expression. She was sure the bejeweled Valdari woman judged her for her outburst. She certainly judged herself.

The Valdari left. Cenric accompanied them down the hill to their tents, because of course he would. Brynn and Cenric had planned to walk together again tonight, but plans had clearly changed. Other people were more important.

Brynn finished her work. She took Guin outside one last time. Guin licked at Brynn's hands, straining on her back legs to leave puppy kisses along Brynn's jaw.

At least Guin's loyalty still lay with her. Brynn fed her another shallow bowl of milk, stroking her coat as she drank. When Guin was finished, Brynn placed the puppy in her basket on Brynn's side of the bed. Guin curled up in the straw and blankets of her basket, making snuffling puppy sounds.

Esa started the fire in Cenric's bedchamber and Brynn dismissed the girl to her own bed by the central hearth. It had been a long day, and they were all tired.

Brynn undressed down to her chemise, but the autumn chill had set in, so she pulled on her woolen shawl. Sitting alone on the edge of the bed, Brynn set to combing out her hair. Things had been going well and she thought things were getting sorted out between her and Cenric, but now…

She was still just a silly girl, sure she could make a stranger love her. How could she be this stupid twice?

Brynn redid her braids and tied them off. She might as well climb into the bed. There would be work to do tomorrow. She reached out, sensing the sleeping figures of the household boys and girls nestled into their beds. All was silent. All was peaceful.

She waited, wondering if Cenric might spend the whole night drinking and carousing with his old friends. Still, she waited up for him. She wasn't sure why.

It was some time before Brynn sensed Cenric coming by his *ka*. He entered the bedchamber quietly, letting Snapper in first. The dog trotted over to Guin's basket as Cenric shut the door after him. His face was a mask of shadows by the firelight.

"You were waiting for me?" Cenric sounded surprised.

Brynn pulled her shawl closer around her shoulders, avoiding looking at him. "Your friends are well?"

"They're fine." Cenric approached the bed, circling around to her side.

She cleared her throat. "Good."

Snapper realized Guin was asleep and made a disappointed sound, dropping back on his haunches. He curled beside the basket, settling down for the night.

"I apologized for you." Cenric sat down beside Brynn, the mattress shifting under his weight. "Hróarr forgave you as soon as he tasted the wine."

Brynn's hands clenched into her shawl. So, he agreed she had done something wrong. Brynn had been beating herself up for hours over her outburst, but it still stung Cenric took Hróarr's side.

"So, what happened?" Cenric fixed her in a steady gaze. He didn't sound upset, which made it worse.

"I don't know." Brynn was so angry, so upset, so frustrated. Her whole life, she had done her duty. She had followed the rules and done the right thing. Yet she never seemed to get a right result.

She had been the dutiful, sweet, and hardworking wife to Paega, but he had been cold to her to the day she left. Despite that, despite how unpleasant it was for both of them, she'd bedded him so she could conceive a child. When that child had come, something in her life had finally been good. She had done everything she knew to do for that child, but in an instant, he had been murdered. Senselessly. Pointlessly.

Now Brynn did everything she knew to do in her new role as lady of Ombra. She served its people, did her best to please Cenric, and tried to make peace with his neighbors. But it had been nearly a month, and despite his heated kisses among the cairns, he hadn't bedded her. He had to be unsatisfied with her somehow. That was all she could think of.

She'd told Cenric she was willing. But she had all but begged Paega to pay his marriage debt. She didn't want to have to plead yet again for a man to swyve her.

She was tired of begging for men's attention when other women seemed to attract it effortlessly, even when they didn't want to.

Cenric rested his hands on his knees. "You said you were fine with my Valdari cousin visiting."

Brynn kept her attention on the fire. "I will do better in the future." It was a phrase she had uttered a thousand times to Paega—*better in the future*. Because she had proven herself not good enough. She was never good enough.

Cenric exhaled a long breath. "Hróarr has heard there's a raiding party headed for Leofton, a village north of here."

"What?" Brynn's whole body stiffened.

"It's more than a day on foot, but it's in my lands."

Her heart raced, pounding in her ears. "Hróarr told you this?"

"He's heard rumors." Cenric grimaced. "I'm taking a few of my thanes with Hróarr's crew to see if we can head them off."

"You're leaving?" Brynn wasn't sure why her voice cracked at that. "You're just going to take your thanes and leave us in the middle of the harvest season?"

"I am leaving most my thanes here." Cenric spoke slowly the way he might to a small child. "We'll wait a few days to see if the raiding party shows and if not, we will return."

Inexplicable fear clawed its way up Brynn's throat. "We're set to begin slaughtering animals in mere days. We need you here."

"As I said, I will be leaving most of my thanes. I'm only taking Anders and Kalen with me. Edric will remain here in charge of defense."

"You can't be serious." Of everything he might have said, Brynn had not predicted this. "You can't just leave. There's still so much work to be done before winter. What if the raids come here? What if more of your neighbors come?"

"It's only three of us, Brynn. You'll be able to manage a few days."

Cenric was leaving them. He was leaving her.

"Why?" she whimpered. "Have I done something? Have

I…" She trailed off, realizing how ridiculous she sounded.

"What?" Cenric cast her a confused look.

"Nothing." Brynn's voice cracked. She coughed, clearing her throat. "Have you spoken to Edric?"

"I have. He's on your side, if that makes you feel better." Cenric stood and walked to his side of the room. He opened one of the cedar chests and pulled out a leather satchel. "He thinks he should go, and I should remain here."

"So why don't you?" Brynn shifted on the bed, something oddly like desperation rising in her chest.

"Because I am the alderman of Ombra." Cenric placed a rolled blanket inside his satchel, followed by what might have been a whetstone or a flint. "If I can't defend these people, I have no right to expect their tribute or their service." He went to the stand where his armor stood guard over the room.

It made sense. Brynn hated it, but it made sense. "Can you take more men?" she asked. "Are there more thanes you could summon from the countryside?"

"There are," Cenric conceded. "But I want them to stay here and protect the main estate."

"I just don't like you leaving with so few of your own men." Brynn thought that must be it, but she wasn't sure. "Hróarr is going to commit his men to a fight for you?"

"He's asking for silver in exchange, but I can't expect mercenaries to fight for free." Cenric shrugged.

"So, he's taking silver to solve a problem only he knows about?" Brynn tried not to sound condescending, but she probably did, all the same. "What's to say these raiders aren't his friends and he's planning to split your payment with them once he pretends to chase them off?"

"You don't trust Hróarr," Cenric sighed. "Rowan never liked him, either."

Brynn didn't think her husband had meant to hurt her with that, but the words stung all the same. She couldn't look at him.

Cenric seemed to realize his mistake a moment later. "I

didn't mean it like that." He smeared a hand over his face, almost like he was trying to scrub the words away. "I trust Hróarr, and I need you to trust my judgment in this one."

Brynn couldn't argue with that, but she still hated everything about this situation.

Cenric pulled something from beside his kit of armor—a spear with the head wrapped in a protective oilcloth. "Edric will see to constructing the scaffolds and final preparations for the animals while I am gone. The work won't stop, and we should be back before the end of the week."

"I don't want you to go." The words were out before she considered them.

"I will come back as soon as I can." Cenric set his spear and packed bag against the wall. "But I have to go, Brynn."

Brynn clenched her fingers tighter together. She had known they might be raided. She had accepted this, but something about Cenric leaving with the Valdari grated her.

"Vana will be staying here." Cenric seemed to think that would be a comfort.

Brynn did not consider it comforting at all. "You're going to leave, no matter what I say."

"That's hardly fair," Cenric countered. "I'm not the one planning a raid on Leofton."

Brynn bit back her response. Everything she wanted to say would only make this situation worse.

She almost asked him to take her along. She could battle as well as any thane and she could heal anyone who might be injured in the fighting.

But no.

It made sense for her to stay here and tend the main estate in her husband's absence. It all made sense. Painful sense.

Brynn held her tongue and watched as her husband continued packing.

20

CENRIC

"You realize I'm not paying you if these raiders don't show?" Cenric faced Hróarr, moving one of his pieces across the tafl board.

Typically, the board would be balanced on their laps, but they had placed it atop a barrel between them to make it easier if they had to rise suddenly.

Hróarr chuckled. "Seems fair."

They spoke in Valdari, crouched under the eaves of a smithy, watching and waiting. The glowing coals in the smithy's forge served for light.

The people of Leofton had panicked upon seeing Hróarr's obviously Valdari ship, but Cenric had managed to calm them.

The headman of the town was an elder named Leofric with one eye and two teeth. His family had founded this fishing village, and he had been none too happy about another thirty or so men to feed, even if only for a few days. Like Brynn, he seemed skeptical that any raid was coming.

Cenric was not sure how he could have parted with Brynn on better terms, but he couldn't shake the feeling that he should have.

Vana had kissed Hróarr in front of everyone, standing on her toes to whisper lovers' secrets in his ear before kissing him one last time.

Brynn had inclined her head to Cenric. "Return safely, lord," she said. Her words had been all stiff formality and icy acceptance.

Cenric pressed a kiss to her forehead all the same, hoping they could sort this out when he returned home. For just a moment, Brynn softened. Her hands squeezed his forearms tight until he had to pull away.

When he withdrew, she took a shuddering breath, almost like she was fighting tears. She pulled herself together a moment later, standing straight and stoic.

Cenric left his wife standing on the riverbank, her face as hard and unreadable as a shield.

"Not sure what's keeping them," Hróarr muttered. He nudged one of his pieces across the board. He had chosen to play Valds, the dark pieces. "Must be the weather."

Tafl was played on a checkered board with pale pieces, Hylds, and dark pieces, Valds. The Hylds started at the center of the board, surrounded on all four sides by the Valds. The Hylds won when their king piece reached the edge of the board, escaping. The Valds had no king piece, but they won by capturing the Hyld king.

It had started raining, so perhaps that was what had kept the Valdari raiders at bay. From where Cenric and Hróarr sat playing tafl, they could see the mouth of the river that opened into the sea. That would be the direction any raiders would likely come from.

Several of Hróarr's men lay napping around them. Any attack would likely come at night, so they had spent last night and the night before watching and waiting.

Two nights of nothing. Two nights of sleeping on the hard ground when Cenric could have been in his own bed, lying next to his own wife. Here it was the third night and Cenric was ready to call this whole thing off if they didn't see enemy ships soon.

If it turned out Cenric had left Brynn, had argued with her for no reason, he was never going to let Hróarr live it down. He didn't believe his cousin would deliberately trick him, but it was infuriating all the same.

"How is Ovrek?" Perhaps Cenric should have used the Valdari king's title, but that seemed like a Hyldish thing to do. Cenric tossed the bone dice, which came up with four marks. That meant he could move any of his pieces a total of four spaces. He paused, considering his next move on the board.

Hróarr's pieces were converging to one side, trying to break through the formation Cenric had set up around his king piece.

"Good," Hróarr replied. "Strong as an ox and healthy as a boar."

"Aelgar is sickly." Cenric looked pointedly up to Hróarr. "Some people think he won't last the year." Cenric was offering brutal honesty, signaling that he wanted honesty back.

Hróarr's dark brows twitched.

"So, I will ask again." Cenric placed one of his Hylds, not the king, in front of Hróarr's advancing line. That was two spaces. He moved two others forward by one space each, ending his turn. "How is Ovrek?"

Hróarr inhaled a breath, studying the board. "He's past fifty." Hróarr tossed his dice before moving a few of his own pieces, advancing on Cenric's line. "But I expect he has more than a few good years left."

"Aelgar's aldermen are loyal," Cenric said.

"Ovrek's jarls are learning to have a king," Hróarr admitted. "But they are learning fast."

What Hróarr meant was that Ovrek still struggled to unite his jarls. It was a hard thing for many of them who had been their own masters for as long as anyone could remember.

"Who would be king after Aelgar, do you think?" Hróarr asked the question offhandedly, not looking from the tafl board.

"Hard to say," Cenric admitted. "I hear Alderman Torswald is powerful. Paega of Glasney could make a claim, but I doubt he has the ambition." Cenric's fist clenched at the thought of Brynn's first husband.

Hróarr cocked his head at Cenric, seeming interested. "Of course, a man who recently took the king's niece for himself might have his own ambitions."

Cenric shook his head dismissively. "I'm not an atheling."

Hróarr frowned, not recognizing the foreign word.

"I don't come from kingly stock," Cenric explained.

"If a man had enough spears at his command, no one would care," Hróarr countered. "Hire a few thousand mercenaries."

Cenric smirked at that. "And where would I get the silver to pay them?"

This was conjecture, nothing but fancy. Cenric and Hróarr had often made plans like this as boys, speaking of adventures that would never be had and conquests that would never be undertaken.

Hróarr shrugged. "Where'd you get the silver to pay the men when you retook Ombra?"

Cenric's cousin already knew the answer to that. "Ovrek."

The Valdari king could be a hard ruler, but he was generous with those who were loyal. He'd given Cenric two ships and thirty men to reclaim his inheritance.

Ombra had been years without an alderman by that time and Cenric had assumed he'd have to fight to retake the shire. Despite that, Cenric had ended up doing far less fighting than he or Ovrek had expected. Cenric had turned up to find his aunt Aegifu running the house and the main estate.

Aegifu had declared Cenric the rightful alderman and scurried back off to her own farm. Some of the wealthier thanes had objected, but most had come around to swearing loyalty to Cenric. Olfirth was one of the last hold outs.

"And they are my men now, not mercenaries," Cenric corrected.

The men Ovrek had sent with him were former thralls who had been granted freedom in exchange for fighting for Ovrek. Edric had been one of them. Those men had been in Valdar too long to return to their old lives, but there was too much suspicion between them and the Valdari for them to stay in Valdar. They now made up the core of Cenric's thanes.

Hróarr stroked his beard, seeming to consider that. "You're right. You're too poor to be a king."

Cenric laughed, taking his turn to toss the dice. "I have enough to do managing my own people. I don't need to deal with the rest of Hylden. The other aldermen dislike me as it is."

"Which does make me wonder." Hróarr's dark eyes watched as Cenric moved his pieces across the board. "Why is such a poor man, so disliked by the other aldermen, marrying a king's daughter?"

Cenric bristled this time. "I've already married Brynn. And I'm not *that* poor."

Hróarr waved his hand at Cenric's tone. "For a king, you are. Which means you are poor for a king's daughter."

Cenric glared at his cousin. Calling him poor once was a jest. Calling him poor three times in a row was venturing into insult.

Hróarr studied the tafl board, not meeting Cenric's glower.

"If there's something you want to ask me, ask it." Cenric didn't like where this was going. There had been a time when he and Hróarr had nothing and no one but each other. They had been closer than full-blooded siblings, closer than twins.

Somehow, Cenric had taken for granted that they always would be. But now his cousin was a Valdari mercenary, and he was a Hyldish alderman. Things were more complicated.

"Why did you marry Aelgar's niece?" Hróarr's question was blunt and bordering on accusation, but Cenric was glad to be getting to the point.

"Ombra needs a sorceress," Cenric said. "Brynn was the first one willing."

"A king's daughter volunteered to marry you?" Hróarr's skepticism was bordering once again on insulting.

Cenric almost began to defend himself, but the best defense was often an attack. "Brynn didn't want me to come here."

Hróarr grunted. "Hyldish women are like that, I hear.

Fearful, whimpering things."

"She thinks you're lying about this raid." Cenric cocked his head at Hróarr. "Or if it's real, she thinks you're working with the raiders and planning to split the silver I pay you once you repel them."

Hróarr's brows rose. "Well, that's a good idea." He looked back to the mouth of the river. "Clever, actually. I should try that one some time." He turned back to Cenric. "I don't suppose you know of any particularly gullible landholders along the coast?"

Cenric made his moves on the board and passed the dice back to Hróarr. "Brynn is my wife. No matter who else she might have been."

"I see." Hróarr tossed the dice and paused, counting how many moves he would be able to make next. "She doesn't seem too happy about you being Valdari."

"I think she just doesn't like you."

"Why? I'm nothing but charm." Hróarr chuckled to himself at that.

Cenric stared toward the mouth of the river. If these raiders would just show themselves, then Cenric could fight them, kill them, and go home. "I let you have Vana."

Hróarr bristled a little at that.

"She chose you," Cenric said before his cousin could argue. "And I accepted it." Cenric had hated it, but he'd accepted it.

The two of them had found Vana trying to build a shelter in the forest. She had been one of many orphans struggling to survive in the wake of Ovrek's war. She had been a nobody, just a farm girl in the wrong place at the wrong time. Sifma, Ovrek's wife, had taken her on as a servant in much the same way Ovrek had taken on Hróarr and Cenric.

The three of them had been little more than children. Then one day they weren't children at all.

Cenric had fancied himself in love with Vana. Her rejection had stung, but he'd understood. At the time, Cenric had little to recommend him. He'd had no land, and little wealth. Hróarr had already been the leader of a ship and a small mercenary company. His cousin could offer stability and safety that Cenric hadn't been able to provide.

Now, Cenric could see Vana's rejection was for the best. It had given him the push to retake Ombra. Without Vana turning him down, Cenric might not have reclaimed his family lands, certainly not as quickly as he had.

Not to mention, Cenric never would have met Brynn.

Hróarr made a dismissive gesture as he moved his tafl pieces. "So I should just accept your Hyldish witch, is that what you're saying?"

"If you want to be welcome in my house, yes."

Hróarr leaned back against the brace of the smithy, studying Cenric. "Well," he said at length, "she does serve good wine."

Boats.

Cenric turned at the thought from Snapper.

Boats! The dog leapt out of the darkness, coming into the light of the smithy. He had been roaming in the dark, but it seemed he was the first to sense the approach of their enemies.

Where? Cenric reached for Snapper, stroking the dog's coat.

Snapper sent back an image of the river mouth with two dark shapes crouched low on the water.

Cenric turned back to Hróarr. "Looks like you didn't lie."

Hróarr glanced down to the tafl board. "Good thing for me, too. Your king has almost escaped." Hróarr kicked at the man nearest to him. "Good news," he barked. "Time for killing." The excitement in his voice was impossible to miss.

Cenric roused Anders and Kalen, both who had slept in their battle gear. He himself had worn his armor and now pulled on his helm.

Kalen stood close at his back. The boy's nervousness made his borrowed mail shirt rattle, but Cenric ignored it. He would only embarrass Kalen by pointing it out.

Anders was more experienced. He stood at Cenric's side with easy confidence. They marched out of the smithy, into the crisp night air.

Like a pack of wolves circling their prey, Hróarr's men came out from between the wattle and daub houses. They'd had the villagers move to the far side of the village, the half farthest from the water.

As the raiders drifted closer to shore, the village appeared asleep and unprepared. What they didn't know was that Hróarr's heavily armed mercenaries lay ready to strike.

Cenric passed his spear to Kalen and drew his own sword. Adjusting his shield on his left arm, Cenric waited a moment until Hróarr marched up beside him. Under cover of darkness, they joined Hróarr's men as they slank from the shelter of the buildings into the narrow streets of the village.

Snapper stayed close to Cenric's side, sensing the change in mood. *Friends?*

No, Cenric sent back. *Enemies.*

Snapper didn't argue as he usually did.

Back, Cenric ordered.

Snapper obeyed, falling back a few steps to let Cenric go in front.

The raiders would have to approach from the narrow inlet, up the main street of the village. "Street" was a generous term. More accurately, it was a mostly straight passage between the wattle and daub huts, but the important thing was that it would force the raiders to come from a single direction.

Cenric and Hróarr broke off at the agreed signal, drawing two groups of warriors to either side. They crouched in the shadows of the huts, waiting.

It would be easier to conceal themselves inside the huts, but most of the huts had only one door. There was too much risk of becoming trapped inside if their enemies managed to spot them and block the entrances.

Hunkered in the shadow of the huts, Cenric waited. Across from him, he could see the vague outline of Hróarr and Hróarr's warriors waiting. At Cenric's back, Kalen had stopped shaking.

Snapper waited by Cenric's feet, ears up, body stiff.

Cenric couldn't hear anything over the rustle of the wind and his own pounding heart, but Snapper could. *See them?*

Snapper snorted and trotted out from between the buildings. He kept to the shadows, his black and grey coat helping him blend into the darkness.

The dog disappeared around the hut, trotting toward the shore. *Boats,* Snapper said. He shared his view of the raiders, showing two longships on the dark water, oars dipping silently as they glided toward shore.

Watch, Cenric ordered.

Snapper sent back the impression of frustration and dropped to his haunches.

Snapper?

Boats. Now Snapper could see the longships gliding closer, running up the shore.

Cenric tensed, ready to give the signal.

Friends? Snapper's question followed the image of dark shapes with axes and spears leaping ashore.

Back, Cenric ordered. *Snapper, come here.*

Whining, Snapper nonetheless obeyed. He leapt to his feet and scampered back up the hill.

Cenric let off a whistle meant to sound like a bird, the signal that the enemy had landed. Across from him, he saw Hróarr wave, signaling that he'd heard.

Snapper skidded to a stop in front of Cenric, looking up in confusion. Snapper often had trouble understanding that people might want to hurt him. After all, he hadn't done anything to deserve it.

Good boy, Cenric sent. His hands were full with his sword and shield, but he made sure the dog understood. *Good Snapper.*

Snapper's tongue lolled happily out the side of his mouth. *Snapper good boy!* came his joyous response.

Stay here, Cenric ordered.

Snapper responded with confusion, but he dropped onto his

haunches again. After the incident with Nettles, he seemed to understand that Cenric was serious.

The raiders moved quietly, but their excitement got the better of them. As they came closer, their footsteps turned into a pounding a moment before a roar went up, men's voices yelling with the goal of striking terror.

That was the signal.

Cenric let off an answering war cry, raising his sword. Hróarr's great bellow came next followed by the roars of the rest of their men.

They swarmed out from between the houses, falling upon the raiders the moment the men came in sight. It was dark, but Cenric could see the outline of a man with a long axe. He had the element of surprise and cleaved across the man's ribs before his foe had the chance to defend.

Cenric wished it had been light enough to see the raiders' faces. Instead of frightened villagers, they were met with more than thirty armed and ready warriors.

Cenric's shield smashed into another man's earning a startled yelp. Anders clung close to his side, edge of his shield pressed against Cenric's, guarding his lord's flank.

Kalen hovered at Cenric's back, using the spear to jab at any man who came too close.

Cenric could hear Hróarr and the other men yelling war cries, but beyond that there was only the fleshy targets in front of him.

The raiders faltered. Cenric and the mercenaries advanced. Cenric's foot caught on a fallen body, but he kept his footing. They pressed forward.

The raiders broke, turning and running back to their longships.

Cenric and the others gave chase, charging down the hill toward the water. They cut down raiders as they were able to catch them, bellowing and roaring the whole time.

The raiders fled, not looking back. They were like polecats

who had tried to raid a henhouse, only to find it guarded by bears.

The raiders scrambled aboard their ships, trying to shove the vessels off the beach and back into the water. Hróarr's men swarmed the nearest vessel, cutting down the raiders who struggled to reach it.

To their credit, the raiders put up a fight, slashing and stabbing. Cenric's allies pressed in close around him, though not quite in formation.

The nearest ship jostled, men scrambling to leap aboard and take the oars while others worked to push it free of the riverbank.

Cenric pursued, wading into knee-deep water after their quarry. He cut down the first man he reached, his sword shearing through an unarmored back. Cenric swooped on the next, stabbing through the raider's spine.

A rope flew over his head to loop over the prow of the ship. Several of Hróarr's men grappled it from the beach, using the rope to stop the boat from going back out to sea.

The raiders inside the ship spun, turning to stab down with spears at the mercenaries on the ground.

The flash of a spear in the moonlight dove for Cenric's head. He raised his shield at the same time a spear shot past him, stabbing up into the man overhead.

Kalen was putting his borrowed weapon to good use. The boy yanked the weapon free, ready to strike the next man.

"Good hit, Kalen!" Cenric shouted, grinning fiercely as he cut down another raider.

The rope around the prow dragged the boat backward and Cenric scrambled out of the way. Kalen skittered close behind him.

Hróarr's mercenaries leapt up on the other side of the ship, hacking and stabbing anything onboard that moved.

Past them, Cenric made out the dark shape of the second longship fleeing back down the river. Cenric hoped they would spread tales of a well-defended and well-armed Ombra.

Slogging back to the shore, Cenric picked out Hróarr's dark figure towering amongst the other men.

"Are we getting paid?" Hróarr asked, humor in his tone.

Cenric laughed under his helmet, out of breath, but riding the euphoria of victory. "You're getting paid."

Sunrise saw the villagers of Leofton reluctantly thanking their lord as they piled the bodies of the raiders in midden heaps.

Hróarr's mercenaries had killed some twenty or so raiders, probably over half of the group that had come on the two ships. The raiders had likely matched them for numbers last night, but these were poorly armed men, probably farmers who had been able to find weapons and ships.

None of the men had armor beyond a few leather breastplates and bracers. A few of their weapons were halfway decent, but they had never stood a chance against veteran mercenaries.

Among the defenders, the only man among them who wasn't a veteran was Kalen.

Kalen sported a new silver ring, proudly displayed on his forearm. He'd only killed one man, but he'd been steady and fought for his lord when it mattered. It was only a matter of time before he would earn his own war-gear.

Snapper ran in circles, barking at the village children in some game only they understood.

Hróarr's ship had been hidden downstream, but it had been dragged out and they were preparing to head back.

"I don't think that headman is grateful," Hróarr muttered, looking over to the elder in question.

Cenric shrugged. "So long as he remembers to pay his

tribute, I don't care."

The elderly man inspected the former Valdari ship. Hróarr had wanted to keep it for one of his men, but Cenric was letting the village have it. The vessel was small, but sturdy and should help the villagers forget that they'd had to house and feed thirty mercenaries.

"We should have you home by nightfall, then," Hróarr said.

"Good." That was the best news Cenric had heard all week.

It had been four days and Cenric was more eager than ever to return home. He had work to do and, more than that, he missed his wife. He felt as if he owed her an apology, though he couldn't have said what for.

"What's this?" Hróarr cocked his head at a commotion near the edge of the village.

Cenric glanced up to see a figure scrambling along the beach, trying to dodge rocks from the shrieking villagers. Several stones struck the stranger, but he kept moving.

It appeared to be a man covered in mud, pale as a fish and his beard braids wet and stringy. He looked remarkably like a drowned rat.

"Lord!" the figure cried out in Valdari. "Lord!" Half-running, half-crawling, the figure scrambled low toward Hróarr. "Mercy, lord!"

The villagers converged, men, women, and children snatching up sticks and stones, ready to beat the stranger to death.

"Hold," Cenric ordered, raising a hand. They ignored him the first time, so he stepped forward, raising his voice. "I said *hold!*"

The people jumped at that, seeming to remember suddenly the corpses they had cleared from the beach this morning—and who was responsible. They glared at the stranger, but let him half-crawl to grovel before Hróarr.

Hróarr did not move closer, but he motioned for his men to allow the stranger to approach. "So, you survived, but your friends left you behind?" Hróarr shook his head. "I hate it when that happens."

The stranger bowed, hands planted on the ground before him. "You are a Valdari lord." It was not a question.

"Aye," Hróarr answered. "But I'm fighting for Alderman Cenric, here. Took money to stop you and your friends, unfortunately."

Throwing oneself on the mercy of the highest-ranking person present was a humiliating, if recognized practice. There was a chance at life, but there was also the risk of an ignominious death and even if mercy was given, a stain of shame.

"Take me back to Valdar with you, lord," the stranger pleaded. "I just want to go home."

Hróarr grunted. "Found out the raiding wasn't to your liking? You should have thought of that before you came raiding."

The stranger fumbled with something on his hand, holding up a metal object covered in mud. "I offer this, lord. You can have this, just take me home."

Hróarr did not reach for the offered object, he was too clever for that, but one of his men stepped forward and collected it for him. Hróarr's mercenary handed it to his lord.

Hróarr studied what appeared to be a finger ring. "We could just kill you and take this anyway," he pointed out.

"Please, lord."

Hróarr exhaled, sounding bored. "What do you say, alderman? Is it sufficient to buy this raider's life?" He extended the ring to Cenric.

Cenric took it, a little surprised. None of the other raiders had much of value on them. There had been iron amulets and one or two silver arm rings, but aside from their bloody clothing—which the villagers had salvaged anyway—nothing worth looting.

This, on the other hand, was a gold finger ring set with a sizable ruby. The craftsmanship was impressive, and it had even been engraved inside the band. That wasn't unusual. Many pieces this elaborate were commissioned as gifts with the name of their giver inscribed as a permanent reminder for the receiver. *AE* caught Cenric's eye. He looked closer.

PAEGA HAD ME MADE.

Cenric's heart stuttered for a moment. He scrubbed at the dirty band, wondering if he'd read it wrong, but no. His first reaction was the hate he had started feeling at any mention of Brynn's first husband. A moment later…how was this possible? What were the chances?

"Where did you get this ring?" Cenric demanded, spinning on the raider.

The man was already prostrate, but if possible, he sank lower. "I won it."

"Won it how?" Cenric demanded. "Who gave it to you?"

"Cenric?" Hróarr cocked one eyebrow.

Cenric shook his head, indicating he would explain later. He looked back to the raider. "Tell me where you got this."

"Kyrna!" the raider stammered. "We stopped in Kyrna on our way here and I won it in a dice game."

Cenric's fist clenched around the ring. "Who? Give me a name."

"I don't remember." The raider shook his head quickly, then seemed to realize his life was depending on this. "I think he was with Ielda's crew. They're planning to winter in Kyrna."

Ielda. Cenric didn't know the name, but he looked to Hróarr.

His cousin nodded carefully, watching Cenric. Hróarr switched into Hyldish, probably so the raider wouldn't understand. "He's a new warlord or wants to be. Recently started doing mercenary work last year."

"This ring has the name of Brynn's first husband," Cenric said in Hyldish.

Hróarr frowned at that. "His name wouldn't happen to be a common one, would it?"

Cenric shook his head. "His shire was raided in the spring."

"I see." Hróarr knew what Cenric did—that only a full-time mercenary who didn't have to worry about spring planting could have done it.

"They killed her son." Cenric looked back to the raider.

The raiders who'd murdered Brynn's son had taken the gold and silver in the estate. That was the way raids worked. They had probably taken this ring, too, and headed back to Valdar. Somehow it had ended up with what appeared to be a random farmer.

Morgi had delivered a sign straight into Cenric's hands—quite literally.

Brynn said she didn't dare ask for justice, but she had to want it. Who wouldn't? The desire for justice gnawed at Cenric and Osbeorn hadn't even been his son.

Hróarr exhaled a long breath out his nose, almost like he was giving himself time to think. "Kyrna is only a day's sail from here."

Kyrna was a southern town in Valdar, but it was still in the far northern sea. That would mean another two days away from Brynn, not including the time they might need to spend searching Kyrna.

Cenric tried to think. What was the right course? He looked over to Anders, standing with his shield slung across his back. "I need you to take a message to my wife, Lady Brynn." Cenric pointed to Leofric, the village headman. "Your people will take him to my estate on this ship I've just gifted you."

Leofric scowled, but he seemed to know better than to argue.

Anders shuffled his feet, but also did not argue. "What should we tell the lady, lord?"

"Tell her I will be home in another three days from now." Cenric looked briefly to Hróarr. "I have business to attend in Kyrna. Business about Osbeorn."

Anders frowned at that. "Osbeorn?"

"She'll know." Cenric didn't want to say any more than that

through a messenger. They had no scribe or monk in this town, so it wasn't as if he had the tools to write her a letter. Cenric would tell Brynn the rest in person.

21

BRYNN

"Lady, riders!" Gannon panted, rushing into the paddock.

"How many?" Brynn set down the leg of the donkey she had been healing. It seemed the little animal had stepped on something sharp and gotten infected. She'd spent the better part of the past hour draining the infection and then using *ka* to heal the wound. She might have to drain the wound again if it healed incorrectly, but it was a start.

The animal's owner was a stern woman of middle years who bowed her thanks to Brynn.

"At least twenty!" Gannon gasped.

"Armed?" Brynn washed her hands in the bucket of water she had been using before drying them on her apron. She slipped under the paddock fence.

"Oh, yes!"

Of course they were. And once again, they were arriving while her husband was away. How convenient. "Which direction?"

"The inland road, lady."

They were approaching the longhouse from Olfirth's lands, if she had to guess. Again.

Brynn stifled a sigh. Aelgar had told her that Ombra was isolated and remote and her contact with the outside world would be limited. It seemed he had lied. This was their third batch of surprise visitors in two weeks.

"What will you do, lady?" Esa's voice held a note of fear, though she remained outwardly composed.

Brynn paused a moment to stroke Guin, held in Esa's arms while Brynn had worked on the donkey. "It's probably nothing. I will go to see, but just in case, wait here with Guin."

Esa's chin jerked in a shaky nod. "As you say."

The puppy whined, trying to reach Brynn, but the sorceress wanted to keep her hands free just in case. She left the puppy and her ward in the shade of the stable, following Gannon.

Brynn strode up the hill toward the longhouse, stifling a sigh. What fresh ordeal was this?

Thorn came trotting after Brynn as she walked up the hill. The grey-speckled dog followed like a second shadow.

Brynn spied the group of riders as they wended down the path. Once again, Gannon had exaggerated.

Brynn counted perhaps ten riders, and a covered wagon pulled by a team of mules. White mules.

Brynn's heart sank. Surely not. Surely it wasn't...

She reached out with her sense of *ka* as she drew nearer. As she felt the *ka* surrounding the newcomers, her fears were confirmed. They were using spells. Simple ones that appeared to be holding cloaks in place or soothing blisters on their hands, but spells nonetheless. At least three of the guards were sorcerers, if weak ones. There were also three others of considerable power.

Brynn's heart raced as she drew nearer. She wished Cenric was here. Surely, he would have stood by her in this. If there was one thing she knew about him, it was that he hated disrespect.

Brynn marched into the yard as the caravan pulled in front of the longhouse. At least they had not beaten her to the front door.

"Lady Brynn!" called one of the riders encircling the caravan. She recognized him as one of Cenric's thanes posted to guard the road after Olfirth's surprise visit. The thane inclined his head to her. "They said they were here to see you."

"Thank you." Brynn raised her chin as the caravan trundled to a halt. She'd known this confrontation would come eventually. It might as well happen now.

One of the caravan guards dismounted and bowed to her. "It has been a long time."

"Not long enough, Neirin." Brynn cocked her head at the man. "Never long enough."

Two women rode behind the wagon on two more white mules, wearing black dresses. Black and white, the colors of the moon goddess. The women were twins, almost identical in outward appearance. They dressed alike, had similar mannerisms, and trained their voices to sound alike.

Many made the mistake of thinking they were the same person in different bodies, but Brynn knew better. Tessaine was dispassionate, so aloof she seemed more like animated stone than living flesh. Anselma was like a dandelion on the breeze, ever flowing to and fro on gusts of emotion.

Brynn was never sure if those were their natural personalities, or if they had adopted mirrored ones for the sake of their performance. Because that was what their lives were, a performance. It was a farce to lend power and mystique to the woman they served.

"Lady Brynn!" Anselma cried, her face alight. "So good to see you!"

Brynn met the greeting with stony silence. She folded her arms across her chest. Perhaps she should feel some kinship. She didn't.

Gaitha and the household girls gathered at the front of the longhouse, watching carefully. The stable boys peered from the entrances to the barns. All seemed to be waiting to see what Brynn would do. They were taking directions from her and accepted her as their leader, at least in Cenric's absence.

Her husband's dyrehunds barked and howled at the strangers like they did with all newcomers. Ash bounced around the wagon and tried to get pets from Neirin before trotting over to Brynn's side and plopping down. Brynn stroked the dog's ears, focusing on the silky fur of her coat to steady herself.

Thorn lumbered up to Brynn's side. He didn't growl, but his whole body was rigid as he remained standing.

Brynn was lady of Ombra. She was married to Cenric. It didn't matter that he hadn't bedded her yet, she was his wife in the eyes of the king and the people of this shire and that was all that mattered.

There was nothing anyone could do about it, not even Selene of the Istovari.

The curtains of the wagon stirred and out stepped a woman with raven black hair streaked with silver. As a child, Brynn had always wanted that raven black hair instead of her grandmother's dirty blonde.

Selene's gaze was warm, motherly, and deceptively marked with smile lines. Her smile fell on her daughter and Brynn felt the predator closing in.

"Brynn! My dear girl." Selene tripped as she stepped down, though it might have been an act. She laughed as she righted herself. "Oh, clumsy me."

Brynn was unmoved, though she could see the people around them relaxed. No one should lower their guard around Selene. Brynn would prefer Hróarr and ninety-nine of his kin over this woman any day.

Selene came toward Brynn, adding a slight wobble to her step. Selene was nearing fifty, but Brynn had seen her feign infirmity too many times to trust it now. She sensed no errant *ka* in the woman's body.

"My sweet daughter, it has been too long." Selene wrapped Brynn in an embrace. "I was so sorry to hear of what happened. Such a tragedy. Such a shame."

Brynn didn't move. She stared straight ahead, giving her mother nothing. One lesson she had learned from Paega, apathy was much harder to fight than outright rejection.

Selene pretended as if nothing was unusual. "I came as soon as I heard." She lowered her voice. "Wassa told me Aelgar forced you to marry. Without your mother's permission? Unacceptable."

"I didn't need your permission." Brynn kept her voice devoid of emotion. She stepped away from her mother, folding her arms back across her chest. She raised her voice so that the onlookers could hear. "The king was kind enough to arrange a marriage at my request."

Selene's jaw ticked, the only sign she was displeased. "Yes, so kind of him." That eternal smile never wavered. "Neirin, help the girls take our things inside."

The guard headed to the back of the wagon where Tessaine and Anselma were unloading bags.

Brynn raised her voice to make sure everyone heard. "You can set your tents on the field below the longhouse." If it was good enough for Hróarr and his Valdari, it would be good enough for Selene. Hopefully, being so close to Vana would be as uncomfortable for Selene as it had been for Brynn these past few nights.

"I am sure there's room for us in the house," Selene chuckled good-naturedly. "We don't need that much space, my dear."

Gaitha stepped down from the doorway. "Brynn, if you would like, we can—"

"The field." Brynn spoke the words firmly, shooting Gaitha a significant look.

Gaitha frowned for just a second, making the freckles around her nose scrunch. Then she caught on. "Yes, the field is quite lovely. The girls can show you the way."

Selene looked to the longhouse. "But such a grand house as this…"

"Is full," Brynn snapped. If her mother wanted to keep pushing the matter, she was willing to simply say the woman wasn't welcome. "It is a pity you did not give us warning of your coming. Perhaps then we could have prepared for you."

Selene laughed good-naturedly, but Brynn knew her mother caught the meaning of her words—*I know you tried to catch me off guard and this is your punishment.* As Paega's wife, Brynn had learned to manage an estate, care for crops, and mediate disputes. But she had learned the art of politics as Selene's daughter.

All her life, her mother had taught her the subtle art of getting what you wanted by giving people what they wanted. Selene had learned early on that Brynn hungered for her mother's praise and acceptance. Like a good politician, Selene had withheld both until Brynn had complied with whatever her mother demanded. Whether it had been studying her spells, attending her prayers, or marrying a man some forty years her senior.

But for the first time in Brynn's life, she was the one with all the power. Because she had something that Selene wanted.

And Selene had nothing Brynn wanted.

22

CENRIC

"So, you think this will make your wife fall in love with you?" Hróarr sounded on the verge of laughter.

Cenric had explained the situation to his cousin before they left, but Hróarr still seemed deeply amused by the whole thing. "It can't hurt," Cenric answered.

"I only mean that she's Hyldish. Hyldish don't believe in vengeance the way we do. They think a bit of coin is enough to end a feud."

Cenric frowned. "You mean blodgild?"

Blodgild was the payment of silver or in some cases gold owed by a murderer to the family of the victim. It was the Hyldish way of preventing the manner of violent retribution that could spring up on Valdar.

Hróarr grunted. "Exactly. They aren't like us."

Us. Valdari.

While most people were unsettled by Cenric's Valdari half, Hróarr never acknowledged his Hyldish half. To most of the world, they seemed to be oil and water, unable to mix, but Cenric's veins were proof it was possible. Cenric had never felt like a proper Valdari, but he never felt entirely Hyldish, either. He was both and neither.

It was dark, but Cenric glared at Hróarr all the same. "You can wait with the ship if you don't like it."

"And leave my cousin alone in the streets of Kyrna? My mother's spirit would spit in my mead." Hróarr grunted. "Besides, I never liked Ielda."

Wet, Snapper complained, slinking along beside Cenric. *Inside?*

Soon, Cenric answered. They should be out of the rain in a few moments.

Kyrna was not a city when compared to Ungamot. But Kyrna was home to some thousand or so permanent residents, which made it a city by Valdari standards.

The streets were crooked, intersecting at odd angles with irregular widths. Unlike Ungamot, this was not a place used to horses and most of it had to be accessed on foot.

Cenric didn't have his full armor with him, but he had his bracers reinforced with iron slats. He doubted he would need them, but one could never be too careful with Valdari.

They had rowed all day to reach Kyrna shortly after noon. The men were tired and Cenric was sore with fresh blisters on his hands. But after a few hours' rest, he had dragged the others into the city.

Hopefully, Ielda would still be here.

Cenric and Hróarr led the way, their cloaks drawn over their heads against a misting rain. At their backs followed Kalen and a pair of Hróarr's warriors.

Kyrna's streets were dark, but light spilled out of doorways and through cracked windows. The city wasn't large enough to have a proper red quarter the way Ungamot did, but it was generally understood that raiders wouldn't have to go far from the docks to waste their newfound riches.

"This way," said their guide, the surviving raider. He walked stiffly ahead, his shoulders hunched against the rain. The man was jumpy and anxious, probably aware of how tenuously his life hung in the balance.

The raider led them around the street corner to a large structure that looked like a barn or warehouse of some sort. The rain washed the air of any smells that might have provided clues.

"Here." The raider pointed to the entrance. "In there."

Snapper inspected the dark building. *Meat. Fire.*

The dyrehund could smell something cooking inside. This was probably the right spot.

Cenric tossed the raider a pair of silver coins. "Don't let me see your face again."

The raider snatched the coins out of the air before scampering off into the dark. If word got back after tonight that he had been the one to give Ielda away, the raider's miserable life would likely be cut short in an even more miserable manner.

"Let the fun begin." Hróarr rubbed his hands together before pushing the door open.

Cenric worked to contain his own excitement. There was nothing quite like the thrill of the chase, of outsmarting your prey. Valdari called themselves wolves and wolves were meant for the hunt.

Inside, someone had built a large fire at the center of the room. A hole had been cut in the roof with an elevated cover to let the smoke out, but not elements in. All the same, not all the smoke escaped properly, filling the large building with smog.

It was a wonder the building hadn't gone up in flames yet. Cenric would need to be mindful of the exits.

Over the fire hung a large kettle, filled with some sort of stew based on the smell. Figures sat around on makeshift tables, using overturned buckets and stools as chairs. Some forms lay passed out on the ground. It was getting late, but not that late.

A pair of men beside the stew pot accepted coins in exchange for bowls of steaming food. Two more guarded what appeared to be several casks of ale, most likely stolen based on their mismatched sizes and the color of their wood.

Off to the back, Cenric espied a guard at the foot of a staircase leading up to the attic. That would be where the whores could be found.

Snapper stepped into the shelter of the barn, letting off a

great shake of his whole body, flinging water in all directions. *Good shake,* Snapper thought appreciatively.

Hróarr cursed, shielding his face from the flinging droplets. Cenric didn't understand the point since their cloaks were already damp.

Friends? Snapper cocked his head, lowering his snout to study the smells. He headed off, circling the barn like he did with most new spaces.

Cenric stepped over the legs of a comatose man as he entered. This was not the most derelict establishment he had visited, but it was not the best, either. Though perhaps *establishment* was the wrong word. This was probably a group of independent people who had gathered in this storehouse for the night with or without the owner's permission.

"There's Ielda," Hróarr said under his breath. "The one losing his guts in the corner."

Cenric spotted a figure doubled over, currently vomiting onto the dirt floor.

That would mean that many of these men were likely Ielda's crew.

Hróarr threw back the hood of his cloak, swaggering into the smoky building. "Ielda, my friend!"

Cenric followed his cousin, discreetly. He had not been to this part of Valdar in some time. His cousin was well-known to these men as a brother-in-arms, or at least a colleague.

The man vomiting in the corner finished emptying his stomach long enough to straighten. He smeared a fist over his mouth, pretending he hadn't just been losing his ale all over the floor.

"Hróarr," Ielda hiccupped. "I thought you were headed south." His words were slurred, the rolling tones of Valdari skidding awkwardly off his tongue.

"I was," Hróarr grinned. "Tomorrow, as it happens. But tonight, I am here. Come, let me buy you another drink."

Ielda shook his head. "Enough."

Cenric stole a glance across the storehouse to where Hróarr's warriors slunk into the shadows, waiting for if they were called. Kalen kept close at Cenric's back, watching the room.

Hróarr wrangled Ielda to a table, making himself at home. In no time, Hróarr had cups of ale for himself, Cenric, and another for the protesting Ielda.

It was a testament to the men's lack of loyalty that none of them stepped in to help their leader.

"How goes trade?" Hróarr asked, leaning on one elbow. "This is my cousin. Cenric of Ombra."

"The Hyldish one?" Ielda hiccupped, face pinching with disdain.

"Half, but he's a wolf where it counts," Hróarr chuckled.

"I don't care for the Hyldish," Ielda muttered.

Cenric smiled at that, resting his elbows on the table. "It looks like you have encountered good fortune lately." Cenric examined the cup he had been handed. It was worn with use, but he could make out the circles and crescents to honor Eponine, the goddess of sorceresses. Almost like it had been taken from the home of one. "Were you raiding this summer?"

"We raided this spring," Ielda said, confirming Cenric's suspicions. "A grand house. A few leagues inland, but well worth it."

Cenric forced himself to show only mild interest.

"We were told it would be undefended and that was true. No real fights and I didn't lose any of my men."

Cenric grinned to hide his excitement. "No wonder you're so rich these days."

"The haul was good." Ielda glanced around. "And the money we took for the raid."

That sounded wrong. "Money?"

"Someone hired us to kill the alderman of Glasney."

Cenric shot a glance to Hróarr to find his cousin looking back to him. Hiring Valdari to kill Hyldish explained a great deal—why the raid had come out of season, why it had been so far inland.

It also raised many, many more questions. Why go through all this trouble to kill Paega, to start? From what Cenric understood, the old man would approve of his own assassination.

"You were hired?" Cenric thought he did a good job of making his voice sound casual.

"We were." Ielda pressed his fist over his mouth for just a moment. "Don't know who paid us, though."

Hróarr laughed. "You took a job from the sprites?"

"A real person," Ielda snapped, too drunk to tell the other man had been joking. "Hyldish. Red hair, shifty eyes, always jumpy like he was about to crawl out his own skin. He paid us half, then never showed to give us the second half." Ielda paused to give several choice curses.

Cenric tried to think of someone who might match that description, but it could be anyone.

Ielda continued. "Doesn't matter too much. We took enough silver to live like kings until next spring."

"I see that." Cenric gestured to the smoky storehouse.

"It's bad news for you, Hyldishman." Ielda shook his head. "People paying Valdari to kill aldermen? Means your country is a pile of peat moss ready to burn."

For all he appeared to be a drunken fool, Ielda was right. If someone had wanted Paega dead and had wanted raiders to take the blame for it, that meant there were larger webs being woven. Aelgar had barely stabilized his rule. For someone to be trying to kill off his aldermen, an alderman with kingly blood no less, was a bad sign.

And why Osbeorn? One child in three made it to adulthood. Brynn's son had only just reached his first year. It seemed excessive.

"It's good news for me!" Ielda cackled. "Lots of work for mercenaries."

Cenric did his best to bury his impatience. How to find out which man had killed Brynn's son?

They couldn't drag Ielda's entire crew back. Neither King Ovrek nor the jarl of Kyrna would stand for that and they didn't have the manpower to do it. A life for a life, that was the way of Valdar.

"You sure you weren't hired by an impatient son wanting his inheritance?" Cenric thought he did an excellent job of sounding bored.

"No." Ielda shook his head, spittle flying as he did. "Old man lost his first batch of sons in the war. He had a new one by some wife a third of his age. Wasn't hard for Svendi finished that one off."

Svendi. How obliging of Ielda to give them a name. They didn't even have to ask.

"Though, the brat looked barely a year old. You wouldn't think a man that age could still get it up." Ielda shook his head. "I think his thanes must have been topping her behind the old man's back."

Cenric chose to ignore the insult to his wife. His prey was close.

"Svendi?" Hróarr screwed his face up as if he was thinking. "With only one eye?"

"Svendi has his eyes," Ielda coughed. "As many as you."

Hróarr stroked his beard, contemplative. "I always get your men mixed up. Which one is missing his eye?"

"That's Svein. My brother."

Hróarr made a grunting sound of understanding. "Then which one is Svendi?"

Ielda pointed a drunken finger across the barn to a pair of men playing tafl. "That one," Ielda slurred. "Both eyes."

Hróarr squinted. "The left one or the right one?"

"Right one!" Ielda was getting frustrated.

Cenric marked the man on the right—carrying two swords, one longer than the other. His beard was braided in two forked strands bound by tiny silver rings. A lot of men had started doing that after Ovrek became king of Valdar.

Cenric made sure not to stare at Svendi for too long. He was going to enjoy what came next.

Loyalty was like a good palisade. It gave order to the world and protection from chaos, but it could also be used by your enemies to trap you if you weren't careful.

In Svendi's case, a little more loyalty might have served him well.

Hróarr and Cenric left Ielda groaning in the corner to slink over to the tafl table and their prey.

Arm of iron and tongue of silver—that was a line from an old song about Havnar, the First of Fathers. He was a great warrior, poet, and persuader. Hróarr must have been blessed by the First of Fathers tonight.

Cenric faded into the background, letting his younger cousin use his reputation as a successful mercenary to their full advantage.

It took a few drinks, a couple coarse jokes, a skillful balance of flattery and insults, and Svendi was ready to join Hróarr's ship. Though in fairness, Svendi took very little persuading to leave.

Before the night's stew was finished, Svendi trailed along, Hróarr's massive arm around his shoulder like the oldest of friends. Svendi had collected his shield and the satchel that probably contained all his worldly goods. He was walking away into the dark with a band of strangers.

Truly, a little bit of loyalty might have helped Svendi live much longer.

Cenric followed close behind, watching his prey while

Snapper, Kalen, and Hróarr's two warriors followed up from behind. Cenric's fingers itched with the anticipation of a fight.

They reached Hróarr's ship, dragged ashore for the night. It had stopped raining and most the men had already bedded down for the evening, cook fires built along the shore.

"Ho!" Hróarr called to the men. "Time to be sailing back to Hylden."

Svendi flinched, looking up at Hróarr. "In the middle of the night?"

"No sense in wasting time." Hróarr turned back to the men who were already packing up their belongings.

Neither Hróarr nor Cenric had expected to find Svendi this easily. Surely Morgi must be on their side.

Hróarr's men moved to obey. No one questioned their leader, but no one was rushing, either.

"What is this?" Svendi asked, suspicion lacing his tone as he wriggled away from Hróarr.

The time for trickery and deceit was over. Out here, in the darkness of the beach, there were no witnesses close enough for a good look.

The shield slung over Svendi's back blocked his peripheral vision. Cenric swept in close and kicked the back of Svendi's knee. Svendi stumbled and Cenric lunged after him, but the whoreson was fast.

Svendi backed away from Cenric, facing all of them, but he had the ocean at his back and Cenric and Hróarr in front of him. He was trapped. "What is this?" Svendi demanded. "What treachery?"

Cenric grinned, not sure the cookfires gave Svendi enough light to see it.

Svendi drew a large knife that was almost a short sword. He waved it threateningly, eyes on Cenric.

"Don't play with him too long," Hróarr muttered. "I want to get back to Hylden before another rainstorm rolls in." As he spoke, Hróarr tossed a spear to Cenric.

Cenric caught the spear, testing the weight. It was a good weapon, balanced. Hróarr always had appreciated fine blades.

"What is this?" Svendi demanded again. "I've done nothing to any of you!"

"No," Cenric agreed, stalking closer. "Not to us."

Svendi's gaze whipped between Hróarr and the others. To his credit, he didn't call for help, but maybe because he knew that no one would come.

Cenric raised the spear, advancing on the other man. His weapon had the longer reach and both of them knew he had the upper hand.

But Svendi was not going down quietly. Cenric could respect that.

The Valdari raider lunged for Cenric. He feinted and spun to avoid the sweep of Cenric's spear, rolling under the blade. He swept under the spearhead and grabbed the shaft. Rushing with his knife out, he slashed at Cenric's head.

Cenric! Snapper cried, barking in fear.

Cenric ducked and dropped into a crouch. He smashed his fist into Svendi's forward knee.

Cenric! Snapper lunged forward, but Hróarr caught him by his scruff, holding him back.

"Steady, son." Hróarr crouched down beside the dog.

Good. Cenric didn't want Snapper getting caught up in this.

Svendi's leg shot out from under him, sending him sprawling into the sand. Cursing, Svendi scrambled away, struggling to get his bearings.

Cenric chased, stabbing down with his spear as Svendi rolled away.

The raider was good. Cenric could see why the man had been arrogant enough to think Hróarr wanted him for his crew—he had the skill to back it up. A pity he'd murdered Brynn's son.

Svendi leapt back up to his feet, watching the other men on the beach, but none of them made to join in. Hróarr seemed to be content to let Cenric handle this one. Maybe he knew it had been a while since Cenric had gotten to fight—really *fight* a worthy opponent.

Cenric dropped his spear, beckoning for Svendi to come closer.

"Cenric…" Hróarr's voice was low, a warning. "Now is not the time for antics."

"Lord?" Kalen sounded genuinely worried.

Cenric faced the Valdari raider, motioning the man closer.

"You're either mad or stupid," Svendi grated, long blade held in front of him.

"We'll see." Cenric smiled, morbid excitement shivering down his spine.

Svendi swept in, aiming for Cenric's gut. His knife was long, but it brought him in close, within grappling distance.

Cenric blocked the knife with his forearm. The blade screeched as it scraped along the iron in his bracer. He felt the blade catch, the impact would leave a bruise, but it didn't meet skin.

Svendi couldn't recover in time to avoid Cenric's fist.

Cenric's knuckles slammed into the side of Svendi's face. The man's whole head snapped to his right, and he sprawled into the sand.

Cenric slammed a boot down over the man's knife hand. Dropping to the ground, he straddled Svendi, slamming his fist into the man's jaw a second time.

Svendi grunted, bringing his left arm up to block. Something flashed and Cenric noticed in time to block a second smaller knife. He grabbed Svendi's wrist, using gravity and his weight to pin that hand beside the first before slamming his knee down into the raider's chest.

Svendi cursed, thrashing ineffectively.

"Are you done showing off?" Hróarr muttered, sounding impatient.

With the man pinned under him, Cenric considered his

options. He could bring Svendi's head as he'd told Brynn, but he had a better idea.

"Rope," he called over his shoulder. "We'll take him alive."

Svendi cursed and struggled, flailing uselessly on the ground. Kalen brought the rope, and they trussed up the Valdari raider like a pig for market.

Between Hróarr and Cenric, they hauled him up into the ship as the rest of the men finished loading.

Cenric shook the sting out of his knuckles as they set sail under cover of darkness, leaving before anyone had the chance to miss Svendi or notice they'd left.

They camped on a nearby island for the rest of the night to wait for daybreak. For the first time since marrying Brynn, Cenric had a foretelling.

He was alone on a beach, stumbling over black rocks worn smooth by the waves. The ocean stretched to his left and a wall of pine trees to his right.

It was a place near Olfirth's lands, somewhere along the south portion of Ombra.

Desperation clawed at Cenric as he searched the driftwood, fish bones, and seaweed washed up by the tide. He spotted the pale shape of a body lying at the edge of the water, just washed in by the waves.

"No," he heard himself say. "No, no." Cenric reached the shape and crashed to his knees, reaching to roll the corpse over.

Brynn was white as death, eyes staring into space with seaweed matted in her hair—drowned.

Thick ropes bound her arms from wrists to elbows.

23

BRYNN

According to Anders, Cenric's thane who had returned two days ago, Hróarr had been right about the raid on Leofton. But now Cenric had gone with the Valdari mercenary to Valdar for some reason having to do with Osbeorn.

Brynn was terrified to consider what that might mean, but luckily, she had a much more immediate concern.

"Daughter, we need to talk."

"We are talking." Brynn heaved up the bucket of water in her hands, pouring it into the stone trough running under the wooden fence.

On the other side, Edric along with most Cenric's thanes and the men of the village worked to move the young cows into the pens.

Selene's nostrils flared. "In private."

Brynn glanced over to Gaitha and the other women currently at work carrying their own buckets up from the river. The cattle would only be in the pens for a day or two until slaughter, but they would need water until then.

There was work to be done, and Brynn had to see to it all without Cenric's help. Not only that, but her mother was proving persistent.

"I have nothing to say to you," Brynn replied, picking up her bucket and heading back to the river. She raised her voice so

Gaitha and the others could eavesdrop more easily. "And there is nothing you have to say to me that they can't hear."

Esa worked at carrying water just as Brynn did. The other women pretended not to listen, but Brynn caught their stares. She spotted Rowan among them, eyeing her with that narrow, suspicious stare. Brynn pitied Rowan. She truly did. She was starting to get an idea of just what Cenric put his women through.

"Brynn!" Selene flustered, lifting her skirts as she chased Brynn through the tall grass. "Why are you doing this? Are you trying to punish me?"

"How am I punishing you?" Brynn demanded. "I never asked you to be here."

"Brynn." Selene exhaled sharply, her first real sign of frustration all morning.

The woman had been relentless. Every time Brynn left the longhouse, Selene was there. She haunted her daughter's steps, trying to persuade her of…something. Brynn still wasn't sure what. She only knew it would involve her mother's schemes, desires, and the plots of the Istovari Mothers.

Brynn came to the water's edge and lowered her bucket beside several other women. The women watched Selene with raised brows, though none of them spoke.

Neirin hovered at Selene's back, her faithful guard. At least Brynn's mother wasn't being followed by the twins today.

"You are the daughter of a king." Selene crouched at Brynn's side. "Yet you are here, fetching water for cows like a house girl."

"What is your point?" Brynn drew up another load of water once again.

Brynn had told Cenric she was willing to work, and she had meant it. Anything to keep her from going back to Glasney.

"You are more than this." Selene shook her head, seeming at a loss. "You were born for more than this."

Brynn's jaw tightened. Like a serpent, Selene had chosen the perfect time to strike. With one of the most brutal times for work out of the year and with Cenric gone, she was vulnerable.

"We can get this marriage annulled," Selene whispered. "It's only been a month. You can come with me and—"

"And what?" Brynn kept her attention on the path ahead, marching back to the water trough.

Selene made a frustrated sound. She jogged to keep up, her voice low. "Paega has agreed to take you back."

More likely, Paega had said he wouldn't stop Brynn returning, but finally she knew why Selene was here.

Brynn tipped her bucket into the trough that was now nearly half full. "Tell me, *Mother*," Brynn spun on the woman. "Does the king know you are here?"

Selene gave Brynn a sharp look. "Paega is old, my girl. He probably won't last much longer. You've kept him alive better than anyone expected."

"Better than *you* expected." Brynn headed back toward the river. She had healed Paega's ailments, treated his injuries without him ever once thanking her.

Selene walked after Brynn, probably looking like a fool to the onlookers. She had to hate that. Selene never liked being embarrassed. "This isn't just about you," Selene insisted. "Your marriage to Paega was a great thing for our people."

When Brynn had married Paega *for the good of their people*, she thought it was so that sorceresses could live in Glasney. Instead, her mother had made constant requests for resources. Gifts of grain, furs, linen, and sheep. The gifts had been requested for this sorceress, or that sorceress, and Brynn had happily obliged.

Glasney had been wealthy enough to afford it, but when they'd had a bad harvest two years ago and Brynn had not been able to send as much as her mother requested, they'd had their first real fight.

"Brynn, you can do nothing for us here," Selene said.

"Perhaps that is the point." Brynn had reached the river again and refilled her bucket. She faced her mother. "I am done, Mother."

"With what?"

"All of it." Brynn marched back toward the trough. "Politics. The Istovari. You."

"You don't mean that."

"I do." Brynn emptied the bucket once again. "I do mean it."

"You would stay here being a workhorse and a broodmare for some northern savage?" Selene's voice frayed on the last word.

"Careful, Mother. That's the alderman of Ombra you're talking about." Brynn fixed her mother in a hard stare.

All around them, Cenric's people paused, watching their exchange. Edric and the other men were too far away, but Gaitha leaned against the fence on one arm, watching Selene with interest as did several others.

Selene's eyes widened and she seemed genuinely at a loss.

"Can you finish this?" Brynn asked Gaitha, gesturing to the water trough. "I am going to go check on the kitchen."

Gaitha kept her eyes on Selene. "Of course."

Brynn handed her bucket to Esa.

"Should I come with you, lady?" Esa also watched Selene like the older sorceress might attack at any moment.

"No, stay here and help Gaitha."

"As you wish, lady." Esa canted her head, returning to her work.

Brynn began the trek up the hill to the longhouse. Ash leapt up from where she had been dozing in the grass and bounded after Brynn. She had noticed one of the dogs always trailed her these days. Was it coincidence or had Cenric given them the command to guard her?

Selene struggled to follow, panting. Brynn would have felt sympathy if it had been anyone else.

She reached the longhouse and Selene followed her inside. Brynn forgot she was barring her mother from the house for a moment.

Selene hovered over her shoulder while Brynn looked after the house girls' progress. "Please, Brynn. Just allow us to speak in private. Please. Only once."

It was a small concession and Brynn hated to give even that, but if she let her mother have this, perhaps she would realize her efforts were useless.

The household girls already had the cakes of bread in the coals and were at work chopping vegetables for the evening stew. Several chickens had been plucked and cleaned for roasting. Everything was in order.

"Fine," Brynn exhaled. "Once."

Selene's face glowed with triumph. It was almost enough to make Brynn go back on her word.

She led her mother into the bedchamber she shared with Cenric. The bedchamber where she'd been sleeping alone for the past two nights. Her mother didn't need to know she had spent those nights missing Cenric and remembering how it had felt to have him hold her.

Ash swaggered in after Brynn, shamelessly inviting herself inside.

Neirin waited outside, though they kept the door open.

Selene sat on one of Brynn's trunks by the wall. She indicated the place next to her, but Brynn ignored her. Selene exhaled, as if dealing with a petulant child. "Brynn, this is bigger than you."

"Isn't it always?" Brynn stepped over to the basket where she had left Guin. Scooping up the puppy, she stroked under Guin's muzzle.

The puppy whimpered, standing on her back legs and straining to lick Brynn's mouth. Ash looked on, watching the puppy with perked ears.

Selene glanced to the door, then back to Brynn. "Aelgar is sickly. Every day it seems he has a new ailment. Not even Wassa can keep up with all his healing."

"Good thing he has a son."

"A toddler," Selene corrected. "A child who will no doubt disappear the moment his father is dead." Selene said it with morbid certainty. "You know how these things go."

Brynn did know. Peace lasted as long as a king was alive. When he died, new contenders arose. Even men who had sworn to serve their ruler's son would scramble for the right to be called king.

It was also custom to kill all the male relatives of the late king, just to be safe. That was what Brynn's grandfather had done when he had seized power after Offa.

When Aelgar had risen to power after Brynn's father, most people had been surprised the sickly brother had managed to draw enough support. There had been fighting across nearly every shire, except here in the north, it seemed.

Many aldermen and warlords had tried to subjugate their neighbors, to assert dominance and carve up a piece of Hylden for themselves, but the sorceresses had backed Aelgar. That had been enough. Kingmakers, they were called now, though butchers might have been more accurate.

The slaughter of the two hundred or so animals in the coming days would be nothing compared to the bloodshed Brynn had witnessed. She and the other sorceresses had carved a path of destruction through Aelgar's enemies like threshers in a field. Never before had the sorceresses gone to war like that. Brynn hoped they never would again.

Most of Aelfwynn's warrior women had died that day along the Cerin. They had paid for their loyalty in blood.

In exchange, Aelgar had agreed to find husbands for their daughters, sisters, and nieces among his thanes and aldermen. To honor them forever in his household and lands.

He had made good on his promises so far. All the same, he had been too happy to ship Brynn off to the farthest corner of his kingdom at her earliest request. She was a liability to him. Everyone knew it.

"You will find a new king," Brynn answered, looking down

at Guin. "I am sure there are volunteers. Every contender will be trying to win over the Istovari first."

"Many of them now have Istovari wives," Selene sighed. "It makes the situation delicate."

"It is not my problem." Brynn let those words hang along with the implication that her mother would have to deal with this alone.

"Torswald of Orland has made us a generous offer in return for our support. As soon as you get another child by Paega, you can marry Torswald instead."

Brynn's spine stiffened. "No."

"Have you consummated this marriage yet?" Selene demanded.

"Of course," Brynn snapped. As soon as the words were out, she wondered if she had said them too quickly.

Selene sniffed. "Don't act so offended. It did take you years the first time."

Brynn had to force her jaw to unclench. "You think a northern savage would leave his broodmare untouched?" She threw her mother's words back in her face, knowing as well as her mother did that there was no way to prove Brynn *hadn't* consummated her marriage to Cenric.

Selene studied Brynn, brows raised. The silence lasted a moment too long, but Selene let the matter drop. "Your uncle is not long for this world, my dear. One way or another."

"I said no." Brynn's jaw clamped down hard. "Keep me out of this."

Selene stood, coming toward her daughter, a look of rapture on her face. "Torswald is willing to make you queen, Brynn. He will keep the title of alderman."

Panic began to claw up her throat. It was happening. Her mother was trying to drag her into a scheme again. One that would entrap her for longer than a war, or the lifetime of a single broken old man. Brynn clung tighter to the puppy in her arms, the reminder of her new life in Ombra.

"Hylden does not have queens. We never have." Not even the wives of kings took that title.

"That can change. Things can always change." Selene's eyes took on a feverish light. "Everything we have worked for, Brynn. Generations of planning, of seeing plans fall apart, of making new ones."

Brynn shook her head. "I will not do it."

"Do this for your people, child. For your family. Do this for your mother."

"You wanted me to fight in the war, so I did. You wanted me to marry Paega, so I did. You wanted me to have a child by him, so I did." Brynn almost choked on the words as memories bubbled up.

Paega had been impatient and rough. *You asked for this,* he had said, *stop crying.* At least he had gotten it over with quickly and they had only had to do it for a few months before she conceived.

Brynn knew the kind of appetites some women endured and maybe she was lucky, but she had never felt so. The pain of being unwanted was a sting that had never lessened.

"A child will make it easier for you to keep ahold of Glasney." Selene sounded like she was considering something. "A child with Paega would be ideal. If you can't get another in a few months, I am sure we can arrange something."

Brynn blinked at her mother. "I already had a child by Paega. Just like you told me to. And I buried him in Glasney." Brynn refused to cry, though mention of Osbeorn threatened to make her do just that.

The puppy squirmed in her arms, noticing Ash on the ground and trying to reach the larger dog.

"If you had just kept him with you, this wouldn't have happened," Selene snapped. "Those Valdari raiders wouldn't have stumbled upon him."

Brynn frowned. "How did you know they were Valdari?"

Selene shrugged. "I don't, but it does seem like their tactics.

Striking at night and all. Even if a spring raid is unusual."

Brynn wasn't sure what to make of her mother's statement. It couldn't be, could it? Surely her mother hadn't known anything about the raid? She had been in the far south.

Immediately, Selene changed tactics. "I am sorry, my dear. It is terrible. I too buried my firstborn and—"

"Do you remember what you said to me when my son was born?" Brynn set Guin down and the puppy sprang toward Ash. "Because I do."

"I believe I congratulated you."

Brynn raised her chin. "You said not to worry because I was young, and I could still try for a girl."

Selene's brow wrinkled. "I never said that."

"Yes," Brynn hissed. "Yes, you did." She would never forget her mother's words as long as she lived. She'd been exhausted, still covered in sweat and gore, breathing in the scent of her slimy, squirming child, and her mother had tsked in disappointment.

"I would never say something like that."

"Why are you lying?" Brynn asked the question coldly, voice low. "Always I have done as you wanted." Brynn's throat grated and she fought to keep her voice from cracking. "But that was before." Before Osbeorn. Before she realized she wasn't the only one who would pay the price for her mother's schemes.

It would never be enough. There would never be an end to the demands.

"Stop being selfish," Selene snapped. "You're being childish."

"Childish?" Brynn laughed, though her eyes stung.

"Someday, you will have your own daughter, and when—"

"When I have another child, you won't be permitted anywhere near them."

"You think I wanted to swyve your father?" Selene demanded, composure cracking. "You think I wanted to birth you or your sister?"

Some part of Brynn had already known that for a long time. Unwanted—that was what Brynn had been her whole life. Paega hadn't wanted her, neither had her mother. Brynn knew little of her father, but she knew full well he had hoped for a son.

Selene seemed to recover herself. "Your grandmother said to me what I am saying to you—this is not about you."

On the floor, Guin and Ash bounded in circles, oblivious to the argument taking place over their heads. Guin let off little puppy squeaks that might have been growls and Ash pranced in circles, tail lashing wildly.

"No," Brynn agreed. "This isn't about me at all." She inhaled a long, slow breath. "I must be married to someone. I know that." An unattached sorceress was a target, especially one of her notoriety. She needed a husband to offer her safety, to be a buffer against competitors for her loyalty. "But I have chosen Cenric. And when we have children, you will stay away from them."

Selene's eyes widened. "How dare you."

"I dare," Brynn grated.

Neirin coughed, indicating that someone was coming.

Brynn sensed two sources of *ka* nearing from the main entrance to the longhouse. It was probably Gaitha coming to check on her and another one of the dogs.

"What is so special about this Cenric?" Selene demanded, her voice lowering to a hiss. "As far as I can tell, he has abandoned you less than a month into your union. What makes you so loyal?"

In that moment, Brynn almost forgot she had argued with Cenric before he left. If her mother was against Cenric, that was a strike in his favor.

The two figures were coming closer. Neirin moved to block them, but they didn't seem deterred.

Selene started speaking faster, realizing her time was running out. Whoever was here was probably going to end their audience. "What about him is different from any other man?"

Brynn was ready for them to be done. "He's honorable, generous, and brave and I'd rather be his wife than anyone's queen."

"You are a stupid girl. A stupid, stupid girl." So, Selene was resorting to insults now? That might have cowed Brynn a few years ago, but she was beyond caring now.

"Get out," Brynn ordered, her arm sweeping toward the door.

"This is a mistake." Selene stepped toward Brynn, shaking her finger in her face. "You will regret this."

"I believe my wife told you to get out."

Brynn jumped. "Cenric." Her face heated. How much had he heard? "You're back."

"I'm back." Cenric leaned one arm against the doorway. It looked as if he'd shoved Neirin aside and why shouldn't he? It was his house, after all. A scab marked his lower lip and the knuckles of his right hand bloomed purple. Had he been in a fight?

Something in her chest unclenched at the sight of him. He might have been in a fight, but he was home.

Snapper bounded through the door, nearly crashing into Ash and Guin. The newcomer's tongue lolled out the side of his mouth in a doggy grin as he left slobbery kisses over Guin and Ash spun happily to greet him.

Cenric's attention remained on Selene. "Why are you still here?"

Selene's eyes widened, her back stiffening with indignation.

"You will speak to Lady Selene with respect!" Neirin said.

"Respect is for guests," Cenric answered. He seemed perfectly unthreatened by Neirin, but Brynn noticed his right hand remained free, ready to grab the sword at his side. "This woman has been told to leave. That makes her a trespasser."

"This is not over," Selene grumbled to Brynn, moving toward the door.

"I think it is," Brynn snapped, putting the weight of her final decision into the words.

Selene and Neirin stormed out the bedchamber and back to their camp in the field, which should now be mostly occupied by Valdari. That would make her mother uncomfortable. Good.

"Is that your mother?" Cenric jerked his head in the direction Selene had gone.

"Yes." Brynn wasn't sure why she felt suddenly self-conscious.

"Edric mentioned she'd showed up." Cenric scratched at his beard, still leaning against the doorframe. He cleared his throat. Was he…*nervous?*

"Anders said you'd gone to Valdar because of Osbeorn." Brynn still didn't understand. She suspected, but she was afraid to know.

She didn't want to find out that her son had been murdered by Hróarr or another of Cenric's friends. Just now, it might be her worst fear—the fear that Cenric might bring her son's killers into their home, to their table.

"I wanted to find you answers." Cenric exhaled softly. "I would want answers, and I would want the man to answer for it."

Brynn shook her head, her voice coming out as a whimper. "At what cost?

Cenric's brow furrowed. "What?"

The words tumbled out all at once. "I…I didn't know what to think and I…" Brynn's voice cracked. "Was it anyone you know? Was it Hróarr?"

"No, of course not." Cenric blinked at her, seeming genuinely surprised.

That was some relief. At least she wasn't going to have to serve her son's murderer at feasts. "Alright."

"But I did find him." Cenric looked to his bruised knuckles. "We brought him back with us."

Brynn's chest coiled with a thousand feelings at once—sickening dread, anger, and the desire to run. At the same time her hands clenched with the impulse to strangle someone. "How do you know it's him?"

"Come." Cenric stepped away, toward the end of the longhouse. "It will be easier to show you."

24

CENRIC

Honorable, generous, and brave? Cenric's chest might as well have glowed with the swell of pride.

After last night's foretelling, he'd pushed Hróarr and the mercenaries to rush home to be sure she was safe. His one comfort was that Morgi only sent him foretellings of things he could prevent, which must mean there was still a way to save his wife.

Perhaps the foretelling was a warning of Brynn's mother.

He didn't like that Selene was trying to talk her out of their union, but Brynn had warned him of that. He liked it less that Selene had chosen to insult his wife in her own home.

But Brynn had defended him. She'd praised him, even if it had been to slight Selene. Despite everything that happened before he left, some part of her still thought highly of him. She wanted to stay with him, at least.

Cenric led the way, swelled with excitement even though he wasn't sure how Brynn would respond to his "gift." Hróarr had cautioned him quite a bit.

"What's this?" Brynn walked behind him, her puppy tucked under one arm.

Up ahead, Hróarr and several of his Valdari came up the path to meet them. Hróarr swaggered, thumbs in his belt, Vana at his side.

"They are bringing your gift," Cenric answered.

Snapper trotted happily in a large circle, sniffing at the ground and greeting the other dogs. As usual, he was oblivious to the impending violence.

Hróarr stepped aside and two Valdari marched forward, leading a bloodied and bound figure between them.

Hróarr's men forced their captive to his knees. Svendi resisted, but like all his efforts over the last day, it was useless.

Esa hovered beside the Valdari warriors, even paler than usual. She looked to Cenric, then back to Brynn.

"Cenric?" There was fear in Brynn's voice.

Cenric stepped to the side, giving her a clear view. "This is Svendi, formerly a mercenary in the service of Ielda." He looked to Esa, then back to Brynn. "The raiders attacked Leofton. We killed or repelled most of them, except one."

Brynn's eyes snapped to Cenric. Her face was neutral, but there was something intent, something coiled tight and ready to spring. A she-wolf about to pounce. Whether she was about to pounce on him or his captive, he wasn't sure, but he kept speaking.

"The raider had this ring." Cenric held out the gold piece to her, still smudged with dirt.

Brynn took it with shaking hands and turned it over, studying the object patiently, deliberately.

Cenric waited. Hróarr and his men waited. Svendi waited. The whole world seemed to be holding its breath.

Then Brynn lowered the ring, clenching it in one hand. "How?" she rasped, her voice trembling.

"The raider told us he'd gotten it from a man who sails with the mercenary Ielda. We found Ielda in Kyrna, where he plans to winter."

Brynn remained focused on the bloodied mercenary on his knees before them.

Cenric spared another glance for Esa. "Ielda also told us who killed the alderman's son."

Svendi let off a string of curses, but a kick from Hróarr's men silenced him.

Cenric nodded to Esa. "As soon as we docked, your girl confirmed it for us."

"It's him, lady," Esa whispered, grasping Brynn's arm as she came to stand beside her. "That's the man who killed your son. I swear it." Tears welled in the girl's eyes.

Svendi tried to struggle again, but Hróarr's men held him in place.

Brynn still didn't speak. She pushed Esa to the side, gently but firmly. "Hold Guin for me."

Esa took the puppy, though the small animal whimpered in protest.

All her attention on Svendi, Brynn stepped toward him. She moved slowly, but it was the slowness of a predator closing in.

"You killed my son?" Brynn's voice was a whisper, a rustle.

Cenric repeated the question in Valdari. "She asks if you killed her son."

One of Hróarr's men stomped down on Svendi's foot, making him yowl in pain.

Svendi spat, adding curses in Valdari. "What if I did, bitch?"

Cenric didn't translate, but his wife seemed to understand.

Brynn shook her head, looking down to the ring in her hand.

Svendi writhed in his captors' grip. "Not her." He looked to Cenric. Seeming to realize he wouldn't receive any quarter there, he looked to Hróarr. "Don't let me be killed by a woman. Please."

Hróarr grunted. "Is that not good enough for a self-proclaimed baby killer?"

Svendi looked back to Brynn. Like all warriors, he knew death followed him like a shadow. But most assumed that their death would come by an accident, illness, or the hands of another warrior.

Brynn was a warrior, in her own way. Cenric saw no shame in letting a man meet his death at her hands, but Svendi disagreed. He struggled, but Hróarr's men held firm.

"Why?" Brynn whispered, her voice little more than a whimper. "He was just a baby." She shook her head, eyes misting. "He couldn't have done anything to you."

"She wants to know why you did it," Cenric translated.

"Why not?" Svendi tried to spit again, but they hadn't given him water and it seemed he was running out. "He was right there. Marked out in those fine little clothes with embroidered edges. Did you make those for him?" Svendi had given up begging for his preferred executioner and now seemed set on taunting Brynn. "Well, then know you marked him for death yourself, whore."

Cenric belted a fist into Svendi's teeth. Blood flew from the raider's mouth.

"Cenric." Brynn grabbed his arm, pulling him to the side. "No."

Cenric wasn't about to let a prisoner insult his wife, even if she didn't understand the language.

"I don't want this." Brynn tugged Cenric away from the prisoner.

Cenric jabbed a finger at the Valdari captive. "He just confessed."

Tears flooded Brynn's eyes. She shook her head quickly.

This was not going at all the way Cenric had expected.

Hróarr muttered under his breath in Valdari. "I told you so."

Cenric searched his wife's face, more confused than anything else. Nothing could bring back murdered loved ones, but in Cenric's experience, vengeance was the next best thing.

Brynn tilted her head back, her nose reddened and tears sliding down her cheeks. "This isn't what I want."

Cenric wanted to give her what she wanted. He would give her anything she wanted, but he'd thought this the greatest gift he could give her and now she stood whimpering and backing away. He had made a terrible misjudgment of his wife. Now half the shire appeared to be looking at them along with Hróarr and his entire mercenary company. Embarrassment shot through him, mingling with confusion.

"What would you have us do?" Cenric asked, doing his best not to sound frustrated.

"I just—"

A man yelled.

Snapper barked.

"Cenric!" Hróarr bellowed.

Svendi leapt off the ground, having wrenched a knife from one of his guards. He barreled straight for Cenric.

Cenric shoved Brynn out of the way, raising his forearm to block the knife slash.

Svendi's entire body went ramrod stiff. It was like stakes had been driven through all his limbs. Fear flooded the raider's eyes along with confusion. His legs buckled and he hit his knees even as his arms remained reaching for Cenric.

Brynn had gotten her hands on the man's wrist, her nails digging into his skin like talons. Her breath came in heaves, and she trembled, but her hold didn't falter.

Hróarr's men made to come forward.

"Stay back!" Brynn ordered. Even with the language barrier, they stopped in their tracks.

"Brynn," her mother called to her softly, swooping in like a vulture the moment she saw her daughter's distress. "This isn't you." She held out her hand as if to beckon Brynn to her. "This isn't you, child."

"*You* didn't fight in the war." Brynn looked up to her mother and something in her seemed to snap. "You don't know me at all."

Svendi still didn't move, and his jaw seemed locked in place. Only his eyes swam back and forth in panic.

Cenric watched with sick fascination. He hadn't known his wife could do this.

"You think because I choose kindness, I am incapable of cruelty." Brynn's words were soft enough to be a caress yet held all the foreboding of a dark cloud on the sea. "But I can be cruel." Brynn looked to Hróarr, singling him out amongst his men. She spun back around.

For a moment, Cenric thought she spun to glare at him, but then he realized she was staring past him, where her mother stood.

"I hate killing. I *hate* it." Brynn looked back to the kneeling raider paralyzed in her grasp. "But I am good at it."

Those last few words were spoken so softly, Cenric almost missed them.

Brynn grabbed a fistful of Svendi's hair and snapped his head back. Blood sprayed and suddenly the Valdari captive was in two pieces.

Brynn held his severed head by its hair as the decapitated corpse crumpled to the ground.

Snapper and the other dogs yelped, skirting back. Gasps and whispers went through the gathered crowd. They were all used to death, but this was different. Abrupt. Unexpected. None of them had known Brynn had that kind of power.

Brynn dropped the head, her hands shaking as she stared down at the corpse.

Around them, everyone had gone quiet. A small crowd had gathered, including Gaitha, Edric, Kalen, many of Cenric's thanes, and people from the village.

"Brynn?" Cenric stepped beside her as she stared at the bloodied ruin in the grass.

"I'm fine," Brynn rasped, her voice strained. She didn't look away from the mutilated corpse.

Cenric had expected rage. He had expected to see her cruelty and a victorious triumph after she took revenge.

That was not what had happened at all.

He touched her arm, unsure if she would welcome it, but she didn't pull away. "I'm sorry," he whispered. "I thought—I was wrong."

"My son is avenged." Brynn stared down at the corpse.

"There is nothing to forgive."

Ever the pragmatist, Hróarr picked the gold ring off the ground where Brynn had dropped it. It was a fine piece, expensive. He offered it to Brynn.

Brynn shook her head. "I don't want it."

Hróarr shrugged and turned to his men, gesturing at the corpse. "This ring for whoever disposes of the body."

A man jumped forward eagerly to claim the prize.

Hróarr handed it over, nodding in approval. "And whatever else is in his pockets for whoever helps."

Hróarr's men descended on the body, grabbing arms and legs. Another followed carrying the head as they headed down toward the river.

"Be sure to leave it past the marker," Cenric called after them. He didn't want that body floating ashore and turning rancid on his beach.

Ash bounded after them, her tail wagging as most the younger dogs joined in.

Snapper sniffed at the bloody ground, tail stiff.

Brynn turned toward Cenric, her face a mask once again. "Supper should be prepared shortly. Will Hróarr and his men be joining us?"

"Yes." Cenric studied her, the blood of a dead man staining her apron. "Are you alright?"

Brynn swallowed and he spotted that flicker of something vulnerable, something just beneath the surface. "I don't know," she answered, her voice small.

Cenric caught her hands. He pulled her into his chest, cradling her against him.

"You're not afraid of me?" she whimpered, all the wrath and vengeance gone out of her.

"No," Cenric answered. It seemed Brynn could kill a man in ways he hadn't even thought possible, but he was a proficient killer himself. There was no more reason to fear her than him.

"I'm a monster," Brynn rasped. "Not safe."

"You're a wolf," Cenric corrected. "So am I."

Brynn might not be Valdari and her tears might have blinded him to the danger lurking in her delicate hands, but she was a wolf as sure as he was. He should have been put off by her lethality, but somehow it felt right. Cenric was a warrior. Why shouldn't his mate be?

Cenric rubbed her back, watching her mother and her mother's guard as they spoke in hushed tones. The memory of last night's foretelling came to him. "Stay close to me for the next few days, alright? I've had a foretelling."

Brynn nodded, still trembling. Soft whimpers turned into quiet sobs as she began to cry.

Cenric looked up to Selene. "You're leaving my lands tonight."

25

BRYNN

Killing her son's murderer had been cathartic for all of a heartbeat, and yet, when the man fell limp to the ground, her son had still been dead.

It was an empty sort of closure. Yes, she had the revenge she hadn't dared hope for, but what was the point?

Brynn couldn't help but wonder if there was a woman somewhere on Valdar waiting for a son who would never come home. Had Brynn created yet one more grieving mother?

She didn't blame Cenric for what he had done. He had been raised Valdari and blood was the Valdari means of justice. In his own way, Cenric had done the greatest thing he could do. He had acknowledged her son's life as worth avenging and gone to Valdar and back to prove it.

Exhaustion weighed Brynn down. She had worked all day and there was the usual tiredness of hard labor, but this was more. She was at the point of numbness, like she had experienced too much pain, and her soul had decided oblivion was better.

Brynn didn't remember if it had been Cenric's idea or hers, but he shuffled her off to bed with Esa's help. Brynn had intended to rest only for a few minutes. She laid down with Guin nestled against her side. The puppy seemed to sense her distress and whimpered, licking Brynn's cheek as she snuggled close.

Esa returned when it was dark, carrying a cake of hot bread, a bowl of stew, and several choice cuts of meat. From the portion sizes, Brynn assumed Cenric had sent it.

Through the door, Brynn could hear voices. It must be well into supper. She should be there, but instead of going into the other room, she ate what she could and sent Esa away with the leftovers. Esa took Guin outside so that Brynn could keep resting.

Brynn wasn't sure how long she slept, but she woke the second time when Cenric came into the room. He entered quietly, but she felt his presence like a shift in the air.

Snapper entered after him, sauntering in like it was his right to be here.

"You can go," Cenric said, voice low. "I will bank the fire."

A figure rose from beside the hearth. Brynn realized one of the house girls had been watching the fire while she slept. The girl bowed to Cenric as she slipped out the door past him.

The longhouse had gone quiet. Cenric took his time to ease the door closed. He sat on the chest at the foot of the bed to pull off his boots and remove his woolen leg wraps. He undressed stealthily, carefully, trying not to wake her.

Guin yipped at the sight of Snapper, hopping to the edge of the bed.

"Shh," Cenric whispered. He scooped up Guin and she growled at him.

Guin was still holding a grudge against him, it seemed. Nonetheless, the moment he set her down, she scampered over to Snapper and the older dog dropped to her level. He rolled onto his back, letting Guin pounce on top of him. Snapper let off a playful growl as the puppy tried to pin him to the rug.

While the dogs wrestled in front of the hearth, Cenric removed his belt. His tunic came next.

The fire outlined muscular shoulders and a toned back. Cenric cracked his neck to one side and then the other, sending ripples through the lines of muscle. He usually slept beside her bare chested, though his trousers had stayed on. All the same, the sight of him now made heat pool in her low belly, and it was suddenly hard to sit still.

"Cenric?"

At his name, he shifted, facing her. "I didn't mean to wake you."

Brynn pushed herself up onto her elbow. "It's fine."

Cenric rose, leaving his clothes on top of the chest. He sat on his side of the bed, stripped down to his trousers. The mattress shifted under his weight as he settled beside her, watching the flames.

As distracting as his body was, Brynn noticed the crease in his brow. "Is something wrong?"

"I had a foretelling."

"A foretelling?"

"Of you." Cenric looked at her wrists, not making eye contact. "Your hands bound and…you drowned in the sea."

Brynn hesitated. "Does that mean I'm going to die?"

"No," Cenric said the word with a ferocity that left no room for argument. "It means we need to be careful, probably for the next few days. Stay close to me, alright?"

Brynn tried take heart in his confidence. "Alright."

"I won't let anything happen to you, Brynn." Cenric spoke the words like a vow.

"I believe you." And she did. Cenric would protect her, if nothing else. That was one promise she didn't doubt from him.

Cenric exhaled another long breath, watching the flames in the fireplace.

"Is there something else?"

"Ielda…" He hesitated, looking back at her. "The mercenary who attacked Glasney. Who led the longship Svendi sailed for."

Brynn braced herself for the grief to well up again, but instead of rising, this time it remained steady. The sadness was still there, a massive lake in her mind, but its waters were calm for now. "Yes?"

"He said they were paid to kill Paega."

Brynn straightened at that. "Paid?"

"Yes." Cenric brushed something off his eye. "He didn't mention being paid to kill your son. Just Paega."

Brynn frowned, trying to think. "That doesn't make sense."

"It doesn't, does it?" Cenric agreed.

"Paega is…" Brynn shook her head. "Ever since the war, he has waited for death."

Brynn had tried to be sympathetic about his grief, but she was finding less and less pity for him now.

She'd lost her child, yet she still forced herself to keep living. She still took care of the people around her and those who depended on her. She hadn't just laid down and given up the way he had.

"I don't suppose you know who might have done it?" There was no accusation in the question, but Cenric's tone was low, serious.

"No," Brynn answered. "And it wasn't me."

"No," Cenric agreed. "No, you could have made his death look like an accident quite easily, I imagine. This would have to be someone tired of waiting for it."

"My mother," Brynn said without thinking. A sick sensation churned in her gut. Had her mother caused her child's death? The woman had mentioned she'd assumed Brynn should have had her son with her that day.

"Your mother?" Cenric sounded interested, but not surprised.

"She…" Brynn hesitated a second as she wrestled with how much to tell him.

Cenric watched her quietly, patiently. He'd been trustworthy so far. Maybe she could risk continuing to trust him.

"My mother knew it was Valdari who attacked."

"I see." Cenric considered that. He must know as well as Brynn that wasn't definitive proof. Cenric himself had guessed as much and Brynn probably could have guessed it herself if she hadn't been so grief stricken at the time. "She and her people have left, but we can hunt them down if you wish."

Brynn shook her head. She didn't want to risk Cenric's thanes for the possibility that her mother had a hand in her son's death. If she went after Selene, she would need to be sure.

"But I thought she wanted you married to Paega?" Cenric asked.

"She came because she had another husband for me. For after I had another child by Paega." Brynn looked away. "I don't want him. I told her I don't, but…she's been planning it for some time. She thinks Aelgar will die soon and wants to have someone to take his place."

Selene had wanted Brynn's son alive to help her hold onto Glasney, but killing the boy had apparently been all the Valdari. That hadn't been part of their patron's plan. Would Brynn ever know for sure? It wasn't as if Selene would admit to it.

Cenric didn't seem surprised. "Your mother wants your next husband to be king?"

Brynn's stomach tightened, but she'd already made the decision to trust him. "No," she whispered. "My mother wants me to be queen."

Cenric shifted back, probably thinking through the same objections Brynn had leveled at her mother. Hylden didn't have queens. There was the occasional tribal chieftain and clan leader who was a woman, but for the aldermen to kneel before a woman and pledge fealty would be more than their pride could bear.

"I can see why," Cenric mused, scratching at his beard the way he did when he was thinking. "If anyone could be the first queen of Hylden, it would be you."

Brynn shot him a sharp look. Had she misjudged him? Was Cenric more ambitious, and power hungry than she thought?

"You are clever. Charismatic. And fierce enough that they would come to respect you. Eventually." Cenric was quiet for a long moment, as if carefully considering his next words. "But

Hylden would never accept a queen married to me." He spoke each word slowly, cautiously. "They only tolerate me because no one else wants the lands this close to Valdar. Aelgar knows this. You know this."

"I don't want to be queen," Brynn said quickly. "I want you."

Cenric looked up at that, meeting her eyes. The firelight reflected in dark pupils as he studied her. His whole body shifted as his full attention narrowed on her.

That look sent chills through her whole body and made heat pool deep in the pit of her stomach. She wanted to touch him, to reach out and clench her fingers into the hard lines of his shoulder, but she was afraid to move. She had the undeniable sense that something would happen if she moved, she just wasn't sure what.

"Brynn?" He spoke her name like an invitation, a dare, and a request all at once.

"Cenric."

That must have been the answer he wanted. Cenric closed the space between them, framing her face in his hands and tugging her toward him. He kissed her as he had done many times, but this time was different.

This wasn't teasing, challenging, or questing. This was confident, sure of himself as his mouth moved against hers.

Brynn's heart raced in a mixture of excitement and fear. She didn't know what to do.

Where was she supposed to put her hands? Was she supposed to take her clothes off now or did he want to do it?

"Cenric!" Brynn shoved against him, panic getting the best of her.

He released her immediately, brow furrowed in confusion. "Brynn?"

Her chest heaved with a swirl of emotions.

"I'm sorry." Cenric shook his head. "I thought...I'm sorry." He shifted away from her, putting space between them.

Brynn grabbed his arm. His muscles were delightfully firm

under her fingers, threatening to distract her. "No," she panted, embarrassingly out of breath. "I just…I'm not good at this."

Cenric studied her hand on his arm. He didn't draw toward her again, but he didn't pull away any further. "What do you mean?"

Oh, this was humiliating. Brynn's face heated and she looked away.

He was going to be disappointed. So disappointed. Brynn always tried to do the right thing, but this was one area she'd never gotten right.

"This." She swallowed down her shame, trying to find the right words. "Pleasing men. I'm not good at it."

Cenric still didn't seem to understand. "Pleasing…men?"

Brynn closed her eyes. To be fair, she'd only been with one man, but when that was the sum of her experience, it had a way of diminishing a woman's confidence. "Paega was never pleased." She didn't know how else to explain it.

That did not seem to answer any of Cenric's questions. "You had a child."

"Yes, but it wasn't a good experience." Brynn thought her face might catch on fire.

"He hurt you?" Cenric's tone turned hard. He shifted toward her again, like he could protect her from the past.

Brynn didn't know how to answer that. It had been rough, but Paega hadn't forced himself on her. She wasn't sure she was allowed to say the man had hurt her when she was the one who had asked him for a baby.

"It wasn't good," Brynn answered, her voice small. "For either of us."

Cenric muttered something in Valdari under his breath—a curse on Paega if she had to guess from the tone.

Brynn gathered her courage again. "I want to please you." She dropped her hand, letting it fall near his on top of the blankets. "But you're going to have to tell me how."

Cenric shook his head, letting out a long exhale. Some of the tension left his shoulders. "Brynn." He shifted on the bed to close the distance between them again. "My sweet wife."

Brynn's heart leapt at his endearment, her body tingling as he drew close again.

He cradled her face with one hand, resting his forehead against hers. "You already please me." He kissed the tip of her nose. "Everything is better since you came here." He kissed just to the side of her mouth. "The air is cleaner." He brushed his cheek against hers as he lowered his head to kiss her jawline. "The mead is sweeter." He kissed her throat, the barest touch of his lips on her skin. "The fields are greener."

"It's autumn," Brynn whimpered, pressing closer against him. She wasn't sure where this was going, but she hoped he wouldn't stop.

Cenric chuckled. "Well, then we can say you make the fields more golden, if you insist." He caressed her neck before sliding her collar aside to kiss her collarbone. "But you make everything better. You are my fondest delight." His lips teased her skin, sending shivers of heat straight to her core.

Brynn gasped, struggling to contain a moan. She wrapped her arms around him, hoping that was alright. His back was broad, rippling. Solid. Comfortingly warm. Alive. "What should I do?" she whispered. "Tell me what to do."

"Take your clothes off." Cenric nipped her ear lobe before pulling back.

Nerves fluttered in her stomach. She didn't want to disappoint him, but maybe if he kept telling her what to do, it would be fine.

She pulled away, feeling a sense of chill at the loss of his nearness. Brynn stood, undoing the belts and ties that held her dress in place. Brynn stripped down to her linen shift, setting her wool dress and outer clothes aside.

Cenric's eyes had gone dark watching her. He gestured to her shift. "All of it. Off."

Brynn trembled as she obeyed, removing the last of her

clothes. She pulled off her stockings for good measure, standing in front of him naked as the day she was born.

Her heart raced. She wasn't quite sure where to put her hands. Self-consciousness burned in the back of her mind. Brynn had never thought herself vain, but in that moment, completely bared in front of this man, every flaw seemed magnified tenfold.

But Cenric wasn't looking at her like she was flawed. His eyes slid over her slowly, appreciatively. His gaze hot and hungry.

A slow smile spread across his face. He crooked one finger in her direction, beckoning her to him.

Brynn climbed back onto the bed, meeting him at the center. Her stomach churned nervously yet she wanted to reach out and touch him, to kiss him again. To have his mouth on her again.

It was just sex, she told herself. People did it all the time, and it meant nothing. It had always been just a means to an end for her. A duty.

But already it was different with Cenric. She'd been vulnerable with him, allowed him to see her deepest, most broken places. She couldn't keep him out of her heart when she had already let him in.

Cenric rested his hand on her side, stroking his thumb over the curve of her hip bone. He nuzzled her neck, inhaling the scent of her skin. He eased her back onto the bed, sinking onto his elbow beside her. He kissed her throat, one hand stroking languidly up and down her side.

Brynn pressed closer against him with a soft whimper.

Cenric lowered his mouth to her breast. He sucked at her nipple, making her gasp and her back arch under him. He leaned over her to kiss her other breast, drawing his tongue in spirals around the nipple until he took that into his mouth, repeating his ministrations.

Brynn bit back a moan, clenching his back. The sensation fluttered between pleasure and pain, a blinding intensity teetering between the two.

Cenric moved back up to kiss her collarbone, her throat, until they were cheek to cheek, his mouth against her ear. "How can I best pleasure you, love?"

Brynn squeezed her eyes shut at the endearment, her fingers digging tighter into his back. "I'm not sure."

"Do you know what I mean?" Cenric was kind enough not to sound mocking as he asked the question.

"I know what you mean, I'm just not sure that I…can." Her cheeks flushed with heat again. Cenric really was going to drag out every single one of her sad little secrets.

Cenric pulled back so they were eye level again. He cradled her face, brushing his thumb along her lower lip. "You've never touched yourself?"

Brynn squeezed her eyes shut. When she had started bedding Paega, she'd asked his elder sister Ulstrid for help because she hadn't known who else to ask. Ulstrid had told her how to touch herself and Brynn had tried it during intercourse, hoping that would make it hurt less. Paega's look of absolute disgust had filled her with more shame than she'd ever known up to that point. She'd never been able to try it again without remembering his face.

"It didn't work," Brynn answered quietly, her voice so soft she wasn't sure Cenric would hear it. "I've never…" She shook her head.

Cenric was quiet for a long moment, then he kissed her forehead. "We'll work on fixing that. If not tonight, then however long it takes."

"I'm fine," Brynn said. "You don't have to go through the trouble."

Cenric tilted his head to the side. "And leave my wife unsatisfied?"

"You might find it frustrating." Brynn didn't want Cenric to be disappointed. She didn't want anything like that spoiling these moments.

"Let us try, love," Cenric murmured, his mouth drifting to kiss her jaw, her neck, back down her collarbone. "Can you trust me?"

Brynn took a shaky breath and adjusted her shoulders to be more comfortable. "What should I do?"

"I am going to do things to you," Cenric said. "And you tell me if you like them or not."

Despite her reservations, Brynn's whole body shivered in equal parts anticipation and nervousness. "Alright."

Cenric leaned back on his elbow, so he had a full view of her naked body. He ran a hand down her side, over her hip, and down her thigh. He took his time, feeling her curves and contours with gentle thoroughness. "How is this?"

"Fine." Brynn enjoyed the feel of his hands on her, if nothing else.

"Good." Cenric reached her knee and feathered his fingers over and down, so that his hand was on her inner thigh. "This?"

"Yes." Brynn's heart thudded harder as his fingers dragged up the inside of her leg. She shifted, parting her legs for him as he drew closer toward the apex of her thighs.

Cenric reached the top of her thigh, close enough to stroke the dark curls between her legs before he withdrew. He repeated the ritual on the other side, asking her at each interval how it felt.

"Fine," Brynn gasped, pressing up toward him as he drew his hand up her inner thigh a second time.

"Good," Cenric purred, his voice heavy in her ear. "What about this?" Instead of withdrawing this time, he stroked two fingers on either side of her entrance, watching her face as he did.

Brynn felt exposed in a way she'd never been before. Being the center of his attention was as exciting as it was terrifying. "That's alright."

"Hmm. And this?" Cenric parted her with his fingers, but instead of pushing inside her like she expected, his touch found the bud at her peak.

Brynn flinched.

Cenric let go. "What's wrong?"

"It's fine." Brynn inhaled a quick breath. "I think your hand is too dry."

"I see." Cenric stroked his fingers through the slit between her legs, coating them in her wetness. "Is this better?"

Brynn gasped. "Oh. That's…that's good."

"Good." Cenric breathed the word against her cheek, watching her as his hand worked between her legs. "Does this please you?"

"Yes." Brynn closed her eyes as a flurry of sensations overtook her. Ecstasy radiated through every nerve ending from her scalp to her toes as Cenric teased pleasure from her sex.

"Stay with me, love," Cenric murmured. "Eyes on me."

Brynn obeyed, opening her eyes to find him smiling down at her.

"Good. That's good. Let me see you." He dipped his fingers down into her cleft, coating them in wetness again before resuming his ministrations. Cenric lowered his head, his mouth finding her breast even as his hand continued to work between her legs.

Brynn bit her lip as the pressure built deep in her core. She could feel her body tensing, rising toward something. She reached toward that feeling, trying to grasp it.

Cenric kept stroking her with one hand, cradling her with the other while his mouth coaxed pleasure from her breast. From where he lay beside her, she could feel his hardness through his trousers pressing against her hip. This aroused him. He was enjoying this, too.

"More," Brynn pleaded. "Please."

Cenric complied, his fingers stroking faster, harder, but that was too much.

Brynn flinched, yelping under him.

Cenric stopped, lifting his head to search her face. "Was I too rough?"

Brynn's breath came in heaves, her body flushed with heat. "I think your fingers dried out again."

Cenric kissed her forehead. "I have a solution for that." He shifted away from her.

Brynn pushed up onto her elbows, suddenly feeling cold. "Where are you going?" She didn't want him to stop. Whatever he had been doing, she desperately wanted him to keep going.

"Trust me." Cenric climbed off the bed. He gripped her behind her knees and dragged her to him, so she was barely seated on the edge.

Brynn reached for him, hoping that was alright. Cenric met her in the space between them, touching the side of her face as he kissed her cheek, her nose, her eyes.

"Let go, Brynn." Cenric lowered to his knees between her thighs and Brynn's chest clenched. She didn't think any other man had ever knelt to her, much less an alderman. He stroked down her legs, bowing to kiss the tops of her feet, then stroking up her calves. His mouth trailed a line across her knees, up her thighs.

Brynn wasn't even sure what to call this. What Cenric was doing to her was more than reverence or homage, greater than any of the words she would have thought to use. The only thing that she could think to call it was *worship*.

Seated on the bed, Brynn watched him, speechless. It was too far beyond anything she had experienced or expected to experience. The way Cenric touched her made her whole chest feel as warm and pliant as melted beeswax. She was defenseless and yet it didn't frighten her.

She gasped as Cenric nudged her legs apart, leaving kisses along the soft skin of her inner thighs. Was he going to…?

Cenric nuzzled the dark hairs between her legs, inhaling deeply. It was vulgar and animalistic and—she liked it. Brynn liked it far more than she ever would have thought.

He grinned up at her, as if somehow he knew, then he dropped his head and his tongue slid between the apex of her legs.

Brynn choked as fiery sensations flared through her entire body. How could such a small thing make her feel so intensely through every bone and sinew?

She leaned back, wanting to give him better access for whatever he was doing. Cenric caught her, pushing her down onto the bed.

Whimpering, Brynn let him, staring up at the crossbeams of the ceiling as the whole world seemed to narrow and expand around what his tongue was doing to her.

Cenric's hands found her breasts and teased lightly along her nipples. Despite the calluses, his fingertips worked deftly and skillful, pinching and stroking and teasing with the perfect tempo.

Brynn moaned, her back arching into his hands. How could anything feel this good?

Tingles of ecstasy radiated from between her legs and her breasts to coil deep in her core. The pressure built, rising faster than Brynn could think about it. She leaned into that feeling, focusing on the sensation of his mouth and hands on her. Brynn strained and it was no longer about just wanting to please Cenric.

She wanted this, whatever it was. She *needed* this.

Then it hit her.

Brynn's climax struck hard. A sob ripped out of her as she slammed upward doubling over Cenric, clinging to him as shudders wracked her whole body.

She couldn't control it as her body contracted and convulsed with a lifetime of pent-up emotions. It was terrifying.

Cenric held onto her, laughing victoriously as she writhed against him. There was nothing dignified or composed as she shuddered against her husband, her body completely and totally beyond her control.

Brynn whimpered, finally collapsing against him as the shudders subsided into little aftershocks.

"Good girl." Cenric stroked her back, voice flushed with

pride. "I knew you could do it for me."

Brynn panted, her mind hazy. Everything felt warm and golden and beautiful.

"You have a nice scream." Cenric straightened, still holding her to him as he kissed her shoulder.

Scream? Oh no. "Did I disturb the rest of the house?"

Cenric shrugged. "They'll be fine." He pressed his lips to the side of her neck. "I am so proud of you."

Brynn giggled nervously, flushed and hot and feeling…what was this? Happiness. She was happy, happier than she could remember being in a long time.

She kissed his neck, emboldened in the afterglow of her climax. She snuggled closer, wrapping her legs around him. She traced a finger down his chest, admiring the planes of muscle that rippled down his abdomen. He was gorgeous. A warrior god wrapped in flesh.

When she had been younger, Brynn had ogled her fair share of men and boys her own age. She'd had the fluttering of nervousness at the sight of a beautiful man before and had experienced more than a few moments of desire.

Then she had been married and found her marriage bed to be filled with nothing but resentment and pain. But Cenric…

"I want something," Brynn whispered.

Cenric's brows rose, and his mouth quirked slightly. "Do you?"

Brynn licked her lips. It wasn't like her, but there wasn't much point in propriety after what had just happened. She pressed a hand over the bulge in his trousers. Brynn didn't know how to explain what she wanted, but her husband seemed to understand.

Cenric's mouth spread into a wicked grin. He stood, undoing the ties of his trousers.

Brynn watched from the edge of the bed, heart pounding in her ears. It was going to happen. But it would be alright this time. She was with Cenric.

Cenric kicked off his trousers and faced her, outlined by the firelight. His cock hung free, hard, glistening at the tip, and much larger than she'd expected.

He was magnificent. Gorgeous. She wasn't sure what she was doing, but she slipped off the bed and knelt as he had done for her, reaching for his arousal.

It was hard to read his expression with the backlighting, but she felt him watching her. Intent. Hungry. Pleased.

Brynn had heard about this, even if she'd never done it herself. She grasped his shaft and hesitated, but Cenric's groan of pleasure gave her the courage to continue. She took him in her mouth.

Cenric let off a low growl, tilting his head back. "That's good."

He was too big for her to take the entire length of him, but she used her hand at his base and her mouth at the top half. She sucked and stroked, wanting to tease the same pleasure out of him that he had drawn out of her.

Cenric groaned in appreciation, rocking his hips. He rested his hands on her shoulders, but she had the feeling that he was holding back, restraining himself.

He liked this. He enjoyed this.

Brynn felt a little thrill at that as he hardened even more.

"No." Cenric pushed her back by her shoulders.

Brynn looked up, chastened. "Did I do something wrong?"

Cenric shook his head. "Be sure to remember that because I will ask you to do it again." He pulled her up to her feet so that they were eye to eye once again. "But I want something else tonight." He kissed her before pressing her back toward the bed.

Brynn let him ease her down, yielding as he leveled on top of her. She shifted, spreading her thighs for him, but he didn't rush it.

Cenric hovered over her, his hands rooted on either side of her head. He studied her for a long moment, searching for something. Whatever it was, he must have found it. He dropped down onto his elbows, so they were pressed together. Face to face, belly to belly.

He stroked the head of his cock up and down along her entrance, urging her open and coaxing more wetness from her until they were both slick. He eased inside her a little at a time—gentle and ever so patient.

Brynn gasped as he pushed his entire length inside her.

He paused, searching her face. "Are you alright?"

"Yes." She wrapped her arms around him. "Don't stop. Please."

Cenric kissed her again, then began to thrust his hips. He started out slow, almost torturously slow.

Brynn pressed her face into the crook of his neck, clinging to him. She wrapped her legs around his waist, wanting to be as close to him as possible.

"Beautiful creature," Cenric panted. "Beautiful, beautiful girl, you feel so good."

"You feel good, too," Brynn whispered. And he did. She didn't think she could climax like this, but she loved the weight of him, the way his muscles coiled around her, the sensation of being filled when he pushed inside her. Sighing, Brynn dug her nails into his back, rocking her hips in time to his rhythm. Her hands roved over him, touching, petting.

"What are you doing with your hands?" Cenric chuckled.

"You're doing all the work," Brynn said, feeling awkward. "I want to do something."

"I'll tell you what to do." Cenric caught her wrists, pinning them over her head. "You're going to lie there and take my cock."

Brynn shrank from him, feeling rebuked. Had she made him angry?

Cenric's mouth found the side of her neck and he scraped his teeth along her skin. He didn't bite her, not quite, but he seemed to be holding back, barely restraining himself from devouring her. "Stop trying to earn everything." His voice softened, but he didn't release her wrists. "I'll get my pleasure, love. Focus on yours."

Brynn nodded shakily. He wasn't angry with her, even if it felt strange that her enjoyment was important to him.

So, this was what it was like to make love. Not just sex. This was true intimacy with someone she wanted, who wanted her back.

She watched the play of the firelight on Cenric's shoulders and how his muscles surged with each thrust. It was a magnificent sight. Enough to take a woman's breath away.

"Brynn," Cenric groaned, gritting his teeth. "I'm getting close, but I can last longer if you want me to."

Brynn shook her head. She strained, pressing up against him. "Take it," she whispered in his ear. "Take what you need."

Cenric growled, a deep, masculine sound that sent a shiver through her. Something primal came over him. Something that frightened her almost as much as it thrilled her. With her hands held down, he thrust into her harder, faster than before.

"Yes," Brynn gasped. He wanted her fiercely, desperately, and she could feel it in every surge of his body. In this moment, she was the focus of his existence, and she had never felt more desired than she did with her wrists pinned in his grasp. "Yes."

He might have been generous earlier, but he demanded it all back now. Cenric slammed in and out of her like he couldn't get deep enough.

Brynn wanted to pull him closer, but he held her wrists down. Again, she felt the need to do something, but he was forcing her to surrender and just receive.

She had no control. She couldn't *do* anything. And it felt amazing.

Cenric climaxed with a guttural oath in Valdari. He thrust deep inside her and held there for a set of heartbeats as the tension released in his face. Cenric feathered kisses all over her forehead, her lips, her cheeks, her jaw, and her eyes before he finally let go of her wrists. He pulled out of her and collapsed onto the bed, sweat shining on his forehead.

He beckoned her to his side, and she curled against him, resting her head on his heaving chest. Cenric ran his hand up and down her naked back.

"Incredible," Cenric sighed. "You were wrong about pleasing men." He kissed the top of her head. "You please me and that's all that matters."

Brynn pressed closer against him. Her throat tightened for some reason. "Thank you," she whispered. "Thank you for everything."

Cenric trailed his fingers along her back. He shifted, tucking her under his chin. "Beautiful, beautiful girl."

In front of the fire, Guin had settled down between Snapper's front paws and he was engrossed in giving her a tongue bath. Snapper was a natural nanny.

Brynn felt safer, happier, and more at peace than she could ever remember.

She was in love with Cenric, she realized. Maybe it was the effects of her climax still echoing through her body, but she didn't have another word for this feeling. It was like being engulfed in a cloud of *ka*, like having a warm hearth in her chest.

For the first time in her life, Brynn was happy and in love.

26

BRYNN

Brynn woke up to Guin whining. Snapper woofed, scratching at the door.

Cenric still slept, sprawled across his side of the bed with one arm over Brynn. She knew he had no dreams, but perhaps the nightmares had been kept at bay for tonight. She extricated herself carefully, not wanting to disturb him. She remembered his warning not to go anywhere alone for a while, so she would stay close to the longhouse and well away from the water.

Brynn pulled on her shift and boots, but didn't bother with her dress or veil. Guin whimpered as she picked her up, licking at Brynn's face. The puppy had nearly doubled in size over the past weeks and soon she would be too large for Brynn to carry comfortably.

Snapper trotted along, sticking close at her feet.

Dawn had still not broken so the longhouse slept peacefully.

Brynn could hear the geese beginning to stir, but the land was caught in the grey haze of pre-dawn. As a child, Brynn had loved these early moments. Aelfwynn used to wake her, and they would use the time to braid each other's hair, dress, and prepare for the day before anyone took notice of them. In that stolen hour between first light and sunrise, they had been truly free.

Guin sniffed at the grass, doing her business and trotting in circles. Several of the other dogs including Thorn came leaping from the other side of the house.

They pounced on Guin, tails wagging and tongues lolling.

Guin growled up at Thorn. The bigger dog's tail stiffened, ears laying back at the insubordination.

Brynn straightened, worried Thorn might bite Guin, but then Snapper knocked Guin over with a paw. Guin scrambled upright again, little teeth bared in indignation. Thorn's lips curled in warning, but Snapper cocked his head and smacked Guin with a paw again, sending her sprawling.

Brynn didn't interfere. It was best Guin learned now to get along with the other dogs. She might be as big as them one day, but they would all have to live together.

One of the other dogs trotted up, carrying a bone. For a moment, Brynn feared it might be the remains of that Valdari raider—the one who had been thrown in the river. Then she realized it was a sheep's foreleg, bits of fur still clinging to one end. It had probably been fed to the dogs as scrap.

Brynn looked down at her hands. She'd killed a man yesterday, but he hadn't been the first. She had lost count a long time ago.

Songs and poems were written about those who wielded swords. Aelfwynn had also been a great healer and had helped dozens if not hundreds of people, but she was remembered for those she had killed.

History sometimes seemed to be made of stone—the only way to make a mark on it was through violence.

The irony was killing was frightfully easy. Brynn could break bodies effortlessly, but putting them back together was the hard part.

It was much easier to kill a rival thane than to make him your friend. Brynn could have easily killed Olfirth, though perhaps not all his thanes at once. It had taken true skill to make them sit and sup at her table.

Osbeorn had been killed with barely any effort from the man who had hurled him over the wall. Yet not even Brynn's massive power and skill could bring him back.

Death could be controlled. Life could not.

Why was killing praised when it was the easy way out?

The dogs stopped their play, ears pricked. Thorn let off a low chuffing, ears flicking back and forth.

Brynn went still, listening. A rumbling shook the earth, like the growl of thunder.

Brynn reached out with her power on instinct. She could sense the sleeping figures within the house, the animals in the stable and the village beyond, but something was moving, something alive and massive.

The dyrehund patriarch took off, barking with his tail raised. The rest of the pack followed, Guin scrambling to keep up.

Brynn rose to her feet, chasing after them. She scooped Guin up in her arms and ran around the corner of the longhouse.

A black swarm bore down on the village, and it took a moment for Brynn to realize what she was seeing.

The young aurochs had broken free of their pens and descended on the village in a stampede. They smashed into fences and houses and screams rose over the rumble of their hooves.

Brynn gaped in horror. The animals were too far away and moving too fast for her to do anything.

The cattle ripped through the camp of Hróarr's men below, smashing through tents like they were nothing.

"Cenric!" Brynn spun around, but her path was blocked by Neirin. What was he doing here? Hadn't he left with her mother? "Move!" She tried to shove past the sorcerer, but he grabbed her arm. Brynn pulled on *ka*, ready to fight him to the death, if need be, but magic slammed into her back.

She felt *ka* forcing its way through her veins and worming through her nerve endings. She dropped Guin and the little dog snarled. Neirin kicked the puppy, and she yelped, flying out of Brynn's view.

"No!" Brynn reached for the puppy on instinct right before

magic engulfed her and she lost control of her jaw. She collapsed, struggling, fighting to draw magic, to cast her own spells, but the hem of a black skirt came into view.

Neirin grabbed Brynn under her arms and dragged her behind the house. The spell held her immobile, the *ka* tight and forceful. It was the same spell she had used on that Valdari raider to hold him immobile.

Screams and shouts rose from the house and the village below.

Brynn's mother must have planned the stampede as a distraction. People would be hurt, maybe even killed. The young aurochs that had been intended to feed these families through winter were being used against them.

One of the twins knelt and held something over Brynn's nose and mouth. They were drugging her.

She'd been distracted and let her guard down for barely a moment and they'd gotten the best of her. She had forgotten Cenric's warning like an idiot.

Brynn knew the Istovari were against her, but she had never thought they would go this far.

The people down in the village needed her. Hróarr and Vana needed her.

Cenric needed her.

But she had been stupid, and innocent people were paying for it.

"Relax, my dear," Selene crooned, her voice coming from beside Brynn's ear. "If you'd just done the right thing, we wouldn't have to do this."

Brynn tried to resist, but she couldn't stop herself from breathing. The cloying scent of the drug found its way into her lungs and the world darkened.

27

CENRIC

Cenric bolted out of bed at the first screams. In an instant he had his trousers on and a sword in his hand.

"Brynn!" He could have sworn he heard her call his name. He'd had another foretelling, one that was eerily the same—discovering Brynn's drowned corpse on an abandoned stretch of beach.

Her puppy and Snapper were both gone. Where was Brynn? Why hadn't she awakened him first?

Snapper? He sent out the thought to be meant with emptiness. It must mean his dog was too far away. *Thorn? Ash?*

Silence.

A touch of fear whispered along his spine. Cenric reached the door of the longhouse, tearing out to a view of the village below.

Some hundred auroch yearlings barreled through everything in their path, ploughing through Hróarr's camp and the village. The yearlings were not fully grown, but they were each a block of pure muscle, easily the height of a man with massive, arched horns.

They left a swath of destruction in their wake, screams and cries rising in the early morning.

The cattle galloped into the forest on the other side, following the curve of the river. Some of the animals tripped only to be trampled by their fellows.

They trailed past the village and into the forest, loping into the trees. It would be a nightmare to get them out and rounded back into the pens, assuming the pens were still intact.

The distant barking of dogs rang out from the village. At least he knew where the dyrehunds had gone.

"Brynn!" Cenric searched left and right. She couldn't be down there, could she? She'd brought her pup outside, that was all. He was sure he'd heard her call for him…

"Lord!" Kalen came rushing out of the house. He looked down on the destruction below and his face went white. "What happened?"

"I don't know yet." Cenric's heart raced as he cast left and right. "Find Lady Brynn at once. If you see her, tell her I've gone down to the village, and we need her." People would be hurt. Edric and Gaitha's house was in the village as were many of Cenric's thanes.

That was probably where Brynn had gone.

"Yes, lord." Kalen sprinted back into the house.

Cenric sheathed his sword, buckling it on as he ran down the path toward the field.

He had posted guards over the cattle, like they always did. What had happened? Was this some foul play from men sent by Olfirth? Had the old man decided that he didn't want to be neighborly after all?

"Hróarr!" Cenric reached the first of the Valdari tents.

Something moved under the torn canvas and the bent tent poles. Cenric pulled aside the flotsam, revealing a Valdari man on the ground, leg crushed beneath the pole that had smashed down on him, along with three others who seemed more confused than hurt.

Cenric saw them upright before running to the next tent.

Figures stirred from beneath the flattened tents. Though poles had been knocked over and, in some cases, trampled, most people had not been struck directly by the animals.

Cenric found Hróarr and Vana's tent at the center. It looked like an auroch had smashed into the side and gotten tangled in the ropes. The outside stakes had been ripped up, making the tent collapse.

"Hróarr!" Cenric dove into the partially collapsed tent to find his cousin on the ground, head bleeding.

Vana knelt beside him, disheveled with a gash on her shoulder. It looked like she'd been cut by a falling tent beam.

"Vana." Cenric dropped into a crouch beside his cousin, nearly weeping when he saw Hróarr's chest rising and falling.

"I'm fine," Hróarr grunted in Valdari, one hand to the cut on his forehead. "But I'm going to skin the damned cow that made my woman bleed."

Vana rolled her eyes, though she favored her injured shoulder. "What happened?"

"I don't know yet," Cenric answered, looking back outside.

Hróarr made to sit up, then groaned. "I might need a moment."

"Brynn will be able to help." Cenric didn't doubt his wife could heal this. He'd seen her mend broken ribs, after all.

"Where is your wife?" Vana looked up as if expecting to see Brynn.

"I'm trying to find her."

Vana's brows rose, worry creasing her entire face. "You don't know?"

Cenric tried not to let those words incite fear. He needed to stay calm and find her. His people needed him. Surely Brynn was alright. Surely—

"I will find her," Cenric said. *Alive,* he vowed silently to himself. "I'm going into the village. See that one doesn't push himself too hard."

"I will," Vana promised.

Hróarr cursed. "She's my *frilla*, not my wet nurse."

Vana ignored him, holding a wad of cloth to his cut. "Lie still a little longer."

Cenric helped Hróarr outside the fallen tent and left him in the care of Vana before racing down to the village. The people in the village had been more protected, solid buildings more resilient than canvas tents.

But aurochs had smashed through garden fences and in a few cases, through solid walls. A clothesline had been snapped, probably by one of the animals' horns. Children's tunics and stockings lay scattered on the ground, stomped into the earth.

A goose shed had been demolished, scattering feathers and the crushed bodies of geese in all directions. The gardens had been mostly harvested already, but those that hadn't had been trampled into oblivion, hoofprints leaving deep gouges in the earth and whatever else had been on the ground.

One of the aurochs had gotten inside a house, knocking over a broom into the fireplace and goring the thane who lived there before smashing out the opposite wall. The thane now lay bleeding while his wife and children scrambled to put out the fire.

Cenric joined in with several others throwing buckets of water onto the flames. They had been able to catch it early, so they saved most of the house, but the man still needed Brynn's attention.

Cows! Snapper leapt up at Cenric's side, seeming to appear from nowhere. *Bad cows! Bad!*

A knot of fear relaxed in Cenric's chest as he patted the head of his old friend. *Brynn?*

Brynn? Snapper dropped onto all fours. *With puppy.* That meant Snapper had seen her, at least.

Find puppy, Cenric ordered.

Snapper woofed and took off running back up the hill.

Ash, Thorn, and the other dogs trotted around, inspecting the damage. They barked or woofed, sending errant thoughts. Cenric tried calling to them, but they were too distracted to pay attention at the moment. Thorn especially was upset that so many people had been hurt.

"Cenric!" Edric rushed up to meet him, covered in dirt and soot, but looking fine. "Most the damage is closest to the longhouse."

"The house itself is fine," Cenric answered shortly. He looked past his friend. "Your wife?"

"A little angry, but well. A cow took out one of our doors."

That was bad and would need to be fixed before winter, but not what some people had suffered.

"What happened?" Edric glanced at the destruction surrounding them.

"Get your sword. See if you can find men who can fight." Cenric looked up the hill to the cattle pens where he had left four thanes to guard the animals last night. "We're going to find out."

Edric nodded, jaw tight.

Cenric paced through the village, assessing damage. No more houses had caught fire, and no one was dead yet, but his wounded thane would be in danger of infection. They needed Brynn. Where was she?

He looked toward the house at the top of the hill. No sign of Snapper, Brynn, or Kalen. Where was that boy?

Cenric kept searching for Brynn in the village. Perhaps Snapper had missed her, and she had already come down to help with the injured people. That would be like her.

Cenric searched house by house, asking after injuries and damages and if they'd seen Brynn. None of them had, but there were a few broken bones, bruised ribs, and smashed fences.

Cenric paused at a familiar house. He knew all the houses in his village, but this one better than most. He didn't want to see her right now, but Brynn might have come here. Cenric knocked on the door of Rowan's family home, hoping for her brother, younger sister, father, or mother. Anyone but her.

It swung open, revealing Rowan. Shit.

Cenric suddenly remembered he hadn't bothered with a tunic before running down from the longhouse. "Rowan."

"Cenric." Rowan's face had gone hard, impassive. She held eye contact with a rigid determination, not looking below his nose.

He asked the same question he had asked at each house. "Are you and your family well?"

"Fine," Rowan answered. "Our goat pen was broken, but nothing else. We will be heading into the village to help the others as soon as we catch the last of the animals."

"Good." Cenric looked back toward the harder-hit portions of the village. "Have you seen Brynn?"

Rowan swallowed, just the slightest tick of emotion. "No."

Cenric tried not to show anything at that, though recollections of his foretelling flashed before his eyes. "Thank you. You and your family's help would be most appreciated at the house of Deidrei. Her wall was broken down and I'd like that to be fixed by nightfall." Deidrei was an elderly woman currently raising three of her grandsons, ranging in age from four to eleven.

Cenric stepped away from the door, ready to head to the next house.

"Is Lady Brynn missing?" Rowan took a step after him.

Cenric wasn't sure why he felt like he shouldn't answer. "I'm not sure." He inclined his head once before marching away and back outside the fence. He shut the gate after himself out of habit, though it wouldn't do much good with the smashed fence.

Edric and three other thanes met him back on the path between houses. "Lord!"

All four men carried swords and spears, like Cenric had instructed. They appeared unhurt, if a bit disheveled. They'd probably been helping to put out the fire and move broken slabs of wood from smashed buildings.

"Let's go see what happened." Cenric led the way through the village and up to the cattle pens.

28

BRYNN

Brynn's head smacked against the side of the wagon again. Grunting, she rolled onto her side. Her mind worked slowly, trying to remember how she had gotten here.

"Are you waking up, my dear?"

At her mother's voice, Brynn snapped upright, her hands yanking backward.

Her hands had been tied from wrist to elbow behind her back and a metal collar locked around her neck, not unlike the thrall collars the Valdari used. Brynn reached for *ka* and it came to her, but no spells formed. The collar around her neck soaked up her power as soon as she wove spells.

Brynn faced her mother, nostrils flaring.

The first thing she noticed was Esa. The young girl's tear-streaked face watched her, trembling at Selene's feet. Her hands had been tied and a dark bruise spread over her eye and another over her jaw.

Selene had one hand on Esa's braid, holding it like a leash. "Esa?"

"I'm sorry, Lady Brynn," Esa whimpered. "I'm so sorry."

"You should be proud of your girl," Selene sneered. "We wanted to have her draw you out and make this whole thing easier, but she refused. Even when I threatened to kill her."

"Esa." Brynn straightened. "It's alright. You're going to be alright."

Tears tracked silently down the girl's cheeks.

"Yes," Selene agreed. "You are going to be perfectly alright because your guardian is going to do exactly as I say."

Brynn inhaled and exhaled ever so slowly. "What did you do?"

"We needed a distraction. It took a bit of effort. Anselma and Tessaine had to rile them up for nearly an hour and it was a miracle no one heard, but we were able to use those cows." Selene glared at Brynn. "I didn't want to hurt anyone, Brynn. I hope you understand this."

Brynn flexed her wrists behind her back, testing her bonds. She'd been tied thoroughly.

The inside of the wagon was furnished for living with silk cushions and padded seats. Her mother had it built during the war when she had been constantly on the road between encampments and forts. It was plush, comfortable, and woven entirely from black and white fabrics. Chimes made of silver hung from the ceiling, hammered in the shapes of the moon cycles. Selene was nothing if not devout.

"What about Cenric?" Brynn demanded.

"You mean your latest form of rebellion? I don't rightly know."

Anger bubbled up in Brynn's chest, but she kept it under control—for now. "Did you hurt him?"

Selene shrugged.

"Answer me!" Brynn shrieked, her voice fraying. "Did you or any of your people hurt him?"

Selene rolled her eyes. "No. Though someone as impulsive and reckless as him is bound to get himself killed sooner or later."

Brynn understood the meaning. Her mother was saying if Cenric was stupid enough to come after them, they would use deadly force to keep her.

"What if I agree to go to back to Paega?" Brynn asked. "I'll put aside Cenric, but you have to spare him."

Selene seemed to consider it for a moment. "If you are willing to be reasonable, I might consider it."

Brynn's chest writhed with fear, anger, and dread. That wasn't good enough. "What is this?" She gestured to the collar around her neck.

"That? It's called dark iron. Alchemists in the southern empire developed it. The intent is to store power, but it works quite well for other things, too." Selene smiled smugly.

Brynn had never encountered anything like it before. No matter how much power she drew to herself, every time she tried to cast spells, the collar consumed it.

Brynn looked to Esa. "Do you plan to hold my ward hostage forever?"

"No." Selene tugged on Esa's braid enough to make the girl flinch. "Just until you have another child by Paega."

Brynn kept her face blank to hide her disgust. "That's quite bold of you."

"I am your mother. You will do as I tell you."

"You lost the right to tell me what to do the moment you killed my son."

Selene cocked her brow. "What are you talking about?"

"The Valdari who attacked Glasney were paid. I know it was you. You wanted Paega dead, didn't you? As soon as he gave me an heir."

Selene scoffed. "Why would I want your son dead? His death was very inconvenient for us."

Brynn suspected Osbeorn had been an accidental casualty, but her mother's words stabbed all the same. "Inconvenient?" Brynn had kept a cage around her temper for longer than she could remember. She had kept her head down, had complied. She wanted to do the right thing, always the right thing. "That was my child." Brynn's voice dropped so low not even she recognized it. "My *only* child."

Selene hesitated for just a second, then seemed to blink away whatever had made her nervous. "You can have others."

Brynn imagined what it would feel like to have her mother's neck under her hands.

"Your sister was a good girl." Selene's voice changed slightly in pitch. "She knew her duty."

"She defied you," Brynn spat. "So, you made sure she died."

Trust me, child. Those had been the words Selene had spoken to Aelfwynn when Brynn's sister had agreed to hold the river against Winfric's thanes. In hindsight, Brynn wondered if her mother might have planned it.

Selene's eyes flashed. "How dare you."

"You stopped the reinforcements."

"Your sister died because of a miscommunication among your cousin's men. Aelgar never was a warrior."

"My sister died because you thought I would be easier to control." Brynn's eyes stung with tears.

Selene exhaled a long breath. "Your sister was a strong-willed girl, but I really expected you to be beyond her influence now."

The wagon hit a bump in the road, making all of them jostle. Low voices came from outside. Brynn could sense what she guessed to be the twins as well as Neirin and several of the other soldiers.

"Aelfwynn tried to have you removed from the Council of Mothers," Brynn said. "She told me. She knew it was the only way to make you stop pushing for her to marry Aelgar."

Cousin marriages were common enough. Selene had argued that an uncle and niece of the same age were not that different. Aelgar was only half-brother to their father, after all. Aelfwynn was hearing none of it.

"Be grateful you will never know what it's like to have a child plot against you," Selene snapped.

Brynn would have happily accepted a thousand plots from Osbeorn if it would bring him back.

"You have never had adult children, Brynn," Selene said.

"You cannot understand."

Rage poured through Brynn's veins. Always there was this excuse—always Selene's reasons were incomprehensible to Brynn because of some shortcoming or lack of experience. First it was because Brynn was a child herself, then because she didn't have one. After Osbeorn came, it was because Brynn didn't have a daughter. Now it seemed that the boundary stones had been moved once again.

"You aren't my mother," Brynn spat. "You never were. Aelfwynn, she was my mother. And I hope that someday I'm half the mother my sister was."

"You are insolent," Selene barked, jerking back on Esa's hair.

Esa whimpered, squeezing her eyes shut.

Brynn clenched her hands into fists. In that moment, everything that was wrong in her life could be blamed on this woman.

"You will go back to Paega and you will fulfill your duty to our people." Selene shook her head. "Throwing your life away on some random thane? Really, Brynn?"

"He's an alderman."

"Bah." Selene seemed about to spit for a moment. "An alderman who cuts his own grain and salts his own fish? It was an insult for Aelgar to arrange the match."

It didn't matter what Selene thought. Aelfwynn would have liked Cenric. Maybe not at first, but she would have grown fond of him. If nothing else, Aelfwynn would have accepted him when she realized he made Brynn happy.

And Cenric did make her happy. For the first time in her life, if only for a brief moment, she hadn't been afraid. She hadn't had the shadow of Selene's expectations hanging over her, the threat of death, or the slow torment of Paega's quiet condescension.

Brynn didn't even care if it was selfish to want Cenric. She was going to get back to him if she had to fight the world to do it.

"Cenric is my husband," she said flatly, defiantly. "I belong with him."

"You belong where I tell you," Selene snapped. "And if this Cenric tries to come for you, he will face consequences."

"If you hurt him," Brynn vowed, voice cold, "not even Eponine will be able to save you from me."

Selene tsked at that. "Try to avoid blasphemy, child. And are you really willing to sacrifice your ward for him?"

Brynn looked at Esa, crying quietly at her mother's knees. She was determined to get out of this and save them both, but if it came down to it? Brynn didn't know what she would do.

"We are meeting a ship down the coast that will take us south," Selene said. "I have the word of Olfirth to let us pass."

"Does he know you've taken me captive?"

"You are not captive," Selene argued.

"No?" Brynn cocked her head. As angry as that response made her, the deflection told her that no, Olfirth didn't know she was being taken against her will. The old thane probably didn't know she was here at all. "What are these ropes, then?"

Selene made a frustrated sound. "You *will* see reason, child."

Brynn disliked violence. Hated it. But even she knew when the time came for it.

Selene had made herself Brynn's enemy. There was no going back from this. As soon as Brynn got the chance, she would kill her mother.

29

CENRIC

Cenric's thanes were dead.

They found the four men lying in puddles of blood, throats cut and still warm. Whoever had attacked them had done so in the early morning hours when they were most tired, close to the end of their watch.

Edric swore, crouching beside the body of Handal, a man who had supported Cenric from the first days of his return. "Olfirth?"

Cenric wished it was Olfirth. It would give him an excuse to fight the old man instead of suffering through awkward dinners, but he didn't think so.

He had four new widows to care for and at least six children between them. But who was to blame?

As they made their way back across the field, Cenric spotted a familiar figure rushing toward them. He dared to hope for just a moment, but then Kalen's face came into view.

The boy arrived breathless, face betraying that he had bad news. "Lady Brynn is missing, lord."

"Missing?" Cenric spoke the word slowly, sure he had misheard. A sick dread tightened in his chest. The foretelling of her pale, lifeless body flickered before his eyes.

"Esa is missing, too." Kalen made a coughing sound. "That's her maid."

Cenric looked across the cattle pens. Someone had broken the fence in multiple places before driving the animals uphill toward the village and the field with the camped Valdari. "Where are the Istovari? The sorceress Selene?"

Kalen glanced over his shoulder. "They left yesterday, lord."

"They took her." Cenric raked a hand through his hair. "They created a diversion and took her."

"Are you sure?" Theodren, one of his thanes, glanced around at the damage. "After seeing what she did to that Valdari, I doubt anyone could have taken her."

"Are you saying my wife left me?" Cenric demanded, whirling on the man.

Theodren flinched. "No, lord."

"Cenric." Edric's tone was level, but stern. A warning.

Cenric shook his head, taking a step away from Theodren. "She was taken." *She wouldn't have left me*, he thought silently. Not after last night.

Last night had been too intimate. She'd let him see her fears, secrets, and desires. It had been more than baring her body, she'd bared her soul.

The memory of his foretelling flickered across his thoughts—Brynn drowned on a beach, and her hands tied.

"Where's her puppy?" Cenric whirled on Kalen.

"Her puppy?"

"Her puppy wasn't there when I woke this morning. Where is it?" He still hadn't heard from Snapper.

"I'm not sure, lord."

Cenric spun back to Edric. "The rest of you get back to the village and post guards. We might be attacked again. I will join you shortly."

"Cenric…" Edric looked between his lord and the house back up the hill. "If she has been taken, we can't chase after enemy sorceresses."

Cenric knew that, deep down. He didn't have the men to attack Brynn's mother and her entourage. Before the attack, they would have been hard-pressed on such short notice, but now…

In the vision, he had been searching alone on that beach. Was this why?

He didn't know how to fix this. What could he do?

If his village had been attacked, he would have known what to do. If Brynn had been taken, he would have known what to do. Faced with both, he was torn.

"Go! I will either join you or send word soon. Kalen, help Edric." Cenric ran back toward the longhouse. He crossed the field not sure what he would find or even what he hoped to find.

There was still time to change the foretelling. Cenric refused to believe otherwise.

He reached the longhouse to find a number of the Valdari being tended by the household girls. Water had been brought to clean away blood, bones were being set, and wounds bandaged.

Cenric skirted the outside of the longhouse, marching along the outer wall. *Snapper?* he called out, searching the tall grass. *Have you found Guin?* Cenric wasn't even sure what it would prove if he found the pup, he just knew Brynn would have worried about her and it was something to *do*.

Pup.

A low whine drew Cenric's attention.

Snapper crouched beside the corner of the longhouse, lying with his tail thumping softly. He pawed at the edge of the wall, letting off a snort.

Cenric jogged over to the dog and dropped to his knees. The puppy had crawled partially under the corner of the house, making a small burrow for herself.

She growled as Cenric reached in, grabbing her by the scruff of her neck to haul her out. She whimpered in his grasp, tail wagging meekly as soon as she was in the daylight.

"Where's your mother?" Cenric asked, feeling like a fool.

The puppy whined, pawing at the air. She was young, but Guin should be communicating by now.

Brynn wouldn't have left her behind. Even if she had taken

Esa, she wouldn't have left Guin.

Cenric tucked Guin into one arm. She squirmed for a few moments, then went still against him.

Snapper woofed, curious.

Cenric petted the puppy, trying to think. There was so much to be done.

He needed to see to the damaged houses. He needed to help round up the lost cattle. He needed to see that his people were safe. But most of all he needed to rescue his wife.

How?

He didn't have enough men. He didn't know where to start looking. If Selene and her people were strong enough to overpower Brynn, what chance did he have?

In the foretelling, he had found her on the beach, which must mean she was being taken out by sea. But it would take him time to comb every beach alone, time he didn't have.

Cenric marched into the longhouse, the puppy still tucked under one arm. Inside was abuzz with the work of people helping the injured and the wounded.

Brynn would have been able to help.

Brynn.

Cenric returned to their bedroom and dumped Guin back in her basket. She howled in protest, then settled down.

Puppy! Snapper leaned over the basket, licking the puppy comfortingly.

Cenric could chase after Brynn alone to find her dead or he could abandon her. How to change his vision? What could he possibly do differently?

He grabbed his tunic and pulled it on. He finished dressing, hands moving out of habit.

Choices usually seemed easy to him. One option or the other. But right now, he hated both.

Would taking Snapper or more of the dogs with him be enough? They were Morgi's animals, but somehow, he doubted it.

Cenric sank onto the bed and dropped his head into his hands, groaning. "Damn it, Morgi," he growled, cursing the goddess under his breath. Why did her warnings have to be so vague? Why hadn't Brynn listened to him? Why—

"Cenric?" At her voice, he jumped.

Rowan? Snapper trotted over to greet her, seeming confused.

"Rowan." Why had she followed him here? Cenric rose off the bed, pacing away from her.

Rowan shut the door to the bedroom, closing them off from the rest of the house. She briefly acknowledged Snapper before turning back to Cenric. "I heard Lady Brynn had disappeared."

Word traveled fast. Cenric grimaced, raking a hand through his hair. "She was abducted."

"I see." Rowan looked away, like she knew this wasn't her place anymore. Why was she even here?

Cenric inhaled sharply. He hadn't spoken properly to Rowan, not since she had left his house for the last time, and their relationship had breathed its final, shuddering gasps.

Rowan looked toward the empty hearth. "I have received an offer from one of Olfirth's thanes. His name is Evred."

"Olfirth?" Cenric wasn't sure why she wanted to discuss this now.

"Yes." Rowan pointedly did not look at him or the bed. "He's well-respected in Olfirth's household and has been given his own farm. I plan to accept."

"I see." Cenric paced, adjusting his collar, his belt, unable to keep himself still. He was already agitated, but having this woman here, this former lover who he still didn't know how to handle, made it worse. He had been alone with her in this room many times, but he didn't like it now. This room was Brynn's place.

"Would you have married me if the baby lived?" Rowan blurted out the words in a tumble, as if they had been sticking to her throat and she had to force them out.

Cenric stopped. Rowan had a miscarriage in the early spring.

She hadn't been very far along, not showing yet. In a way, the pregnancy hadn't felt real to him. There hadn't even been a body to bury. But perhaps it had felt more real to her.

Cenric would have acknowledged the child, of course. Raised them in his household, certainly. Maybe there was a right answer to give Rowan. Maybe there was something compassionate, something considerate, but Cenric chose to answer honestly. "No."

Rowan's eyes closed and the tension in her face eased, almost like she was relieved.

Cenric shifted, realization setting in. "You thought I blamed you for the miscarriage?"

Rowan shrugged, still not meeting his eyes. "I wondered."

Cenric exhaled a long breath. "We were a bad match." He shook his head.

He was a Valdari in all but name and an alderman. Rowan was the daughter of a modest former thane who had never left the shire of Ombra. Cenric had been fresh from Ovrek's war, eager to prove himself, and convinced a strong sword arm was all it took to be a leader. More than that, he had been lonely, and Rowan had been awed by the attention of her alderman.

She had smoothed many of his rougher edges and he had expanded her horizons, but it was not enough. In the end, neither of them had been able to give what the other needed.

Had she left him, or had he sent her away? Cenric wasn't sure.

When she had told him she was going home for a few days, just to be with her family, a part of him had known it was over. Their nights together had become fewer and further between until one day Cenric found himself promising to pay her dowry whenever she found a husband—not him.

"We were a bad match," Rowan softly agreed.

Cenric wasn't sure what else to say. This was too much on top of everything else.

"What Lady Brynn did." Rowan paused, then continued.

"When Olfirth came with his thanes? I could never have done that."

"What are you saying, Rowan?" Cenric tried not to snap at her, but he was on edge and his wife was still missing.

Rowan straightened, like she was a warrior bracing for the impact of an enemy shield wall. "You need her."

Cenric hadn't expected that, but Rowan wasn't done.

"I was…unkind…when she first came to us." Rowan clenched her hands in front of her. "I can't be friends with her. I *won't* be friends with her, but she helped my father and sister anyway. She helped my family. She's already helped people across this village. Protected people across this village." She inhaled a long breath and met his gaze. "You need to get her back."

"How?" Cenric demanded, all his frustration exploding out of him in that one word. "How should I do that? I don't have enough thanes. Those I have, I need to guard the village and gather the cattle, or we risk a lean winter. Hróarr is injured as are most of his men. It's just me. What exactly am I supposed to do?"

Rowan retreated until her back hit the door. She had gone pale, shrinking before his anger.

Snapper whined, stepping between them. *Cenric?*

Cenric realized he had been advancing on her and took several quick steps back. He hadn't meant to take it out on her like this.

Rowan spoke, her voice barely above a whisper. "What would Brynn do?"

"Something clever," Cenric muttered. "Something I'm not thinking of."

"And what are you not thinking of?"

Cenric wanted to hit something. How was he supposed to know that?

With that wagon, Selene's people would have to take the roads. That would mean going through Olfirth's lands to reach the sea.

What had Brynn said to him? That men only cared about their pride. That meant Brynn would do something he was too proud to see.

Something humiliating, but possibly effective.

"You're going to marry one of Olfirth's thanes," Cenric muttered, scratching the stubble on his chin.

"Yes." Rowan frowned.

"Olfirth has thanes." Cenric braced himself. This was going to sting, and he hated it. If this had happened even a few days ago, he wasn't sure he would have tried it, but this was Brynn. And he was desperate.

Rowan still sounded confused. "He does."

Cenric snatched his helmet off the stand on his side of the bed. He set it aside as he grabbed the mail shirt and pulled it over his head.

He had a plan, a desperate one, but a plan nonetheless. Cenric rarely wasted time after he made a decision.

"You know what you're doing?" Rowan sounded hopeful.

"Have my horse saddled. Tell Edric I'm going to Olfirth."

Rowan opened the door and fled, leaving it open.

Cenric tied on his greaves, reinforced with steel slats, and his bracers reinforced with the same. He had no idea if they would help him against a sorceress, but they might help him against her guards. There was something cathartic in moving and having a course of action again. He buckled his sword belt over his armor, reaching for his wolf helm next.

Go? Snapper asked, tail wagging.

Go, Cenric answered.

By the time he strode out in his full battle gear, the longhouse went quiet. No one spoke, but the household girls and the injured Valdari stared.

Selene had killed his thanes and taken his wife. Cenric was going to make her pay.

Cenric headed straight for the stables where Gannon was

already saddling up Bada. Cenric murmured a blessing on Rowan for her thoroughness.

"Going somewhere?" Edric called, trotting up on his bay steed in his own lamellar armor, helmet under one arm.

"I'm going to ask Olfirth for help," Cenric said, though the words tasted like bile.

Edric's nose wrinkled at that. It was one thing to ask help from a friend like Hróarr, but it was quite another to seek the help of a man who'd been your unspoken enemy for nearly two years.

The peace with Olfirth was new, and Cenric suspected it was still more an alliance with Brynn than himself. This would be seeking aid from a foe.

"Well, I once swore that if you died fighting, I'd die with you."

"You have Gaitha to consider. And the people."

"Gaitha can take care of herself," Edric scoffed. "Who do you think saddled my horse? And Theodren has gathering the cattle under control."

"We might be going to our deaths. If Olfirth doesn't kill us on sight, the sorceresses might."

Edric rested his spear on one shoulder. "Ready when you are, lord."

Cenric stifled his grin at that. He took Bada from Gannon and used a stump to mount the chestnut stallion.

Bada snorted, prancing under Cenric as his rider mounted. He heard the jangle of mail and recognized the battle sound.

"Do you know the way to Olfirth's farm?" Edric muttered.

Cenric had only been there a few times, but he knew it was somewhere along the main roads. "This way." He turned Bada toward the southeast and nudged the stallion into a canter.

Go! Snapper cried with glee, loping alongside them.

Edric followed close behind.

Olfirth's longhouse was massive, aged, and weathered. Cenric had to admit, begrudgingly, that it was fine even compared to his own.

At the sight of two warriors in full battle regalia charging along the path, Cenric heard shouts of warning go up. Gritting his teeth, he reined Bada into a walk.

Edric slowed his horse behind him. The animals snorted, tails wringing.

Olfirth's longhouse was situated atop a hill overlooking a collection of homes surrounded by a wooden palisade. The gate was open, probably so farmers and household servants could go about their work. It was still the middle of harvest season, after all.

Cenric rode all too slowly up the path to Olfirth's home. He came to a stop in the yard before the main entrance, surrounded by the thane's barns and grain stores.

Unlike when Olfirth had ridden to Cenric's hall, this was still early in the morning. The men had not yet left for the fields. Cenric felt Olfirth should see that as a courtesy, but from the way the old man glared at him, Cenric doubted that was the case.

Olfirth stood on the steps of his hall, arms crossed, feet shoulder width apart. He had no armor, but his axe rested on the ground, leaning against his hip.

Younger thanes surrounded him, carrying swords, spears, and axes. They might not be armored, but they did outnumber Cenric and Edric almost ten to one.

Predictably, Snapper rushed up to them, tail wagging. The men ignored him.

"Young wolf," Olfirth grunted, raising his chin. "I believe my invitation was for more than a week from now."

Looking at the old man's face, Cenric almost changed his mind and turned around.

But this was for Brynn.

Cenric wasn't sure what to say, so he acted instead.

He dismounted and handed his reins to Edric. Turning back to Olfirth, he removed his helm, tucking it under one arm.

An armored warrior on horseback was nearly untouchable. A bareheaded man on foot was much less so.

Olfirth's brows rose, arms still folded. "I cannot wait to hear your explanation for this."

Cenric gritted his teeth, holding back every retort that sprang so readily to his tongue.

Brynn.

His dead warriors.

He would worry about his pride later.

"My people were attacked this morning." Cenric managed to keep his tone level.

Olfirth grunted. "Raiders?"

"Sorceresses."

Something flickered in Olfirth's face for just a moment. Something like surprise.

"They stampeded the young aurochs through the village. My four thanes guarding them were found with their throats cut."

"And you suspect your new wife did it?"

"No," Cenric snapped, perhaps a little too sharply. "She was with me when they were murdered."

Olfirth glanced to one of his men, a fellow with an axe by the door. The man gave no visible reaction, but Olfirth looked back to Cenric. "It's a shame. My sympathies. But it wasn't us."

"I know." Cenric nearly yelled the words, then took a deep breath, steadying himself. This wasn't going well, but what had Brynn said? Most people were reasonable.

"Then why are you here, young wolf?" Olfirth exhaled a long breath, cocking his head to the side. "In full battle-gear, no less?"

"They took Brynn." Cenric didn't know what else to say.

Olfirth gave no visible reaction, though several of his men looked to him for guidance.

Snapper, realizing he would not be getting any pats from the men, trotted back over to Cenric and plopped down.

"I have heard much of this new wife of yours." Olfirth drew out each word slowly. "She's a king's daughter, isn't she? Hardly the usual wife of a northern alderman. One who isn't even invited to meetings of the Witan."

Cenric fought to keep his calm. He could trade insults with Olfirth another time. "The sorceress Selene has been trying to persuade her to leave for days. They fought. My wife told Selene to leave."

He couldn't explain Morgi had warned him of this. There wasn't time and he wasn't sure Olfirth even believed stories of his family's gift.

Olfirth glanced to the man with the axe again. "The sorceress Selene asked permission to pass through my lands. She has a ship meeting her at an inlet near the coast."

Cenric's heart leapt, even as it sank. Selene was here somewhere, but time was running out. They needed to stop her before she made it to the open water.

"You think she took Lady Brynn against her will?"

"I know it." Cenric braced himself. "But I don't have the men to hunt them down."

Everything in Cenric screamed against the admission of weakness. He hated to tell his rival he lacked warriors right now, that they were vulnerable. It felt almost like he was betraying his people by confessing their weakness.

Olfirth's thanes eyed him suspiciously, but Cenric kept his attention on Olfirth. This would be the old man's decision. Cenric waited, hating everything about this.

"I don't like you, young wolf," Olfirth grunted. "You're arrogant, impetuous, and far too prideful for someone so inexperienced."

Cenric clenched his jaw until his teeth ached. If the old man wanted to trade insults, Cenric had a long list on the tip of his tongue.

Olfirth stroked his beard, like he was thinking. "You remind me of myself when I was your age."

Cenric frowned at the same time several of Olfirth's thanes looked to the old man. They were like hounds readying for their master's call.

"I don't like you," Olfirth repeated. He heaved a great sigh and uncrossed his arms. "But I am a sentimental old man. And I'm quite fond of your wife."

Cenric didn't dare hope. He kept his eyes locked on the old man until Olfirth stepped back into the hall.

"Battle gear and spears," Olfirth ordered his thanes. "We're going hunting."

Cenric glanced to Edric. Already, he had changed his vision just a little. He only hoped it would be enough to save Brynn.

30

BRYNN

"I'm sorry, lady," Esa whimpered, crouched in the cart beside Brynn. "I'm so sorry."

"Shush, it's alright." Brynn did her best to comfort the weeping child. "I won't let anything happen to you."

"This is all because of me," Esa wept.

Brynn hated her mother for everything she'd done to lead to this. It was unfair. Unjust. Wrong.

Tessaine and Anselma rode on their white mules at the back of the wagon. Neirin and the other thanes surrounded them.

From what Brynn could see, they were heading down an unfamiliar road. Not that Brynn had much time for exploring since arriving in Ombra.

They were headed for the sea as best she could tell. Brynn remembered Cenric's warning, his vision of her death, and a sinking sensation pooled in her gut.

Brynn tried to pull at more *ka*. It rippled toward her eagerly, that wasn't the issue. But the moment she tried to push magic outward, the collar soaked it up.

"How did you make this?" Brynn demanded. "This collar."

"I will tell you some other time," Selene answered mildly. She stared behind them down the road, frowning.

"Afraid I'll find a weakness?" Brynn snapped, even though she knew the answer.

"My dear, I am not a fool." Selene was still staring down the road, past Tessaine and Anselma.

"You will have to take this collar off me eventually."

"Will I?" Selene answered mildly.

"Are you going to have me raped, Mother?" Brynn raised her chin. "Because I will not go to Paega willingly."

Selene exhaled a long breath out her nose. "You are too old to be having your rebellious phase, Brynn."

Brynn seethed. Perhaps she should have rebelled sooner. Then she never would have married Paega in the first place.

"The Mothers are tired of waiting. We have planned this for generations, but your father had to get himself killed before he named your sister heir." Selene grimaced. "Then the fool girl refused to marry Paega's son."

Paega's eldest son had been approaching forty and unmarried. He had several sons with a concubine, but they'd all died young. Then Paega's eldest son had died, along with his other four, and Aelfwynn died shortly thereafter.

That had left Paega and Brynn.

"Your claim would be stronger with a child from Offa's line," Selene sighed. "Even if we had to make do with a boy, we could have married him to a sorceress when he was older."

Brynn bristled. "Offa's line?"

There were kings in Paega's family line. His mother had been the daughter of Offa, one of the greatest kings in living memory. Offa had ruled the largest portion of land the north had ever seen and received tribute from as far south as Phaedrun.

Kingship was a fickle thing. Oftentimes, it only lasted a generation or two before some warlord who happened to be richer, stronger, and more powerful than his neighbors started thinking perhaps he should be king instead.

When that happened, the male line was usually wiped out. Brynn and Aelfwynn had been spared because they were girls and because they had given allegiance to their uncle.

Brynn groaned, leaning against the back of the wagon. She

had been a fool. Naïve.

Her marriage wasn't about Paega's lands, but bringing King Offa's bloodline into the Istovari.

Offa's blood might not be enough to guarantee any claim to kingship, but it would help. If Brynn's son had lived, he would have been a sorcerer and the descendant of three mighty kings—Offa, Brynn's grandfather, and Brynn's father. Osbeorn would have been the perfect figurehead for the sorceresses to claim control, true control, of the country.

Brynn had always known her mother was a schemer, but she had never realized how far-reaching or persistent her mother was. "Who is a part of this?" she asked, feeling oddly numb. "Do all the Mothers know?

"This plan has been in motion before your conception," Selene answered calmly. "You cannot fight it."

Brynn wrestled against her bonds all the same.

After her sister had died, she had stopped fighting.

Brynn had done her duty. Married a man she didn't want. Had a baby. Accepted Paega's quiet condescension and resentment. Even marrying Cenric was her way to follow the rules with the blessing of her king. For years, she had submitted to authority and bowed to the will of others.

But not anymore.

The desire to fight, to rebel—it burned inside her, hot, angry, and demanding.

Aelfwynn's death had convinced her that was the cost of disobedience. Death and pain were all that had come from daring to challenge the rules.

So, Brynn had done everything she could to be a good daughter, a good wife, and a good mother, but it had made no difference. She still lost her son, and once again she had buried the person she loved most in the world.

Brynn had defied tradition and lost Aelfwynn. She had followed tradition and lost Osbeorn.

And Cenric…

He was gentle with her in a way Paega never had been. Cenric respected her. He listened to her even when he didn't like what he heard. She was trying to make things work, but so was he.

Perhaps that was the difference.

Brynn had spent her whole first marriage reaching out to be met with emptiness. When she reached for Cenric, he reached back.

Closing her eyes, Brynn kept pulling at *ka*. She dragged it into herself in great swaths. She pulled it in until her head went light, and she thought she might pass out. But whenever she tried casting, the collar consumed her spells.

Selene tsked. "You're going to make yourself faint."

Brynn didn't care. She was not going quietly this time. She had found something in this remote northern land. She didn't yet know what it was, but it was worth the fighting for. It was worth the daring.

Everything had limits, so perhaps she could pull enough magic to overwhelm the collar. Perhaps if she forced it to consume enough of her spells, it would break or stop working.

Gritting her teeth, Brynn kept reaching. Her abilities to sense and draw *ka* were unhindered. She could pull on as much of it as she wanted, reach as far as she wanted.

She could count all ten of her mother's soldiers and feel the mild spells being worked by Tessaine and Anselma. Brynn could tell the horses were mostly healthy, though one of them might be developing saddle sores.

Past them, she could feel the forest. The trees were alive, blooming, and bright. Woodlife scuttled through the greenery.

Brynn pulled power from all of it. She soaked in strength the way she hadn't in a long time. She pulled in so much *ka* that she felt her own aches and pains fading as her bruises and the chafing on her wrists healed.

Brynn kept reaching, reaching…

A burst of *ka* flared into her awareness. Large and clustered together, probably a herd of animals.

Careful to keep her face neutral, Brynn kept reaching, prodding at the new source of power in her awareness. There were twenty or more large animals following them down the road. Horses?

At this distance it was challenging to tell, but Brynn thought she sensed additional shapes on their backs. Riders? Was it possible?

Twenty was too many for a casual group of travelers. Could it be? Dared she hope?

Cenric? Was he bringing his thanes after her?

Brynn wasn't sure if she wanted it to be him or not. Her mother wouldn't hesitate to cut him down and neither would Tessaine, Anselma, and the others.

It might be him, it might not. Either way, Brynn continued gathering and releasing spells as fast as she could.

Selene rolled her head in Brynn's direction. She would be able to feel Brynn drawing in massive amounts of magic. Maybe she was worried. Maybe she knew the limits of the collar and would take steps to keep it from breaking.

Regardless, Brynn had no way of stopping Selene from sensing her power, so she kept drawing.

31

CENRIC

"You stay with me, young wolf," Olfirth grunted.

Cenric bristled under that. He was in Olfirth's lands, surrounded by his thanes, but he bristled. "You think I'm leading you into a trap?"

"I think I'm riding straight toward something with only your oath that it's not a trap."

Cenric bridled at the implied insult. "I honor my oaths."

Olfirth laughed at that, as if something about that was truly funny. "We'll see."

It had been much easier to be civil to Olfirth when they had been speaking at Cenric's table. Cenric was starting to realize Olfirth had been on his best behavior then. He had fewer reasons to behave now.

Olfirth had all the power and Brynn wasn't here. There was nothing stopping Olfirth and his men from turning on Cenric and Edric and leaving their bodies for the carrion birds. Distantly, Cenric wondered which of these men was Rowan's suitor or if that man was here at all.

"Lord." One of Olfirth's thanes rounded the bend, having ridden ahead to scout. He was a slim fellow with a dappled grey stallion. "Horses ahead with a wagon. About a mile."

Cenric's heart sped up. He caught himself standing in his stirrups on impulse, trying to see.

Bada sensed his movement and stomped, tail wringing. The stallion was still fresh and could feel his rider's unease. The animal knew a fight was coming and was tired of waiting for it.

"Anyone we know?" Olfirth grunted.

"Can't tell," the thane answered. "Too far away. There's a pair of white mules at the back, though."

Olfirth rubbed his jaw, frowning.

That pair of white mules ridden by the twin sorceresses might be impressive, but they were also recognizable. It was likely the sorceresses hadn't expected pursuit.

Brynn? Cenric looked down to Snapper.

Horses. Snapper answered. *Hunt?*

Maybe, Cenric sent back. If Brynn was in a wagon, it would be hard for Snapper to find her scent trail, but there might still be something the dog could do.

"Well." Olfirth inhaled, hands crossed over the front of his saddle pommel. "There are a few inlets in this area."

"The nearest one is to the west," the thane answered.

Olfirth seemed to think. "We can cut around to the beach and sweep down it."

"They'll see us coming," Cenric pointed out.

"If they're sorceresses, they don't need to see us." Olfirth drew himself up. "But if we can spot their ship, we might be able to head them off." He jerked his head toward the trees. "Evred, lead the way."

A thane on a chestnut swerved off from the main group at a trot, heading into the trees. This part of the forest was sparse enough for horses to pass through, but the men still had to duck under branches.

Cenric wanted to move faster, wanted to spur Bada into a gallop to reach the shore. But even if the way ahead hadn't been thick with fallen logs and unseen flaws in the earth, there was safety in numbers. Even if these men may or may not be friends.

As they rode, he wondered if Olfirth might be in league with Selene. Even if he wasn't, the old man might just want Cenric and Edric far away in the wilderness before turning on them. This whole thing was a risk, but Cenric couldn't see how to avoid it.

The forest thinned and Cenric caught the sound of the waves before the sea came into view. The horses skittered out onto the pebbled beach, the wind whipping up off the water. Bada raised his head, nostrils flaring at the sudden gust. The stallion chomped at his bit, mirroring Cenric's frustration.

The beach ran north and south in either direction as far as the eye could see, disappearing around a bend of trees. Aging driftwood littered the pebbles and dark stone marked where the ocean had receded.

Cenric's stomach knotted in sick realization. This was the beach—the beach from his foretelling. He could only hope they weren't too late, but he found himself desperately searching the shore all the same.

Fish! Snapper cried. *Seagulls!*

Brynn? Cenric was almost afraid of the answer this time.

Snapper woofed. *No Brynn.*

"The tide is going out," called Evred, the scout. "They'll have to move quickly if they have a ship coming into the inlet."

Cenric searched the swath of ocean before them. White waves peaked, swelled, and broke against the beach. A few birds circled overhead, but this shoreline appeared mostly deserted. From the dark lines on the stones, the water would rise nearly to the trees at high tide. No sign of a ship yet.

What if the sorceresses were taking Brynn another way? What if they'd already lost their quarry?

Olfirth's horse snorted and stamped, but the animal kept its head down. Everyone around the old man showed discipline and control, even the animals.

Cenric found himself respecting Olfirth more with each moment, if begrudgingly.

Evred led the way down the beach, his horse trotting in the lead while the rest of the thanes fell in behind him. Their spears and shields jangled, but the sound was mostly covered by the murmur of the sea.

"I don't need to tell you we're keeping whatever we find," Olfirth said.

Cenric glanced to the older man.

Olfirth continued. "Should we happen to fight, I mean. Your enemies' horses. Their gold and silver." A spark entered the old thane's eyes. "Maybe even a ship, from the sound of it."

That was the way of things. The reward for battle was the bounty of your enemies. Attacking was always preferable to defending because it had the greater promise of reward.

Another time, Cenric might have argued, but there was only one thing he wanted. "If I get my wife back, I don't care."

Olfirth chuckled again. "You're a sentimental *young* man, I see."

Cenric was sure that was meant as an insult, but Brynn would have ignored it, so he did, too.

"Ship," Evred called as soon as they came into earshot. "Entering the inlet."

Cenric's scalp prickled at the confirmation. Entering the inlet, that meant the sorceresses hadn't met it yet. They weren't too late.

Cenric and Olfirth rode forward, keeping to the shade of the trees so they would be hidden from the men on board. They rounded the bend and sure enough, the tail end of a ship was gliding into the inlet, upriver.

Olfirth adjusted his reins, heaving a great sigh, turning back to his men. "Do we have the rope? Good." He worked his jaw, seeming to think for a moment. "Well." He cast a cynical grin at Cenric. "Now we just hope that Lady Brynn actually wants to be rescued."

Cenric had no response to that.

32

BRYNN

Brynn felt the group of animals veer into the forest and her heart sank. Perhaps it had been a herd of deer.

"Did you do anything to Cenric?" Brynn looked straight to her mother.

Selene exhaled sharply. "You need to forget about him."

Brynn straightened, her back resting against the wagon as she glared up at her mother. "Did you or your people do anything to my husband?"

"He is not your husband," Selene snapped. "You married him without my permission."

"He was fine when we left." Anselma volunteered, looking down from her white mule.

Selene narrowed her eyes at the girl, but she only smiled down at Brynn.

"We created a distraction and there were a few losses with that, but the alderman was alive."

Relief flooded Brynn's chest along with dread. Who had been hurt? Kalen? Gaitha and Edric? The people in the village? Hróarr and Vana? Brynn might not like Hróarr, but he was important to Cenric.

Selene scowled. "You slept with him last night, didn't you?"

Brynn's first impulse was to look away, but she forced herself to hold her mother's stare.

"How many times did I tell you not to be sentimental about sex?" Selene demanded. "Nothing good comes of it."

Sex with Cenric was different. It had been true intimacy, with vulnerability and trust in both directions. Paega had touched her like it was a wretched chore, Cenric touched her like it was an honor, an indulgence of the most decadent kind.

Whatever it had been, Brynn wanted more of it. She hadn't guarded her heart because she felt her heart was safe with him. Maybe it wasn't. Maybe even if she escaped and found her way back to him, he would break it.

But she had gotten just a taste of what a life with him could be like and she wanted it. Wanted it desperately enough to risk, to dare. To hope.

The horses trundled to a stop. Esa whimpered at Brynn's side as Selene stood.

"The road is too narrow for the wagon ahead." Selene jerked her chin at Brynn. "Stand, girl."

Brynn watched her mother, not moving.

Selene grabbed Esa's hair, and the girl cried out in the sorceress' grasp. "Will you cooperate?"

Brynn pressed her tongue against the top of her mouth, her mind racing for a way to save Esa. "You leave her behind when we board the ship. Unharmed."

Selene rolled her eyes. "You want me to abandon your ward away from civilization?"

"Esa's a clever girl." Brynn kept looking at her mother. "She'll be fine."

Silent tears fell down Esa's face, but she remained silent—steady.

"Fine." Selene rolled her eyes. "You come with us, and we will leave her behind on land."

It wasn't much, but it was something. If Brynn didn't have to worry about her ward, she would be free to resist. Her mother would have nothing to hold over her anymore.

Brynn rolled onto her side, awkward with her hands lashed

behind her back. She crawled and flopped her way to the end of the wagon.

Neirin grabbed her arm as she reached the edge. "Sorry," he muttered, pulling her after him.

Brynn studied her mother's hound. He was a sorcerer, the son of a sorceress who had served Selene for years. At one point, he was supposed to serve Aelfwynn when he came of age, but she had been dead before then.

Neirin took her on foot into the trees, another of her mother's guards grabbing Brynn's other arm.

Brynn kept pulling at *ka,* drawing it into herself and letting it gust out of her. The collar kept soaking it up, gluttonous and insatiable.

She feared wearing herself out by the time she was able to get free. What if she managed to break the collar but was too tired to use magic by that time?

Selene led the way, still holding Esa by the hair. Guards flocked around them, Tessaine and Anselma close at their heels.

They left the horses behind with a few of the servants. Those would probably travel the slow route down south, planning to meet Selene in Glasney, or perhaps Orland.

Brynn felt sick at the thought of Orland and Torswald, its alderman. The alderman her mother wanted her to marry after she had a daughter by Paega. She wouldn't do it. She would die first.

They marched through the forest, weaving between trees, over fallen logs. Selene's skirts caught on sharp twigs, and she cursed, yanking them free.

The forest was alive with a haze of *ka* to Brynn's senses. Life glowed all around her. It rushed in to meet her as easily as it ever had, but she still couldn't force spells to form.

Selene and the twins had to be able to sense her gathering massive amounts of power. But they were either confident in the collar's ability to hold her back or good at disguising their concern.

The only hint they noticed was Anselma's wide eyes as Brynn drew in a particularly large surge of power. The girl glanced to her sister, who remained predictably impassive.

Brynn pulled in more power. There had to be a limit to this device. There were limits to everything. Nothing was truly infinite.

They stumbled through the forest. Brynn could sense the bodies of men up ahead and the lazy, winding *ka* that marked fresh water.

They broke out of the trees to the back of a narrow inlet. It wasn't deep or large enough to be truly useful and appeared too shallow for much use outside of high tide.

The ship was unfamiliar as were the men on board. Hyldish men, from the look of them. Not that it meant anything.

Brynn dug her heels in, shoving back against Neirin. "Let my ward go," she ordered. "If you want me on that ship, you let her go."

Selene cast Brynn a dark look over her shoulder. "Do you not trust me?"

"No." Brynn growled back.

Selene heaved a sigh. "Neirin, bind the girl to one of the trees back there and then join us."

"You said she would go free," Brynn protested.

"No," Selene purred. "I said I would leave her on land."

"You bitch!" Brynn spat.

Neirin took a coil of rope from his belt and stepped toward Esa. The girl wept as he dragged her to a sapling hidden from view of the river and forced her to sit back against it. He set to lashing her in place, her hands bent backward around it.

"Let her go," Brynn pleaded. "Mother, please."

This inlet was remote and away from any nearby settlements. Esa would be left alone in the wilderness with little chance of rescue. She might be able to free herself, but she had been beaten and Neirin looked to be taking his job seriously. She'd likely be here until thirst or the wild animals finished her off.

"I have already made one concession, child," Selene reminded her. "I will not be making another."

Brynn wanted to argue, but she had few options. Her mother might change her mind and decide to bring Esa after all—or kill her.

Brynn allowed herself to be led to the edge of the water. They had to wade into the river, the icy water past their knees. The ship was lightweight with only six oars, meant for speedy movement and navigating shallow rivers.

The crew appeared to be regular men, though another sorceress waited at the prow. She was dressed much as the men in tunic and trousers, but Brynn could sense the *ka* fluttering around her like fireflies. Her eyes were lined in kohl, as were those of her sailors. Her tanned face was framed by gold rings that hung from her silken headband. "Lady Selene," the seafaring sorceress bowed to Brynn's mother. Her accent had an odd tone Brynn couldn't place. "Everything go according to plan?"

"So far," Selene sighed, even as she shivered with the cold water. "Are you ready?"

"Ready. The tide is going out, so we had best move quickly." The stranger looked to Brynn, squinting like she was used to the glare of the sun off the water. "Lady Brynn?"

Brynn didn't answer.

"This is my daughter," Selene said.

The seafaring sorceress took in Brynn's bound and collared state. "Why is she bound?" The stranger's gaze snapped to Selene.

Brynn opened her mouth to reply, but the collar around her throat twitched. It was slight, but she'd felt it.

Something was happening.

Brynn focused on dragging in more power and letting it flow out of her again. She no longer bothered with trying to shape specific spells. Brynn tried to blast power out of her in a tidal wave. The collar kept drinking her magic, lapping it up greedily.

The stranger's frown deepened at Brynn, probably able to see her feverish efforts at magic.

"Let's be going," Selene said quickly. "No sense in waiting."

"I didn't agree to abduct or enslave anyone." The seafarer looked to Selene. "I'm not Valdari."

Selene's mouth pinched. "You want answers. I understand. I will happily provide them, but just right now, we are being pursued by some twenty armed men."

Brynn's chest jolted. Was her mother lying? Or had she sensed the riders as Brynn had?

The seafaring sorceress sucked her teeth. "When we get out to sea, I expect answers. And if your answers don't suit me, the deal is off."

Selene's nostrils flared, but she demurred. "Of course."

Neirin splashed up to the vessel and climbed over onto the deck. He settled at Brynn's side, taking her other arm once again.

Esa remained on the riverbank hidden behind the trees, tied and helpless. Brynn was trying to help. Had she doomed the girl?

The seafarer set to calling the oarsmen, giving orders for the ship to be pushed back out the way they had come. The water grew deeper the farther they went, moving fast—too fast.

The collar around Brynn's neck twitched again. She was close to something. So close.

"Brynn." Her mother came into her vision, standing in front of her with eyes wide. "You need to stop."

Brynn met her mother's gaze. She kept drawing in *ka.*

The world was alive. So alive. So full of power.

The collar rattled faintly, shaking against her collarbone. It warmed against her skin.

"Lady Brynn." Anselma stepped forward, then stopped, hands wringing in front of her. "Lady Brynn, no."

Selene spun on the girl. "How is she doing that?"

Anselma blanched. "I don't—"

Selene didn't wait for a response. She whirled on the seafarer. "Get us out of here!"

"What is happening?" the seafaring sorceress demanded.

Selene ignored her and spun back to Brynn. "Brynn, stop!"

Brynn didn't stop. She reached and dragged and released power even as her head became lighter and her thoughts muddied.

Selene spun to Anselma. "Do you have more of the sedative?"

"I—"

"Quickly, girl!"

If they drugged Brynn again, they might undo whatever she'd managed to do. They might find a way to permanently bind her.

The ship sailed swiftly, carried by the current. It rounded a bend in the river and the ocean came into view. Brynn fought, straining to gather more power as the ship glided ever closer to the open sea.

Anselma fumbled with her bags as they swept toward the sea. The ship jostled and she dropped her pack.

Neirin forced Brynn onto her knees, clutching her hands behind her back. "Stop!" he hissed in her ear. "Stop!"

Brynn had no intention of stopping. The ship swept by the last of the pines and the quiet forest. Past...

There were living things in the trees. Things larger than squirrels or deer. Brynn might have missed them if she hadn't been reaching for *ka* so desperately.

There were men in the trees. Too many to be an idle hunting party or a harmless group of fishermen.

Selene shook her head, crouching in front of Brynn. "Brynn, if you keep fighting, you risk—"

The ship slammed to a stop.

Everyone toppled off-balance.

Neirin stumbled, slamming Brynn down into the deck. Selene screamed and the sorceresses raised defensive spells. Shouts rang across the deck and the familiar sounds of clanging steel burst around her.

Growling, Brynn dragged still more magic into herself, still pinned by Neirin.

"Stop!" the sorcerer panted, trying to pull her up.

A scream overhead cut him off.

Brynn kept dragging in power. She didn't care what happened. If she died, so be it, but she would take her mother with her.

The collar buzzed as Brynn continued to feed it magic. It heated, stinging her skin. She braced herself, pulled in yet more power, then released it.

Neirin was becoming frantic even as a battle raged around them. "If you overpower the trammel, it will—"

The collar exploded in a surge of golden light.

33

CENRIC

Cenric crouched on the bank of the river, keeping to the shadows of the trees. The ship had sailed up the narrow inlet and disappeared some minutes ago.

The water had been shallow enough for some of the horses to cross to the other side. Olfirth's men tied ropes to the trees on the far bank, then crossed back. Under better circumstances, they would have blocked the inlet with stones and logs, but they had limited time.

They used rocks to weigh the ropes beneath the surface, stones that would be small enough to fall free as soon as the ropes were drawn taunt.

Cenric crouched in the shadows of the trees, hands wrapped around one of the lengths of rope.

One of Olfirth's riders remained mounted, another coil of rope at the ready. His job would be to lash the prow of the ship and drag the craft to the side.

Cenric waited with his shield slung over his back, gripping the rope tight. He caught snatches of voices from upriver. Women's voices.

Was one of them Brynn?

"This is going to be funny if it turns out to be some harmless fisherman," Edric whispered at Cenric's back.

Cenric shot a hard look to his thane.

Edric shrugged. "We were all thinking it, lord."

Cenric looked back up the river, where he could see the water through the trees. In moments like these, a heartbeat seemed to last a lifetime, and a breath could last an age.

Either they were about to fight at least three sorceresses and their sorcerer bodyguard, or this was all for nothing and Brynn was lost.

Cenric shifted his stance, adjusting his grip on the rope one more time. Olfirth's thanes gathered around him, all holding onto their own ropes, ready for the fight. Tension rippled through all of them, that kind of excitement tinged with dread.

Olfirth stood beside Cenric, axe resting against one shoulder. He held his shield loosely, waiting.

The trees made it impossible to form a shield wall with any cohesion. Forests were pernicious, cruel battlegrounds that hated everyone equally. Cenric could only hope that the pines would protect them from any attacks from the sorceresses.

Brynn had told him living things were easier to attack. Perhaps the trees would absorb some of the magic.

Cenric? Snapper's confused question filtered through.

Wait. Cenric didn't need the dog getting underfoot or caught in the middle of a battle.

"Ho," one of Olfirth's thanes called softly.

Up ahead, the ship glided back into view. There were several new figures on the deck, including the familiar form of Selene, his mother-in-law.

Then he saw Brynn.

She was dressed exactly as her corpse had been in his foretelling—in a tattered shift and bound with ropes. She stood between two men, her arms lashed in ropes from her wrists to her elbows. Something that had not been in his vision was locked around her neck—a locking band made of dark metal not unlike a thrall's collar.

Fury burned in Cenric's chest at the sight of her bonds, washing out the relief he might have felt at seeing her alive. How dare they. How *dare* they.

Cenric adjusted his grip on the rope one last time, looking to Olfirth. The old man lifted his hand.

If they raised the ropes too quickly, the people on the ship might be able to cut them before the cords hooked the front of the hull. If they were raised too late, the ship could sail past.

Cenric cracked his neck, a shiver of anticipation went through him.

The ship glided to the mouth of the inlet. Olfirth shifted, then his fist dropped.

As one, Cenric, Edric, and Olfirth's thanes yanked the ropes taunt. They leaned hard to the left, bracing around the trunk of a large pine as the ship jerked into the lines.

The horseman sprang into action, looping his rope over the prow of the ship and veering his animal back into the trees. With a line connected to the vessel, the horse jerked it sideways, pulling the craft partway onto the shore.

Cenric spotted the shapes of men and sorceresses knocked against the deck of the ship. Several appeared to be recovering, drawing weapons and shouting in alarm.

But he'd lost sight of Brynn.

Armed men leapt from the ship, several rushing to try and cut the vessel free, but Olfirth's thanes charged to meet them.

With the ship immobilized, Olfirth's men swung their shields from their backs onto their arms and Cenric did the same. Battles cries split the air as the first of Olfirth's thanes clashed with the sorceress's men on the riverbank.

The spear wasn't going to be much use in such close quarters, so Cenric drew his sword. He rushed toward the ship, Edric at his back.

Olfirth let off a war cry and leapt into the fray.

Cenric made it to the edge of the trees before the air itself seemed to crack. There was a sound that was not so much a sound as the absence of sound, like the silence before the crash of thunder.

A blast of power burst from the ship. Everything exploded into golden light, blinding and disorienting.

Cenric went weightless, hurling through the air. He smacked into the earth onto his back. Air was forced out of his lungs and everything in his vision turned white. His ears rang with a high-pitched shriek.

For a moment, he blinked and gasped at the sky, blind, deaf, and unable to breathe. It felt like forever, but air slowly filled his lungs again and he made out the shapes of trees overhead.

Cenric! Snapper's panicked cry flooded Cenric's thoughts. *Cenric hurt? Cenric!* Snapper hovered over him, licking his face and pawing at him frantically.

Edric's voice filtered through the ringing. "Cenric? Cenric! Are you alive?"

"Alive," Cenric grunted, ruffling Snapper's ears to reassure the dog.

Edric lay a few steps away. Around them lay the shapes of Olfirth's thanes. The men stirred, groaning as they struggled to rise.

Rolling onto his side, Cenric clawed his way to all fours.

The blast of power had pushed back the nearest trees, bending great trunks like reeds for a basket. Several of those nearest the bank had been flattened entirely, pushed out by the force of that spell.

The surge had gone in all directions, forcing up water, silt, river plants, and rocks. The ship was gone, or more accurately, it lay in pieces. Boards scattered among the mud and broken trees like the feathers of an unfortunate wooden bird.

"Brynn." Fear rose in Cenric's chest. She had been on the deck of the ship. Where was she now? *Stay away from the strangers,* he ordered Snapper.

Strangers? Snapper cocked his head, tail stiff.

Stay back.

Bodies littered the beach, thrown in every direction. Most of them appeared to be moving, but that had been a massive amount of power. Even if Cenric's experience with sorceresses was limited, he knew that hadn't been normal.

Those who had been closest to the blast had been thrown back into the trees. The surge of power had forced the water up and away, but the river continued to flow, washing pieces of the broken ship and flotsam of the blast out to sea.

Cenric found his sword and snatched it up. He came across a shield and though it wasn't his, he picked that up, too, slinging it over his left arm. His shoulder ached and his whole body felt tender after being stuck by the blast, but he ignored that for now.

Armed, he didn't wait for the others to join him. The warriors for the sorceresses that had been closest to the blast were helpless right now.

Cenric came to the first man lying on the riverbank, groaning and scrabbling at the ground for his dropped weapon. He sliced down sharply through the man's neck, severing the spine in a clean blow.

Not far away, a young woman lay on the beach. It was one of the twin sorceresses who had served Selene. She whimpered as she rose, bedraggled, black dress covered in mud. Blood flowed from a cut on her temple as she tried to claw away from him.

"Where is Brynn?" Cenric demanded, stalking after the girl.

She looked to still be in her teens, her dress wet and sticking to her like a shroud. She shook her head and raised her hand in his direction.

Cenric realized what she was doing the next instant and raised his shield on instinct.

A blast of fire rippled across the wood, then winked out.

Cenric batted it aside and lunged. He stabbed straight into the girl's chest, just below her collarbone.

She screamed, her whole body seizing. She looked down in shock at the blade, her wide eyes making her look even younger.

Cenric yanked his sword free and slashed sideways, the force of the blade shearing through her cheekbone and into her brain.

Her body hit the mud in a gory mess, and he stepped over it toward the wreckage.

Where was Brynn?

More of Olfirth's thanes staggered through the trees to the riverbank, rushing on the men who had served the sorceresses. Some of the men recovered, drawing weapons. Others were slaughtered in the mud where they lay.

"Anselma!" screamed a female voice.

Cenric spun around to see the other twin sorceress clawing to her sister's side.

"You killed my sister!" the girl screamed.

Cenric raised his shield to face the girl. He had seen what Brynn could do and wasn't sure a shield would be enough, but there was no way out of this fight.

The girl's nostrils flared and her eyes were wide in horror and rage that Cenric knew well. She raised her hands, and he could only guess she had drawn power and loosed it.

The lashes of magic clawed across Cenric's shield, scoring like whips but not piercing.

Cenric didn't hesitate. He charged and swung in with his sword.

The young sorceress lashed out again, but her spell glanced off Cenric's helmet, failing to find purchase on the metal. It was a single mistake, but it cost her life.

Cenric's sword caught her in the ribs, ramming up from her side to pierce her heart. There was a moment's shocked horror where she stared with wide eyes at the man who had killed her.

He ripped his blade free and let her fall to the ground. Hopefully, Brynn would forgive him for this.

34

BRYNN

She was weightless. Formless.

There was peace in the silence. Rest.

Brynn felt as if she floated over an endless void, at the precipice of infinity. All she had to do was wait.

Brynn.

She knew that voice. Brynn tried to turn her head, but she didn't seem to have a body.

Get up, Brynn.

That couldn't be right. Brynn tried to open her eyes, tried to see, but she couldn't.

Get up.

Aelfwynn?

There was the sense of a sigh, though not quite the sound. *You're underwater. You're going to drown if you stay here.*

Wynn, is that you?

Who else?

But you died.

And so will you if you don't move.

Brynn made an effort to shake her head, but she still couldn't seem to feel anything, much less move anything.

You need to get up.

Brynn couldn't even tell which direction was up. *How can I hear you?*

Because you're dying, idiot. Now get your head out of the water.

Dying. How strange. Was this what it felt like? Oblivion? Blackness? This was not so bad.

If you join us today, I will make you sorry, the voice said. *Very sorry. Do you hear me?*

That was Aelfwynn. It had to be.

Who is us?

The dead, little sister. Aelfwynn's voice was full of frustration. *The dead.*

Brynn felt a tremble go through her formless being.

Live, Brynn. For me. For yourself. For Cenric.

Cenric?

That name clanged against her awareness and for just a moment she felt water rushing into her mouth, clogging her lungs.

Wake up, Aelfwynn ordered. *Wake up.*

Osbeorn? That name rose to Brynn's awareness. She needed to know.

Mildreth is taking care of him.

Paega's wife?

I was never much good with babies.

This had to be real. Brynn would have never imagined such a thing as Paega's precious dead wife looking after Osbeorn.

I like Mildreth, Aelfwynn added quickly. *She saw how you always left offerings for her and her children's graves. She's grateful.* The impression of Aelfwynn's snicker came from the voice. *She has a large stick she's been saving for when Paega gets here.*

Brynn would definitely not have imagined that.

Will you wake up now? The humor of Aelfwynn's voice was gone, replaced once again by annoyance.

Yes.

It seemed that agreeing was all Brynn needed to do.

Her awareness slammed back into her body and with it, pain. A burning sensation seared through her chest, her throat, and radiated down her back.

She was underwater, just as the voice had said.

Survival instinct took over and Brynn thrashed. She scrambled for the surface, but she couldn't reach it. She was caught in the current, rushing along too fast, being swept out to sea.

Cenric's vision was coming true. Brynn was going to drown with her arms tied, just as he had seen.

Large hands seized her roughly from above. Someone caught her elbow, yanking so hard it nearly jerked her shoulder out of socket. A male voice she didn't recognize shouted overhead.

"I have her!" the stranger called. "I have Lady Brynn!" It was a man with most his face covered by a helmet.

Brynn coughed and hacked. Her arms were still bound but the collar was gone. She was nowhere near where she'd last seen.

A dog barked, frenzied and fearful.

They appeared to be on a beach lined by pine trees, a rocky expanse with black sand stretching in both directions. She could see the mouth of the river, but it seemed she had been swept out along with the rest of the remains of the ship that bobbed and floated on the waves.

The dark-haired stranger sloshed out of the water, dragging her along as the rope tied around his waist guided him back to the shore.

"Who are you?" Brynn's voice came out as a croak.

"I'm Evred, thane to Olfirth."

Brynn's half-drowned mind caught up as he dragged her ashore, hauling her onto the beach like a sack of eels. "Olfirth?" She collapsed on the muddy riverbank, gasping and choking.

A black and grey shape slammed into Brynn, slobbering a rough tongue over her face.

"Snapper?" Brynn coughed.

Snapper barked at his name, batting at her nervously.

"We wouldn't have found you if not for the dog." Evred crouched beside her, looking her over as he removed the rope from around his own waist. It seemed several men on the shore had helped pull him back out of the river's rushing flow. "The water is shallow here, but the current is fierce. Deadly, if you're not careful."

"Best be going," another of the men said. "There's a fight upriver from the sound of it."

"Cenric," Brynn gasped. She pulled in magic and this time, *ka* rose to do her bidding. The ropes were made of flax twine and though the fibers had been dead a long time, they took in her power and with a little guidance melted off her in wet clumps.

Brynn flailed as her arms came free, wincing as feeling rushed into her strained chest and shoulders. She pulled in more *ka*, letting it settle around her joints and muscles. The ache lessened, but she would probably be sore for some time.

"Why didn't you do that sooner?" Evred wondered.

Snapper whined, nosing at Brynn's side.

Brynn stumbled to her feet, sand squishing between her bare toes. She'd lost her boots in the river. "Where is Cenric?" She faced down the three armored thanes in front of her.

Where was her mother, for that matter? Esa was back upriver and—

"Where is my husband?" Brynn whirled on the three men, spotting their horses tied behind them up the beach.

Cenric was here somewhere, he had to be. Brynn knew it with a desperate certainty that clawed at her like talons.

"You're safe, lady," one of the other men assured her. "Olfirth gave us orders to find and guard you if we found you. You're in no—"

These men didn't understand. Brynn wasn't worried for herself at all. "Cenric." She looked to Snapper, meeting the dog's eyes.

Snapper whined, going rigid.

"Cenric." Brynn repeated the name in a plea.

Snapper spun around, racing back into the trees.

Brynn tore after him.

"Lady Brynn! They're fighting!"

Brynn was out of breath, coughing, and barefoot, but the thanes were fully armored and partially waterlogged.

She raced after Snapper back toward the river. Her mother would kill Cenric if she got the chance. Once again, the person Brynn loved most was in danger and she wasn't there, couldn't protect him.

Sticks and rocks lashed at her feet, but she kept running. The trees near the river had been bent back, as if forced by some great maelstrom. Silt and mud had been forced up, smearing the surrounding trees in what had once been the river bottom.

Snapper's paws made a soft pattering sound as he led the way.

Brynn had never seen anything like this before. Even more shocking, she had been the one to make it happen. She could sense the figures along the riverbank, a cluster of bodies in two groups facing down one another.

Battle lines. A shield wall. Just like Aelfwynn.

She sensed Snapper had stopped beside a figure ahead and rushed toward it, thinking it might be Cenric or another of Olfirth's thanes.

Neirin appeared around the tree, bleeding, covered in mud, and stumbling awkwardly on one foot. He grabbed her arm. "Lady Brynn, we must flee."

Snapper woofed, seeming confused.

She pulled away from Neirin. "Let me go."

"Lady Brynn, I beg you," Neirin pleaded as both of them shivered with the cold.

"Release me," Brynn growled. "Now."

Neirin lunged for her, wrapping her in a bear hug.

Snapper nipped at Neirin in outrage, sensing Brynn's distress.

Brynn slashed with her power, slicing across Neirin's face.

Neirin caught part of it, reshaping her spell as it met his skin.

Her attack left shallow scratches instead of deep cuts.

But Brynn had an advantage—he needed her alive.

She rammed her knee between his legs. Aelfwynn would have been proud.

Neirin cursed, but that gave her the opening to get in close. Brynn grabbed his neck. Neirin snapped up his own spell, trying to defend himself.

He might be able to overpower her body, but he was no match for her magic.

Brynn's power sliced through him in a single, clean stroke. It had been a long time since she had been in the war, but the killing spells came to her as easily as a familiar song.

Neirin's eyes went wide in shock and then his head tumbled back, followed by his body a moment later. The corpse collapsed against her, and she shoved it, scrambling away.

Snapper yelped in surprise, skittering back.

The three pursuing thanes caught up in time to see her mother's bisected guard thud to the forest floor. One of the men cursed and made a strange gesture, Evred and the other just stared.

Brynn needed to find her husband. "Cenric?"

Snapper whined, looking toward the shieldwall. He seemed torn. Had Cenric ordered him to stay out of the way?

Brynn scrambled through the trees, branches catching at her hair and shift. She was cold, deathly cold, but she couldn't think about that right now.

She reached the edge of the devastation where the broken and flattened trees began. The two forces came into view.

Olfirth's thanes had drawn up into battle lines, their shields forming a single row, though there was not quite enough space for a full shield wall.

Where was her husband? She couldn't spot him in the tight press of bodies.

A flare of power caught her attention.

Her mother stood facing down the thanes with a small force

of her surviving warriors, four of them appeared to have magic of some kind. The seafaring sorceress crouched in the reeds not far away.

"Where is Brynn?" roared Cenric. "Where is my wife, you bitch?"

Despite everything, Brynn's heart leapt. He had come for her. Cenric had come to rescue her. He was alive.

"You dare attack me?" That was Selene, indignant to the end. "You have murdered my servants! Innocent girls!"

"They were guilty the moment they helped you take my wife." Cenric spat the words without the slightest trace of remorse. "Now where is she?"

Brynn didn't dare speak. Her mother was too focused on the thanes, but even a word now would ruin the element of surprise. She was outnumbered. She needed to strike first.

"You will pay for this, upstart," Selene sneered. Brynn's mother sounded truly angry. Not even Brynn had heard her this angry before. "You attack innocent sorceresses, murder my warriors, accost—"

"Will you tell me what happened to Brynn, or shall we get back to the killing?"

This was a distraction. Brynn could sense the vague outline of several of the seafarer's men beside her, lending their power to a spell. She realized with some surprise that at least two of them were also sorcerers, but she had missed it before. Brynn's mother faced Cenric and his thanes from farther down the riverbank, but it was a distraction while the seafarer prepared to strike them from the left.

Power swirled around Selene, though it would be invisible to Cenric and his thanes. Same for the seafarer and her small group of surviving oarsmen.

If the amount of magic being gathered was any indication, they were trying to catch Cenric and the thanes in the middle of two attacks.

Brynn crouched in the shade of the broken pines, her first

impulse was to draw in power, but she didn't want to alert the other sorceresses to her presence.

Cenric was in a trap, and he didn't know it. Fear tried to wrap its icy claws around her. Brynn forced herself to be calm, to think.

Brynn's mother released her first spell. Selene was no battle sorceress, but her power was significant.

Fire roared straight for Cenric and the line of shields even as the seafaring sorceress sent invisible claws straight into the line of thanes.

Most blows glanced off the shields, greaves, and helmets, but the heat was too much. Fire was one of the most difficult things to create, but it could be effective.

The line buckled, the men curling in behind their shields as they drew back.

They were going to die.

Brynn didn't have time to think.

She clawed like a madwoman out of the trees, hands sliding on rock, silt, wood splinters, and debris. She skidded down the side of the riverbank, half falling, half rolling between the two lines.

She doubted she was strong enough to take on eight other magic users, but it didn't matter. The other sorcerers might kill her, but it didn't matter.

On her hands and knees between the thanes and the sorceresses, Brynn pulled directly on the others' spells. These were killing spells, burgeoning with power, but simple.

Magic was just *ka* expressing the will of a mortal. Brynn might not match their combined strength, but she had honed her focus for years. She imposed her will on their spells, dragging the power toward herself.

Pain exploded across her skin as unseen blades sliced her and fire turned the water soaking her clothes to steam.

Blood splattered as their spells sliced through her shift, but the spells barely made it skin deep before she absorbed them, drinking them into her body. The *ka* healed her instants later, some of it mending the damage it had done and some of it flowing through her, ready to be put to another use.

The pain sliced and cut and burned, but she planted her hands in the silt beneath her and focused. Magic was nothing without focus. Runes, patterns, and weaves were all useful for magic, but only because they helped focus.

White-hot agony covered her whole body and Brynn screamed with the effort of taking in so much so fast. She had thought her mother, and the others might hesitate to attack her, but it seemed they were more concerned with saving themselves.

They showed no mercy. Brynn's vision went gold, nearly white from all the pain and power assailing her from what felt like every angle.

On her hands and knees, Brynn gritted her teeth, building a shield. Screaming, she bent their power back, refusing to let the spells reach past her—refusing to let them touch Cenric.

"Brynn!" Cenric cried her name, but a scrambling sound told her someone held him back.

Good. She wasn't sure how long she could hold this shield. Panting, she held the barrier between her mother, the seafarer, and Cenric and the line of thanes at her back.

Brynn was still soaking wet, her hair a mad tangle, covered in dirt, silt, and bleeding from countless cuts from head to foot, facing down at least eight other sorcerers and sorceresses.

Eight other spell weavers she had just overpowered. Six of them were men and likely not as well-taught, but still.

"Brynn," her mother gasped. "How?" Selene watched her with a strange expression that was half fear, half anger.

The seafaring sorceress and her men edged back, but where could they go? Their ship had been destroyed and they were stranded.

"When Aelfwynn died, I was helpless," Brynn croaked, voice shaky from the cold. "I will not be helpless again."

Years of practice, of pushing herself, and using her magic

every single day had made her stronger. Brynn's discipline had matured. She might not be able to overpower Selene and the others outright, but if they wanted to keep throwing spells at her, she had the control to impose her will on their magic. Their killing spells were child's play compared to the nuance and complexity of the healing spells she had worked almost daily for years.

"I wanted to be left alone." Brynn's voice came out as a rasp, a whine. "I only wanted to be left alone."

Selene shook her head slightly. "Brynn…it doesn't have to come to this."

"You brought it to this." Brynn's words ended in a whimper.

"Brynn." Selene shifted. Was she going to run? "Brynn, don't. We can talk about this." She spread her hands, releasing *ka*.

Brynn looked to the seafaring sorceress and her men. They didn't attack, but they still held onto magic. The seafarer looked to Brynn's mother, a question on her face, but Selene was looking to Brynn.

A hesitant smile shaped Selene's lips, probably meant to be cajoling. "Trust me, child."

Those words. The exact words her mother had spoken to Aelfwynn before sending her sister to an unmarked grave.

Brynn sent a lash of power straight for her mother. The spell struck Selene in her exposed neck, slicing through skin, cartilage, and bone.

Selene's eyes locked with Brynn's—shock, horror, and abject disbelief—before she crumpled to the ground.

One of Selene's surviving thanes hurled a javelin. Brynn ducked and the missile struck one of the shields at her back.

That attack had been meant to strike her chest.

Brynn gathered power for a counterattack, but a hatchet struck the enemy thane in his temple, caving in his skull. The man toppled, and one of his fellows made to run.

In an instant, the remaining men tried to flee, but they were tangled in the rushes. The line of thanes at Brynn's back rushed past her to fall on them, hacking, stabbing, and spearing at the men with ruthless ferocity.

Brynn watched the bloody work with a distant kind of horror. They were her enemies. This was the way of war, the way of the world.

The seafaring sorceress dropped to her knees, hands going up. She held no weapons, but Brynn could see she released *ka*, too. "Mercy, Lady Brynn."

Brynn stared at the woman, feeling oddly numb. Should she let these people be killed?

"Mercy for me and my sailors." The sorceress scrambled to Brynn, half-crawling as the fighting turned to butchery. "Mercy!" The seafarer bowed low at her feet.

Brynn clamped a hand down on top of the woman's head, throwing up her arm to stop Edric from swinging a second hatchet. "Hold!" Brynn ordered.

The small thane scowled but blocked one of Olfirth's men who tried to stab the woman with a spear. "Alas, Lady Brynn says no."

Brynn was risking treachery from the woman, but both knew this stranger and her four surviving sailors were as good as dead without her protection. "What is your name?"

Panting, the seafarer kept her head bowed, shoulders relaxing just a little. "Keeva, daughter of Thesrin."

Brynn's thoughts snagged on the name. "Thesrin Green-Mantle?"

Thesrin Green-Mantle had been one of the sorceresses who had died alongside Aelfwynn. She had been a kind woman of middle years, but she had followed Aelfwynn to the end.

"Yes, lady." Keeva remained bowed as her sailors came scrambling close behind her, hands in plain sight and heads likewise down. Brynn realized that one of the sailors was another woman, though she hadn't noticed that before.

"Brynn!" Cenric grabbed Brynn, pulling her into his chest

and covering her with his shield. "Brynn, are you alright? You're bleeding. So much blood."

"I granted them sanctuary," Brynn mumbled between chattering teeth. "We're letting these five go."

"Whatever you want." Cenric glared past her to the kneeling sorceress and her cohorts. "Get out of here."

"If you haven't noticed," Keeva sounded almost annoyed as she rose to her feet, "our ship is in pieces."

"Walk," Cenric growled. "If you start south now and move through the night, you'll be out of Ombra by sunup."

"You expect us to *walk* through the night?" Keeva stood carefully, her sailors close at her heels.

"Be thankful you're alive after you abducted my wife," Cenric spat back. "Now get out of my lands."

Keeva hesitated for just a moment, probably realizing she addressed Brynn's husband and an alderman, not some random thane. "Apologies, lord, but I never agreed to abduct anyone. Selene misled me."

Whatever explanation Keeva might have, no one else seemed interested in hearing it. Olfirth's thanes had finished off what remained of Selene's men and were picking over the bodies. Several glared in the direction of Keeva and her survivors, particularly at the gold temple rings she wore.

"Start moving," Cenric ordered, jabbing his finger southward. "My wife may be in a merciful mood, but I am not."

Brynn could have argued with him, but he was right. Just because she had decided to spare these people didn't mean they wouldn't head straight back to the Mothers with the tale of what had happened.

Keeva seemed to realize she and her sailors were still in danger. She motioned for them to follow. "We'll be going, then." She jerked her head and one of the sailors led the way, heading toward the south.

"Just follow the coastline," Edric called out helpfully. "Can't miss it. It's got a whole bunch of water next to it."

Keeva shot a glare toward him, but wisely didn't snipe back.

Snapper trotted out of the trees, coming to stand hesitantly beside Cenric. The two of them shared a look and Brynn thought they must be speaking in their minds.

Brynn watched to make sure Olfirth's thanes didn't try to attack the survivors, then she let her eyes close.

She had killed her own mother.

"Brynn?" Cenric's entire demeanor changed the moment he looked down to her. Everything about him softened, turning gentle in the space of a breath.

Brynn curled against the hard overlapping plates of his armor, wishing she could feel his chest. "It's pointless. All pointless."

"What is it? What's wrong?" Cenric shifted, catching her as she slumped against him.

"This." Brynn looked at the carnage scattered across the riverbank. "The Istovari won't leave me out of their games. More will come."

"Then we'll kill them, too." Cenric said it like a vow, like he was daring the Mothers to try it.

"For what?" Brynn shook her head, leaning against him.

Cenric was solid, steady as he dragged her closer, holding her up as her legs buckled. "For freedom. For peace."

"And throw away all these lives?" Brynn stared down at her hands, stained with her own blood mingled with Neirin's.

More would come. She was too valuable to be allowed to go free. If what her mother had said was true, and the Mothers had been planning this for generations, they would not allow her to escape even now. If not her, then perhaps her children—if she and Cenric had any.

"If they come against us, they throw away their own lives," Cenric growled. "You owe nothing to the people who would enslave you."

Those words seemed selfish, strange. Her whole life she had been told what she owed her family, her mother, her people, her kingdom. Cenric was the first person besides Aelfwynn to say the world owed her something, but perhaps it did. It at least owed her a choice. The right to choose her own destiny.

"Oh, love." Cenric looked her over. "You're shivering."

"The water was cold." And the fire of those spells had warmed her for only a moment.

"You're covered in blood."

"The cuts are mostly healed," she mumbled. "I will be fine."

"Brynn." Cenric rubbed her back, tucking her against his shoulder. "We'll get a fire going and get you into dry clothes. Then we'll get you home and I'm never letting you out of my sight again."

Brynn wanted him to take his armor off so she could feel his body heat better. She was cold, sore, and weary from using so much magic. *Ka* sped the body's natural healing process and could grant extra strength, but it did not fix exhaustion.

She was numb. So much death. So much blood.

She'd killed Neirin and her mother and the riverbank was littered with corpses—all of the sorceresses and their men.

"Any more of them?" Edric sounded just a little too cheerful as he yanked his hatchet from the skull of a dead man. He pulled something shiny from the man's belt pouch, inspecting the silver coins appreciatively.

"You said we could keep whatever treasure we found," grumbled one of Olfirth's thanes.

"Ho, friend. I killed this one," Edric quipped.

"No fighting." Olfirth lumbered up to the two men, glaring between them. He carried a bloody axe.

"Indeed." Edric divided the coins he'd taken from the corpse. "What do you say we share?"

The strange thane snatched the offered half with a grumble, leaning over to rummage over other bodies.

"Esa." Brynn pushed away from Cenric, alarm rocking through her at the memory.

"Esa?"

"They left her tied to a tree upriver."

"I'll look." Edric gathered up his hatchets and looked to the thane he'd just shared silver with. "Care to help?"

The stranger looked to Olfirth, but the old man nodded.

Edric and Olfirth's thane headed upriver at an easy jog. Esa had been left close to the river. It should be easy enough to find her and bring her back.

Brynn wasn't sure she had the strength to heal the girl just yet, but she would as soon as she could. Brynn's mind moved slowly. Perhaps she was in shock, but she turned to the old warrior a few paces away. "Olfirth?"

The old thane inclined his head in the ghost of a bow. "Lady Brynn. I've never seen a ship ripped apart before. Most impressive. I was looking forward to taking it, but that was impressive nonetheless"

Brynn looked to Cenric, confused.

Olfirth answered. "Your husband came to me this morning and all but begged me to help find you."

"I did not beg," Cenric countered.

Olfirth shrugged. "Might as well. Removed your helmet and dismounted your horse and everything. Even asked nicely."

Brynn looked to Cenric.

Her husband's jaw tightened, and she could tell he didn't appreciate this spin on events. "The rest of my thanes were either injured or needed to gather the cattle," Cenric argued. "I didn't have much choice."

"People were hurt?" If injuries were severe, she might not be able to help for a day or so and that could cost lives.

"Yes," Cenric admitted. "No life-threatening injuries besides my four thanes who were watching the cattle pens last night." Cenric glared at the partially beheaded body of Selene. "Their throats were cut."

"Oh." Her mother had been willing to kill four random men and seriously injure if not murder others.

"So, your husband asked me for help," Olfirth repeated. He

scratched at his beard, looking over the carnage on the beach. "We should probably burn these bodies."

Brynn turned back into Cenric so that he filled her entire vision, hiding her from the corpses. "You asked Olfirth for help?"

Cenric's throat bobbed. "I had to do something." His anguished expression said what remained unspoken—his foretelling, the one that had warned of her death.

Cenric had gone to a man he despised, admitted his weakness, and asked for help. That would have been a blow to anyone's pride, but to a young warrior constantly accused of being an unworthy upstart?

Brynn had known many warriors and many fighting men. Most of them would rather let their mistakes kill them than admit to being wrong. To them, meekness was worse than physical injury and humiliation was worse than death.

But Cenric had been willing to sacrifice his pride for her? Something caught in Brynn's chest.

"You love me." Embarrassment burned her face the next instant. She shouldn't put words in his mouth. She shouldn't expect—

"Yes." Cenric's answer cut off her doubts. "Yes, I love you, wife."

Brynn's throat tightened and she thought she might have tears left after all. "I love you," she whispered, leaning in close, keeping the words for just the two of them. "I've never been in love before, but I'm in love with you."

Cenric smiled, creasing the dirt smeared over his face. He brushed his thumb across her cheek, sweeping away the tears. They weren't sad tears this time, but perhaps happy wasn't the right word either.

Hopeful.

For the first time in a long time, Brynn had hope. The future, if still shrouded in mystery, did not seem quite so dark.

Cenric brushed her hair back from her face, gently, tenderly.

"Let's go home, love."

At their feet, Snapper let off a happy woof.

Thank you for reading!

You can expect more soon from Brynn and Cenric! (And Snapper and Guin, too!)

Visit my website elisabethwheatley.com for latest news, updates, and early bird sign-ups.

ABOUT THE AUTHOR

Elisabeth Wheatley is the author of High Fantasy with Epic Romance. She lives in Austin, TX with her husband Christian and their Jack Russell Terrier, Schnay, and cat, Yumi.

You can find her at elisabethwheatley.com